CATS, CHOCOLATE, CLOWNS...

CATS, CHOCOLATE, CLOWNS, and other amusing, interesting and useful subjects covered by newsletters.

Edited by Greg Mitchell

DEMBNER BOOKS / NEW YORK

Dembner Books
Published by Red Dembner Enterprises Corp.
1841 Broadway, New York, N. Y. 10023
Distributed by W. W. Norton & Company, Inc.
500 Fifth Avenue, New York, N. Y. 10110

Library of Congress Cataloging in Publication Data
Main entry under title:

Cats, chocolate, clowns, and other amusing, interesting,
and useful subjects covered by newsletters.

Includes index.
1. Handbooks, vade-mecums, etc. 2. Newsletters—
United States—Directories.
I. Mitchell, Greg.
AG106.C37   031'.02   81-17240
ISBN 0-934878-13-7 (pbk.)   AACR2

Acknowledgments

Cats, Chocolate, Clowns ... would not have been possible without the cooperation of hundreds of authors, illustrators, editors, and publishers. Throughout the book, credit for reprinted material appears at the foot of each item. In the Directory, you will find the addresses and further details about the periodicals, including organizations that have so generously extended permission to reprint from their publications.

Introduction

Pick a subject, any subject, and chances are that somewhere in America someone is publishing a newsletter, journal, or bulletin about it. In this book I have collected some of the funniest and most informative material that has recently appeared in these *very* special interest publications.

The number of daily newspapers published in this country continues to dwindle, and mass-interest magazines are struggling to maintain a profitable share of the market, but business in the specialty field is booming. There may be as many as 100,000 newsletters. Most are put out by companies or community groups and are read only locally; there are 35 in-house bulletins in the U.S Agriculture Department alone. But some have wider appeal. By various estimates there are between 5,000 and 10,000 highly specialized periodicals that achieve national readership. Although they never see the light of day at a newsstand—they are sold by subscription only—their number is growing steadily.

Most are written, edited, and pasted-up by one or two individuals working out of their own homes. Once a week or month or year these journalist/entrepreneurs mail their publications to several hundred or perhaps several thousand devoted readers. These are person-to-person operations; the only thing between editor and reader is the mailman.

Some of the publications have been around for 50 years; others are less than a year old. Some are typeset on typewriters; others use computer graphics. Some are printed on smudgy scrap paper; others on slick stock. Some are solid copy; others have beautiful illustrations or photographs. Only a few accept display advertising, but many have long classified sections. There are four-page mimeographed newsletters and 64-page quarterlies that almost look like "real" magazines. And there are 128-page, superbly bound journals that look as respectable as *Foreign Affairs* but deal with slightly offbeat subjects—such as cursing or out-of-the-body experiences.

What many of these publications have in common is that each, in its own obscure and often peculiar way, explores a fairly esoteric subject generally ignored not only by the mass media but by other special-interest periodicals as well.

The variety is almost infinite.

There are journals about people (Laurel & Hardy, Millard Fillmore, Richard III, Sherlock Holmes, Horatio Alger), places (Paris), and things (marbles, mushrooms, model rockets).

There are bulletins for blind bowlers, chimney sweeps, garlic lovers, inventors, stone-skippers, puppeteers, punsters, unicorn hunters, and survivors of the sinking of the *Titanic*.

There are newsletters for people with a passion for grade-B movies, for people who collect beer cans, for people who think Teddy Bears are tops. You've heard of Save the Whales—but you probably have never come across *The Beaver Defenders*.

If you believe that the earth is flat, or the metric system obscene, that Lizzie Borden was innocent, Edsels were great cars, or that procrastination pays off in the long run—there's a publication for you.

There's a newsletter solely for people named "Mike."

There is even a *Newsletter on Newsletters*—and a society of newsletter publishers, the Newsletter Association of America. (Naturally, the NAA publishes its own newsletter, *Hotline*.)

Who are the people behind the publications? In the brief profiles I have written for the book, editors explain how they got their start and how they've kept their newsletter alive (if not always on schedule). Few had any background in journalism when they began. Among them is a former dog catcher, a housewife, a clockmaker. The enjoyment they have gained from their experience—and the quirky quality of much of what they publish—is a tribute to their passion, vision, and ingenuity.

Some would argue that God put out the world's first newsletter, in the form of the Ten Commandments. But that doesn't quite qualify; it was only a one-shot deal.

The first regularly published periodical in America was called *The Boston Newsletter,* founded in 1704 by John Campbell, but it is considered a *newspaper*. The publication that is generally acknowledged as the first "modern" newsletter was the Whaley-Eaton *American Letter,* launched in 1918 by Huntington Whaley. It was an immediate success. Another business-oriented venture, the *Kiplinger Washington Letter,* has since become—with more than 400,000 subscribers—the most prominent publication in the newsletter field. Like many of the more "serious" newsletters, it appeals to readers willing to pay a premium for inside information unavailable to the general public. (One Washington newsletter, the *Daily Report for Executives,* currently charges $2,150 for a yearly subscription.)

In the world of politics, *I. F. Stone's Weekly*—a four-page digest of news and opinion—began attracting considerable attention in the 1950s. Stone's fame and success—when he retired in 1971 he had more than 70,000 subscribers—inspired hundreds of political reporters (and others fascinated with politics) to start their own weeklies.

Although inside-Washington newsletters and Wall Street tip sheets may be—numerically speaking—the leading entries in this field, this book pretty much ignores them. Many have already received a lot of publicity; Joe Granville's *Market Letter,* for example, has been given the credit, or blame, for sparking several stock market upheavals. In this book I have focused on publications that are cranked out in basements or slapped together on the kitchen tables of middle America. The only inside-Washington newsletter in this book comes out of *St. Petersburg, Florida.* It's called *The Washington Crap Report.*

Few of these periodicals have a circulation over 2,000; almost all are produced for fun, not profit. Many are put out by collectors—for collectors. Others encourage readers to clip coupons, enter sweepstakes, solve puzzles. Although I've shunned fan-club bulletins, I have listed, in the Directory in the back of this book, some of the dozens of periodicals dedicated to famous authors: from Shakespeare and Blake to Evelyn Waugh and Anais Nin. They are not "fanzines"; they are distinguished-looking journals in which scholars discuss the historical background of—and symbolism in—their favorite author's work. For decades many readers have wondered why the final chapters of *Huckleberry Finn*—otherwise, a masterpiece—are so weak. Thanks to *The Mark Twain Journal* I now think I know. It seems that Twain was distracted, as he was writing the conclusion of the book, by a brainstorm; he spent several weeks away from his desk attempting to market a board game based on British royalty!

Cats, Chocolate, Clowns . . . is not meant to be a survey. The Directory in the back is by no means complete. I have examined almost 1,000 "little" publications but there are others I did not see. I have merely tried to shove out of the shadows a few publications that are particularly interesting to me, and potentially interesting to many others. I have been surprised and impressed by the quality of writing and the humor in many of these periodicals.

What makes this book more valuable, I hope, than most of the recent spate of almanacs and catalogs is that the items and articles do not just sit on the page; in a sense they have a life of their own. Each is still firmly attached to its source—a living, breathing, intriguing newsletter or journal, whose address can be found in the back of the book. There's a lot more fun and information where this came from, and thanks to the Directory you have a chance to tap into it directly.

So get into the spirit of things. Or go all the way and start your own newsletter! A few dollars, a couple of reams of paper, envelopes, stamps, and access to a duplicating machine is all you really need. If there is a message in this book, this is it: In the field of extra-specialty publishing there's always room for one more.
                                                    —G.M.

For Jenny M.

Contents

Chapter 8. Animals & Other Living Things

Chapter 9. That's Life

Chapter 10. The Arts

Chapter 11. Serious Stuff

Chapter 12. Collecting & Hobbies

CATS, CHOCOLATE, CLOWNS...

Facts & Figures

THE NEWSLETTER THAT HELPED START IT ALL

Whaley-Eaton's *American Letter* may have been the first "modern" newsletter but the man whose name is synonymous with *newsletter* today is Willard Monroe Kiplinger. It was Kiplinger who gave the newsletter *style* and practically made the underscored word an art form.

A lot of the credit has to go to the so-called Panic of 1920. Banks were closing in droves. "Kip" Kiplinger, 28, had just been hired by the National Bank of Commerce of New York as its Washington eyes-and-ears. In the midst of the panic, the bank decided to cut expenses by allowing Kiplinger to free-lance for other clients. The Federal Reserve Board, Federal Trade Commission, and something called "income tax" had recently been instituted. Kiplinger felt (as he would later describe it) that businessmen everywhere had an "uneasy feeling that strange, interesting, and sometimes disturbing things were going on in Washington." To many, it seemed that newspapers were not covering this beat very well.

W. M. Kiplinger

Austin H. Kiplinger

Kiplinger secured 20 clients, whom he advised from his office in the Albee Building on 15th Street. To make ends meet he wrote articles for the *New York Times Sunday Magazine* and served as an adviser to Cordell Hull, then a congressman from Tennessee. (Hull paid him $150 a month.) Kiplinger and a group of other investors (including Henry Wallace) formed the American Institute of Agriculture in Chicago, a kind of farmers' correspondence school on marketing. It flopped and Kiplinger lost his entire life's savings of $4,000.

It was then that Kiplinger and his partner, Melvin Ryder, decided that sending the *same* weekly report to all his clients would be a time- and labor-saving device. It was not intended to be profit-making itself—it was "just a kind of bonus or dividend," Kiplinger said. "We had a basket on the front desk; and every time we interviewed anyone we would jot down a condensation of what he said, assuming it was of interest to the business world, and drop it in the basket. Then on Wednesday night after work, we would spread these scraps of paper out on a big table, sort them and arrange them, and have them typed into our weekly letter."

The first few letters were very popular with the handful of clients. Kiplinger and Ryder decided letters should be provided separately from the firm's other services. They found a printer on G Street who would print, fold, stamp, and mail 500 copies of the one-page sheet for $21. The first *Kiplinger Washington Letter* rolled off the press on September 29, 1923.

The lead item advised clients that "rumors of an international German loan . . . are foolish." Then there was an item on the possibility of government regulation of the coal industry. Then, a look at an upcoming case before the Supreme Court, "involving the question of whether national banks may legally establish offices, or branches, within the same city. . . ." And then this classic—indicative of so many Kiplingerisms to come: "Radio, what a lot of valuable research by government departments is available on this popular subject! But government documents suffer under their age-old reputation for mustiness."

A covering letter notified readers that they could receive a page of information like this every week for $10 per year. The first mailing brought 21 subscriptions. Growth was modest but steady. Kiplinger's partners continued to do other work for clients, such as finding out, for an advertising agency, what kind of gloves President Coolidge wore.

By this time, Kiplinger's editorial style—the one-line sentences, punchy words, and underlining—had settled into a comfortable (soon to be much-copied) groove. "When I started the letter," Kiplinger later wrote, "it had no more style than a postcard from Niagara Falls." But it was designed to transmit information, fast; Kiplinger knew his clients were busy people who wanted predictions made for them, as succinctly as possible.

Circulation has soared in the past 50 years. The *Washington Letter* now goes out to over 500,000 subscribers, who pay $42 a year for it. The Kiplinger conglomerate on H Street in Washington now produces biweekly *Tax* and

Agricultural letters and monthly letters for readers (or investors) in Florida, Texas, and California. Circulation for these five publications ranges from 19,000 to 104,000. Like the *Washington Letter* they are four-page, 2,000-word sheets, *sans* illustrations, filled with pithy facts and forecasts. Since 1947 Kiplinger has also been putting out *Changing Times* magazine.

W. M. Kiplinger's son, Austin, a lifelong journalist, took over the editorial reins in 1961. (W.M.K. passed away in 1967 at the age of 76.) Twenty-two editors in all put out the letters. Their job, as Austin Kiplinger says, is "not to espouse any position, to praise or condemn. Our role is to evaluate the prospects." But Austin Kiplinger's outlook and philosophy were pretty well stated at the close of a June 1981 letter, when he wrote:

"Been traveling a bit recently to various parts of the country . . . . Big cities, smaller towns.

"Most areas seem to be doing fine. Lots of activity and growth, hometown pride, vigor, enthusiasms over what they have and what's ahead. . . .

"There's a growing mood of confidence among most business people. Not Pollyannish or ignoring inflation, interest rates, other problems. But a feeling the country will now take the medicine . . . and get results, which means a stronger and more stable economy, less influenced by gov't. . . ."

BASE PATHS

A novel idea inspired Kenny Trainor's entrance into the newsletter field. A poet and fiction writer, Trainor sat down to write a book about baseball but realized he knew very little about the "private and daily lives of ballplayers." So he read about a hundred books on the subject and devoured *The Sporting News* and *Baseball Digest*.

He never did finish that novel. Instead, in 1978, he compiled statistics on every big-league team for a sports service in Baltimore. That winter he self-published the stats in a "fact book." He then used the book "as a premium to get people to subscribe to my weekly newsletter in 1979," Trainor recalls, "and the whole thing sort of skyrocketed from there." He was profiled in the *Philadelphia Bulletin* and *Baltimore Sun* and spoke at seminars in Las Vegas and Atlantic City.

Baseball Fact Sheet is published weekly during the baseball season. Many of its 350 subscribers are reporters and gamblers, Trainor says, although some of the statistics and tables could interest anyone who follows baseball on a game-by-game basis.

Each six-page issue includes records of how pitchers have fared in the past against the coming week's opponents; a running log of how each team has performed this season at home and away, in day games and at night, versus left-handed pitchers and righties, on artificial turf and natural grass. Trainor's sole source of information: box scores published in daily newspapers.

"Special Features" in each issue might include an analysis of how the size and type of home crowds may affect a team's performance. Trainor compiled a table, for example, that showed each team's won-lost record from 1979 to 1981 for different days of the week. He discovered that the Toronto Blue Jays were 29 and 69 playing before few fans Mondays through Thursdays—but won 20 games and lost only 14 before big crowds on Sundays! The Baltimore Orioles, he said, draw about equally well on Fridays and Sundays—but their Friday home record was 19 and 6, their Sunday mark 14 and 16. His explanation: "The Friday night crowd in Baltimore consists of fans who drink a lot of beer and make a lot of noise to support their home squad. However, on Sunday afternoons, the stands are filled with families with small children."

Trainor, who now lives in Trenton, New Jersey, divides his time between baseball and poetry. One of his poems was included in the 1981 *Yearbook of Modern Poetry*. He is 31 years old, "but when you read as many box scores as I do," Trainor reports, "you have a tendency to get old before your time. . . ."

Longest Caves in the World

1. Flint-Mammoth, Kentucky   224.70 mi.
2. Optimisticeskaja, Ukraine   88.86 mi.
3. Holloch, Schwyz, Switzerland   86.87 mi.
4. Jewel, South Dakota   66.61 mi.
5. Ozernaja, Ukraine   64.62 mi.

NSS News
(National Speleological Society)

If a cat died in ancient Egypt, family members were required to shave off their eyebrows as a sign of mourning.

Funny Funny World

Who is Taxed the Most?

The Gross National Product of the United States was 2156.1 billion dollars in 1978. That year the total value of federal, state and local taxes raised was 647.1 billion dollars. This means that the percentage of GNP represented by taxes in the U.S. was 30.2. According to the Organization for Economic Cooperation and Development these are the percentages for several other countries in the same year.

Sweden	53.5
France	39.7
West Germany	37.8
Britain	34.5
Italy	32.6
Canada	31.1
Japan	24.1

- Sweden has the highest *income* tax, France the lowest.
- Japan has the highest *corporate* tax rate, Sweden the lowest.
- Britain and the U.S. have the top *property* tax; Sweden and Italy have *none*.

Dollars & Sense

A rattlesnake can bite you even after it's dead. Its reflex action can last as long as a half hour after it dies.

Funny Funny World

How You Can Save With a Woodstove

Stove, Pipe, Installation, etc.	$458.00
Chain Saw	149.95
Gas and Maintenance for Chain Saw	44.60
4-Wheel Drive Pickup, Stripped	8,379.04
4-Wheel Drive Pickup, Maintenance	438.00
Replace Rear Window of Pickup (Twice)	310.00
Fine for Cutting Unmarked Trees in State Forest	500.00
Fourteen Cases Michelob	126.00
Littering Fine	50.00
Tow Charge from Creek	50.00
Doctor's Fee for Removing Splinter from Eye	45.00
Safety Glasses	49.50
Emergency Room Treatment (Broken Toes-Dropped Log)	125.00
Safety Shoes	49.50
New Living Room Carpet	800.00
Paint Walls and Ceiling	110.00
Chimney Sweep Services	45.00
Log Splitter	150.00
Fifteen Acre Woodlot	9,000.00
Replace Coffee Table (Chopped Up and Burned While Drunk)	75.00
Divorce Settlement	33,678.22
Total First Year's Costs	$54,632.81

The Chimney Sweep News

A Hairy Theory on Preventing Colds

"I have been a family practitioner for the past 40 years, and my records reveal that about 70 percent of my male patients who have beards exceeding two inches in length and heavy mustaches that extend from the nasal cavities and cover the upper lip appear to be spared from most viral or other upper respiratory conditions." Those words come from Sinet M. Simon, M.D. (writing in *Modern Medicine,* February-March, 1981). It is Dr. Simon's belief that "extensive hairy growth over the face and chin and above the lips acts as a repellent or as a filter of viruses or allergens that might cause these infections."

Executive Fitness Newsletter

When lions make a kill, the leader of the pride has first dibs on the liver.

Funny Funny World

DON'T KICK THE CAN

Where Have All the Breweries Gone?

Americans today are drinking more and more beer, at relative bargain prices, but there are fewer and fewer breweries. Just before Prohibition, some 1,500 breweries were slaking the thirst of this country's beer drinkers. When the great experiment was over in 1933, fewer than 800 breweries resumed operations. By the time the beer can was introduced on January 24, 1935, only 730 brewers were still in business. In 1952, just 350 breweries remained. Some 210 survived until 1963, and by 1975 that number had dwindled to fewer than 70. Some industry experts predict only four breweries will be marketing their product by 1990. There will still be dozens and dozens of brands then, but they will be just like the Buick Apollo, Oldsmobile Omega and Pontiac Ventura are today—Chevy Novas, all produced by the same company, but with slightly different trim on each model.

The Beer Can

The "underground economy" (barter, informal co-ops, untaxed income) may make up as much as 27 per cent of the Gross National Product, according to University of Wisconsin economist Edgar Feige. That represents $700 billion—more than the total official GNP of France. In the last 10 years, he calculated, the "unobserved economy" has expanded at roughly triple the rate of the official GNP. Underground prices are 20-40 per cent lower, and unemployment may not be as extensive as statistics indicate.

Leading Edge Bulletin

Radio Facts and Oddities

The distress call ••• – – – ••• is sent as ONE letter!!! It has *no* meaning, it is not really SOS, nor does it mean "Save Our Souls"!

S   O   S
•••   – – –   •••

The Distress Call
•••   – – –   •••

Sparks Journal

The Japanese shut down the Tokyo Zoo for two months out of every year to give the *animals* a vacation. Ten months of chatty people with prying eyes, that's enough. Those beasts get nervous. They need the rest.

Funny Funny World

If You're into Numbers, Here's a Bit of Trivia for You.

Unlucky 13 is one of the most common superstitions; even today, many hotels and office buildings do not have a 13th floor. Thirteen's bad name supposedly started with the Last Supper, when 13 apostles dined together. But to the founding fathers of the United States, there certainly did not seem to be anything unlucky about the number 13—it was, after all, the number of colonies that wished to break away from England to form a new republic.

In fact, the number 13 went on to become the keynote of the Great Seal of the United States. If you examine it carefully, you will see 13 stars, 13 clouds, 13 stripes, 13 laurel leaves, 13 berries, 13 main feathers in the eagles right wing, 13 feathers in his left wing, 13 feathers in his tail, 13 letters in the facing motto, *E Pluribus Unum,* 13 letters in the reverse motto, *Annuit coeptis,* 13 times 3 letters in the words, "The Coat of Arms of the United States of America." In fact the number 13 is repeated 13 times in the Great Seal!

Turtle Express

Q: Who first said, "What this country needs is a good five-cent cigar"? Vice President Thomas Marshall or Speaker Joe Cannon?

A: It was our 28th Vice President (in the Woodrow Wilson administration), Thomas Riley Marshall. Marshall, a long-time Democratic Congressman, was born in 1854 in North Manchester, Ind. and died in 1925. He made the remark to John Crockett (then chief clerk of the U.S. Senate), and it became widely cartooned and quoted by contemporary artists and columnists. For instance, Franklin P. Adams, the columnist and radio wit, transposed the saying to "What this country needs is a good five-cent nickel!"

The Pipe Smoker's Ephemeris

Twinformation

- Twin rates in U.S.: 1 in 93.2 white births, 1 in 73.2 non-white.
- Triplets: 1 in 10,200 white, 1 in 5800 non-white.
- Quads: 1 in 490,000 births.
- Quints: 1 in 55,000,000 births.
- There is one set of sextuplets surviving in South America.
- In USA, 34% of white twins are identical; 29% of non-whites.
- The fertility of twins is no different from that of single-borns!
- Lightest recorded surviving twins were born in Peterborough, England, in 1931, weighing 16 oz. and 19 oz.
- A twin labor is only slightly longer than for a singleton. Because twins tend to be smaller in size, labor is usually not as severe.
- Siamese twins occur very rarely, perhaps once in 100,000 births.

- Mothers who have had 1 set of twins have a greater chance of repeating.
- A Yale University study has shown that women who become pregnant within two months after they stop taking the pill double their chance of having twins.

NOMOTC Notebook
(Mothers of Twins Club)

Here's a way to win a bet! Get someone to bet that Cuba produces the most cigars. (Actually, it doesn't. Holland produces the most cigars per capita and the U.S. the most in actual numbers.)

Funny Funny World

Going to Extremes

Ketchikan, AK, has the highest zip code, 99950, while the Reader's Digest Assn. of Pleasantville, NY, has the lowest—00401. . . . The longest postal rural route in the U.S. is in Leakesville, MS—170 miles. Shortest is in Mt. Angel, OR—1.8 miles to a high-rise. . . . The PO at Hinsdale, NY, is the nation's longest operating facility, continually occupying the same quarters since 1816. . . . Ridley Park, PA, is the U.S.' first total solar energy facility. . . . Barrow, AK, is the northernmost PO. . . . Moses Walter delivers the mail in Stella, KY, on his pony, "Patsy." Walters, 83, has delivered mail on horseback for 40 years. . . .

PMCC Bulletin
(Post Mark Collectors Club)

Bolts From the Blue

For the most recent 20-year period, 15% of the recorded lightning victims in the U.S. were taking cover under trees, according to the National Oceanic and Atmospheric Administration. Another 12% of the fatalities is made up by people boating, fishing or swimming. From 1959 to 1979, 2,210 deaths were due to lightning; Florida had the most of any state with 223.

Natural Hazards Observer

The Most Prized Autographs of All Time

1. Julius Caesar—worth an estimated $2 million (none has ever been found).
2. Shakespeare—$1 million (only six exist).
3. Christopher Columbus—$1 million (eight exist).

The Pen and Quill

The largest bird's nest on record is one 9½ feet wide and 20 feet deep, built by bald eagles near St. Petersburg, Florida, estimated to weigh more than 2¼ tons.

The Raptor Report

There are an estimated 50,000 caves in the United States. Missouri has more than any other state—at least 3,000.

NSS Bulletin
(National Speleological Society)

Beer Can Collectors of America

The Oldest Brewery in the U.S.

In continuous operation and under the same family name, according to the United States Brewers Association: D.G. Yuengling & Son, Inc., Pottsville, Pa. (est. 1829).

The Beer Can

Baseball Leaders in "On-Base Percentage"

(On Base Percentage: Hits + Walks *divided* by At Bats + Walks.)

All-time		Current (as of 1981)	
Ted Williams	.483	Mike Hargrove	.407
Babe Ruth	.474	Ken Singleton	.401
John McGraw	.464	Joe Morgan	.399
Billy Hamilton	.456	Rod Carew	.397
Lou Gehrig	.447	Gene Tenace	.389

Baseball Historical Review

As evidence of the nasty effect of the force of gravity on back problems: The families and doctors of U.S. astronauts aboard the 84-day voyage of Sky-lab in 1974 were more than a little surprised to find the spacemen nearly two inches taller upon their return. "With no grav-

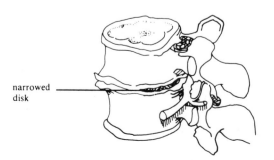

narrowed disk

ity . . . their disks fattened up with moisture, making their spines longer and the men taller," Dr. [Hamilton] Hall [author of *The Back Doctor*] explains. "Once they returned to earth, gravity took over again, and within a few days the astronauts were back to normal size." Since that mission, space suits have been designed to allow for such growth.

Executive Fitness Newsletter

World Series Facts

Game-by-game breakdown of winning percentage for the *home* team in World Series play in the past 50 years:

Game 1. 64%
Game 2. 54%
Game 3. 63%
Game 4. 48%
Game 5. 45%
Game 6. 60%
Game 7. 32%

Note that in the seventh game the home team has won less than one-third of the time, dropping 15 out of 22 before the home fans—including the '79 Orioles and the '75 Red Sox, the last two World Series match-ups to go seven games.

Another item—the team with the best winning percentage during the regular season has gone on to win the series 57% of the time. In recent years, the team with the best percentage has won five of the last seven championships. . . .

Baseball Fact Sheet

. . . .If a person were to live for seventy years, or three score and ten, and if his average heart rate during an average day were eighty beats per minute, the heart would beat approximately ten billion times during his lifetime. Occasionally we may miss a heart beat; but if a few are missed in a row, we would most likely faint away. How much work does this heart do in a lifetime? It has been estimated that the heart may pump a hundred and fifty tons of blood in a lifetime or have done enough work to raise a ten-ton weight for ten miles. Most of us in our modern day world take this for granted and rarely reflect on what is happening minute by minute, day by day within our breasts. . . .

Heartbeat

The Basis of the Metric System

A cube of water ten centimeters to a side has a volume of one liter and weighs one kilogram.

Footprint

The money required to provide adequate food, water, education, health and housing for everyone in the world has been estimated at $17 billion a year. It is a huge sum of money . . . about as much as the world spends on arms every two weeks.

World Federalist Newsletter

Tax Advantages of Investments

(In order of advantage)

1. Personal residence
2. Real estate
3. Timberland
4. Oil and gas
5. Corporate stocks
6. Equipment leasing
   "Hard" money and currencies (tie)
   Exempt bonds (tie)
9. Cash value insurance
10. Deferred annuities
11. Savings accounts

—Vernon K. Jacobs
Tax Angles

The Boy Scouts of America's First Eagle Scout

Arthur R. Eldred, age 17, of Rockville Center, N.Y., August 21, 1912. There have been 600,000 since.

Scout Memorabilia

Husbands in the Delivery Room

In recent years it has become quite customary for husbands to be with their wives while their children are born, an experience which unites the couple at a very critical time in their relationship. The prestigious New England Journal of Medicine reports that the mothers concerned have far fewer complications during childbirth; that their labor is normally only half as long, and that they are more affectionate toward their newborn infants. This refutes the objection of some physicians that husbands who are present on this occasion are a nuisance.

However, the report goes on to say that a mature woman friend, present with the wife at the time of childbirth, can be even more helpful, because some husbands are too nervous to give their wives the necessary reassurance!

Marriage Enrichment

Can Tranquilizers Foil a Lie Detector?

Taking a mild tranquilizer such as Miltown allows persons to lie without detection in lie-detector tests, according to study results reported in the journal Science. Their study of the tranquilizer, whose chemical name is meprobamate, showed that normal people outwitted the stress-sensitive tests after taking one 400-miligram dose, considered the effective minimum.

Police Times

Permanent Birth Control Choice of 12 Million Americans

AVS' estimate of numbers of sterilizations performed in the United States reveals that, over the past decade, 12 million Americans chose permanent birth control as their protection against unwanted pregnancy and childbirth. And, during 1979 alone, approximately 921,000 individuals sought and obtained a sterilization: 435,000 were for men (47%) and 486,000 for women (53%).

Why permanent birth control? Because it's safe, effective—almost 100%—extremely low in complication rates and side-effects, and now, finally, it can be accomplished as an out-patient procedure under local anesthesia for women as well as for men.

AVS News
(Association for Voluntary Sterilization)

Cars Most Likely to Be Stolen

(According to the Highway Loss Data Institute)

1. Lincoln Continental	6. Eldorado
2. Corvette	7. Fleetwood
3. Mark V	8. Brougham
4. Buick Riviera	9. Firebird
5. Versailles	10. Toronado

The California Highway Patrolman

Cars Least Likely to be Stolen

(According to the Highway Loss Data Institute)

1. Volare	3. Datsun 310
2. Subaru	4. Concord

The California Highway Patrolman

More than 224 casket companies have gone out of business in the past 14 years—and the decline continues—according to a report of the Casket Manufacturers Association. As of early 1980, there were less than 450 casket companies serving funeral directors in the U.S.

The percentage of growth in job opportunities for funeral directors is projected at 0.0%,

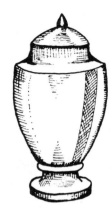

according to a recent study by the Bureau of Labor Statistics of the U.S. Labor Department. In 208 selected categories projected over the next 10 years, the funeral director category is the only one which projects neither growth nor decline.

Continental Association of Funeral and Memorial Societies Bulletin

California throws away more food than some countries produce. In 1974, 49 million people could have been fed with so-called "waste" food that was thrown away. In most cases this food was edible, but not saleable or available for a variety of reasons. One answer to using this "waste" food is to make it available through food banks, emergency food centers, and "weekend meal" programs. . . .

TRANET

A rattlesnake won't eat cold food.

Funny Funny World

From 1974 to 1980 the number of telephone subscribers in France increased from 6 to 16 million and public telephone booths quadrupled to 100,000. France's telephone network, revamped and modernized, moved from one of the most backward in Europe to the most progressive.

Ten years ago it was the only western country where the telephone was rationed with 400,000 requests for lines to be filled and a wait of six months to three years.

Letter from Paris

A Record 15,161 Airports Now Available in U.S.

The number of airports, heliports and other landing facilities in the U.S. broke the 15,000 mark in 1980 for the first time. In all, there were 15,161 landing spots available to civil aircraft at year's end. This represented a net gain of 415 over 1979. Included in the year-end totals were 12,240 airports, 2,336 heliports, 527 seaplane bases, and 58 short takeoff and landing (STOL) airports or runways. Texas continued to lead all states with 1,375 landing facilities, followed by Illinois 942, California 825, Alaska 731, Pennsylvania 694, Ohio 652, Minnesota 491, and Florida 485.

The 99 News

Reginald Jones, chairman of General Electric, stated foreigners now receive 37 percent of all U.S. patents while in 1960 the comparable figure was just 20 percent.

Lightbulb

High on the Hog

For a number of years the White House has been using oversized monogrammed damask dinner napkins for state dinners. Guests often take them home for souvenirs. They are purchased from Le Ron's, a Fifth Avenue linen shop catering to the wealthy. They cost about $900 per dozen.

Washington Crap Report

50 percent of a beaver's lifetime is spent swimming.

Funny Funny World

Approximately 275,000 persons are being arrested annually in California for driving under the influence of alcohol or other drugs.

The California Highway Patrolman

More than 30 windpower plant manufacturers are gearing up to sell 20,000 to 30,000 very large wind machines to electric utilities and about one million smaller ones to industries, farmers, homeowners and others before the year 2000. The number of wind power units sold in 1980 was about 1,500 and the American Wind Energy Association, 1609 Connecticut Ave., N.W., Washington, DC 20009, USA, forecasts 15,000 units will be sold in 1981.

Solar Energy Digest

Supermarket Facts

The average shopper spends three minutes in the produce section, which works out to a little over a second for each of the 125 items that are typically on display.

The National Supermarket Shopper

Buddy-Buddy

The General Accounting Office did a study of 256 randomly selected consultant contracts valued at $2.6 *billion* awarded by the Defense Department.

Three-fourths of the contracts went to former Pentagon employees. 82 percent were awarded without competition. In all but one of the 256 contracts studied they found waste and mismanagement.

Washington Crap Report

Food & Drink

COCOA LOCO

When Milton Zelman was growing up in New Orleans his great-aunt was the proprietor of a baking and catering company. Little Milton folded pastry boxes for her. Now Milton lives in Brooklyn, works as an art director at American Express Company, and publishes his own newsletter about chocolate.

Zelman eats a quarter-pound of chocolate a day, so he knows what he's talking about. Since he is only five foot three, he should be shaped like a Hershey kiss, but in fact he weighs only 120 pounds. A few years ago Zelman noticed that the one thing most of his friends craved above all was chocolate. He felt there was something "eminent" about chocolate, something "profound"; it was a tragedy, he believed, "that not enough attention was paid to chocolate."

From left to right: Lisa DeMauro (contrib. writer), Bun Kaseguma (production), Anne Montgomery (assoc. editor), Milton Zelman (publisher), Boyd Hunter (editor), Patty Van Benthuysen (contrib. writer)

And so he set out to "heighten chocolate consciousness" and "expedite the chocolate cravings" of chocophiles and chocoholics.

The first issue of *Chocolate News* rolled off the presses (printed on light-brown paper scented with a near-chocolate aroma) in January 1980. Issued every two months, the 16-page publication now has over 10,000 subscribers and has become a profitable operation. "We're in the brown," Zelman boasts. *Chocolate News* is well written and, as one would expect from a professional art director, extremely attractive to look at. An average issue might include a Chocolate Chip Cookie taste test, a visit to the Lindt plant in Switzerland, an interview with a chocolate-loving celebrity, another chapter in the History of Chocolate, a mail-order guide, a book review, and several recipes. *Chocolate News* recipes are richer than Rockefeller.

Zelman's taste was revealed when he described "How to Make a Milton." This "fantasy sundae," he wrote in *Chocolate News,* is comprised of "a scoop of vanilla fudge, a scoop of chocolate and, yes—why not—a scoop of chocolate chip. Some sliced bananas, peanut butter chips, chocolate coffee beans, Kahlua, mandarin orange segments, crumbled chocolate mint wafer cookies (the Girl Scouts sell the best), hot fudge sauce, walnuts, whipped cream and, of course, a cherry on top. The kitchen sink was too heavy to lift." Zelman claims he is compiling an exposé of "death-by-chocolate"; certainly anyone eating his sundae would be a candidate for an OD.

When Zelman invites friends over for fondue they dip into melted chocolate, not cheese. He is choosey about his guests. "The more interesting the person and the more dynamic the personality," he says, "the more one seems to be attached to bittersweet chocolate. . . ."

An Interview with Vincent Price

"The Candy Kid"

A man of superlative taste, Vincent Price is equally at home playing delightfully dapper villains in ghoulish film hits, lecturing on primitive and modern art at universities, and cooking up a gastronomical storm in his own kitchen. Born in St. Louis, he attended Yale and London University and made his N.Y. stage debut in *Victoria Regina* in 1935. A distinguished film career followed soon after, highlighted by such chestnuts as *Elizabeth and Essex, Dragonwyck* and *Laura,* in addition to his well-beloved Edgar Allan Poe series of shockers. Recently, he has been dazzling stage audiences with his *Diversions and Delights,* a one-man *tour de force* based on the life of Oscar Wilde. Somewhere along the line, he found time to write a cookbook *(A Treasury of Great Recipes).* As Mr. Price chatted with us from his home in Los Angeles, it was obvious that he is as warm and gracious in real life as he is deliciously dastardly on the screen.

Is it true that your father was a confectioner?

"Absolutely. We shared the same name exactly—I'm Vincent L. Price, Jr.—and he was president of the Confectioners' Association at that time and personally knew Mr. Hershey and many of the other chocolate potentates. It was very convenient having a confectioner for a father. You could take a girl on a date and bring her a 25-lb. box of chocolate, which made quite an impression, as you can imagine. I was known as "The Candy Kid," in fact. That was the title inscribed on a little medallion I received which I was very proud of as a youngster. I gave it to my daughter who now wears it on her charm bracelet."

You must have quite a few chocolate memories that go back to an early age.

"Yes, indeed. I remember one of my father's friends sent us The Life of Brer Rabbit in chocolate—all the Uncle Remus characters made from old German molds, I believe. At Christmas, when Santa would come, we kids always left a piece of chocolate for Santa. . . . Dad, of course, was Santa."

What are your particular preferences when it comes to chocolate?

"Well, my mother liked milk chocolate and I always preferred bittersweet. My wife, who's English, loves good chocolate of all kinds. Her favorite shop is on Old Bond Street in London. We can't wait to go back . . . just for the chocolate."

Chocolate News

The raisin is the only plausible justification for the invention of Bread Pudding.

Raisin d'Etre

No Place Like Home

I have found, for example, that my many European friends who come here to visit do not really appreciate being taken to that little French, German, Italian or whatever-style restaurant that will remind them ever so much of Paris, Berlin or Rome. Many of them actually wallow in Big Macs, although even Ronald McDonald has found his way overseas. And so, I feel that those of us with certain ethnic backgrounds tend to take that particular style of cooking for granted, find it pedestrian and fail to realize the interest that others may have in sampling what is, to them, a new form of dining. Let us never forget that Mrs. Roosevelt had the King and Queen of England for lunch and gave them hot dogs! Bravo, Eleanor! And just to carry that particular reference a mite further forward—some years, not too long ago, I was in England and watched a television program devoted to the Royal Family at leisure on a picnic, and featured there were pictures of H.R.H. the Duke of Edinburgh, stoking the fire so that H.R.H. the Prince of Wales could cook the hamburgers! I suppose it's all from what vantage point one looks.

Le Campion Gourmet Club

How to "Sweetin' a Pot"

Almost every cook in the country has at least one cast iron cooking utensil. Generally, this will be a skillet that has been passed down from mother to daughter. Rarely will you find other iron pots in today's modern kitchen and there's a reason for this—seasoning new iron cookware is assumed to be a difficult job, especially pots that will be used to boil foods in.

All too often an iron pot is tried out, but the cook discovers the food prepared in it has turned black and has a very distinct bitter taste to it. This is caused by cooking in a pot that has not been properly seasoned.

"Sweetin' a pot," as the old-timers called it, is a job that requires know-how and only a bit of patience.

Wash the skillet or kettle inside and out with a mild dishwashing soap. Dry thoroughly. Heat the oven to 350 degrees Fahrenheit. Using unsalted shortening or lard, grease the iron-ware inside and out. If there's a lid, do the same with it. Bake the greased ironware for five hours. Remove from oven, allow the pot or skillet to cool for a few minutes, then wash them again in hot, soapy water. Repeat this greasing-baking. After several applications of shortening, heating and washing, test the pot to see if it's broken in.

A "sweetened" pot will not stick when used for frying, nor will it give off iron deposits that turn foods dark when boiled. If your pot doesn't pass the test, repeat above procedures until it does.

After the pot has been seasoned, never allow it to sit in sudsy water. This will cause it to rust and stick. And finally, never place cold water in a hot skillet or pot!

Farmstead

Lovers of the Stinking Rose

526 Santa Barbara   Berkeley CA 94707

odors being "offensive." But if they persist, we recommend that their ads should conform to scientific fact. . . .

Garlic Times

It is useless for the sheep to pass resolutions in favor of vegetarianism while the wolf remains of a different opinion.

Turtle Express

Boycott Mouthwash!

It has come to the attention of LSR [Lovers of the Stinking Rose] that Signal Mouthwash, a product from Lever Brothers, is being intensely promoted through television and magazine advertising. The gimmick behind the campaign is that Signal halts bad breath caused by the "strongest of all" mouth odors—garlic and onions. Not only is this claim questionable, but it suggests further that garlic and onion odor are socially undesirable, a view that LSR cannot let go unchallenged.

In this age of sophisticated culinary tastes, the lingering odor of garlic and onions on one's breath is a sign of cultivation. The ruin of any outstanding French, Chinese or Italian meal would be to kill the fragrant after-taste with a commercial mouthwash.

But on another level, the so-called clinical studies by Lever's own "specialists in oral hygiene" don't make sense. First, other clinical studies (objective studies *not* paid for by the product's manufacturer!) have shown that garlic odors come not from residual particles of garlic in the mouth, but from the lungs—the mouthwash is at best a *temporary* masking agent. Chewing clumps of parsley can also reduce the odor from garlic consumption.

More importantly, the Lever ad, by claiming that Signal combats garlic and onion odors in the mouth, suggests that garlic odor is emitted only from the mouth. The fact is that the odor of garlic is exuded in the normal process of perspiration—you could hold your breath indefinitely and *still* smell from garlic! And need we add that oral and dermal activity are not the only two outlets for garlic odor? Need we elaborate on the third?

LSR insists that Lever Brothers discontinue its disparaging remarks about garlic and onion

Wild Turkey and Wine

Roger Latham, in his book, *Complete Book of the Wild Turkey,* said this: "The surest way to ruin the rich natural flavor of the wild turkey is to fill it full of all kinds of junk, season it to high heaven and pour a bottle of wine over it. The fancy recipes are for fancy people, not me."

Well, no greater expert on wild turkeys than Roger Latham has ever lived, but there are those of us who are just winebibbers at heart and like a touch of the grape with our favorite meal.

Sylvia Bashline, one of the country's experts on cooking wild game, said in her cookbook, *The Bounty of the Earth,* that wild turkey deserves to be complemented at the dinner table with no less than champagne.

It's traditional to have cranberry sauce with turkey. Next time try adding two tablespoons of sherry to a pound of whole berry sauce, for added zing.

For a rich sauce to serve over slices of turkey, mix one third port, one third jelly (currant or blackberry), and one third butter together and heat.

Want something beside soup to make of the turkey leftovers? Try this turkey in cream and wine sauce.

Turkey in Cream and Wine Sauce

2 cups boiling water
1 diced small onion
2 stalks celery
1 teaspoon salt
½ teaspoon pepper
1 cup heavy cream
2 tablespoons flour
3 tablespoons any red wine

Simmer turkey chunks in the boiling water. Add onion, salt, pepper, and celery. Cook one half hour, then remove turkey chunks from water. Strain the broth and add cream. Heat to boiling. Stir in blended flour and 2 tablespoons water. Stir until thick. Add turkey chunks and red wine. Serve over biscuits.

—Shirley Grenoble
Turkey Call

Try This on a Sweet Tooth. . .

Complex carbohydrates (starches) could taste a heck of a lot more like the sugars we crave if we'd only give them a chance.

You don't think so?

Then try this. Take a piece of bread and chew it for a full 30 seconds. Then pay close attention to how it tastes. Sweet.

The chemical reason is that salivary juices contain an enzyme, called amylase, which is capable of converting starch into sugar—*in the mouth*.

So who knows. Maybe if we all ate more complex carbohydrates (as we did in the old days), and chewed them longer, we wouldn't even think about hot fudge sundaes.

Executive Fitness Newsletter

Can bad food be souring your marriage? "Nutrition is involved in 90 percent of my cases, and in 75 percent of them it's a major factor," says Mary Jane Hungerford, Ph.D., founder and former director of the Santa Barbara, California, branch of the American Institute of Family Relations. Dr. Hungerford tells of one typical couple (husband testy, wife depressed) that got along "like honeymooners" as soon as the two cut down on sugar, refined flour and coffee. Many marital spats, it seems, stem from a condition known as hypoglycemia (low blood sugar), which these foods have been known to cause.

Executive Fitness Newsletter

How to Avenge "Montezuma's Revenge"

Here is a formula that works, according to the U.S. Department of Health:

Prepare two separate water glasses, as follows:

Glass No. 1

8 oz. orange, apple, or other fruit juice (rich in potassium); ½ oz. honey, corn syrup, or table sugar (fructose—provides sugar necessary for absorption of essential salts); 1 pinch table salt (rich in sodium and chloride). Stir together until sweetener and salt are dissolved in juice.

Glass No. 2

8 oz. water (carbonated or boiled); ¼ tsp. baking soda (sodium bicarbonate). Quickly stir soda into water.

Now drink alternately from each glass. Supplement this "prescription" with carbonated beverages or water and tea made with boiled water, as desired. Avoid solid foods and milk until final recovery.

The PanAngler

How to Cut a Cheesecake

To avoid the inevitable flaking and sticking that occur when using a knife, use dental floss to cut a cheesecake. Take a long strand, stretch it taut, and press it through the cake with a slight sawing motion. When you reach the bottom, simply let go of one end and pull the floss out. If the crust is too resistant, you can finish off by pushing a knife gently into the cuts made with the floss. Either waxed or unwaxed floss are good for this, but try to avoid the mint-flavored.

Chocolate News

It took agriculture researchers seven years to cultivate a potato that was ideally suited to the potato chip business.

Spotlight

German Food

There is no doubt about it! German food is solid, hearty fare, and about as recognizable and distinguishable from French cuisine as the respective languages of these neighboring countries differ in tonality from one another. . . . I do think the Germans tend to go in for quantity as well as quality, and perhaps the American habit of overloading dinner plates stems in part from that German heritage translated to American shores. The French don't do it! The British *do!* But we must also remember that the present English royal family is directly descended from the German. . . . I have a German Encyclopaedia of Cooking published in Leipzig in 1910. At the back of the second volume are page upon page of menus of famous dinners served to royal personages, not only in the various states of Germany itself, but also those served to H.M. Queen Victoria. How these people made it even into early middle age beats me, because I should have thought they would all have died much sooner, either of acute indigestion, obesity, or cirrhosis of the liver.

The Grand Duke's Court Dinner, April 2, 1889

Mulligatawny Soup (in itself a meal)

Truffles in Burgundy (money no object? but then truffles were cheaper, I suppose)

Roast Beef with Roast Potatoes

Miniature Patty Shells a la Talleyrand (Probably mushrooms in cream—roast potatoes weren't enough?)

Pureed Snipe (Are you ready for *that?*)

Young Chickens—roasted (Are you beginning to see what I mean?)

Cardoons with Beef Marrow

Victoria Pudding (I'm not sure exactly, but believe it was full of bread, gelatine and cream)

Pineapple Ice Cream

Nachtisch (which simply translates as an "after-dish," or dessert)

This particular pot-luck supper was thrown for Prince Albert of Prussia, who was also Regent of Braunschweig (of liverwurst fame), at the palace in Braunschweig.

And we think we eat too much today.

Le Campion Gourmet Club

The Story of Chocolate

Origins

Frankly, our favorite food has origins which go back, like most natural life, to obscurity. The roots of chocolate are sunk into the soil of myth, supposition and circumstantial evidence. The original cacao (cocoa) trees (whence comes the cacao pods, seeds, nibs and chocolate), according to botanists, likely developed wild in the Orinoco (Venezuela) or Amazon valleys more than 4000 years ago. The earliest archaeological records left by early Latin American civilizations indicate that a chocolate drink was part of their daily lives. The Mayans are usually given credit for the first cultivation of the cacao tree, taking it with them on their migration to the Yucatan around the seventh century A.D. The ancient Toltec tribe, who lived in the area later occupied by the Aztecs, attributed the introduction of the cacao to their god of the moon, Quetzalcoatl —thus chocolate was the food of the gods. The Aztecs, who also worshipped Quetzalcoatl, evidently carried cacao seeds as they wandered throughout Central America. So revered did the cacao tree and its pods become that the seeds or beans were used in religious rituals and became a standard of currency for both Mayans and Aztecs. Could there have been Aztec bums who said, "Hey, buddy, can you spare a bean?"

From the Halls of Montezuma

It is claimed that Christopher Columbus was the first European to encounter chocolate, when he arrived in Nicaragua in 1502. The natives were using the beans as currency and drinking chocolate as a common beverage, much as we drink coffee today. Surely someone must have offered him a cup. But Chris was obsessed with finding a new trade route to India, and as usual, he couldn't recognize a good thing when it was placed right under his nose.

Luckily, Cortez was more astute. Welcomed in Mexico in 1519 by the Aztecs, who mistook the blond-bearded sailor for their lost god Quetzalcoatl, Hernando was entertained lavishly in Montezuma's court. The great Aztec emperor was exceedingly fond of chocolate and reportedly drank 50 tankards a day.

It is probable that Montezuma's potion demanded an acquired taste. The Aztecs drank chocolate as a stimulant, eschewing sweeteners in favor of spices to enhance the sharp, bitter flavor. Whatever Cortez thought of the royal drink, he admired the gold chalice in which it was served.

Learning of the use of cacao beans as a currency of exchange and being taught by Montezuma how to cultivate the precious trees, Cortez returned the hospitality shown him by plundering the Aztec Empire and sailing back to Spain with the first chocolate beans ever to reach Europe. These beans, planted in Mexico, Trinidad, Haiti and Africa, gave the Spanish a monopoly on chocolate that lasted 100 years.

"Choco, Choco, Choco . . ."

The earliest accounts of how chocolate was made and what it tasted like are from seventeenth-century histories and diaries. Joseph Acosta, a Jesuit missionary writing about the customs in Mexico and Peru in the late 1500s, says, "The chief use of this Cocoa is in a drincke which they call Chocolate, whereof they make great account, foolishly and without reason; for it is loathsome to such as are not acquainted with it, having a skumme or froth that is very unpleasant to taste. . . . Yet it is a drincke very much esteemed by the Indians, whereof they feast noble men as they passe through their country."

A more thorough and flattering portrait comes from the explorer Thomas Gage who devoted a whole chapter to "Chocolatte" in his *New Survey of the West Indies.* The following comes from the third edition, published in 1677: "This name Chocolatte is an Indian name, and is compounded from *Atte,* as some say, or as others, *Atle,* which in the Mexican language signifieth water, and from the sound which the water (wherein is put the Chocolatte) makes, as *Choco, Choco, Choco* when it is stirred in a cup. . . ."

Chocolate News

Presidential Sweet

Nancy Reagan's Vienna Chocolate Bars

2 sticks butter
1½ cups sugar
2 egg yolks
2½ cups flour
1 ten-oz. jar jelly (*Chocolate News* recommends raspberry jelly or apricot preserves)
1 cup semisweet chocolate bits
¼ teaspoon salt
4 egg whites
2 cups finely chopped nuts

Cream the butter with the egg yolks and ½ cup sugar. Add the flour and knead with fingers. Pat batter out on a greased cookie sheet to about ⅜″ thickness. Bake for 15 to 20 minutes at 350° until lightly browned. Remove from oven, spread with jelly and top with chocolate bits. Beat the egg whites with salt until stiff. Fold in remaining cup of sugar and nuts. Gently spread on top of jelly and chocolate. Bake for about 25 minutes at 350°. Cut into squares or bars.

Chocolate News

The Morel of this Story. . .

An old legend has it that Christ and Peter walked over the country-side begging bread. Some gave them hard brown bread of poor quality, while others gave them soft white biscuits of good quality. As they walked through the forest eating, the bread crumbs fell and where the brown crumbs fell poisonous mushrooms sprang up, but where the white crumbs fell delicious edible mushrooms grew. Surely these were morels! We have heard all sorts of names for morels and related species. Dryland fish, murtles, mountain fish, snake-heads, etc., but no matter what the name, these are the most sought-after fungi in the world!

The Mycophile

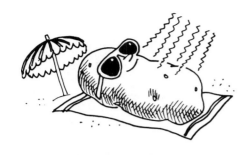

A Potato a Day Keeps the Doctor Away

Potatoes are often credited with special medicinal powers. Because they retain heat or cold well, they are handy compresses.

•

In Ireland, water from boiled potatoes is rubbed on aches, sprains, and broken bones.

•

A stone or pebble boiled in the pot with potatoes is believed to have great curative properties.

•

In Holland it was necessary that the potato be stolen to be efficacious as a cure. In Yorkshire it must be dried in the morning sun and protected from the afternoon sun.

•

In Newfoundland, a sliced baked potato is placed in a stocking which is then tied around the neck to cure a sore throat.

•

In Texas, scraped raw potato is placed on burns and frostbite.

•

Potatoes with their high vitamin C content saved many sailors' lives on long voyages by preventing outbreaks of scurvy.

Spotlight

From Bean to Bar

For those naive chocolate devotees amongst us (myself included) who assumed that chocolate was probably made by grinding up beans from a "cocoa bush" into a powder and adding water, the 30-minute film, "From Bean to Bar," produced by L.S. Heath & Sons, will be something of a revelation. With the aid of vibrant color photography, we are straightaway whisked off to the tropics where we discover, much to our dismay, that there is no such thing as a "cocoa bush." Chocolate comes into the world as a pretty five-petalled blossom which soon develops into a heavy cocoa pod that looks something like a Hubbard squash and hangs imposingly from the sturdy branches of a good-sized tree.

Harvesters select the ripened pods, cut them down from the tree, and slash open the shells, extracting the beans that are encased in a slimy, whitish pulp, which has a Mango-like taste. One pod can produce 20 to 50 beans, and 400 beans are required to create one pound of chocolate.

With the pulp still clinging to their skins, the beans are sent off to fermenting sheds to "cure" and are then spread out on massive "drying roofs" to dry fully in the sun, whereupon, according to the film, the beans are polished by native workers.

The next stop on our journey is Robinson, Ill., the home of the Heath Chocolate Company, where we find batches of raw beans undergoing rigorous quality control tests in the lab as they are analyzed for fermentation levels, screened and cleaned by machine and then air-blown to storage silos. Next, we bear witness to the drying and roasting process, after which the beans are cracked open and the hard outer skins are separated from the "nibs," which are composed of half cocoa butter and half cocoa solids—the essence of what we know as chocolate.

If this sounds a trifle complicated, be apprised that our saga of the bean has only just begun. The nibs are ground up to form a dark, syrupy "chocolate liquor," to which sugar, cocoa butter, and milk powder for milk chocolate, are added. The resulting "mixer paste" undergoes compression for smoother texture and consistency and emerges a light powder. We then observe the "conching" process, which uses frictional heat to liquefy and thereby remove all traces of bitterness from the milk chocolate compound. Finally, the film takes us on a guided tour of the assembly line as English toffee bars are mixed, cooked, cut, covered with a milk chocolate coating (that gets an "air wave" treatment for that familiar ripply effect on top), wrapped, boxed—all by machine, of course—and sent on their merry way to consumers hither and yon at the rate of 1¾ million bars a day.

—Boyd Hunter
Chocolate News

Garlic Ice Cream

Soak:
  1½ teaspoons gelatin in ¼ cup cold water

Heat to the boiling point:
  2 cups milk
  ¾ to 1 cup sugar
  ⅛ teaspoon salt

Dissolve the gelatin in the hot milk.
Cool, then add:
  2 tablespoons lemon juice
  2 cloves minced *garlic*

Chill the mixture until slushy. Add when whipped until thickened, but not stiff:
  2 cups whipping cream

Still-freeze in a mold or foil-covered tray.
Top portions with fresh strawberry topping.

Garlic Times

World's Oldest Wine

Commanderia may be the world's oldest wine. As far back as the seventh century B.C., the Greek poet Hesiod sang the glories of Cyprus Nama, a wine made from grapes exposed to the sun. And even before that time, worshippers of the goddess Aphrodite celebrated with it. In the twelfth century when the Knights Templar set up their headquarters, or Grand Commanderie, near the city of Limassol [in Cyprus], the wine was renamed Commanderia. While the name changed, the method of making the wine has remained essentially the same as it was when Hesiod described it 28 centuries ago. All three companies exporting wine to the U.S. [from Cyprus] send a Commanderia.

The Friends of Wine

Tucson, Ariz.—The *Arizona Daily Star* has some suggestions for heat-wave gourmets who are getting bored with fried eggs served up on a piece of sidewalk.

The newspaper calls it car cookery. Any of the dishes can be whipped up in areas where this summer's scorching heat wave has struck:

Wrap a standing rib roast or a turkey in foil and place it gently on the front seat of your car. Large hams should be strapped in a seat-beat in an upright position.

Unscrew the knob on the gearshift lever and slide four marshmallows over the hot metal rod. Most turn-signal levers will accommodate a single hot dog, skewered from end to end.

The dashboard beneath the windshield—the hottest spot in most parked cars—doubles as an energy-free broiler. Slices of garlic toast can be arranged along the dash and, if watched closely, steaks and hamburgers can be char-broiled on the radio-speaker grill so the hot grease can drain properly.

To warm leftovers, park under a shade tree.

Funny Funny World

Just why the prune has received the majority of the publicity pertaining to wrinkles is a mystery which we raisin fanciers of Fancy Raisins will do our best to penetrate.

The canard, for example, that "No matter how old a prune may be it's always full of wrinkles" has been discredited time & time again by the Research Foundation of the IF/R [International Friends of Raisins] in countless scientific experiments in our new spotless laboratories manned by white-coated technicians.

Working with the latest sophisticated abacus, our theoretical physicists have established beyond a shadow of a doubt that year in and year out, and year for year, the raisin is more wrinkled, per unit of wrinkle, than is the prune.

Of course, the big Prune Trust, underwritten as it is by the Rockefeller and Ford foundations, has unlimited resources to spread these lies about the raisin. We look to brighter and happier days and a cleaner and purer world where the prune is at last discredited . . . and the raisin is raised to its proper place in the supermarket display.

Raisin d'Etre

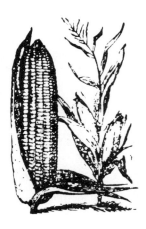

Domestic Beer Found Full of Corn

Why are the nationally distributed American beers so different from the daily drinking beers of Europe?

Europeans think corn is for the birds

The answer to that is a real maize. Not Maze, but maize. And you can blame it on Squanto and Massasoit who taught John Carver and William Bradford to like and cultivate corn. In northern Europe, where it is little seen—and generally imported from America at that—it is still often called "Indian Maize."

But no European would make beer out of corn even if it were more available. Nearly all beer there is made from barley-malt (malted barley grains) and water, aided by yeast and the great flavoring agent and preservative, hops. In Germany, the pure beer laws allow only barley, hops, yeast and water—except for the specialty wheat beer, weizenbier or weisse. The brew cops of Switzerland, Norway and Finland enforce similar laws to guarantee the quaffer good body and flavor.

But, in the U.S. we brew with a little malted barley, some hops, the yeast necessary to get fermentation going—and adjuncts. That's a term for other grains. The most common is corn, followed by rice. Adjuncts are used partly to make a lighter product; lighter in body and lighter in flavor. But, they are also used for another, more important, reason.

Corn is quick, economical

In the U.S., barley is barely produced, but we have corn running out our ears. Barley is dear, corn is cheap.

Further, malting barley—getting it into a useable form—is a slow, expensive process.

Barley grains are rock hard and would take forever to break open and release fermentable starch. The barley is spread on a floor or a moving belt and soaked until it starts to germinate. Germination is stopped by controlled heating. This softer product is malt.

Corn, however, can be prepared for fermentation merely by cooking it quickly and cheaply.

So, just as the American nation grew up on whisky because it was a compact and easy way to carry corn to the West—and had far more kick per canteen-full than the same amount of wine—American beer drinkers have been growing up on light brew made quickly and cheaply and largely from corn.

But don't sneer at the American's taste in beer, other than the present fad for light beers actually labeled "Light" or "Lite". A good balance of barley-malt, hops and corn (or, in the case of Budweiser, rice) can produce a nice, clean beer with thirst-quenching qualities and some taste, especially if it is not served too cold.

Schlitz learns a lesson

If you don't believe the American beer drinker cares, just look at the devastating lesson he taught Schlitz. Over the years the Jos. Schlitz Brewing Company turned out a proud product. After all, Schlitz made Milwaukee Famous. Just a few years ago I preferred Schlitz over Bud with my Chinese dinners because there was more flavor, more character. The company was pretty well fixed. Then Miller started catering to a perceived taste for lightness and blandness, and Budweiser became aggressive on the marketing scene, and Schlitz began losing market shares.

Schlitz did what many companies do in such straits; they cut costs. It costs money to age beer—even if only for days or a couple weeks. So they cut the aging time. And barley-malt costs a lot more than corn, so they followed accounting advice there.

I dropped Schlitz. So did millions. Little kids were looking skyward and pleading, "Joe, tell me it aint true." But, it was, indeed, bottled Grimsville.

The new product reminded me of the output of an ultra-modern brewery constructed near the Boordy Vineyards of that disciple of H.L. Mencken and pioneer of Eastern American hybrid wine, Philip Wagner. As we drove past one day, he pointed to the beer factory and remarked: "Modern miracle. Guaranteed less than 24 hours from the horse to your glass."

Business at Schlitz went from bad to awful. Then they brought in a new president. Frank Sellinger not only came over from Anheuser-Busch where he learned to sell Bud and Michelob, but he came up, not through accounting, but through brewing.

So, he knew what was wrong. The beer was lousy. And his first move was to fix it. After a lot of trial blends and tasting room conferences, he settled on the "new" Schlitz. There is less corn and more barley-malt and hops. And it is aged longer. It even tastes like beer.

—David Pursglove
The Friends of Wine

Federal Bread

The federal definition of *bread,* or *white bread,* or *rolls,* or *white rolls,* or *buns,* or *white buns* allows the following things as ingredients *without listing them on the label:*

mono- and di-glycerides; carragheenan; bromelain preparations; alpha-amylases obtained from *Bacillus subtilis;* calcium sulfate; calcium lactate; calcium carbonate; di-calcium phosphate; ammonium phosphates; ammonium sulfate; ammonium chloride; potassium bromate; calcium peroxide; azodicarbonamide; tricalcium phosphate; *L*-cysteine; calcium stearoyl-2-lactylate; lactylic stearate; sodium stearyl fumarate; succinylated monoglycerides; ethosyxlated mono- and di-glycerides.

—*Code of Federal Regulations*
Title 21, Volume 1 (1970), 17.1.

Monocalcium phosphate, calcium proprionate, sodium proprionate, and sodium diacetate can also be added, but if so must be listed as ingredients. . . .

Quarterly Review of Doublespeak

Words, Words, Words

FOUL PLAY

Reinhold Aman can curse in over 200 languages, which leaves him, he says, only 4,800 to go. Americans, he has found, are very poor at swearing. "They just don't know how to do it," he comments, "and usually fall back on the same 24 words or so."

He has a tip for lousy cussers: "Look for a distinguishing characteristic. Each of us is deviant in some way. For instance, I wear glasses, I'm five foot seven, 20 pounds overweight, have short hair and a Kissinger accent. So you could start off calling me a fat, four-eyed, runty, reactionary, sewer-mouthed Kraut."

Aman's no-words-barred expertise has led to *Maledicta,* a twice-a-year journal that looks like *Foreign Affairs* or *The Iowa Review* but reads like . . . like nothing else in America. The titles of the scholarly (and mock-scholarly) articles recently published—or about to be published—in *Maledicta* pretty much tell the story:

Spanish Gypsy Curses
American Indian Insults
Swiss Swearwords
Embarrassing Trade Names
Anti-Clerical Limericks
Marlon Brando's Verbal Abuse
American Doctors' Slang
Suggestive Song Titles
Censorship in Dictionaries
Forbidden Auto License Plates
Offensive School Cheers
Sexual Terms in the Bible and Talmud

Aman has been "sowing wild oaths" (the headline on a *Newsweek* profile of him in 1980) for more than a decade. A native of Bavaria, he completed his Ph.D. in linguistics and medieval literature at the University of Texas in 1968. His analysis of 151 battle scenes in the *Parzival* of Wolfram von Eschenbach sparked his interest in the study of aggression, which led to a fascination with aggressive speech. He began studying invective in earnest while teaching German at the University of Wisconsin and got a chance to get into it full time when he was denied tenure at the school in 1972. (His parting comment to his department chairman, Aman says, was: "When I see you, my feet fall asleep.") Aman complains that "people are killed and injured every day because of insults but they [academics] refuse to study them because the subject is disreputable."

Aman began collecting insults—and the stories behind them—with a vengeance. His goal: to analyze every offensive term ever used anywhere in the world. Aman accumulated 14,000 pages of research and 4,500 bibliographic file cards. In 1977 *Maledicta* was born. (He coined the name: think of our English word "malediction," meaning curse, slander, or calumny.)

Soon 2,500 readers in more than 50 countries had subscribed and Aman was toasted as the Wizard of Epithets on *NBC Evening News, Phil Donahue* and the *Today* show. He drew up a business card with the legend, "Have Curse, Will Travel," and took to the lecture circuit. *Time* magazine observed that "with the possible exception of Don Rickles, he is the only American who makes a full-time living out of insults."

Aman believes that cussing is nothing to be ashamed of; it releases pent-up emotions and prevents aggression from being expressed physically. And he feels that the study of swearing has redeeming social and cultural value. He points out that Freud once said: "The first human being who hurled a curse against his adversary instead of a rock was the founder of civilization." He quotes Shakespeare (from *Henry IV*): ". . . to gain the language,/'T is needful that the most immodest word/Be look'd upon and learn'd. . . ." Aman has learned that Catholics seem to specialize in blasphemy; WASPs concentrate on body functions, sex, and excrement; and those who hail from the Middle and Far East are partial to ancestor insults. No language is more aggressive, he observes, than Yiddish. His favorite Yiddish curse? "May all your teeth fall out except one, so you can have a toothache."

Aman, 46, publishes *Maledicta* out of his home in Waukesha, Wisconsin. He does all the professional-looking typesetting himself. In 1980 he estimated that he netted $3,700 a year from the journal and the books he has published under the banner of Maledicta Press. (One was a previously unpublished bawdy story by Mark Twain.) In March 1981, however, as the result of a story in *The Wall Street Journal,* he received 3,000 inquiries about his publication, which led to 2,000 new subscriptions. Aman was happy to get what he called "a $20,000 bonus," but the extra one-man work load led to "one of the worst times in my life."

Aman is still waiting for someone in the media, however, to pick up on his monograph of profanities found in Richard Nixon's White House tapes. His name for this study pretty well captures what he calls his mission in life: "Expletives *Restored.*"

MIND GAMES

Even the names of the people behind *The Enigma* are enigmatic. To other members of The National Puzzlers League, which puts out the 12-page journal, *Enigma* editor Marjorie B. Friedman is known as MANGIE. Treasurer Paul E. Thompson is BLACKSTONE. It's a lot easier to figure out who MANGIE and BLACKSTONE are than to solve most of the puzzles in their publication.

About 300 members receive *The Enigma* every month but according to MANGIE (er, Marjorie), "We really don't have 'readers'—what we have are 'solvers.' " Each issue has one page of news (an upcoming convention/competition, for example), one page of messages from readers, one page of results from last month's issue, and nine pages of puzzles (composed by members for each other) that range from rather simple Spoonergrams to almost indescribable (but apparently not unsolvable) "heteronyms," "metathesises," and "bigram rebus alternades."

Enigma subscribers must be pretty bright. "We have loads of Phi Beta's and Mensa members and Ph.D.'s," says Friedman. "I like to think that the characteristics in common are braininess and a sense of humor." Most of the members are mathematicians, engineers, or computer experts, but Friedman thinks "it's interesting" that "we have quite a few farmers."

The National Puzzlers League is not a passing fancy. It has been around since 1883, and 900 issues of *The Enigma* have been published. ARTY ESS was editor for 33 years and B. NATURAL for 17. Because the NPL has "no desire to expand," according to Friedman (it runs on all-volunteer help and a low budget), it will only accept as members those who are extremely serious about taxing their brains.

Even so, *The Enigma* is mostly for fun. Friedman calls puzzle-solving "a pastime which will give you more pleasure, for less expense, than any other hobby. All of us are in the game to have fun and to perpetuate the puzzlistic art. We do not sponsor contests for big money prizes. *The Enigma* is our battleground where we do our best to entertain each other, where the constructors challenge the solvers, and where wit and humor are the order of the day."

The Associated Press reported that a school principal in Houston sent the following message home to parents: "Our school's cross-graded, multi-ethnic, individualized learning program is designed to enhance the concept of an open-ended learning program with emphasis on a continuum of multi-ethnic, academically enriched learning using the identified intellectually gifted child as the agent or director of his own learning." One father responded as follows: "I have a college degree, speak two foreign languages, and four Indian dialects, have been to a number of county fairs and three goat ropings, but I haven't the faintest idea what the hell you're talking about! Do you?"

Quarterly Review of Doublespeak

- A PUN is defined ideally as an ad lib, conversational play on words, the lowest form of humor, and is traditionally greeted with a responding pun on the same theme, or groans:

He: I limit my catch to one fish.
She: Don't be a piker. Take 100.
He: That's a whale of a catch.

Shakespeare, as did most Elizabethans, reveled in puns. His plays are filled with them. Most, when explained, are non-broadcastable. Many are complex. This opening from *Richard II* is a double pun. The "sun" is "the son" of York, soon to be King Edward IV. It is also the "sun" of his emblem.

"Now is the winter of our discontent made glorious summer by this sun."

- AN EPIGRAM is a terse, pointed statement, sometimes humorous!

"Not to be born is best"—Sophocles, 400 B.C.
"There but for the grace of God goes God."
    —Churchill, concerning Sir Stafford Cripps
"A fisherman is a long stick with a lot of patience on one end and an old shoe on the other."

This converts to a pun thusly:

"A fisherman is a long stick with a whale of a lot of patience on one end and a wish on the other."

- A GROANER is an extended story, often tediously long, pointing a moral which includes a pun or puns on a familiar phrase.

A witch gave two people one wish. A man wished for $1,000 while the woman wished for $1,000,000. Which proves that "There's a lot more wish in the she."

- A SPOONERISM is the transposition of parts of words—named after Dr. Spooner, an Oxford don:

"Pardon me, madam," he said, entering church. "You are occupewing my pie."

- A MALAPROP is named after Mrs. Malaprop in *The Rivals,* Sheridan's great comedy. This is the use of a word which sounds like it belongs, but doesn't.

Describing a man who was the pinnacle of politeness she said: He is the pineapple of politeness.

- A NON-SEQUITUR is part of a sentence or remark which doesn't logically follow what went before.

"I don't care if the sun is shining, you'll have to carry your slide rule."

- A BON MOT is a French epigram.
- A JOKE is a sometimes funny story.

Punsters Unlimited

Elite Maledicta

During the Vienna Summit, Soviet Foreign Minister Andrei Gromyko, trying to propose a toast, refused the help of a translator and said to Mrs. Dean Rusk: "I offer a toast to this gracious lady. *Up your bottom.*"

Wisconsin's governor, Lee Dreyfus, recently upset the Honey Producers Association by telling the State Honey Queen, Lynn Ludack, that he ate honey, but his wife did not because she considers it "bee poop."

British Prime Minister Margaret Thatcher in private scoffed at her continental allies. She called them "bloody wets," roughly equivalent to U.S. "drips."

Maledicta

Millard Filimore's Last Words

"This nourishment is palatable."

The Fillmore Bu(n)gle

Laws

ABEL'S CONSERVATIVE PRINCIPLE: Never do anything for the first time.
CAHN'S AXIOM: When all else fails, read the instructions.
CAPONE'S LAW: You can get much farther with a kind word and a gun than you can with a kind word alone. (Al Capone)
ETTORE'S LAW: The other line always moves faster.
FELDSTEIN'S LAW: Never play leapfrog with a unicorn.
GILBERT'S LAW: When everyone is somebody, then no one's anybody. (Sir W. S. Gilbert)
HARTLEY'S LAW: Never sleep with anyone crazier than yourself.

HUROK'S LAW: If people don't want to come, nothing will stop them. (Sol Hurok)

JOHNSON'S LAW OF AUTO REPAIR: Any tool dropped while being used to repair an automobile will roll on the floor to the exact geographic center of the vehicle's undercarriage.

KIERKEGAARD'S LAW: People demand freedom of speech to make up for the freedom of thought which they avoid. (Saren Aabe Kierkegaard)

KOMMEN'S LAW: If you look like your passport photo, you're too ill to travel.

LAW OF PREDICTABLE RESULTS: No matter what happens, there is someone who knew it would.

MARX'S THEORY: Military intelligence is a contradiction in terms. (Groucho Marx)

MASSON'S MAXIM: "Be yourself" is the worst advice you can give to some people.

NASH'S LAW: Progress might have been all right once, but it went on too long. (Ogden Nash)

RICKOVER'S LAW: If the Russians would send a man to hell, we'd say, "We can't let them beat us to it." (Admiral H. Rickover)

RUNYON'S RULE: The race is not always to the swift, nor the battle to the strong—but that's the way to bet. (Damon Runyon)

SCHMIDT'S SYSTEM THEORY: Build a system that even a fool can use, and only a fool will want to use it.

STURGEON'S LAW: Ninety percent of everything is crud.

THOREAU'S SECOND LAW: Men have become the tools of their tools. (Henry David Thoreau)

WEST'S LAW: To err is human, but it feels divine. (Mae West)

WILDE'S PERSONALITY THEORY: Only the shallow know themselves. (Oscar Wilde)

Turtle Express

Many West Germans, angered by the unusually cold and wet summer of 1980, sent insulting postcards to the weather bureau.

Maledicta

Dirty Riddles

1. What is it a man can do standing up, a woman sitting down, and a dog on three legs? *(Answer: Shake hands.)*
2. What is it that a cow has four of and a woman has only two of? *(Answer: Legs.)*
3. What is a four-letter word ending in "k" that means the same as intercourse? *(Answer: Talk.)*
4. What is on a man that is round, hard, and sticks so far out of his pajamas you can hang a hat on it? *(Answer: His head.)*

Turtle Express

Some Examples of Doublespeak

Doublespeak	Translation
low income	poverty
sub-standard housing	slum, ghetto
non-retained	fired
for your convenience	for our convenience
encore telecast	re-run
pre-owned	used
therapeutic misadventure	malpractice
negative deficit	profit
correctional facility	prison
change of equipment	something broke down
dentures	false teeth
genuine imitation leather	fake leather
inoperative statement	lie
bathroom tissue	toilet paper
occasional irregularity	constipation
senior citizen	old person
eliminate redundancies in the human resources area	fire employees
life insurance	death insurance
incursion	invasion
nervous wetness	sweat
memorial park	cemetery
tinting, rinsing	dyeing
downward adjustments	budget cuts

Quarterly Review of Doublespeak

***Breaking Wind Saves Heat.* (Headline above an article recommending the planting of wind-breaks around one's house.)**

Maledicta

Linguistic-Cultural Myopia Separates U.S.–World

Former Chairman of the Senate Foreign Relations Committee J. William Fulbright said recently, "Our linguistic and cultural myopia is losing us friends, business, and respect in the world."

Think about it. Among industrialized nations, the United States stands alone in its neglect of foreign language study. Outside of the U.S., only four percent of the earth's population speaks English, while nine out of ten Americans cannot speak, read, or effectively understand any language but English. . . .

The fact that so few American adults are fluent in any language but their own is probably reflective of a kind of smug Americocentric view of the world that assumes that anyone with whom we have need to communicate should learn to speak English. . . .

Carl Rowan, in *The Oregonian*, writes: "Senator S.I. Hayakawa, R-Calif., has said that there are some 10,000 Japanese salesmen in New York City, all of whom speak English; while there are about 1,000 American salesmen in Japan, few of whom speak Japanese. If those figures are close to correct, you begin to see why we have a balance of trade problem."

Similar situations are cited by Charles W. Bray III, deputy director of the U.S. International Communications Agency: "We are being thrown into contact and conflict with peoples whose histories and motivations we scarcely understand."

> *ELNA Newsletter*
> (Esperanto League for North America)

William Penn, Quaker and founder of Pennsylvania: "Never marry but for love; but see that thou lovest what is lovely."

> *Marriage Enrichment*

Ah, Chute!

The "Urban Cowboy" craze and other pop-culture phenomena have begun to create a whole new audience for rodeo. Yet the sport is a subtle, complex art and many people attending their first few rodeos find themselves very confused, unable to understand the special terminology necessary to grasp the real meaning of the sport.

As a public service, I have extensively researched rodeo jargon and produced this compact, easy-to-comprehend glossary of common rodeo terms:

BAREBACK—What you are when you've lost your shirt in a poker game.

BARREL RACE—An informal timed event. Any number of contestants gather to see how quickly they can empty a keg of beer.

CHUTE—A common expletive voiced by cowboys after having been bucked off. (Ah, chute!)

HOOEY—What you'll get on your boots if you don't watch your step in a rodeo arena.

HAZING—What your eyes begin to do if you dismount head-first—or win the barrel race.

LITTLE BRITCHES—Those extra-tight jeans worn by many cowgirls.

MATCH COMPETITION—When a cowgirl takes out a cigarette and seven cowboys try to be the first to light it.

MECHANICAL BULL—Anytime someone brags about how great his pickup is.

LUCK OF THE DRAW—When someone pulls a gun on you, and misses.

PICK-UP MAN—The guy who cleans up the rodeo grounds.

MOUNT MONEY—When your horse makes more than you do.

PIGGIN' STRING—Consecutive visits to greasy-spoon restaurants. ("My ulcer's killin' me—I'm workin' on a four-day piggin' string.")

PULLING LEATHER—Picking up the check at a restaurant and discovering your billfold is empty.

SLACK TIME—That brief interlude between leaving a bull's back and hitting the arena floor.

> —T. J. Gilles
> *World of Rodeo and Western Heritage*

Right or Wrong?

Romans 14:15 Whether it's right or wrong, don't do it if your brother thinks it is wrong.

1 Cor. 10:27 Whether it's right or wrong, do it if your brother thinks it is right.

Romans 14:14 It's right if you think it's right and wrong if you think it's wrong.

> *Exploring the Bible*

How It Works

Ronald Reagan recently issued a half-page memo ordering government agencies to cut back "superfluous" publications. In order to explain the memo, the Office of Management and Budget (the OMB) put out a 10-page bulletin. To explain the bulletin the OMB has now put out a 20-page plan with 8 attachments and a new form to put the bulletin into effect.

As late as the 1930s there was a small sign backstage in each legitimate theater and vaudeville house outside New York City, reading: *The words "hell" and damn", and the name of the deity, are not to be pronounced on this stage.*

Maledicta

The Greatest Pun of All Time?

Attributed to E. W. Hornung, the brother-in-law of Sir Alfred Conan Doyle. "Though he's not very humble, there's no police like Holmes."

Punsters Unlimited

A Variation on the Same Theme

Nero, watching Rome burn, observed: "Though it's beginning to crumble, there's no blaze like Rome."

Punsters Unlimited

The New Jersey Division of Gaming Enforcement in a report to the Casino Control Commission did not use the term "Mob," "Syndicate," "Mafia," or "Cosa Nostra." Instead, the report refers to a "member of a career-offender cartel."

Quarterly Review of Doublespeak

From San Francisco, the Associated Press reported: Gifted flunk IRS form. Only one student in a class of 24 gifted eighth graders here correctly completed an Internal Revenue Service 1040A income tax form that the IRS says is so easy any eighth grader could understand it.

And the longer 1040 form, said to be easy enough for any ninth grader, stumped all 27 ninth graders tested and a class of high school seniors as well.

"Don't ask me how they figure it out," said perturbed Stephanie Chan, a ninth grader at Abraham Lincoln High School. "And to think we have to do it when we grow up!"

"Why can't they just write it in English?" pleaded student Jim Johns.

Quarterly Review of Doublespeak

The First "Form Letter"?

A "bedbug letter" was a public relations term meaning a form letter expressing denial, in reply to charges or inquiries from a large number of complainants. Its genesis was in the early days of railroads when primitive sanitary conditions aboard sleeping cars led to angry letters from customers. A clever form reply, which neither denied nor confirmed the claims, and which tended to disclaim liability for and explain away the predatory insects, was developed. Thus it became easy for a railroad official to tell his secretary, "Send them the Bedbug Letter," rather than to dictate replies.

This response to the complaints about bedbugs likely was the first widely circulated form letter, and for years afterward the term "bedbug letter" became the synonym for form letters of any kind.

Fortunately, the term has been amended to "form letter" and the literary device has become much more respectable, particularly with the advent of the computer-assisted form letter, one of which recently asked me, "How would you like to see *Mrs. Barker* driving her new Cadillac up and down *Box 2228* while the neighbors stood in awe?" I am not married. . . .

Gray Barker's Newsletter

When a flight from Buffalo to Cincinnati landed in Louisville, a passenger asked the stewardess why the plane was landing since it was a direct flight. Without batting an eye, the stewardess replied, "It is indeed a direct flight, madam; it just isn't nonstop."

Quarterly Review of Doublespeak

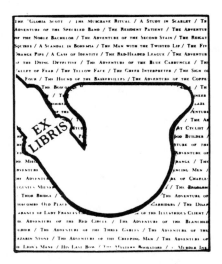

Charles Lamb's Death Wish

"May my last breath be drawn through a pipe, and exhaled in a jest."

The Pipe Smoker's Ephemeris

Banished Words & Phrases!

Unconditional Banishment

- *Ballpark Figure* indicating an estimate. A disservice to a great sport which is accurately documented by statistics.
- *Time frame* replaces "point in time" as a pretentious redundancy. "We have no time frame for his departure." Why not, "We don't know when he'll leave"?
- *Do-able,* as in Mass. Gov. Edward King's statement, "a $500 million rollback we think is do-able."
- *Surely if we can send a man to the moon we can. . . .*
- *Campaign rhetoric,* in that it is a misleading expression wherein politicians mute the idea that they were actually lying.
- *Howard Cosell,* en masse.
- *The reading aloud* by TV announcers of printed words displayed on the screen.
- *Our craft, paying my dues* and *surviving* as used endlessly by some entertainers in interviews.
- *De-plane*
- *For sure*

Limited Banishments

- *Interface,* as used by anyone other than

seamstresses, geometricians, and computer operators.
- *Podium,* when used where one means "lectern." One stands behind a lectern which rests on a podium.

Moratorium

- *The Athens of the. . . .*

Two-Year Probation

- There is nothing wrong with these words, but they are being over-used, particularly by restaurant critics and architects, and in this over-use tend to be pompous:
- *Ambiance*
- *Opt*

Washington Phrase Alert

- *Where you stand is where you sit,* which apparently means that one's philosophy and opinions are based solely on one's job.

The Woods-Runner

***Nuke the Unborn Gay Whales!* (A multi-target bumper sticker.)**

Maledicta

Doublespeak Here and There

The rules committee of the Democratic Party recently decided to drop the term "handicapped" in favor of the term "physically challenged."

•

Thomas Murphy, Chairman of the Board of General Motors, in an interview on "Meet the Press," when asked why the automobile business is so bad, replied: "We are in a period of negative economic growth."

•

The *Los Angeles Times* . . . carried an advertisement . . . for "Real Counterfeit Jewels."

•

A report on the results of a program designed to attack functional illiteracy among adults which was prepared by the National Testing Service Research Corporation of Durham, N.C., said in part: "The conceptual framework for this evaluation posits a set of determinants of implementation which explains variations in the level of implementation of the Comprehensive Project. . . ."

Words That Mean Business

The correct use of the prefix "bi" as in bimonthly and biweekly is hard to keep straight. The problem is that there are so few rules governing the use of "bi" that many of the words are interchangeable. Or, using one instead of the other will do the same thing. For example, bimonthly and biweekly both mean twice a month. But, bimonthly *also* means every other month. And biweekly can mean half-weekly.

One usage expert recommends that words beginning with "bi" should be used only when no other way of saying what needs to be said can be found. For example, "He was famous for stunt flying in a *bi-plane.*" In this case, saying "a plan with two sets of wings," would be too clumsy and might not convey what was intended.

Biennial and biannual are two more words that are confusing. Biennial means occurring every two years. Biannual refers to something that occurs twice a year. But even "experts" have confused them. *Fowler's Modern English Usage* cites the example, "An annual bulletin is our first aim; but biennial issues may become possible if the Association enlarges as we hope." This is from a bulletin issued by the International Association of University Professors of English.

In some cases, it may not make that much difference. But when clarity is important, as in preparing policy manuals for employees, the plainest language should be used to avoid confusion. Instead of saying employees will be paid biweekly or bimonthly, a simple "twice monthly" could be used. This practice can be used in almost all cases: twice weekly, twice monthly, every two hours. You may know what you mean, but it's more important that the reader does, too!

From Nine to Five

Reckshun, Hugh G. (Entry in the Blacksburg, Virginia, telephone directory, circa 1974.)

Fun & Sport

REFUND FUN

"Smart shoppers" who collect coupons have dozens of publications to use as their Bibles. Many are "here today, gone tomorrow" operations that never reach more than a hundred readers. But Claudine Moffatt of Manchester, Missouri, one of the pioneers in this popular form of specialty publishing, is still around, after almost 20 years, wheeling and dealing for the benefit of several thousand fans.

What is refunding? Claudine explains it this way: "A discount program for purchasing a product. This system of rewarding the consumer for purchasing a given product has been used since 1895 when C. W. Post offered a penny on Postum. The company can write it off to advertising, while the refunders add to their household dollars by claiming the discounts or tax-free gifts. Some are satisfied with a few dollars a year while others go all out. By saving only $3 a day you save over $1000 a year. $3 is a very realistic goal. . . ."

The trick—and this is where Claudine's publications come in—is to be aware of every possible refund available *and* be able to obtain the coupons that will earn you a discount. Through her own research, Claudine (who has no connections with manufacturers) uncovers many offers, and subscribers send along quite a few others. She prints about 250 notices in her publications every month.

But this is only half the system; a $1.00-off offer on Hershey's Cocoa isn't going to do a bit of good for anyone who's allergic to chocolate. However, if that person loves peanut butter and has a Hershey's coupon, she can trade with someone who hates Skippy but craves hot chocolate . . . well, you get the idea. Through *Jaybee* (a monthly 12-page tabloid) and the *Refund Hot Line* (which comes out several times a month), Claudine lists all available offers and facilitates trading (by methods that are totally legal, but a bit complicated).

The first national bulletin for refunders was founded by Niles Eggleston of Milford, New York, in 1954. But when *Jaybee* was established in 1962 it set new standards of reporting and used abbreviations and lingo in its listings since adopted by most of the rest of the field, according to Claudine. Many women have started similar businesses—apparently believing Eggleston's statement that housewives could put out these publications "between burping the baby and stirring the gravy"—but dozens have failed to last even a year. Claudine's track record has earned her a position as chairman of the Refund Bulletin Editors Association. She attends many conventions of coupon collectors every year.

There are, Claudine estimates, 15 million Americans who receive $17 billion in refunds annually. But "trading trash for merchandise," she points out, "is not a Johnny-come-lately way to beat the system. I have a water glass and pitcher set my aunt got with soap wrappers 80 years ago. My first doll was obtained that way. Most people were refunders as children—all that cereal box stuff—and quit." It is for those who've kept at it, or returned to it, that Claudine puts out her publications. She does it in her nine-room home, with the aid of four electric typewriters and a couple of mini-computers, which have a way of breaking down or being taken over by her grandchildren (who like to play Space Invaders on them).

"Being a bulletin editor," Claudine says, "is a high risk, low pay proposition, and most of them have more red ink than the government. Printing and postage costs are taking big bites out of every dollar. You learn to expect the run-of-the-mill catastrophe. After 236 issues of *Jaybee* I've learned that Murphy's Law was written by a bulletin editor. Anything can go wrong—and does. Each issue extracts its pound of flesh. That's what I tell people who remark how slender I am—a combination of sweating out each issue and living 20 years on *only* refund food.

"But my teeth sparkle. What a healthy head of hair! R-e-l-i-e-f is spelled a dozen different refund brand names. Headaches cannot occur too often, if we want to claim all those Bayer, Tylenol, Excedrin, and Anacin refunds!"

WETTING A LINE

J im Chapralis has fished in over 30 countries—from the Arctic to Argentina, from New Zealand to Yugoslavia (with stops in Mozambique and Angola). He is a member of the International Fishing Hall of Fame. He won the international distance fly casting championship in Paris in 1955 and the German All-around Championship in 1956. His biggest thrill? "Playing a large sailfish on a fly rod for three hours using a 6-pound leader." He lost the fish. Shows what a good sport(sman) he is.

Jim started *The PanAngler,* an eight-page monthly newsletter from Chicago, in 1976, convinced that "there was a need for news, reports and evaluations of fishing outside of the U.S. Domestic fishing is nicely covered by such publications as *Field and Stream, Outdoor Life,* etc. But they don't do that much international reporting and because of the usual time delays with magazines their tips on a 'hot' new area can be dated by the time it reaches readers." *The PanAngler* gets this news out in a matter of days. Its circulation has passed 5,000  and Chapralis claims that it "might be the 'most quoted' fishing publication that we know of."

Until jet travel became accessible to millions, international fishing was pretty well confined to the Zane Greys and Ernest Hemingways of the world. Now, he says, anyone with a few hundred dollars in hand can fly from Miami to Costa Rica in three hours and find exotic fishing camps that are more like resorts.

The PanAngler covers the waterfront: from big-game fishing to trolling and light-tackle casting. Since they're closer to home, Canada and Mexico (and all of South America) get special attention but marlin fishing off Australia gets covered, too, always in a concise, informative style.

In 1976 *PA* predicted that a snook of over 50 pounds would be taken from the east coast of Costa Rica within the next two years. The odds against this occuring, according to Jim, "were huge since only one snook of over 50 pounds had ever been recorded in the history of sportfishing." Ten months later someone landed a 53½-pounder off Costa Rica.

Chapralis claims that *PA* editorials have inspired the formation of the American Sportfishing Federation and encouraged airlines to change schedules to suit anglers. During the Nicaraguan civil war *PA* campaigned against commercial snook fishing there. "Surprisingly," says Jim, "we heard from Somoza's government, and they even signed a bill prohibiting commercial snook fishing. But the government toppled soon after that."

Readers probably ask us this more than any other question: "How many entries does it take to win in a sweepstakes?" It only takes one entry to win. However, it's rather difficult to say how many entries you should submit in an effort to have that one entry selected as the winning entry. We've always considered contesting a hobby, and we spend as little or as much as we like. If we particularly like the prizes in a promotion, we'll work harder on that one and send in extra entries. But you'll have to decide just how many entries you should submit to any contest or sweepstakes.

Contest Newsletter

How Softball Was Invented

Chicago Board of Trade reporter George Hancock is credited with devising a version of the sport that is generally acknowledged as being the official forerunner of softball that is played today by more than 30 million Americans and 12 million foreign participants in 55 countries.

Hancock's version was called Indoor-Outdoor, the year was 1887, it was Thanksgiving Day and Hancock, wanting to liven things up in the Farragut Boat Club, came up with an idea: a battered boxing glove became a ball, a broomstick for a bat, two sides formed, and the beginning of softball.

From Indoor-Outdoor to Kitten Ball, Playground Ball, Diamond Ball, Mush Ball, and in 1932, the game acquired the name it is now known by worldwide, softball. Walter Hakanson, Denver YMCA director, is credited with giving softball its present name.

Hall of Famers

Chess

Origins

No one knows just who was the inventor of chess, or indeed if it was just one man. Like many other games of antiquity, we know very little about its origins. We can be reasonably certain that the first version of chess was played in India between 100-600 A.D., and most likely around the year 400. *Chaturanga,* the oldest variant of chess that is known, used as pieces elephants, horses, chariots, and foot soldiers to represent the four wings of the Indian armies of the time, as well as a king and minister to guide them. The first chessboards were actually backgammon boards, which at the time were divided into 64 squares and suitably ruled for the older game. Both chess and backgammon used dice at first, though almost at once the superiority of chess without chance playing a role was recognized.

Chess began its slow migration westward, being introduced in Persia circa 550. The Persians claimed to have invented both chess and backgammon in later texts, but no one else agrees with them. . . .

Chess for Blood

Chess can awaken violent passions, though nowadays these furies are channelled into complaints to tournament officials. King Canute executed Earl Ulf over a game of chess when the earl refused to let Canute take back one of his moves. They *were* on bad terms to start with. . . . An Icelandic prince slew a local chessmaster after the master was so impolitic as to win three times in a row. (The reverse behavior could also be dangerous, as one chessmaster was banished from the court of Caliph Al ma-Mun for losing deliberately.) Knut V and Valdemar were at a game of chess when assassins from King Sweyn broke in on them. Knut was killed, but Valdemar used the chessboard as a shield to escape.

Richard, Duke of Burgundy, killed an opponent by braining him with a solid gold king. Condemned to death, he played chess with his jailer and ended up killing *him,* too. After some time, a nobleman who was brave enough and skilled in self-defense agreed to play the duke. They were engaged in a game when the hangman and two guards arrived and attempted to drag Richard off to his appointment. *"Enraged, he did slay one guard with his bishop, the other guard with his knight, and with his king he slew the Hangman."* After which he sat down and finished the game. (Obviously, the set was mightier than the sword.)

The Italian masters Leonardo and Boi died unnaturally of poison, and there is no telling how many fights and brawls were started in taverns over a stakes game in which the favorite had lost. All in all, chess was not a completely safe occupation in medieval times, even if it was sedentary.

The First Great Cue Championship

The origin of billiards never has been definitely proved but whether, as claimed, it began in more or less its present form with the invention of the cue tip by Minguad in Paris in 1823 or in Greece in 400 B.C., as mentioned in the travels of Anarcharsis, cannot alter the fact that the first championship of any consequence ever played took place June 1-9, 1862, at Irving Hall, New York City.

That momentous event was the first chapter in a new book of the game. However, preceding this tournament by about three years was a preface that is considered the real beginning of competitive billiards in America from a public exhibition standpoint.

Several matches for sizeable stakes had been played but in April, 1859, Michael Phelan of New York and John Seereiter of Detroit met at Fireman's Hall, Detroit, in a 2,000 point match for a purse of $15,000.

The size of the stake, the largest ever recorded, excited the country as did the $5 admission fee. If such a purse was unprecedented the admission charge was positively staggering.

These two items alone created such widespread interest that almost overnight billiards became one of the most popular indoor games. However the $5 admission fee was more to keep the undesirables away than for profit and it worked out very satisfactorily as a brilliant gathering of men and women witnessed the match.

The game was caroms with four balls on a 6 by 12 six-pocket table, pushing and crotching being permitted. Phelan, who already had claimed the title, won by 96 points. His average was a fraction more than 12 and his high run 129. Seereiter's average was 11-plus and his best single effort was 157.

Following his victory Phelan was recognized as the first champion of America, a title which he wore with dignity and honor for three years, meeting and defeating the veterans and youngsters who were rapidly coming up to later make one of the most colorful eras of the game.

One of these latter was John Deery of Cincinnati who played a principal role in two of the most famous dramas in billiards—the championship match that caused Louis Fox to commit suicide, and the match in which he stood guard over A. P. Rudolphe. The match with Rudolphe was played in San Francisco, where Deery was a great favorite. The crowd displayed marked partiality and, as Rudolphe was about to make the winning carom, one of Deery's backers stepped to the table, picked up one of the balls and hurled it into the crowd. Deery personally escorted the man back to his seat, replaced the ball and stood watch against any further disturbances as Rudolphe made the point to win the match and the title.

Six feet tall, athletic, fearless and strikingly handsome, Deery was 19 years old when he met Phillip Tieman, also of Cincinnati, and one of the first flight players in the country, in his, Deery's, first important match. It was in November, 1861, and the match was played on a 6 by 12 six-pocket table, Tieman winning 1,000 to 683.

Undaunted the young man invaded New York City in April of the next year and met Michael Foley, an aspirant for Phelan's title, and again was defeated 1,000 to 502. Incidentally at this match, which was played at Irving Hall, Henry Ward Beecher, the distinguished pulpit and platform orator was tendered an ovation upon his appearance as one of the spectators.

Then came the first big championship tournament the following year that attracted all the leading players. Again billiards captured the attention of the sporting world.

Dudley Kavanaugh returned the winner with Fox, Deery, Tieman, Seereiter, Foley, William Goldthwait and Victor Estephe finishing in the order named. Deery eventually was to win the championship.

Foley, the last survivor of this pioneer band, passed on in 1925. During the latter years of his useful and honorable life Foley operated a billiard room in Kansas City, a veritable haven for the old timers who, surrounded by many priceless and venerated relics of the days of their youth, played over and over again those early battles of the green cloth—in easy chairs.

Billiards Digest

Spoonergram

Spoonergram: Exchange of the initial sounds of two words or word parts in the answers: TIE PIN, PIE TIN; TOENAIL, NO TAIL.

Some have a — — — — — / — — — — for driving cars,
While other hapless souls
Can't even locate, so I've heard,
The — — — — / — — — — — or the controls.

Answer:

Sheer gift,
gear shift.

The Enigma

Babe Ruth's First Home Run

On May 7, 1915, a German submarine sank the Cunard Liner *Lusitania* off the coast of Ireland with a loss of 1198 lives. This was one of the biggest news stories of the 20th century. The day before, a young pitcher with the Boston Red Sox lost a tough 5 to 3, thirteen-inning game to the Yankees at the Polo Grounds in New York. And baseball history was also made that day, although it would take a few years before the significance of the event would be realized. For on that afternoon—Thursday, May 6, 1915—Babe Ruth, the 20-year-old Boston southpaw, hit the first of his grand total of 714 regular season major league home runs.

Ruth's first home run came in the third inning off Jack Warhop, the starting Yankee right-hander. He was the first batter in the inning and he hit Warhop's first pitch into the second tier of the right-field grandstand. The ball, a prodigious wallop, landed in Seat 26 of Section 3. Although Ruth had been with the Red Sox for a few games in 1914, his first home run came on only his 18th time at bat in the majors. He went to bat 10 times in 1914 and this was his eighth time up in 1915. It was his fifth major league hit—his other hits up to that time included three doubles and a single.

Among the gathering of 8,000 who witnessed Ruth's first circuit clout were Ban Johnson, president of the American League, Joseph Lannin, owner of the Red Sox, and two baseball reporters who later hit it big in the literary field after graduating from the sports desk—Damon Runyon and Heywood Broun.

Runyan, who covered the game for the New York *American,* wrote:

> Fanning this Ruth is not as easy as the name and occupation might indicate. In the third inning Ruth knocked the slant out of one of Jack Warhop's underhand subterfuges, and put the baseball in the right field stands for a home run. Ruth was discovered by Jack Dunn in a Baltimore school a year ago where he had not attained his left-handed majority, and was adopted and adapted by Jack for use of the Orioles. He is now quite a demon pitcher and demon hitter—when he connects.

Broun penned the following for the New York *Tribune:*

> Pitted against Pieh was Babe Ruth, the remarkable young player discovered by Jack Dunn in a reform school last year. Ruth was put in the school at an early age, but seemingly he quit too soon to be completely reformed. He is still flagrantly left-handed. Babe (he was christened George) deserved something better than a defeat. It was his home run into the second tier of the grandstand which gave the Red Sox their first run of the game, and later he singled twice. He missed a chance to strike a telling blow in the eleventh inning for, with a runner on first and third with only one out, he was fanned by Pieh.

Broun also added this humorous note: "Nobody can take a mark of distinction away from Ruth. He is practically the only left-handed pitcher in the country not called Rube."

—Al Kermisch
Baseball Historical Review

Anti-Hunting Columnist Goes on West Virginia Grouse Hunt

After two hours of grouse hunting, the anti-hunting, big-city columnist would have hailed a cab, had there been one available.

This highly unusual episode began when Bob Greene, who writes for the *Chicago Tribune* and whose columns are nationally syndicated through Field Newspaper Syndicate, wrote a column calling hunters "the sickest of America's sick," among other things.

"They call themselves sportsmen," Greene wrote in a December column. "What a joke. Unlike other sports, hunting takes no physical conditioning, no speed. Any slob with a gutful of booze can go into the woods—and if his weapon is powerful enough—stand a good chance of making a kill."

Greene's column, published in a large number of newspapers throughout the nation, generated a prompt response from outraged hunters. In West Virginia, where an estimated one out of every five residents are hunters, indignant letters and telephone calls came pouring into the offices of the *Charleston Daily Mail.* Angry hunters, thinking Greene was a local writer, came to the newspaper's offices in search of him. They wanted to "talk turkey" to the guy who had called them "sick" and "perverted."

Sam Hindman, *Daily Mail* managing editor, was stunned by the overwhelming reader reaction. Irate letters and calls inquired about Greene's hunting experience. Had he ever hunted or fired a gun? If not, what right did he have passing judgement on hunters? Hindman decided on a course of action. He invited Greene to come to West Virginia and hunt ruffed grouse.

"Put bluntly," Greene wrote later in a special column to the *Daily Mail,* "I had been challenged to quit mouthing off and start looking around. If I was going to characterize hunters as perverts, the hunters wanted me to say it to their faces—in the forest, not from some office in Chicago."

Greene quickly accepted Hindman's invitation.

Three veteran West Virginia grouse hunters, Arch "Bozo" Griffith, an electrician from Boone County; C. D. Duncan, a lab technician, and Roy Blizzard, an official with the state Department of Education, both from the Charleston area, were selected to accompany the Chicago writer on his first grouse hunt.

Sworn to keep the identity of their guest a secret, the three hunters became acquainted with the 33-year-old columnist over a country meal of venison and wild turkey the evening before the hunt. The meal was designed to give Greene "a taste of the fruits of hunting."

The following day the foursome headed for one of Roy Blizzard's favorite grouse coverts. His four-wheel drive vehicle took the party deep into the snow-covered hills of Wirt County, near Elizabeth, about a two hour drive north of Charleston.

Although Greene hadn't used a firearm since boyhood days at summer camp, Blizzard equipped him with a shotgun and shells just in case he had the opportunity and desire to shoot at a grouse. After receiving instructions from Blizzard on how to use the shotgun, Greene took several practice shots at trees before the group began their hunt. However, he carried the shotgun unloaded just for the experience.

The weather, and a six-inch snowfall, had the birds sitting tight in heavy cover and made it difficult for Blizzard's dogs to locate them. However, late in the day, three birds were flushed, but they escaped unscathed. Later, Greene wrote that he was happy that the birds were not killed.

By the time the party returned to the Jeep, Blizzard estimated they had traversed about five miles of steep terrain. Greene reportedly estimated the distance to be closer to 15 miles. Although the hunters slowed their pace to accommodate him, Greene admitted he became leg-weary, but at no time did he feel inadequate.

Now that the hunt was over had Greene changed his opinion of hunting and hunters? Were they still "sick" and "perverted" for wanting to hunt?

In the last of a five-part series of special columns to the Daily Mail, Greene revealed that his hunting experience had not changed his anti-hunting attitude. If anything, his convictions were reinforced that the main attraction for hunters is the thrill of the kill.

"Being outdoors together in the wilderness was a part of it, yes—but there was no doubt in my mind that the thing that truly made them [hunters] feel good was to succeed. To kill," wrote Greene.

Although he had classified all hunters as "perverts" and "the sickest of America's sick," Greene said he liked his three West Virginian companions "a lot" and preferred the time spent with them to that usually spent with the people of Chicago.

"If the opportunity came up to get together with these three men again," Greene wrote, "I would say yes in an instant."

Greene returned to Chicago with "approximately the same view of the morality of sport hunting" that he had when arriving in Charleston. He remained convinced that the act of hunting is "perverted" and "sick" and the killing of defenseless animals is wrong. But, he wrote, he would "never again be so sure that all hunters were people who deserved to be denounced with the strongest of epithets."

As the group parted company to go their separate ways, Greene took off his down-filled, camouflaged hunting coat, newly purchased for the trip, and gave it to Bo Griffith. He said he wouldn't be needing it again.

The Drummer
(The Ruffed Grouse Society)

Joggling

The three balls click like a motor, cascading over and over between my hands in perfect time to my jogging stride. Their beat visibly intensifies my every step every mile of the way.

Joggling, the simultaneous practice of jogging and juggling, harnesses the pumping motion of a jogger's arms for purposes of juggling.

In 1976, seven years after I started jogging, my younger brother taught me to juggle. Immediately hooked on object manipulation, I took three balls along to play with after my daily running routine at the track on the campus of North Carolina State University in Raleigh. For many days that summer I jogged, then juggled. Finally, in a fit of athletic inspiration, I joggled.

So immediately was I struck with the ease and sensibility of this fusion of two great, an-

cient sports that I was astounded by the stares that I drew. "What d'ya mean by that!" I shouted at a small congregation in the stands snickering as I passed. "Haven't you ever seen a joggler before?"

No, they hadn't. And neither have thousands of others who've witnessed my practice since. Whether alone on the street or in the midst of a pack of joggers in a race, my joggling seems unique. Public reaction is mixed. Crowds lining the Peachtree Road Race course in Atlanta for the past three July Fourth's have been largely thrilled at glimpsing three balls floating along in the sea of 25,000 fairly similar runners.

But, most of the after-work and weekend joggers I encounter don't make a show of acknowledging my renegade running style. Some nod and smile, or laugh approvingly. A few have shouted, "Show off!" or other words of disdain, but I write them off to the unfortunate human propensity to hate things they don't understand. "What is there to understand," I reply.

The jogger's natural body rhythm and forward motion actually make juggling on the run easier than juggling standing still. For jogging establishes a right-left-right-left rhythm not only in the legs, but throughout the body, including the arms. The up-and-down arm motion needed for juggling is also inherent in a jogger's stride. Forward speed acts as a gyroscope, aiding body balance and hand/eye coordination. The combination of timing and motion make joggling almost automatic. Tosses from hand to hand require very little additional arm motion beyond what is needed for jogging. There even seems to be more time to correct juggling mistakes as the ball bounce in front of my eyes.

As quickly as the joggling rhythm is set, physical endurance becomes the only barrier to distance. I normally cover 3 or 4 miles, often without a single drop.

For a long while I joggled alone. I was confounded that such a natural fusion would not root and flourish. "What a great sport it is!" I exhorted the curious masses. "The music of juggling moves enlivening the rhythm of running legs—exercise and art in a single stride!"

Failing to spark the joggling revolution in Raleigh and Atlanta, I looked forward to Fargo and the 33rd annual convention of the International Jugglers Association for a following. "Surely there," I said, "the jugglers will take to joggling!" And joggle they did, in the world's first official 100-yard and 1-mile joggling races.

Joggling is a simple, unique way to combine two activities I enjoy. Both jogging and juggling are healthy, beneficial physical activities in an age that's taken a fancy to physical fitness. Those who try will find that when the two motions are coupled, their synergistic energy is sheer delight.

—Bill Giduz
International Jugglers Association Newsletter

How a Blind Bowler Bowls

Although bowlers are never required to accept guidance assistance in any form, most of the totally blind ones rely upon a bowling guide rail while rolling the ball. The rails now in use in leagues and in area tournaments are three feet high and from nine to fifteen feet in length. . . . The rails are placed alongside the bowling approach and they extend back from the foul line. A bowler who needs the assistance of a rail usually slides one hand along its smooth surface while delivering his ball with his other hand. Of course, he is free to use the bowling technique he prefers; many totally blind bowlers use the three or four step approaches used by sighted bowlers, while other totally blind bowlers prefer to position themselves in relation to the rail and to deliver the ball from a stationary stance.

The Blind Bowler

First to Fly

The first book written on fly fishing was by a woman—Dame Juliana Berners, the prioress of a nunnery in England. Some consider it the finest essay on fishing ever written.

The Flyfisher

Caddies vs. Carts

Caddie	Cart
Has name, will respond	Just sits there
Will signal and wave	Doesn't understand
Moves out ahead	Always with you
Holds flagstick	Cannot go on green
Hands you a club	You get it yourself
Weighs 140, no tracks	Weighs 750, makes ruts
Will caddie, rain or shine	Course closed to carts
Finds your ball	Never even looks
Wipes your clubs	Bangs up your clubs
Tires but never stops	Runs out of juice and quits
Picks up clubs	Runs over them
Can judge distance	Blind as a bat
Says, "nice shot."	Has no interest
Cleans your ball	Could care less
Can walk anywhere	Has restricted areas
Rakes bunker	Watches you do it

—Dick Haskell
Golf Journal

Enigma

Enigma: Veiled clues to the keyword; a riddle.

A Briton propels a boat;
An American kicks a ball;
A cosmopolite bets on roulette;
What single word covers them all?

Answer:
Punter.

The Enigma

The Name Game

It's not easy to name a horse. Oh, you can take the easy route and borrow names, or parts of names, from the horse's parents. Like the super-horse Niatross: his mamma was Niagara Dream, his papa was Albatross.

And so you take a little bit from this, and a little bit from that, and you've got Niatross! See? Easy.

Or another way to do it is to establish a "theme" when you're naming your horses. Bruce Gimble, a speedy three-year-old pacer who chases Niatross around the tracks, is out of a mare named Bergdorf. And although the owners spell the horse's name GIMBLE instead of GIMBEL, all their racers have been given names of famous department stores.

The U.S. Trotting Association sets certain restrictions in the registration of harness horses. Names are limited to four words and a total of 18 spaces. Names of living persons cannot be used unless written permission is given with the registration. Or, you can't tag trotters or pacers with names of famous or notorious persons, trade names, or names claimed for advertising purposes. So you won't see Henry Kissinger speeding down the homestretch, unless the former Secretary of State has given the okay to use his famous name. And there won't be any BOB'S PLUMBING SUPPLIES hitched to a sulky either. Too many letters and too much advertising.

As colorful and creative as they may be, horses names will never be as imaginative as many of the men who care for them. These men, for the most part, never asked much out of life. They knew how to muck out a stall and rub down a horse. They slept on cots in the tackroom. Or, sometimes on a couple bales of hay. And a certain peculiarity or habit would provide them with a name that would follow them wherever they went.

There was Freddie The Goose and Mickey The Flea. And we mustn't forget Rattlesnake Pete, Stew Kettle Jack, or Silk Hat Harry. Naturally, you remember Taxi Cab Riley, Buck Tooth Scotty, Monkey Face Murphy, Freddie The Louse and Jack The Liar. Not to mention Dirty Neck Frank, Coconut Head and Pink Eye Whitey. And the world will never forget Loose Horse Harry, Big Foot Tom or Piano Walt.

No self-respecting horse would ever allow himself to be called names like these.

News from the Hall of Fame of the Trotter

Best Places to Fish in the Entire World

(Outside continental U.S., 1981)

Salt Water

Best Variety Fishing: Club Pacifico de Panama and Bahia Pez Vela of Costa Rica. CP provided the better fishing in the winter and early spring. Then Bahia gets our nod.

Best Black Marlin: Australia is the perennial favorite in October and November. After Australia, Panama's Tropic Star, Club Pacifico and Costa Rica's Bahia offered good marlin fishing.

Best Pacific Blue Marlin: Kona, Hawaii, by a landslide. But Bahia Pez Vela is coming up fast. Several blues over 700 lbs.

Best Striped Marlin: Mazatlan, Mexico, in the winter months; Cabo San Lucas in the late spring and early summer. Ecuador's Salinas is making a comeback. New Zealand for "biggies."

Best Pacific Sailfish: Tropic Star in May easily. Then Bahia Pez Vela, and Mazatlan, Mexico (in June).

Best Atlantic Sailfish: Cozumel, Mexico.

Best Roosterfish: Bahia Pez Vela is probably the best via artificial lures. If you don't mind using bait, La Paz, Mexico is still the place.

Best Bluefin Tuna: Prince Edward Island.

Best Tarpon: East coast of Costa Rica (Casa Mar, Parismina, Isla de Pesca). Belize in May and June.

Best Snook Fishing: Same as above. Parismina yielded a 43-½ pounder. Casa Mar and Isla seemed to have better snook fishing in the spring instead of the more heralded fall season. Keller's in Belize offered good snook most of the time, though they ran much smaller than Costa Rica's snook.

Best Dolphinfish: Costa Rica's Bahia Pez Vela; Panama's Club Pacifico and Tropic Star; Dominican Republic.

Best Bonefish: The Bahamas primarily. Deep Water Cay Resort is one of the best places.

Best Permit: Deep Water Cay in the Bahamas for large permit; Yucatan, Mexico (Pez Maya and Boca Paila); and Belize.

Fresh Water:

Best Variety: Alaskan camps. Loesche's, Curtis' Tik Chik, Bristol Bay, Golden Horn and others. They offer five varieties of salmon, trout, char, grayling and even lake trout and an occasional northern pike.

Best Northern Pike: Brabant's Lodge, N.W.T., Lloyd Lake Lodge, Sask., Sickle Lake Lodge, Manitoba and dozens of other Canadian lakes.

Best Muskie: Wabigoon Lake, Ontario.

Best Smallmouth Bass: Rainy Lake (via Fontana's houseboats), Kishkutena Lake and Manitou waters in Ontario. Pine Island Lodge in Manitoba produced good bass fishing in spite of very low waters most of the years.

Best Largemouth Bass: Rainy Lake (via Fontana's houseboats), Kishkutena Lake and Manitou waters in Ontario. Pine Island Lodge in Manitoba produced good bass fishing in spite of very low waters most of the year.

Best Largemouth Bass: Lake Guerrero in Mexico for quantity; Cuba for size.

Best Lake Trout: Kasba Lake, Great Slave and Great Bear and Nueltin Narrows in N.W.T., Waterbury Lake in Saskatchewan.

Best Grayling: Kazan River and Great Bear Lake in N.W.T., Ugashik waters of Alaska.

Best Walleyes: Gunisao, Manitoba; Lloyd Lake in Sask., Manitoba's Island Lake for quantity (though size was a disappointment).

Best Rainbow Trout: Numerous rivers of Alaska; Bow River, Alberta; Patagonia in Argentina; North Island of New Zealand (Lake Taupo).

Best Brown Trout: South Island of New Zealand; Patagonia in Argentina.

Best Brook Trout: Cooper's and Paor's camps on the Minipi watershed (Labrador).

Best Atlantic Salmon: Restigouche in New Brunswick/Quebec by a long shot. No other river produced as many large salmon on a consistent basis. Norway's Alta River was the runner-up. In Iceland, Midfjardara was probably the best.

Best Arctic Char: NW.T. Tree River (it provided a 26 lb. plus char).

Best Jungle Exotic Fishing: The exploratory trips on Columbia's Inirida River for payara, pavon, and other species. Sam Hogan Ecuadorian Jungle Safaris were also productive.

Best Dorado: Argentina's Parana River is still the leader.

Best Pavon: Panama's Club Lago for very fast fishing—though these fish are much smaller than those taken in Colombia, Venezuela and other South American waters.

Roller-skating is the sport that allows you to stand absolutely still while hurtling toward disaster. It's a little like Congress.

Orben's Current Comedy

Letter Changes

Letter changes: Change the specified letter of one keyword to form another; a first-letter change of DESPITE is RESPITE. [In the following, it is a third-letter change.]

Old Mother Hubbard went to the
— — — — —.
Its contents were worthless and
— — — — —.
Goodies were missing, no bone and no
— — — — —.
Both she and her doggie got none.

Answer:
pastry,
paltry,
pantry,

The Enigma

Characteristics of a Successful Contester

What are the characteristics of a successful contester? A successful contester seizes every opportunity to enter each and every sweepstakes and contest. When you receive "junk mail" that has an entry form for a sweepstakes, send it in. Reader's Digest, Publishers Clearing House and many other companies have awarded millions of dollars in sweepstakes over the years. When you pass a new shopping center or new store opening, pull in and sign up for any prizes being offered. Fill out and send in entry blanks you find in magazines and newspapers. In other words, work at it all the time. Contesting must be more than just a part-time endeavor. It requires diligent effort. It must be an all-consuming passion, a driving, singular pursuit.

Entering on a random, hit-or-miss basis will not produce the results you'll achieve by working constantly and deliberately. Remember, the three "P's" of contesting are patience, perseverance and postage.

Contest Newsletter

Contests, Sweepstakes & Other Promotional Activity on Increase

A recent issue of *U.S. News & World Report* had a very interesting story describing how companies are using promotions to lure customers and increase sales. The article said, "Businesses of every type—not just the traditional food and soap companies—are blanketing the country with cents-off coupons, refunds, sweepstakes, rebates and cash prizes."

The story said that 130 million dollars will be won by consumers this year in games, contests and sweepstakes. The article quoted Richard Kane, president of Marden-Kane, a major contest judging organization: "Promotions have exploded. In a recession-type economy, business is finding that promotions are a prime form of insurance."

The story points out that Publishers Clearing House is now offering a top prize of $250,000 in its current promotion, which is double last year's big prize of $125,000.

The story said that "most companies are moving away from merchandise prizes and toward awarding cash to contest winners. In the case of some major awards, the Internal Revenue Service is provided a list of winners, with their addresses and Social Security numbers."

Contest Newsletter

Anagram

Anagram: Apposite words or phrases composed of the same letter as the "base." Thus, NAME FOR SHIP is an anagram of H.M.S. Pinafore.

1. THEY SEE: — — — / — — — —
2. BEAR HIT DEN: — — — — — — — — —
3. I LIMIT LEGACY:
   — — — — — — — — — — —
4. TRUSS NEATLY TO BE SAFE:
   — — — — — — / — — — — / — — — — / — — — —

Answers:

1. The eyes
2. Hibernated
3. Illegitimacy
4. Fasten your seat belts

The Enigma

On the Okayama golf course near Kobe, Japan, is a 28,000-foot-long monorail for golf carts. As you play the course, your golf cart follows you around automatically.

Funny Funny World

Amazing Skiing

Handicapped skiing began in the 1940s in Austria and soon spread to the United States by word of mouth. Twenty years later, organized programs began to spring up in U.S. skiing areas. . . . On the Rockies, the Poconos, the Alps, and other mountainsides, handicapped persons are taking to skis and loving it.

"When they told me I was going to ski, I thought they were crazy," said Tony Ferrar when he was introduced to the 52 Association. Now the blind Viet Nam vet confidently glides down the slopes with over 100 other blind skiers.

Some of the athletes were experienced skiers before they lost an arm or a leg. Others are trying the downhill runs for the first time. Rev. Don Rogers, Eugene, Oregon, is one beginning amputee skier. "Skiing on one leg is easier than on two," he says. "The trouble with two skis is that they don't go in the same direction for the beginner."

The AMP
(National Amputation Foundation)

Wacky Ways to Help Beat Boredom

Find a bug and follow it around the house.

PMCC Bulletin
(Post Mark Collectors Club)

•

Idle hands can be kept busy on a rainy day by having the children remove seeds from a pound of raisins.

Raisin d'Etre

Good Hitters Bat an Eye

What makes a .300 hitter? Concentration and cross-dominant eyesight help, says Donald S. Teig, O.D., an optometrist who recently tested 275 major leaguers. It seems that hitters with cross-dominant eyesight (being able to see better with their left eye if they hit righthanded and vice versa) may get a better look at the ball by virtue of the fact that their "good" eye is a nose's width closer to the pitcher. Only about 20 percent of the general population has cross-dominant eyesight, but in Teig's study of seven major league teams, 50 percent of the players he examined displayed the phenomenon. Leading the pack in team-seeing, incidentally, were the Kansas City Royals, 70 percent of whom see cross-dominantly. The Royals also led the 1980 season in hitting.

Executive Fitness Newsletter

History

TITANIC UNDERTAKING

I n the light of what happened on the night of April 14–15, 1912, it is a little disconcerting that the Titanic Historical Society solicits new members with the greeting: "Welcome Aboard!"

The society is probably the only organization in the world whose honorary members are survivors of a famous shipwreck.

Edward Kamuda, 42, of Indian Orchard, Massachusetts, wasn't even born when that British vessel, the fastest ship afloat, went down on her maiden voyage after hitting an iceberg in the North Atlantic (1,517 lives were lost). But he got interested in the subject when, as a teenager, he saw a movie about the disaster. In 1957 he wrote a letter to each of the survivors of the voyage, requesting recollections, and six years later the THS was born, "for the purpose of investigating and perpetuating the history and memory of the *Titanic*" (and its White Star sister ships, *Olympic* and *Britannic*). Kamuda, who makes his living as a clockmaker, became editor of the well-illustrated quarterly *Titanic Commutator.* A typical issue contains stories by survivors (an estimated 100 are still alive), a picture of an iceberg that might have done the damage, and a tribute to the captain of the *Carpathia,* which raced to the scene of the sinking and rescued more than 700 persons.

The society now has over 2,000 members, including several dozen survivors and sons and daughters of survivors. They have looked into the possibility of raising the *Titanic* (they're not the only ones interested, of course) and are trying to open a museum of artifacts. (Kamuda has an appropriate memento himself—a *Titanic* life preserver.) They also take part every year in the U.S. Coast Guard's memorial services, which are held at sea on the anniversary of the incident, over the spot where the ship may now reside. Through the society, members can order a scale-model *Titanic,* a copy of the deck plans of the ship, the official U.S. Senate report on the disaster, or a "Remember the Titanic" T-shirt.

But what keeps the society (and *Commutator*) going is that several mysteries surrounding the *Titanic* remain unresolved. Most notably: What ship approached the disaster area, shortly after the *Titanic* flared signal rockets, and then drifted away? Why didn't some of the other ships nearby notice the distress calls? Everyone loves a detective story and a lot of people are fascinated by disaster; the *Titanic* saga whets both appetites. One new THS member, an accountant from Long Beach, California, wrote to the *Commutator* and explained that he was interested in the subject "because of the doubt about the greatest sea disaster ever, about why and how so many people lost their lives, about why lifeboats failed to go to help those in the water, and why no one was ever prosecuted for it. . . ."

MIDDLE AGERS

"Picture if you will," suggests an official message from the Society for Creative Anachronism, "a green field encircled by colorful pavilions, pennants flying in the breeze. Lords and ladies in medieval garb stroll about. . . . A minstrel strums on his lute. . . . On the field, armored knights strive with sword and shield for their kingdom's highest honor. . . . During a lull in the fighting a green-cloaked herald steps forth and announces a Royal Court. The people in all their finery begin to gather around the thrones. . . ."

This is not a dream or fantasy, or a scene from a Hollywood movie. It is an event, recreated several times a year by chapters of the Society for Creative Anachronism, an organization that relives the Middle Ages, "as they were and as they might have been."

The SCA's official publication is a forty-page magazine whose title is a takeoff on *Sports Illustrated*. It's called *Tournaments Illuminated*. The contents of *TI* are not, however, tongue-in-cheek. Articles are well-researched (if not quite scholarly) slices of medieval life. Food, fashion, literature, military customs, and legend all get about equal play. Sample articles (all written by SCA members): Livery Maintenance, The Period Palate, A Little Viking Ingenuity, The Three-Hour Crossbow, and On Peasants. The illustrations are pretty good too.

TI is edited by Friar Bertram of Bearington and Eromene Aspasia of Constantinople. Who? In real life they are Dave Schroeder and Ary Guildroy of

Chicago. Like other SCA members they have adopted Middle Age monickers. (They cannot give themselves a title but they can be *given* one—by an SCA "king.") Someone named Bill Keyes, for example, goes by the name Wilhelm von Schlussel; Caryl McHarney is Countess Irminsul the Improbable.

The society was founded in 1966 following what was to be a one-shot back-yard costume party in the Berkeley, California, area. By the early 1970s branches had formed on the East Coast. The society was organized into eight kingdoms, which were further subdivided into principalities, baronies, provinces, shires, and cantons. Each kingdom in what the SCA calls "the Known World" publishes its own monthly newsletter. (The "East" letter is a 32-page booklet called *Pikestaff.*) Headquarters remain in Berkeley. There are currently more than 12,000 members.

Tournaments Illuminated may be historically sound but the SCA is not merely a study (or nostalgia) group. It is extremely social and highly active. Members really get into making medieval crafts, jewelry, food, grog, swords, and shields. But the highlights of activity are the tournaments themselves. Members wear tunics and court dress. (Outsiders are allowed to observe but they are considered "mundane.") Period food is cooked in medieval-style utensils. Participants in melees and jousts make their own armor and simulated weapons. The king bestows knighthood on the victors. And afterward there is dancing, music, archery. Throughout the year, chapters hold revels, banquets, and feasts. At all times true chivalry is practiced!

"For some," says *TI* editors Bertram and Eromene, "the Society is a weekend excursion, for others it's a way of life." Or as another member, Duke James Greyhelm has pointed out: "We try to live up to the really beautiful parts of the Middle Ages and get rid of the draggy stuff, like plagues and famines."

How Did a "Church Key" Come to Be?

Throughout the Midwest during Prohibition the church sexton had a major problem—he could no longer slip away to the corner saloon for his daily nip. While beer was plentiful, it came in bottles with a cap which could only be removed conveniently with a bottle opener.

Most sexton's wives were ardent supporters of prohibition, and/or members of the WCTU—an extreme temperance group—therefore it was not possible to carry a standard bottle opener in a pocket or billfold. The sexton did carry a large ring of keys necessary to carry out his duties. As soon as the problem became known an enterprising novelty manufacturer hurried to fill the need and the "Sexton's Key" was born. The name was soon transformed to "Church key"—a name that is still used by many beer drinkers for any type of bottle opener.

—Don Stewart
Key Collectors Journal

Great Moments in History: 1914

Mary Phelps Jacobs, 19, was so set against the whalebone corsets of her day, she had her French maid make a soft under-garment from two lace handkerchiefs and a pink ribbon. It was the FIRST BRASSIERE!

Her friends loved it. Mary took out a patent on it. She started to make and sell them, but soon failed; however, she did sell her patent to Warner Brothers Corset Company for $15,000. Warner Brothers sold $20,000,000 worth of brassieres in the first two years.

Lightbulb

Ferris's fellow engineers said it couldn't be done. The world's fair directory first granted a concession, then fearfully withdrew it. Only four and one-half months before the fair opened was the concession finally confirmed, and when the wheel was operating there was considerable satisfaction to national pride in knowing that it had taken three years to complete the Eiffel Tower. . . .

—Beekman W. Cottrell
World's Fair

The Ferris Behind the Ferris Wheel

In 1892 George Washington Gale Ferris conceived a plan for the first Ferris Wheel. His idea came with the flash of inspiration so dear to legend, so often literally true. Within the 20 minutes that followed that flash he had sketched out the design and dimensions, and thus the wheel that dominated the Chicago exposition the following year took form. Young Ferris had gone to Chicago to see what was being planned for the Columbian exposition. He heard a banquet speaker berate the mechanical engineers of America who had been able to offer nothing more than a suggestion for a bigger Eiffel Tower. It was a question of national pride, of the absolute necessity for something to swing the world's acclaim back from the Paris exposition of 1889 across the Atlantic to the land that boasted of vigor and new ideas. Ferris attended a chop dinner at a Saturday afternoon club in Chicago soon after the challenge at the banquet. "Before the dinner was over I had sketched out almost the entire details, and my plan has never varied an item from that day," he told a reporter in 1893, when the great wheel was turning smoothly on the Chicago midway.

He was the very type of the young inventor, the epitome of rising American enterprise and imagination. *Dash* was the word for it in the '90s. . . . From the very outset his interest lay with iron and steel, especially with structural steel. . . . He established the G.W.G. Ferris Company in Pittsburgh. . . . Among many of its accomplishments were the Steel Arch Bridge over the Mississippi River at Minneapolis, and another like it at St. Paul. The Ferris Company completed Government Bridge over the Potomac in Washington, D.C., and built a portion of the Third Avenue elevated in New York. . . .

The great wheel itself, true to the tradition of inventing hazards, almost died aborning.

The First Teddy Bear

The Teddy Bear originated more than 70 years ago in Giengen-am-Brenz, a picturesque little German town. Its cobblestone streets and gingerbread houses make a storybook setting for the headquarters of the world's largest manufacturer of stuffed toys.

Born in 1847, Margarete Steiff had polio when she was 2½ years old. The disease paralyzed her legs and her right arm, confining her to a wheel chair for the rest of her life. Margarete became a dressmaker and owned the first sewing machine in Giengen (she had to work it backwards because of her paralysis). In 1877 she opened a women's and children's dress shop, fashioning garments of fabric from the Haenhle felt factory. She did well and hired several helpers. Margarete wrote, "At this point the model of an elephant fell into my hands; felt was well suited to copying it." The finest shearings were used for the stuffing and this little pin-cushion elephant, the first Steiff stuffed toy, was born.

Initially the toys were given as gifts to visiting children, but as the demand for them grew, Margarete's brother, Fritz, realizing their potential, took several to the county fair. Soon all the toys were sold, and Margarete's hobby became a small and flourishing family business.

In 1897 Margarete's nephew, Richard, an artist, joined the firm. He had spent many hours sketching the playful brown bear cubs at the Stuttgart zoo, and working from these sketches, he designed a mohair plush bear with movable joints. The first models were introduced in 1902.

In the same year, in America, President Theodore Roosevelt, an avid outdoorsman, was in Mississippi to hunt bear. After several days during which no bears were sighted, the guide chased a little bear cub out of the brush and cleared the way for the President to shoot it. Mr. Roosevelt refused and shooed the young cub back to his mother.

In the President's party was the political cartoonist for the Washington Post, Clifford Berryman. He was so moved by the President's gesture that he drew a cartoon which showed the President refusing to shoot the cub. After that, the cub appeared in all Berryman's cartoons on the President and Berryman called it "Teddy's Bear."

For the first few years Steiff's bear sales were disappointing but in 1906 the factory was put on an overtime basis by a party at the White House in Washington: the party decorations were Steiff bears dressed and equipped as hunters and fishermen. When the illustrious Teddy Roosevelt, a bear expert, admitted that he couldn't name the breed, a guest said, "Why, they're Teddy Bears, of course." The ensuing publicity brought a crush of orders for the suddenly fashionable Teddy Bear and more than a million were sold that year (a record never equaled). The success of the Teddy Bear enabled Steiff to expand, and now there are plants in Germany and Austria, all still owned by the Steiff family.

Bear Tracks

The American Attic . . . is a vanishing species and on the way to becoming altogether extinct. No split level ranch-type "homes" have attics. No "town-homes" (read row-houses) have attics. No condominiums (condominia) have attics. The desire, and perhaps need, to stash away some of the past for a future perspective and use is frustrated. We really need attics, to have waystations for our minor heritages that can only be reassessed by an objective future generation. To take the place of attics, and to give everyone the fun and knowledge derived from discerning searches, our generation has invented flea markets and garage sales, surrogates for our increasing millions of Americans who have had no attics.

The word itself is an interesting one, derived from the adjective referring to Athens and its province Attica. Architects in the Roman period elaborated upon the basic themes of Greek architecture. In the design of triumphal arches and large civic buildings, they often added a story above the entablature, on top of the normal columnar order crowned by a cornice. This extra stage above the main facade is called an attic story, although no major buildings still preserved in Attica show this feature. The term was applied by neoclassicists in later generations, not by architects in antiquity; Audsley's *Dictionary of Architecture* says the term is a seventeenth-century one!

Attics were especially favored in the Renaissance. An outstanding example is Michelangelo's Saint Peters, which has not only an attic stage above the main order of the building itself, but an attic story added to the central drum before the surge of the dome. From such classical attics descend the garrets or attics of our forbears, minor areas above the main horizontal roof-line of our houses, used for castoffs from the principal rooms below.

Victorian attics have almost all gone. This is a paean in their praise and an acknowledgment of the significant role they played in harboring our past cultures for the future.

—Richard Howland
Nineteenth Century
(Victorian Society in America)

Down Memory Lane

Remember some of the old Burma Shave signs which still provide good safety reminders: "At school zones . . . heed instructions . . . protect . . . our little . . . tax deductions." "When you drive . . . if caution ceases . . . you are apt . . . to rest . . . in pieces." "Drinking drivers . . . nothing worse . . . they put . . . the quart . . . before the hearse."

The California Highway Patrolman

Why the U.S. Does Not Use the Metric System

When the Constitution of the United States was drafted, there was included a special clause to prepare the ground for the adoption of a new decimal system of measures, which was advocated by all enlightened people. When the French Revolution in one of its first steps put into law the decimal metric system, the Congress of the United States considered adopting the French system. But Thomas Jefferson, whom Congress respected as the authority on such matters, opposed the plan on the ground that the French system was inadequate, since it did not coordinate time with length, volumes, and weight. This opposition from inside the camp of the progressive forces doomed the adoption of the decimal system in the United States.

Footprint

Electric cars are expected to be taking a share of the vehicle market after 1985, but battery-powered autos are far from new, says the Automotive Information Council.

The first electric vehicle was built in 1839 by Robert Anderson of Aberdeen, Scotland, but the first practical use did not occur until 1886 when one was introduced as a taxicab in England. The battery had 28 bulky cells and the taxi had a top speed of 8 mph.

By 1904 electrics were somewhat common on U.S. city streets for short runs. The Electric Vehicle Co. in that year made 2,000 taxis, accounting for one-third of the cars used in New York, Chicago and Boston. The owners of the company even forecast a need for a chain of electric-charging stations.

By 1910 the use of electric vehicles had peaked. They quickly lost ground to the internal-combustion engine as the nation's cities and road systems started to expand, and as great improvements were made, such as the self-starter for gasoline engines, plus the availability of inexpensive gasoline and the low price of gasoline-powered mass-assembled cars.

Electric vehicle interest didn't pick up again until the mid-1960s, "sparked" by public concern over air pollution. The fuel availability problems of 1973, 1974 and of today further intensified interest in electric vehicles.

Progress is being made. One new unit can power a car at 55 mph for 150 miles before it has to be recharged. Also in the works are hybrids, which combine electric and gasoline power. General Motors plans an electric in 1985, which would last for 30,000 miles. But batteries would cost $2,000 to replace. GM plans to build 100,000 of the cars—if it perfects its battery.

The California Highway Patrolman

Mother Goose

One of the most-remembered storytellers and verse composers of the period immediately before, during, and immediately after the Elizabethan period was the "person" known as "Mother Goose." Mother Goose was not a real person; the name "mother goose" comes from Charles Perrault's book of fairy tales in French which was subtitled "Contes de ma mere l'oye"—literally, "tales of mother goose," but really an idiomatic expression meaning "old wives' tales." Despite the American legend that a "Mother Goose" wrote nursery rhymes in New England, no evidence of her book has ever been found; the first American "Mother Goose" was a reprint of the English edition.

If there had been a Mother Goose, due to the subject matter of "her" verse, hiding behind such a name at that period was necessary. Even though to the uninitiated Mother Goose rhymes make little or no sense at all, taken in the context of when it was composed we see brilliant satirists at work.

Take for example "Old Mother Hubbard":

Old Mother Hubbard went to her cupboard
To get her poor dog a bone,
But when she got there the cupboard was bare
And so her poor dog had none.

"Old Mother Hubbard" was a nickname given to Queen Elizabeth by her political enemies—the "loyal opposition," if you will. Her lover, the Earl of Essex, was a nonlanded lord and constantly asked Elizabeth for lands so he would have an income. He is "the little dog" because he was forced to walk two paces behind Elizabeth, whose strides cause Essex to trot behind, "like a little dog." When Elizabeth finally asked Parliament (the "cupboard") for a "bone," it replied that all the Crown lands—except hers—were gone. Since Elizabeth would not part with hers, "her poor dog had none."

Elizabeth's father and his court also came in for some gentle ribbing from Mother Goose. Take, for example:

> Sing a song of sixpence,
>   Pocket full of rye,
> Four and twenty blackbirds
>   Baked in a pye.
> When the pye was opened,
>   The birds began to sing.
> Wasn't that a dainty dish
>   To set before the King?

> The King was in the countinghouse,
>   Counting all his money.
> The Queen was in the pantry,
>   Eating bread and honey.
> The Maid was in the garden,
>   Hanging out her clothes,
> When down came a blackbird
>   And snipped off her nose.

The "king" here is Henry VIII. The six-pence song is any song of the day sung in bars, a jolly, happy song. Henry is happy because he has just seized the grainfields ("pocket full of rye") of the friars of St. Augustine (the "blackbirds") and has all their revenues to count. The "pye" is a monk's cowl, and they were allowed to "bake" by Henry's orders. The "queen" is Catherine of Aragon, who is eating of English bread with the Spanish honey—the pledge of the King of Spain to keep her in power as Queen of England. "The Maid" is Anne Boleyn, just returned from France with new frocks. At this time she was at Whitehall Palace (the garden) where Henry first saw her. Cardinal Wolsey is the "blackbird" who snipped off her "nose" (engagement to Lord Percy).

Problems at court were not the only satires bandied about by the populace. The intrigues of Mary of Scotland became "Mary, Mary, quite contrary"; the plight of the people because of the demand for wool (and consequent lack of farm labor needed) became "baa baa, black sheep"; and the fall from power of the Earl of Essex, although another source claims Richard III, became "Humpty Dumpty."

Even innocent verse has gory facts behind it. For example:

> Peter, Peter, pumpkin eater,
>   Had a wife and couldn't keep her.
> He put her in a pumpkin shell
>   And there he kept her very well.

This tale is about a murder. Peter has an adulterous wife ("couldn't keep her") whom he murders, hacks to pieces, and buries in a pumpkin shell. He kept her very well indeed. One source says this ditty was recited while his head sat atop a pike on the road to London.

Finally, there is the nursery rhyme "London Bridge is falling down." This rhyme tells the truth: Periodically the houses and shops built on the side of London Bridge fell into the water, or they burned down, thus giving their heavily-insured owners (but not storeowners) needed mercantile funds. Finally, building bridge-side was prohibited, but long after the nursery rhyme became popular.

So once again even nonsensical rhymes point to historical facts which modern times have forgotten. Such are the legends of which history is made!

—John the Grey of St. Brendan
Tournaments Illuminated

Potatoes first became fashionable when Marie Antoinette paraded through the French countryside wearing potato blossoms in her hair. They soon became the rage in Parisian court circles.

Spotlight

ing small, light watches, the wrist watch became practical. Freedom from winding became more attractive. This bit of history demonstrates how development in a particular field depends on technical breakthroughs.

John Harwood entered the picture in 1922. Harwood was a watchmaker and repairer. In his work, he saw many watches damaged, if not ruined, by dirt, most of which entered through the winding mechanism and by the irregular winding and sometimes over-winding by owners. Elimination of these sources of trouble would increase the life and reliability of watches. Harwood's invention provided enough power to wind the main spring.

In spite of the obvious advantages, watchmaking firms were uninterested until Harwood and several associates organized their own company in Great Britain.

Lightbulb

No Burn by Sherman

Of course, Sherman didn't burn Savannah when he got to the sea, and he did *not* burn one Georgia town on the blazing path and it was Madison. At least he didn't burn the homes—only the train depot, cotton gin, and a clothing factory. All because their resident U.S. senator was a friend of Wm. T's brother, Sen. John Sherman! And they served the marchers a front-lawn picnic of fried chicken and cornbread!

Sons of Sherman's March to the Sea Bulletin

Self-Winding Wrist Watch

This anecdote illustrates that unusual motives sometimes trigger important inventions. The idea of a self-winding watch surfaced two centuries ago. Pocket watches were built using a swinging weight responsive to movement of the wearer to wind the mainspring.

Early designs were not popular because of their bulk, delicate nature, and high expense. These problems motivated numerous inventors and a number of patents were granted on various designs. The selling feature that physical winding was unnecessary was undoubtedly an important motive.

As technology improved to the point of mak-

Neither Snow nor Rain nor Gloom of Knight: Medieval Postal Systems

. . . .Out of the hodge-podge of petty messenger services, which were oftimes the victims of feudal wars and cut-throat rivalry, came the most sophisticated system in medieval Europe. Born in the mind of one man, and patronized by the Holy Roman Emperor, *Torre and Tassis* became the largest privately operated mail firm in Europe's history. It operated continuously for almost six hundred years, until the last fragment was purchased by the Kaiser of Germany in 1867 to be the foundation of his country's own postal system.

In the year 1290, Omodeo Tasso of Bergamo, Italy, started a highly organized messenger system between Milan and Venice, including most of the major towns along the way and maintaining from almost the very first day a rigid schedule of pickups and deliveries. So accurate and successful were his operations that in 1305 the rulers of Venice made Tasso Post Master, with sole authority to handle the city's mail.

Expanding under strict family control, the Tassis reached into every corner of Europe. By 1450 there were Tassos as Post Masters in Venice, Milan, Rome, and Brussels. When, in

1516, the Holy Roman Emperor made Jean-Baptiste Taxis his Imperial Post Master for life, the Taxis family had monopoly contracts with the Kings of England, France, and Spain, the Holy Roman Emperor, the Czar of Russia, and most of the rulers of the Italian city-states, as well as the Pope. So wedded to their posts were the senior partners of the firm that many of them surrendered the Italian spelling of the name: della Torre (the Tower, for Venice) e Tassis (the Badger, for Milan), accommodating to the local language. In France they were De La Tour et Tassis; in Belgium de Tour et Tassis; in Germany von Thurn und Taxis; and in Spain Taxis y Acunha.

This is not to say that life was easy for Torre e Tassis. The Holy Roman Emperor claimed vast domains but ruled indirectly. Even his personal fiefs were in near-constant turmoil. Independent operations for the guilds, the Church, local governments, and petty nobility, as well as competing commercial ventures such as the Hanse, often resulted in beatings, robberies, murders, oppressive laws and savage pricing wars. Life was very much an adventure for members of the firm and family.

Throughout the 15th and 16th centuries, though, the family grew and profited. By 1600, more than 20,000 couriers traveled routes that criss-crossed the length and breadth of Europe. From Brussels, schedules allowed postal runs to Paris in two days, Blois in three, Lyon in four, Innsbruck in five, and Toledo in twelve. Rigidly adhered to, such schedules brought riches, popularity, and worldwide respect, as well as the titles of barons and counts and finally the robes of Imperial princes.

But the growth finally came to an end. The iron-clad contracts that the firm had forced on the rulers of Europe in exchange for near-perfect mail delivery now became its downfall. The kings of France and Spain, eager to reap profits for themselves, forced von Thurn und Taxis to sell for mere pittances, and the new nations that sprang into being after the Napoleonic Wars wrote *finis* to the power of the Holy Roman Emperor. Only the German states remained faithful.

But even that ended when on a fateful day in 1867 the Kaiser ordered a state loan of 3,000,000 marks to buy the remainder of T&T for the New Germany. So died a dream that had lived for six hundred years.

—Eadwine be Bocce Sele
Tournaments Illuminated

Paris is probably the world's most beloved city that has, through a series of historical events, become the most beautiful of all the world's metropoli. There exists in Paris a kind of atmosphere that defies description which has, for centuries, fascinated and attracted writers, poets and painters.

It started in 987 A.D., an important year for Paris, if not France, when Hugues Capet, Duke of France and Count of Paris, was chosen King of France, and the busy commercial Paris area became the nucleus of a rapidly growing crownland. The city was further enhanced by two important historical characters. First the 12th century King Philippe II, fondly called Auguste after the Roman emperor, built a wall around Paris, paved the streets, founded the Louvre and began the cathedral of Notre Dame. From that time on Paris was clearly the center of things in France.

"I want to be a second Augustus," wrote Louis Napoléon Bonaparte in 1842, and when, a few years later, he restored the Empire, Paris became a city of scaffolding, flying dust, noise and falling plaster. Baron Georges Haussmann was hired to build broad new boulevards and avenues, erect public buildings and open parks and squares leaving a permanent impression on the city. Today Paris is also changing in more subtle ways. We will recount these changes and keep those who love the city informed of them. A letter from Paris, which has always held a magnetic attraction to Americans, is like a letter from home.

Letter from Paris

Small Invention That Made Big Money: Patent #188,292

In 1873 Chester Greenwood was so uncomfortable in the harsh Maine winter he got the Idea for "Ear Flaps," later renamed Ear Muffs. He was only 15 years old. His mother and grandmother made them from his description. Soon friends and neighbors were asking to buy the new "Greenwood Ear Muffs!" The Greenwood family took out a patent for Chester and started to make their patented products. They became RICH from *manufacturing* and *selling* Ear Muffs.®

Lightbulb

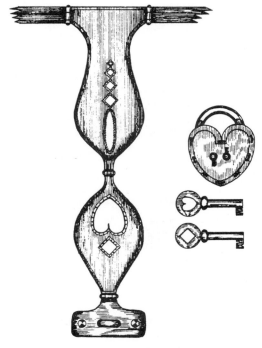

Illustrations by Stanley Smyth

A History of Chastity Belts

The fact that chastity belts did indeed exist, and in fact still do, is now soundly documented. When they were first used is an extremely difficult matter to determine. The earliest recorded reference is during the second half of the twelfth century, though no tangible examples remain of this period. Popular legend has the crusaders fitting their ladies with the device but this was a case of the chroniclers mixing their time periods. It has now been conclusively proved that the belts were a basic innovation of the southern and eastern cultures and were brought to Northern Europe and England at the close of the Crusades. Whether the crusaders brought the devices with them or observed their use and created similar models is a question that will probably remain unanswered.

Venice was a center for the Oriental trade and it is believed the belts were introduced into Italy during medieval times. The sexual customs of the Orient became known and gradually spread throughout Western Europe. Though some variations on strange sexual practices were known and practiced among the upper classes in England as early as the twelfth century it was not common behavior for the masses. Such practices were deeply rooted in the Asian and Arabian cultures. As more and more travelers became aware of these practices the basic design of the belts underwent a design change.

The first belts were simple one-piece devices curved to fit the body and attached to a rather heavy rigid belt. Later models were made in two pieces with a hinge arrangement so the device could be secured to the belt in front as well as the back. This design has prevailed down to the present time.

The use of devices to protect the chastity of young girls and women has its origins in antiquity—long before written history. Such devices included sewing up, inserting metal rings, wearing heavy leather garments and, in one culture, painting parts of the body yellow. Therefore the basic theory behind chastity belts is not something that appeared with the introduction of the present models. The need for protection has always been there. For many centuries, those who could afford to, locked their women up in barred chambers, hired guards and devoted a considerable amount of effort to protecting their property. Women were one of the most valuable commodities, especially wives. The matter of a true heir was paramount to all men of station and property.

With the decline of romantic love at the beginning of the Renaissance, more practical methods were required to protect the man's valuable property. Marriages were arranged for power and practical reasons. Therefore, purity for both mothers and daughters became an obsession. Peer pressure created intense jealousies and a means had to be found to create some peace of mind for the man who had to be away from his home from time to time.

Story tellers, balladeers and scribes delighted in expounding on this theme to the extent that men worried more than ever. Given this climate it is much easier to understand how chastity belts came into widespread use. No such justification can be advanced for the practice today. The use of these devices has not totally disappeared nor will it likely disappear in the forseeable future. In fact on the 16th of March, 1903, Frau Emilie Schafer of Berlin, Germany, applied for a patent for a "Girdle with lock and key as a protection against conjugal infidelity."

—Don Stewart
Key Collectors Journal

Pup Tents

A Little-Known Story. . . .

One day U. S. Grant paid an official visit to Sherman in the role of inspector general. Sherman's backwoods men on the Western front didn't cotton much to discipline. When told to turn out for inspection by Grant, Sherman's men got down on all fours in front of their small tents. As Grant passed by, they began barking and howling in mock imitation of hound dogs. What the general's reaction was is now largely forgotten, for nothing much came of the incident. Except for one thing: Forever afterwards the little shelters used by those soldiers were familiarly known as "pup tents."

Military Collectors' News

The First Parking Meters

The "Snitching Post" was the name first given to parking meters when they initially replaced the old Western hitching posts on Oklahoma City streets way back in 1935.

The nation's first parking meters—150 of them—were the brainchild of the late Carl Magee, attorney and newspaper editor. He dreamed up the device as a means to increase the turnover in parking space on busy city streets. Then, a mechanical engineer from Ohio named Gerald A. Hale developed the clock-operated meter and joined with Magee as a partner.

From this rather modest 150 meter instal-

lation in Oklahoma City has sprung a controversial business—one which has been fought in the courts from the very start. There are now over 1,700,000 on-street metered parking spaces throughout the nation. They earn over $110 million a year. Other off-street parking meters earn another $160 million. New York City leads the pack with over 75,000 parking meters.

The California Highway Patrolman

History of the Windmill

The origin of the windmill is not at all clear. Recent evidence attributes its discovery to Persia or China. Whether the idea traveled to Europe via the East or was spontaneously invented in various places is subject to debate and speculation. By the 12th century, windmills had begun to appear in England and Northern Europe. The idea was brought to America and developed rapidly by both English and Dutch settlers.

It is thought that early windmills were built by seamen and shipwrights because many of the fundamentals of sailing apply to the functions of windmills. The windmiller would need to know not only the particulars of grist grinding, but he would have to have a knowledge of the construction, repair and use of sails, which necessitated an understanding of wind dynamics, carpentry, mechanics and engineering as well as an eye for the weather. Mills are thus a remarkable example of the way that man adapted to life at the edge of the sea, gave a glimpse of the energy of our ancestors, and offer new hope for the future.

—Lianne B. Westcott
Old Mill News

Titanic's Gus "The Cat" Cohen Lives On

At age 85, Gershun Cohen has probably taken his last ocean voyage. His small pension and the high cost of travelling these days has put a damper on one of his primary hobbies—travelling. But wherever he goes, Gus Cohen is almost certain to attract attention whenever he talks about his past life. And what a life he has had! Without the benefit of a rabbit's foot, four-leaf clover or other lucky charms, Cohen has survived one of the greatest peaceful maritime disasters, various bombings during two world wars, a bout with rheumatic fever at age 43, and has broken his wrist three times. As if this were not enough, "The Cat" (as he has been nicknamed) was shot in the head during WW I, and later at the age of 78, was stuck down by a car while he walked towards a Dublin television station to tell about his experiences on the *Titanic*.

Looking back to the year 1912, Gus describes himself as a nice young kid of 19 with plenty of hair at the time. Cohen was an out-of-work printer from Whitechapel, England, when he decided to leave his home and seek his fortune in the United States. He recalls the departure of the great liner:

"We started out on April 10th. In those far-off days, maiden voyages were not considered strange and there were not many people to cheer us off when the boat sailed. . . . I travelled third class, and I believe there were six people in my berth, all comprised of English people, who eventually were drowned.

"We had a fairly good time and played cards and various games to occupy our time. The journey was going fairly well, but I remember that on April 14th, it got very cold. I remarked to various passengers that we must be near icebergs and I was laughed at and told that I was fancying things!

"On the evening of the disaster, we were enjoying ourselves in the lounge of the third class, and later I went to my berth at 10:30 p.m. to sleep for the night. At 11:45 p.m. we were awakened by a crash, but did not take notice of this because we thought something happened in the boiler room and we went to sleep again. We were later awakened again by the master-at-arms and told to put on lifebelts.

"I did not worry about putting one on, because I thought, like many others, the boat would never sink. So far as I can remember, I don't think we had any boat drill. Nobody, outside of some officers, could tell us what happened at the time, at least we were not told of any damage. At this time, we heard the band playing from afar. Realizing there must be something wrong, I went along on the third class deck and saw great lumps of ice and then surmized that we had struck an iceberg! But we still did not think that there was any danger.

"Suddenly there was an order to man the lifeboats, and, as usual, it was women and children first. I had to fend for myself. I had to find a lifebelt, which I did and thought that it was time to save myself. But first I went back to my berth to find some of my belongings and as I walked through the corridor, I was told by some merchant men that things were serious, so I decided to go back on deck.

"As soon as I did so, all the bulkheads were closed to keep the ship buoyant. While walking to the boat deck, I saw quite a few people praying and holding rosaries and thought to myself, 'I will pray when I am rescued.' There were also a lot of people walking around as if at a loss as to what to do. A number of families who were emigrating all stuck together and were not separating from each other because they did not want to be parted from their parents, brothers or sisters.

"In this case, I was glad that I was travelling alone, so I only had to look after myself . . . thank goodness! However, I was very worried if my father or mother heard I was drowned. At this time, the boat was tilting to one side and I realized the precarious position we were all in. It was no use to keep on the third-class deck, because I could see that the first-class passengers were looked after first.

"I tried to get to the first-class deck, but was barred by sailors from going there. Eventually, by various means, I did manage to get on the first-class deck, but by then, things were hopeless! The *Titanic* was at a very sharp angle and I realized it would not be long for the boat to sink.

"There was no direct communication to the other boats, except by wireless telegraphy, and by this method, and by Morse Lamp, the SOS went out. Signal flares were sent up by the *Titanic* but, of course, to no avail. But still we thought we would have help from other boats. At the time, we knew that the *Olympic* (sister-ship to the *Titanic*) was not far away going in the reverse direction. We eventually found out, when we arrived in New York, that it was hundreds of miles away so we had false hopes!

"Now, I knew things were hopeless, and although there was no panic (and I can vouch for this . . . although some reports say otherwise) I knew it was time to really act. Not all lifeboats were full and many left half full. I realized that no more lifeboats would be used—I do not realize the reason why— I had to do something!

"While holding the rail and looking over the side of the ship, I heard one of the sailors in one of the lifeboats shouting for me to jump. It was about 200 feet high from the water where I was standing. I was a lad and did not realize the danger but I knew I must do something. I was standing near the davits with the ropes hanging down, and did something of which I did not realize the danger. I climbed on the davit, crawled across and jumped for one of the ropes. I was wearing gloves and that saved my hands, partially.

"I clutched the ropes and when I got to the end of these, I still found I had to jump into the sea and was kept up by my lifebelt. After being in the water several minutes, I was picked up. The boat that rescued me had many women and children, but was not filled to capacity—it could have taken a lot more. I found out, later, that Mrs. Astor was in the same boat.

"We could see the *Titanic,* which must have been at an angle of about 30°, and all the lights were still on. I would like to add, at this point, that the orchestra on the *Titanic* was not playing at the time when I jumped from the ship, because I distinctly remember them standing about with their instruments. I was given an oar, and we had to pull away fast because we thought the suction would pull us down. When we were at a safe distance, we heard the first explosion — it may have been the boilers, I don't know. Then came the second explosion—what this was I cannot tell. Then the *Titanic* sank altogether!

"For several minutes, all was quiet, and then I heard the cries of people drowning which is never out of my ears! Our boat picked up several men from the water. I believe one or two died of exposure. Then the bung of my lifeboat began to leak, so my job was to bale the water out. We sailed through the night in a calm sea. We were lucky and every star we saw in the sky, we thought were lights from other boats, but they were only mirages. All the lifeboats were kept together by order of some officer who we later were informed was second mate Lightoller.

"At about 6:00 a.m., when it became light, we saw a boat in the distance, which we found out to be the *Carpathia*. We reached this ship by rowing to it. All those who were in good health (if this was possible) had to climb on board this ship by rope ladder. . . ."

Gus remained in the United States for about two and one-half years. In the meantime, World War I surfaced and Cohen decided to return home to volunteer for service in the British Army. Oddly enough, the vessel he chose for his return to England was none other than the White Star Liner *Olympic*. He travelled in third class on this vessel as well. . . .

The Titanic Commutator

Brief Survey of the Controversy Surrounding King Richard III

Life: Born at Fotheringhay Castle, October 2, 1452. Nominated Lord Protector April 9, 1483, by Edward IV. Petitioned by Lords and Commons to ascend the throne, June 25, 1483. Crowned by general consent, July 6, 1483. Slain at the Battle of Bosworth Field, August 22, 1485.

Undisputed Facts: He extended the scope of trial by jury, made laws to protect juries from intimidation, and established the system of bail for prisoners. He caused the statutes to be written in English instead of Latin and ended the system of "benevolences" by which the king exacted money from his subjects. He founded the College of Arms. He was a patron of Cambridge University, of Caxton, the first English printer, and was a great benefactor of the Church.

James Gairdner in his *Richard The Third* (1898) said that as king he seems really to have studied his country's welfare; he passed good laws, endeavored to put an end to extortion, declined the free gifts offered to him by several towns, promoted justice, religion and morality, was very generous to the Church, and declared he would rather have the hearts of his subjects than their money.

The Tudor Story: The picture of Richard as a hunchbacked monster was the creation of a highly organized and ruthlessly executed Tudor propaganda campaign to make him appear capable of having murdered his two boy nephews in order to bolster Henry VII's very weak claim to the throne. Shakespeare seized on this legend of a child-murdering King as rich dramatic material and so unwittingly helped perpetuate it. As more and more contemporary chronicles and other reliable evidence were unearthed, however, the Tudor version became deeply suspect and is now widely discredited. The true fate of the little "Princes in the Tower" remains "non-proven."

The Bones in the Tower: The skeletons of two children were discovered among the foundations of a staircase in the Tower in 1674 and were interred by order of Charles II as being those of the Princes. The bones were privately exhumed in 1933 with no independent witnesses present, and on examination, were declared to be the bones of children of the right ages. Neither sex nor century could be established, however, and present-day anatomists, armed with new knowledge and techniques, ascribe a wide margin of error to the earlier deductions.

The Question of Motive: Since Richard III was freely elected King by Lords and Commons on the grounds of the bastardy of his brother's children, these children *were no threat to him.* But while the "Princes" were known to be alive, their sister Elizabeth could not be put forward as the heiress of York, and so, through marriage to Henry Tudor, consolidate Henry's claim to the throne. Thus, Henry VII is a possible murderer of the "Princes." Another possible murderer is the Duke of Buckingham; he was also the boys' uncle, first Prince of the Realm and Constable of England. He had exactly the same opportunity of date, time, and place, and the authority to order the murder of the "Princes" as has been ascribed to Richard. He also had a motive, which Richard did not: He aspired to the throne that Richard then held. Another view, widely held ever since the eighteenth century but also lacking the final proof, is that the "Princes" were never murdered at all, but were removed from the Tower. The only thing which can be truly said is that after the autumn of 1483 there is no final evidence of what became of the "Princes."

The Ricardian Register

Loyaulte me lie

The Pardoner

The Pardoner was one of the necessary evils of the Middle Ages. The Church, once so pious, had become very materialistic by the 14th century. Churches were grand palaces, the Church coffers were overflowing, and the Church Fathers were lords of their day. Petrarch wrote of the papal city of Avignon: "I am living in the Babylon of the West" where prelates feast at "licentious banquets" and ride on snow-white horses "decked in gold, fed on gold, soon to be shod in gold if the Lord does not check this slavish luxury."

Supposedly commissioned by the Church, the Pardoner would sell absolution for *any* sin from gluttony to homicide, cancel any vow of chastity or fasting, remit any penance for money, most of which went right into his pocket. What the Pardoner was selling was salvation—but a false salvation which preyed upon the people's need and credulity.

The regular clergy detested the Pardoner for undoing the work of penance and endangering souls, as his goods were spurious, and for invading clerical territory, taking collections on feast days or performing burial or other services for a fee that should have gone to the parish priest. Yet the system permitted him to function because it shared in his profits.

Among the party of travellers in Chaucer's *Canterbury Tales* is a "gentil Pardoner of Rouncival" who has just come from the "court of Rome" with a wallet full of pardons. Among the tools of his trade he had a pillowcase which he claimed was "Our True Lady's Veil," a piece of the very sail that St. Peter had when he went upon the sea, a latten cross full of stones, and a bottle of pig's bones ("bones of a saint"). Apparently all he lacked was a piece of the True Cross.

But with thise relikes, whan that he fond
  A povre person dwelling up-on the lond,
Up-on a day he gat him more moneye
  Than the person gat in monthes tweye.
And thus, with feyned flaterye and japes,
  He made the person and the peple his apes.

—John the Grey of St. Brendan
Tournaments Illuminated

Americans in Paris

Paris has been second home to a stream of Americans since pre-revolutionary days. For over 200 years they all went to Paris or dreamed of going. From John Adams and John Jay with their puritanism, Ambassador Benjamin Franklin with his coonskin hat, Robert Fulton with his steamboat, Georges Catlin and his Indian show, Whistler and his painting, Mark Twain with his carpetbag and umbrella, Anna Gould and her fortune, James Gordon Bennett and his newspaper, Mary Cassatt and her portraits, Gertrude Stein and her friend, world heavyweight champ Jack Johnson and his white wife, Ernest Hemingway and his boxing gloves, Isadora Duncan and her long white scarf, Sylvia Beach and her book store, John Dos Passos and his Model T Ford ambulance, F. Scott Fitzgerald and his Zelda, Aaron Copland and his music, George Gershwin and his concerto, Bricktop and her nightclub, Henry Miller and his Tropics, Richard Wright in exile, black musicians with their jazz and thousands upon thousands of students to would-be imitators of the list of famous Americans, they have crowded these shores like the "homeless, downtrodden" who passed through Ellis Island.

Letter from Paris

The Bang Bang United States Essay

The proverbial boiler factory would be a quiet place compared to the United States Postal Service, if the idea of one genius had been adopted by the Post Office Department in the latter parts of the last century. The Post Office never was satisfied with the system for cancelling its stamps. Too many stamps were being cleaned, by having the cancellation removed, and thus subject to being used again. The 1867 grill, which enabled the cancelling ink to penetrate the paper of the stamp, was just one of several schemes suggested. There was no doubt that the Government was losing a considerable portion of the revenue that should have come to it, through the fraudulent use of stamps a second time.

This particular inventor saw a way to solve the problem. It was really simple. The stamp should be one that when used could not be used again, simply by changing its form. To accomplish this, he proposed that every stamp have on the back a bit of gunpowder, exactly similar to the "caps" used in toy pistols even today. The stamp would be affixed to the letter in the ordinary way, and the postal clerk, to cancel it, would simply hit it with a hammer. If he aimed correctly, the hammer would hit the stamp, it would explode into bits, and there was not a chance in the world that it could be reassembled to be used again.

The Post Office actually was interested in the crazy idea, and essays were prepared, not only for postal use, but for documentary use as well. They are not great rarities. They exist, reading U. S. POSTAGE and U. S. INTERNAL REVENUE. The stamps bore the portrait of the then Secretary of the Treasury McCullough. If there was then a rule about portraying living people on postage stamps, no one seemed to mind that this would be a violation of it. We have seen these not only in singles, but in pairs, with one stamp exploded. The used one usually shows definite signs of the charred paper that resulted when the percussion cap was hit, and burned the paper.

Happily the scheme was never adopted for our stamps. The Post Office would be a pretty noisy place, if it had been, especially with these large metropolitan offices which send tens of thousands of letters per hour through the cancelling machines. Aside from the noise, there would always be the possibility that a certain number of letters would catch fire from the sparks that would fly about, resulting in blazes in Post Offices which might require more firemen in regular attendance than postal employees.

Well, today we have machines that cancel stamps, but the old problem of what to do about stamps that do not get canceled is still with us. A fair proportion of the stamps on our mail come through without any defacement, especially if they are placed on the cover in other than the suggested position. Perhaps it is time to resurrect the "cap pistol" stamp!

—Herman Herst, Jr.
Virginia Philatelic Forum

A Wireless Whodunit

The very first occasion in which wireless was used to apprehend a criminal took place in the year 1910.

It was in July of that year that a most notorious British murderer by the name of Crippen escaped the clutches of Scotland Yard and fled to Belgium. There Dr. Crippen and his inamorata, who had been his nurse and secretary, obtained passage on the Pacific Mail Liner *Montrose* in Antwerp. They set sail for Canada, sure that they had successfully evaded the law.

For the voyage, his secretary and nurse had cut her hair short and had disguised herself as a boy to allay suspicion. They kept strictly to themselves aboard ship and avoided all familiarity or social amenities with any of the passengers or ship's officers while walking on deck. They had all of their meals served to them in their stateroom and never entered the dining saloon.

The ship's captain observed their rather peculiar behavior and he was not at all convinced that the boy was really a boy at all. He communicated with his home office by wireless and described the doctor and his nurse (the "boy").

The home office in return immediately sent him a detailed description of Dr. Crippen and his nurse, adding that they were wanted for murder. With this information in hand the Captain was convinced that the two of them were the fugitives and so informed his office.

Upon receiving this information, Chief Inspector Drew of Scotland Yard immediately

sailed on the *SS Laurentic*, a vessel much faster than the *Montrose*.

Then began what seemed a transatlantic race between the two ships. It is interesting to note that the situation was known to the whole world by wireless, though the two fugitives had no inkling that the news of them was being flashed to all quarters of the globe and that the world at large was enthralled by the thrilling knowledge that the escapees were crossing the Atlantic in hot pursuit by Scotland Yard, and secure in their belief that they had successfully escaped and that their identities were completely unknown!

However, immediately upon their arrival in Canada they were arrested by Chief Inspector Drew, much to their astonishment, whereupon they were immediately returned to England to stand trial for murder.

—H.J. Scott
Sparks Journal

Keys to the City

Cities had their beginnings in the need of naturally social mankind to seek safety and mutual protection in some easily defensible location. High walls were constructed around the major area, normally enclosing the leaders' homes, merchants' shops, warehouses, religious shrines and military barracks. One large gate was normally provided for entry and egress, though some cities had more.

The gates of most cities were opened only during the daylight hours. At dusk a trumpeter would mount the ramparts and sound the notice of the closing of the gates. All the serfs working the fields, shepherds and hunters would return to the walled city with the livestock and game. Only citizens and subjects were allowed this privilege. Persons who were not honored guests or who were representatives of other cities were required to leave before the gates were closed for the night.

Originally the gates were locked by a large bar, often so large it required as many as twenty men to raise it into place. The gates were designed to withstand the largest known battering ram. As war machines improved, the large heavy gates and bars became useless as protection. Smaller gates evolved that locked with a key. The primary concern during this period was to keep out spies, beggars, itinerant craftsmen and other undesirables.

At some period, lost in antiquity, an especially astute politician presented a visiting personage from another city the highest honor he could bestow—a special gold "Key to the City." This honor meant that the host trusted the visitor and that he was extended the privilege of citizenship.

Over the years cities have risen and fallen but the idea of presenting distinguished persons with honorary citizenship has continued. While today the keys are purely symbolic, the honor and meaning remains the same.

Keys to the City are among the most desirable of collectibles. They are often hard to find, though some cities will arrange for collectors to acquire a key for a fee. Prices of the keys range from $10 to $30 and upwards.

—Don Stewart
Key Collectors Journal

Small, fuel-efficient automobiles are not new. A rash of them appeared more than 30 years ago.

Following World War II, with a high demand for new automobiles, many small independent automakers sprung up overnight. A few auto companies, along with these new manufacturers, introduced a number of lightweight, small-engine compact cars with high mileage capabilities. Cars with names like the Bantam, Davis, Gregory and the Bobbi Car came on the scene. The small cars were advertised as second family cars for running about town, much like the computer-car concept being touted today.

Unfortunately, the cars failed in the marketplace because the public just wasn't ready to buy small cars. At that time consumers were more interested in horsepower and comfort. The bigger the better.

One small economy car that sold better than most was the Crosley. Its success, however, was short-lived. It had the capability of 36 to 50 miles to the gallon. Its curb weight was just 1,155 pounds. By comparison, most subcompacts of today are about double that.

Another well-known economy car of the period was the Henry J. The car was a participant in several coast-to-coast Mobil economy runs and in the 1952 run, one model posted 30.86 mpg.

Later came compacts such as the Lark, Rambler, Willys, Falcon, Chevelle and Valiant. After a brief flash, they also faded. They were considered to be too small for American tastes. The big car continued to be king until the oil crunch hit in early 1979.

Today's smaller cars, though much larger than their brothers of 30 years ago, offer virtually the same mileage capabilities of those earlier models. . . .

The California Highway Patrolman

Unusual Pursuits

NOT FOR THE SWIFT

"It's a fact that good humor is a tonic for mind and body," says Lloyd D. Hardesty, Grand Imperial Turtle and editor of the *Turtle Express*. "It is the best antidote for anxiety and depression. It is a business asset. It attracts and keeps friends. It is a direct route to serenity and contentment." It's no wonder, then, that the organization headed by Hardesty, Turtles International, has as its motto: "Turtles Have More Fun."

Turtles International was founded "unofficially" in 1914 and officially 17 years later. Today there are said to be several million card-carrying Turtles around the world who follow the Turtle Creed: "Recognize the fact that you never get any place worthwhile in life unless you stick your neck out." When a Turtle meets someone he suspects is a fellow member, he asks the question: "Are you a Turtle?" There is only one accepted answer to this query, and that is: "You bet your sweet ass I am." (The ass is the official Turtle mascot and all Turtles are expected to have one.)

"One night on the Dean Martin show," Hardesty recalls, "'old Dino' opened a closet door, spotted Johnny Carson, and asked, 'Are you a Turtle?' 'You bet your sweet (bleep) I am,' answered Carson—and really brought the house down. There is never a dull moment when Turtles are around."

According to Hardesty, former astronaut Wally Schirra "probably did more to foster the Turtle cause than anyone imaginable. Wally initiated instant and lasting fame for the Turtles when, in outer space as pilot of Apollo 7, he held up a sign reading 'Deke Slayton—Are you a Turtle?' Deke Slayton, who was flight director for Apollo, is a Turtle also. His answer caused the first worldwide TV bleep, and being a plug for Turtles, it was also the very first and only worldwide TV commercial."

Registered Turtles come from all walks of life—from "600 readily recognizable celebrities" to presidents of the United States. (The last six presidents have signed, or been signed, up.) "Turtles are nonpolitical, nonsectarian, nonviolent, nontoxic and nonallergenic," explains Hardesty, "so if you believe that a sense of humor is not only rewarding but highly essential in your everyday encounters with other human beings, you're a Turtle of the highest caliber, regardless of who or what you are."

Hardesty, 49, runs the organization out of his home in Westchester, Illinois. (He is employed as a production manager at a steel company in Skokie.) There are over 70 Turtle chapters (known as Shells or Watering Holes) in the U.S. alone. Members communicate through the *Turtle Express,* an informal, hysterically funny digest, and meet at annual Turtle events, such as the Festival of the Hare, La Fiesta del Burro (to honor the club mascot), and International Turtle Creepstakes (turtle races held around the country). But the organization—believe it or not!—also has a serious side. All proceeds from Turtle activities go to hospitals and institutions for the handicapped and retarded children. During the club's annual "Christmas in May" celebration, members bearing gifts are encouraged to visit hospitalized children and hold "zany, slapstick, outrageous and/or successful" activities to raise funds for charity. The group's latest project involves raising funds to purchase 20 acres of farmland where handicapped children could raise vegetables.

But let's face it, Turtledom is basically a big goof. "Turtles," Hardesty says, "believe that life runs smoother on the oil of humor. That is not to say that you have to get well oiled to appreciate good humor." Hardesty claims that membership is so "diligently sought" that the organization now has several imitators, known as mock-Turtles. In reality, however, *anyone* can join by sending him $1 for a lifetime (sometimes called "100 Year") membership. It costs a little extra to subscribe to the *Express.*

TURTLES officially stands for The United Resistance to Life's Everyday Setbacks. But why was the turtle, of all things, chosen as the club symbol? "The turtle," Hardesty explains, "starts life with a very slim chance for survival and yet the turtle has been around longer than the dinosaur. The turtle is still around because it knows when to stick its neck out and when not to. Democracy is only 200 years old and if our government starts right now practicing the Turtle philosophy, there's a good possibility that democracy just might be around for another 200 years."

CITIZEN RABE

Unicorn Hunters International
Punsters Unlimited
Boulder

The Woods-Runner
Raisin d'Etre
The Society of the Friends of Lizzie Borden

The man behind all of these activities, and more, is William T. Rabe, public relations chief for little (2,400 students) Lake Superior State College in northern Michigan.

It all began in 1968 when Rabe's son John, then three, asked him what all these people were doing throwing flat stones into the waters off Mackinac Island, Michigan, where the Rabe family was vacationing. The fol-

lowing summer, Rabe wrote an article on stone skipping for a local paper and with tongue deep in cheek asserted that there would be a tournament on Mackinac Island on July 4. When Rabe received phone calls from people who wanted to sign up for the big event, he figured, "Why not?"—and the annual July 4 International Open Stone Skipping Tournament was born. (More than 500 entrants, who pay a 50¢ fee, now turn out every year.) Naturally, Rabe had to start a newsletter to cover the action, and that was *Boulder: An Avant-Guard* [sic] *Journal of Stone Skipping Action and Comment.*

Then, in 1970, Rabe, along with Prof. Peter Thomas, poet-in-residence at Lake Superior State, and Prof. John C. McCabe (a biographer of Laurel and Hardy), founded the Unicorn Questers, based on the belief that "every man has a unicorn he is predestined to hunt. It is not necessary actually to track, find and slay this beaste, but only that the Quest be most diligently pursued." On March 20 the Unicorn Hunters at Lake Superior State sponsor an annual Snowman Burning to celebrate the arrival of spring, and from October 5 to 11, Rabe issues Unicorn Questing licenses (he has given out 25,000 so far). The Lake Superior literary magazine, *The Woods-Runner,* has become "the official meeting place of the Unicorn Hunters."

But Rabe was just warming up. He published a one-by-four-inch newsletter about raisins called *Raisin d'Etre.* "It's small," he explains, "because raisins are small." He helped form The Society of the Friends of Lizzie Borden; their motto: "It Ain't Necessarily So!" Members of the society are "not required to believe deep in their hearts that she was innocent, but only to bring to the fore, when necessary, the simple fact that she was found not guilty." He organized Punsters Unlimited "to clarify ownership of puns since they generally cannot be copyrighted." Punsters send puns they want to claim for their own; PU assigns the pun a serial number and returns the pun with a certificate. (Punsters, like unicorn hunters and stone-skipping entrants, help to defray the costs involved by paying 50¢ fees and supplying self-addressed, stamped envelopes.) "If anyone else has a serial number on the same pun," PU informs them, "check the numbers—the lower number indicates the earliest time of origin and the true originator of the pun."

Rabe and his band of merry men also solicit nominations from the public for over- and mis-used words and phrases in the English language that should forever be banished from our shores. On New Year's Eve the Unicorn Hunters meet to pick the "winners"; these selections often get quite a bit of newspaper publicity.

All of this tomfoolery is carried out under the aegis of what Rabe calls The Unicorn, Ltd. Conglomerate. This, he says, "in the traditional American concept, includes a large range of activities put on by a vast assortment of agencies which were founded independently, at various times, but each embraces the tenets of the Unicorn Quest." One of the most inspired activities takes place on the fourth Friday in August. Members of the World Sauntering Society stroll along what is reputed to be the longest front porch in the U.S. (880 feet, at the Grand Hotel, Mackinac Island) "to revive," says Rabe, "the lost art of sauntering rather than rushing thither and yon to no great purpose."

Obviously there are not many more worlds for bearded Bill Rabe to conquer. But in his search for ways to warm and shorten northern Michigan winters he will, he says, "leave no stone unskipped." As his cohort Peter Thomas has said: "The pursuit of the unicorn is a lonely quest, but many more embark upon that journey than teachers or publishers may recognize. . . ."

Tips for Stone-Skippers

Most skippers use the side cast, not neglecting the all-important follow-through. A wide-arc swing, feet spread and shoulders square, seems to work best for most; but there are of course exceptions. . . .

Rocks should be flat, ovoid, and, for best skipping, thin though not wafer-like or they are unstable. The size must fit the conformation of the index finger and thumb of the casting hand. Comfort is most important here. Size is not a measure of a winning skip.

Some skippers follow the Anselm Method of skipping knee deep in the surf. This technique is particularly helpful when skipping in heavy water, enabling the sportsman to cast his stone along the troughs between waves. . . .

Boulder

Garlic Your Way to Good Health

Garlic is a magical plant and I use it for everything and consider it one of the five most valuable and medicinal and cosmetic plants. If you cook it, it loses some of its potent properties, so I use it fresh except for garlic soup which I consider next to chicken soup as a miracle treatment. . . .

The mashed cloves of garlic are applied externally as a poultice for swellings and sores and can be dabbed on pimples and acne to reduce swelling.

Four or five cloves of garlic infused in water, vinegar or wine make an excellent wash for the scalp to stimulate growth and eliminate dandruff. . . .

—Jeanne Rose
Garlic Times

"Nosetalgia"

A Touch of Class from the Past

Called "snorting" by the young, a rage of fancy snuff sniffing is sweeping college campuses all over the U.S. The snorting population seems now to be evenly divided between men and women.

Most people get off to a bad start with snuff. Usually, they try snuff just once and there is a good reason for this. Most chewing tobacco and snuff available in the U.S. is pretty vile. This is because American tobacco companies are really cigarette companies and their snuff and chewing tobacco, if they make any, are by-products made from left-over and reject tobacco—perhaps even sweepings. Well, that's not what snuff is all about. The real thing is a blend of fermented prime tobaccos, finely ground and often mixed with fragrances such as jasmine, heliotrope, lemon, cinnamon, carnation, musk, bergamot, and attar of rose. . . .

Snuff is sniffed and it never reaches the lungs. The nasal membranes actually absorb snuff with a pleasant effect. . . .

The first reference to snuff in the English language is found in John Sparke's "Account of Hawkin's Second Voyage" (1565). In the 17th and 18th centuries, during the era variously called "The Age of Elegance" and "The Age of Enlightenment," snuff sniffing was the universal habit of the upper classes. Tradesmen smoked, sometimes on cool evenings and around the fireplace or brazier, for where else a live coal? Peasants enjoyed their tobacco orally. If the tobacco was in leaf form this was called "chewing"; if the tobacco was ground this habit was called "dipping," to distinguish it from the intended purpose, viz., snuffing. Remember that persons of the lower class did not have pockets and did not carry handkerchiefs. The mouth was a convenient receptacle and, often, a hiding place for a pinch purloined from milord or milady.

—Wade Poole
The Pipe Smoker's Ephemeris

Possibly the Best Swimmin' Hole in Arizona

Verde Hot Springs is about 25 miles east of Camp Verde, and half a mile west of the Childs Power Plant. Gird your loins, that little stretch of "road" past Childs is the worst. Park at the sandy campground and wade across the creek to the hot spring. Send your large "passenger" in first, it may be deep. And stop complaining about getting your feet wet. That's what you're here for. Besides, that creek is a very significant boundary. With the only entry approach being in one county, and the hot spring in another, the bather is reasonably assured of no skinny-dipping hassles.

Across the river, you'll find the ruins of a resort spa, reputedly a hideaway for Al Capone. Big Al knew how to lay low in style. There are two cement hot tubs and several gravelly natural tubs below. The waters weigh in at a respectable 100°. There used to be a hippie commune nearby, but they got rained out a couple of years ago. (We've heard it said that flash floods are just Nature's way of telling you to move on.) One final tidbit: UFO sightings come thick and fast around Childs. The prevailing theory has it that they come to suck up juice from the power plant there. Our suggestion is that they come to take the waters. Whatever the case, when recommendations come from such diverse and disreputable sources as bohemians, gangsters, extraterrestrials and editors it's time to gas up the micro bus and head for the hinterlands.

—Eric Irving
The Hot Springs Gazette

Illustration by Florence Irving

Volunteer to Work at a Winery

A number of the newer, smaller wineries around the country are not yet on a strong financial footing and sometimes welcome help from volunteers during the harvest or at other times of high work load. If you have a week or a few weekends to spend, contact local wineries to see if they would be willing to accept volunteer help. In most cases the wineries cannot pay wages or provide lodging, but may be able to feed volunteers. I have many fond memories from a decade ago when I drove a tractor (something of a thrill for a city boy), pounded in stakes in 100 degree temperatures, picked Chardonnay in the rain, crushed Riesling in a basket press operated by manpower rather than by machine, and tasted all the new wines out of the barrel. For winelovers who really want to get involved, this sort of volunteer work can be most rewarding.

The Friends of Wine

Notable Snuffers

Both Napoleon and Ben Jonson took over one pound of snuff per week and both kept it loose in their pockets.

George III's wife was known to family and friends as "Snuffy Charlotte" because of her prodigious snuffing.

Other notable snuffers of the past include:

Voltaire	Madame de Pompadour
Frederick the Great	Swedenborg
Pope Urban VII	Shakespeare
Pope Benedict XIII	Bacon
Beau Brummel	Dr. Johnson
Saint John Bosco	Jonathan Swift

The Pipe Smoker's Ephemeris

Anyone wanting to take a crack at recovering oil from abandoned fields should find a 1980 report from the U.S. Department of Energy interesting. It lists 676 abandoned oil fields in Texas which produced 250,000 barrels or more and includes information on the field's name, county, discovery date, year of last production, well depth, and other data. Cumulative production from the fields studied—many of which were never subjected to secondary operations—was 760 million barrels and the report says that there should be one billion barrels of oil still in place and subject to secondary or tertiary production. In some cases, in SED's view, these fields would probably respond to flooding with steam produced in large fields of solar collectors. You can order copies of the report, "Abandoned Texas Oil Fields," from the U.S. Government Printing Office, Washington, DC 20402. Document 061-000-00479-3.

Solar Energy Digest

Automobile Inventions That "Didn't Quite Make It"

Gadgets, gizmos and devices that will make a car run better, smoother, faster and cheaper have been appearing on the market since about a day after the first car hit the streets back before the turn of the century. Everybody from scientists to homemakers have come up with inventions on their own that they were certain would make the mouths of automakers water, and in some small way revolutionize the automobile. And, if an idea happened to bring the inventor a little fame and fortune, well, that was okay, too.

Reality, however, has a way of setting in and erasing dreams. Few of the tens of thousands of ideas committed to paper and even patented have ever been tried by automobile manufacturers. For the most part, these inventions have been deemed impractical or too costly, but the high rate of rejection never stopped "inventors" from dreaming up grand and glorious items for cars.

For instance, in 1926, Leander Pelton, of Des Moines, Iowa, apparently grew weary of looking for a parking space, so he designed a car that could be parked just about anywhere.

While conventional automobiles are parked resting on their four wheels, Pelton's design was for a lightweight car that could actually be stood on end and simply rolled into a small parking spot. On the back of his car he designed a vertical platform with heavy duty rollers. All you had to do with Pelton's Vertical Park Car was tip the thing back onto the built-in platform and then push the car into a parking slot slightly larger than a refrigerator.

There were a few flaws in Pelton's design, however. For one thing, it was never explained how you tipped the car up on end. Also, there was the minor problem of fluids such as gas, oil and water running out of the car once it was in the vertical position. It's highly unlikely that Pelton made a lot of money from his idea.

Sophisticated "sound systems" are commonplace in automobiles today, but 70 years ago Daniel Young of Pine Bluff, Arkansas, thought music in an automobile was a good idea even then.

Young invented and patented an organ for automobiles. The keyboard was attached to the back of the front seat, and persons riding in the back seat could play the organ to entertain themselves and the driver as they motored through the countryside. . . .

Driving can be, at times, a bit boring, and apparently Charles Ramage, of Longden, North Dakota, wasn't terribly thrilled with conventional automobiles of his day. He designed a device that he believed would "impart a thrill to the driver and afford great amusement . . . to onlookers." His invention? A somersaulting automobile.

A driver could, when the urge struck him, roll his car end over end in perfect safety with Ramage's invention. Actually, it wasn't a car in the traditional sense. It was a simple chasis with steering wheel, engine, seat, etc., encapsulated in a semi-circular roll cage. A lever below the chasis when actuated would literally push the car over and the vehicle's momentum would carry it around and back onto its wheels. Sounds like great fun, especially on busy city streets. . . .

Now it's important to point out that all the inventions that we take for granted on cars today weren't necessarily devised for cars in the first place. For example, rubber tires were tried on horse-drawn carriages in London in 1876. While they did give passengers a more comfortable ride the police and general public weren't thrilled with the idea. The tires made the carriages "noiseless," and a quiet carriage

was considered a safety hazard to pedestrians.

Even traffic laws were created long before the automobile. In China nearly 2,000 years ago there were laws concerning maximum size and speed of vehicles in certain parts of cities. Even traffic officers were used to control traffic movement at some intersections. Some historians claim that in ancient Mesopotamia there were "No Parking" zones. If a person parked his chariot in a restricted area and got caught, he didn't do it again. He didn't have a chance to—the penalty for violating no-parking laws was *death*. And we think some fines today are heavy!

Even vehicle rental services aren't a modern invention. In ancient Rome, anybody with the right amount of money could rent a chariot or other fine conveyance either for travel or special occasion to impress fellow Romans.

Back to the 20th century. When pedestrians and automobiles tangle, almost always the pedestrian comes out on the short end of the deal. With this in mind, Hanz Karl of New Jersey in 1932 patented a "pedestrian protector." It was a complicated device that practially defies description, but its basic function was to keep pedestrians from being injured should they collide with a moving vehicle. In the simplest terms, the device consisted of a bar that stretched across the front of the car, and if a pedestrian was hit by the bar it automatically slammed on the car's brakes. At the same time, a blanket stored under the car's front bumper shot forward and, according to Karl, "a falling person will fall upon the blanket so the clothes will not be spoiled, but his fall will be softened."

"A new and useful improvement in locomotion apparatus," is the way Z.P. Dederick and Isaac Grass described their contraption to the patent office in 1868. It looked like a man pulling a two wheel cart, but it was really a steam engine that, through a series of levers, permitted the "machine" to "walk" like a man. The cart could be steered, and the stride of the machine varied for slower or faster speeds. There's no record of this device ever being marketed. . . .

The list of good and not-so-good inventions for cars is virtually endless. Some ideas are impractical, others too costly, but in a few cases the "bad" ideas of yesterday, with a bit of refinement, have become today's "better ideas."

—Richard Bauman
The California Highway Patrolman

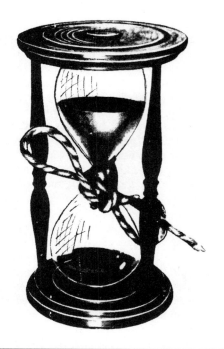

Since the cat ranch will be utilizing rats to feed the cats, it can expense the entire batch of rats purchased during the first year. If it starts with one million rats, at a nickel each, they will have four rats per cat per day, and a whopping $50,000 tax deduction.

The rats will be fed on the carcasses of the cats they skin during successive years. This will give each rat one-quarter of a cat. You can see by this that the business is a clean operation, self-supporting and really automatic throughout. The cats will eat the rats, and the rats will eat the cats, and the ranch will get the skins and the tax benefits! Incidentally, the ecologists think it's great.

Eventually they hope to cross the cats with snakes. Snakes skin themselves twice a year. This will save the labor cost of skinning and will also give the ranch a yield of two skins for one cat.

Turtle Express

Once a procrastinator makes up his mind to take a firm stand on something, nothing in the world can stop him from possibly getting around to it—some day.

Last Month's Newsletter

Do You Need an Interesting Tax Shelter?

There is a cat ranch near Karmossille, Mexico, that has a great idea for a tax shelter. (Disclaimer—Turtles International does *not* advocate killing cats.) Here is their proposal:

Each female cat will average about 12 kittens a year; skins can be sold for about 20¢ for white ones and up to 40¢ for black. Soon, this will provide about 12 million cat skins per year to sell at an average of 32¢, making a revenue about $3 million a year. This really averages out to $10,000 a day, excluding Sundays and holidays.

A good Mexican cat man can skin about 50 cats per day at a wage of $3.15 a day. It will only take 663 men to operate the ranch so the net profit will be over $8,200 per day.

The cats will be fed on rats exclusively. Rats multiply four times as fast as cats. A rat ranch will be started adjacent to the cat ranch. Here is where the first year tax break really comes in.

Religious Clowning

It's as old as the second millenium before Christ, but the story of Jacob tricking Esau out of his birthright for the mess of pottage (we would say "a bowl of beans") has marvelous comic insights that every clown appreciates. The whole scene reads like a script for a gag between two hungry clowns. In fact, I'm reminded of Samuel Beckett's *Waiting for Godot* in which the tramp Didi rummages in his tattered pockets to find a turnip for Gogo to eat: "Make it last, that's the last of them."

So the subject of food and clowns is ancient, but you holy fools can still follow the tradition with modern twists. Remember that you are a "joey" because of the famous Joseph Grimaldi, the English clown who stuffed sausages, cakes and other delicacies in his pockets. He won his audiences with comic songs like "Hot Codlins" (taffy apples), so that in his farewell speech at the Drury Lane Theatre in 1828 he said:

"It is four years since I jumped my last jump, filched my last oyster, boiled my last sausage—and set in for retirement. Not so well provided for, I must acknowledge, as in the days of my clownship, for, I dare say, some of you remember I used to have a fowl in one pocket and sauce for it in another."

Thus Jacob and Esau as well as Grimaldi

and many other clowns have used food to satirize our human concern for the immediate, practical appetites rather than the ideal, long range goals of mankind. It's no wonder then that food has great significance as revealing truth in the religious tradition (remember the forbidden fruit in the garden of Eden and the cosmic pratfall of Adam and Eve).

One of my favorite jester stories which I often use in my church programs concerns a French king presented with a strange complaint by a baker. The baker said that a man sat outside the bakery every day and smelled the bread. "O king," said the baker, "he should pay me for the privilege of smelling my bread." The king thought only his court fool could judge such a case, so the clown was called in. Hearing the facts of the matter, the fool agreed; "Yes, everyone knows how delicious your bread is, so he should pay for smelling it." They dragged in the ragged, thin fellow, and the fool pronounced the sentence: "Rattle the pennies in your pocket!" Then the fool turned to the baker: "Now the *sound* of his pennies has paid for the *smell* of your bread!"

Such a gag, it seems to me, is as telling as any preacher's sermon on the evils of greed, and it would make the basis of a good comic routine if it were acted out. Think of other clown routines that could satirize our misuses of food. What about a gag on the junk-food junkie who turns down wholesome food for those processed things that add little health? Or how you could poke fun at our American habit of littering our lovely countryside with beer and pop cans, cartons from the Dairy Queen, and unsightly gum and candy wrappers?

In short, don't forget food gags when you are doing your religious clowning, for they can be both fun and full of meaning. Remember the humor of Proverbs 15:17, "Better a dish of spinach and love to go with it, then beefsteak and hatred besides."

—Dr. Thomas Niccolls
Calliope

A Brief History of Stone Skipping

(Also known as "Ducks and Drakes")

Record of the sport goes back at least to 1583 where mention is made of oyster shells as well as stones. Tradition holds that the sport was begun by an English king who skipped gold sovereigns across the Thames. George Washington is thought to have popularized it in America by skipping a stone across a river. True, legend has it that this was a silver dollar, but George was close with a buck and would never have done such a thing. . . .

Boulder

Research on "Have a Happy"

Kenneth F. Kronenberg is currently researching the derivation and initial uses of the symbol of the smiling face in the circle which is often accompanied by the phrase, "Have a happy day." It is his understanding that it may have been used by industrial psychologists as a morale booster in industrial settings in the middle to late 1960s. Now its use is, of course, generalized in the entire culture through advertising. His efforts so far have turned up little. Nobody seems to know what the symbol is called, and nobody who uses it seems to know where it came from.

Popular Culture Association Newsletter

"Proof" that the Earth is Flat

According to the natural law of physics, water lies flat. If the world were round, for every six miles of water, you'd have a drop of 24 feet. Lakes would have humps in the middle. Have you ever seen a lake with a hump in the middle?

The Flat Earth News

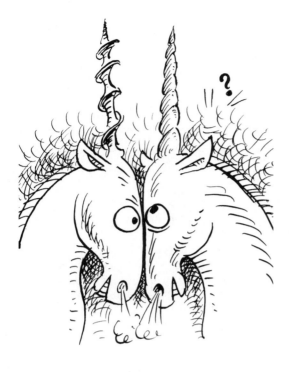

How to Hunt a Unicorn

The following regulations will be enforced by the Wildebeaste (Mythical) Division of the Department of Natural Unicorns of the Unicorn Hunters of Lake Superior State College.

Bag Limits:
1. Only one Unicorn per month. A success ratio higher than this often results in a form of euphoria, which of course requires a mental truss. This is highly undesirable.
2. Female unicorns may not be taken. Since no one has ever sighted a female unicorn it is believed that males reproduce asexually.

Approved Questing Devices. Unicorns may be taken with:
1. Serious intent
2. General levity
3. Iambic pentameter
4. Sweet talk

License.
Actually we prefer not to think of this activity in terms of license, but rather of privilege.

Drawing for Privilege.
In the event that the Unicorn herd diminishes to numbers smaller than five per square dream, a drawing will be held to determine privilege holders.

—Mike Gendzwill
The Woods-Runner

Chimney Sweeps

According to Mary Poppins, "when you're with a sweep, you're in glad company." Apparently you're in pretty creative company, too.

There are an estimated 3000 chimney sweeps throughout the United States, and almost as many clever names.

Cinder-Fella tops the popularity list of fanciful names, while Santa's Helpers in Dallas, Texas, also cashes in on the image of friendly little elves keeping chimneys spic and span.

A trifle more realistic are the folks in Akron, Ohio, who dub themselves Grubb & Grimes Master Chimney Sweeps. Then there's Soot on a Shingle in Coquville, Oregon. . . . Got a sick chimney? Call the Flue Bug in Gresham, Oregon, or Flue Season Chimney Sweeps in French Gulch, California. . . . If you're in a poetic mood, there's Jeepers Sweepers in Denver. . . .

It's an unusual business; it's a sometimes dangerous business. But, it appears that when you climb around on steep and slippery roofs wearing a top hat and tails, it helps to have a sense of levity along with a sense of balance.

—Sharon Timm
The Chimney Sweep News

from "Song of the Democratic Leaf"

by Walt Whitman

I roar with tobacco, I rub it on myself,
Yammering, incoherent, alive with the musk
of the weed;
I throw off my clothes, and run barefoot
From Long Island to Virginia, my beard awash
with blue smoke.
I run touching the street-car conductor, the
clerk, the anarchist, the soldier, the babe-
in-arms;
All, all, I would have them all smokers of pipes,
Drunk with the excellence of the fire.

The Pipe Smoker's Ephemeris

Thanks to:

Congressman Bertram L. Podell (D-NY) who rose on the floor of the House to note that that week was National Procrastination Week, and marked the event by saying "I will put off my remarks on the subject until a later time."

•

Joanne Wheeler for her suggested slogan-of-the-month for 1973: "There's always a future in Procrastination."

Last Month's Newsletter

Inventive genius is needed at the U.S. Patent & Trademark Office about as urgently as anywhere else in the world, just to keep track of all the details of technology and would-be technology being funneled in here from all the inventive genius there is now or has been.

The load of words, numerals and drawings—each meaning something to somebody, and some meaning a new blessing to almost everybody—is far too great to be called merely "enormous." Any one of them might have a bearing of some kind on any other of them, and the problem is to let that bearing be applied at the right time.

Back in 1790, when the patenting enterprise was under the fascinated care of an architect, inventor and statesman known as Thomas Jefferson, just three patents were issued in the first year. Nowadays the annual output exceeds seventy thousand, with about 110,000 applications being received each year.

That's better'n 2,000 a week—just in case you thought the Patent Commissioner would be waiting at the front door, panting for the one you sent in. Somewhere between 1,200 and 1,600 patents get issued each week, too, but not from the flow received the same week—it takes on the average about 18 months from the date the application was received to the date of issuance of a new patent, ready to go forth into a highly skeptical world.

Lightbulb

Why You Should Purchase a Milk Cow

No doubt about it—the economics of owning a family cow make good sense. The question is, "Am I ready to be tied to the milking stool better than ten months of the year, first thing in the morning and again just before supper, every day?"

Annual costs (1980 figures), including purchase price

Purchase of Jersey cow	$500.00
2,900 lbs. grain	$278.25
132 bales hay	165.00
Milk pail and strainer (used)	15.00
Mineral blocks	8.20
Veterinary fee (cut teat)	22.00
Sawdust bedding	15.00
Milk filters	5.10
	$1,008.55

Returns

1,020 gals milk	$1,836.00

Profit

First year	$ 827.45
Second year	$1,327.45

Farmstead

All the World Loves a Clown

I was very nervous, that day that I first entered the main office of the Peace Corps in Washington, D.C. "They'll think I'm a kook"... "Nothing like this has been done before"... "They will laugh me out of the office"... the thoughts raced through my mind. But I was determined, so in I strode.

What I proposed to the people at the Peace Corps that day was a unique idea. I wanted to travel around the world and give free performances for children at schools, hospitals, and orphanages in celebration of the International Year of the Child. I asked the Peace Corps if they could find me places to perform, a roof to sleep under, and a bowl of beans now and then. I was surprised at the response I received.

Letters were written to the Peace Corps directors of each country the Peace Corps operates in. In time, I received invitations to twenty-four nations across the globe. A school for the deaf in Thailand ... a kibbutz in Israel ... an orphanage for war orphans in Lebanon ... a children's hospital in Costa Rica ... a UNICEF telethon in New Zealand ... a center for "street boys" in Colombia, these are but a few of the places I was invited.

Having places to perform, and an act (developed by five years of clowning experience in the Ringling Brothers Circus and other clown scenes), the next step was to find a sponsor to cover the cost of my airfare. But alas, my fund-raising efforts did not produce anything substantial. Undaunted, I decided to make a tour of the nations near to the U.S., and then return home to renew my efforts to raise money for my world tour. What follows is an account of each of the countries I visited.

St. Vincent

I came here at the request of Peace Corps director Bob Barnes to clown at evacuation centers for the refugees of a recently active volcano. Last April, Mt. Soufriere erupted and sent 20,000 people (about one quarter of the population of this tiny Caribbean island) scurrying for cover, most to various schools and churches which became overcrowded refugee centers.

A good dose of clowning was just the tonic they needed. The people of St. Vincent, unaffected by television's mass-mind boggling, really knew how to laugh! Many had never seen a clown before. And, although many still believe in "real magic," they had never seen anyone perform magic illusions before. It was not uncommon, after seeing my torn and restored newspaper illusion, for some people to approach me with two odd bits of paper and ask me to put them together, for real!

Guatemala

Here, I joined a group of 14 Peace Corps volunteers who had taken time off from their usual projects to form a traveling road show. This small-time circus, a program for the International Year of the Child, put on funny skits, puppet shows, skill displays, and music all dealing with various Peace Corps themes: nutrition, hygiene, health, education, reforestation, friendship, and cooperation. Besides myself, the players included a music band and nine people who dressed up as different vegetables to bring off the message of good nutrition.

For two weeks we traveled by dirt road to remote Indian villages all over Guatemala's countryside. We had to hike in to some of the areas. For many of these villagers, this was their first look at any form of outside entertainment.

I found Guatemala to be a fascinating country. The Indians who live there (descendents from the Mayan People) have retained, more so than many other conquered people, their cultural identity. . . .

Honduras

One memorable performance was in a small village in Honduras named Marcala. Here, the

Peace Corps volunteers had been advertising my arrival for over a month. In a town like this, which had never seen any entertainers at all, this whipped quite a bit of excitement. When my jeep arrived, after 4 hours on a bumpy road, it was immediately surrounded by screaming school children. After a brief parade through town, the show started in a small hall. It was a riot. The people were screaming so loud, they could not hear me. The room was so narrow that few could see me. And their amount of contact with the outside world was so slight that I don't believe many understood me. But nevertheless, the whole town seemed to be in the midst of a Beatlemanic frenzy just because of my mere presence. Shades of Ed Sullivan.

Another memorable performance was at a Red Cross camp for refugees from the Nicaraguan conflict. This was in Choluteca, Honduras. Over 3,000 people were there, and their situation was very sad. Most were very poor people who had left everything behind them when the fighting in Nicaragua became too intense. Dislodged from their homes, uncertain of the whereabouts and condition of family members, and bereft of any sense of security for the future, it would seem that these people would be the last to laugh with a clown. But just like a high pressure system replacing a low pressure system, humor has a way of bubbling most energetically when it's been suppressed the longest. The laughter from the Nicaraguan refugees was full, gushing, hefty, and hearty. They had much to forget.

—Rick Davis
Calliope

A Sample of Refunds Offered Every Month by Major Companies

DRY SACK $1.00 REFUND OFFER . . . $1.00 for 375 ml or larger Dry Sack sherry front label. . .

•

LUNCH MEAT OFFER . . . free pkg for 5 Armour Star lunch meat pkg. . .

•

FREE FLAIR PEN OFFER . . . free Flair for 2 El Marko cards. . .

•

FREE MIGHTY DOG OFFER . . . 3 free cans for 15 Mighty Dog labels. . .

•

NABISCO . . . World Series book for Fig Newton, Nilla wafers and Nutter cookies pop seals, + 35¢ p/h. . .

•

POLAROIDS FIVE DOLLAR FILM OFFER . . . $5.00 for three Time Zero or other Polaroid film colored end panels. . .

•

$1.00 CASH REFUND OFFER . . . $1.00 for five 3 oz yellow bursts from Raisinets, Goobers and Sno-caps. . .

•

RED FOX . . . trial pkg of Red Fox chewing tobacco for requesting it. . .

Jaybee

Letters to the Editor of the Procrastinators' Club Newsletter

Steven Z. Nison, Chicago, tells us that for fun, he goes to O'Hare Airport to watch people miss planes. . . .

•

Betty Moore, Huntington Beach, Ca., in recommending membership for her husband, Woodrow Wilson Moore II, wrote that he bought a 1939 Pontiac in 1970, got an engine for it in 1971, and it's still in the garage.

•

Stephen Alexander, Oreland, Pa., claims he is alive today because he was too late to catch any of "all those boats and planes that crashed in the last 20 years. . . ."

•

About 14 years ago, an attorney in Edwardsville, Ohio, wrote asking the first step in forming a chapter. We sent him information. Recently, he wrote again, asking, "What's the *second* step?"

We're gonna have a great chapter in Edwardsville!

Last Month's Newsletter

Stocking Up

Most supermarket shoppers wishfully remember the roll of paper towels they bought on sale at 59¢, when they pay 99¢ and $1.09 week after week, waiting for another sale. But, there are other shoppers, and for want of a better name, we will call them "stockers," who look for sales, and when they find them, use all their smart shopping skills to buy a large quantity at the lowest possible price. Sometimes this quantity is enough to last as long as a year or two. Other stockers carefully plan their purchases to last until the next sale.

Is it really worth it to stock up?

Because of inflation in general and skyrocketing food prices in particular, many stockers are now looking at their stock as an "investment." Investing in the food that you will eventually eat has some very interesting advantages. First, it is an investment that isn't likely to go down in value. In the foreseeable future, food prices are only going in one direction . . . up, up and away! And with food and household products you don't have to worry about finding a buyer when you get ready to unload your investment, because you yourself will consume it or use it.

Shirley Lindner of Cumberland, Maryland, calls the pantry in her home "the stock market." Here is how she explains why it pays to stock up. "Putting money in the bank only earns 6% interest, and the higher rate of inflation makes your money worthless. But, putting my money in the supermarket products that I stock up on, easily earns me 20% and more over the course of a year."

If, like Fay Butte, of McLean, Virginia, you invested in chickens at 39¢ a pound, and were still eating them today, as she is, you would have earned almost 100% on your investment!

Many experts believe that food prices will rise almost 20% this year, led by substantial increases in meat prices. This is all the more reason to consider stocking up to be a "gold plated" investment opportunity.

—Martin Sloane
The National Supermarket Shopper

Klope Sets Stone-Skip Record!

A 20-year-old systems engineering student shattered the world record Saturday at the Mackinac Island Stone Skipping Open Tournament.

Warren Klope stepped up to the water line and on his first cast in tournament play hurled a 24-skip stone. Klope, a student at Oakland University near Detroit and resident of Troy, Michigan, threw a thin, flat, grey limestone for ten plinkers and 14 pittypats (the little skips at the end of the run).

Saturday night's awards banquet at the Grand Hotel was highlighted by several dull technical papers read by various tournament officials. Traditionally, the current winner of the tournament does not attend this formal affair.

However, the Loys of Flint did attend to present an appeal on a ruling by the judges. Glen A. Loy, Jr., was the 1971 tournament winner and placed fourth this year with 22 skips.

One of Loy's stones, the fourth in a six-set, split in half on the first plink. Both halves continued to skip. The judges panel ruled that only the half which skipped the largest number of times was counted.

Loy claimed that skips of both should be counted.

After a tedious debate which continued through the appetizer, soup and salad, officials referred the matter to the winter rules committee.

Loy made an immediate appeal to State Supreme Court Justice G. Mennen Williams at a nearby table, but Justice Williams said the matter was out of his jurisdiction. He handles only Frisbee cases.

Governor William Milliken, who was also dining at the Grand Hotel, said he was delighted that the championship had been brought back, "not only to the U.S.A., but to Michigan."

Boulder

Famous People

MILESTONES WITH MILLARD

Phil Arkow, publisher of *The Fillmore Bu(n)gle*—a 12-page journal put out "once every Haphazard"—is employed as public relations director for the Pikes Peak Humane Society in his spare time. Arkow explains how the *Bu(n)gle* came to be:

"SPERMFLOW (Society for the Preservation and Enhancement of the Recognition of Millard Fillmore, Last of the Whigs) was started in 1975 as the braindrizzle of one George Gladney and myself, who got together one night in the Top Hat Bar behind a bowling alley in Colorado Springs and decided we needed an excuse to get together regularly to get drunk. We decided to form SPERMFLOW as the only American society dedicated to the celebration of mediocrity in American life, as best epitomized by Millard Fillmore, generally acknowledged as the most mediocre president we ever had. Not the worst, mind you: just the most fair-to-middlin', with the emphasis on the middle.

Phil Arkow, vice-president of S.P.E.R.M.F.L.O.W. (second from left), with a group of fellow Fillmorons installing a new officer in the Imperial Order of the Melted Mystic Mint. (Photo By Hook/Crook)

Millard Fillmore

"Since that time we have grown to over 180 members in 30 states plus Malaysia, Liberia, Guatemala, West Germany, India and the Bermuda Triangle. Our members are called Fillmorons. They collect Fillmorabilia. They visit all the towns and counties named after the Old Boy, the 13th and unluckiest prez of the U.S. of A. They belong to any number of other mediocre-based organizations, including the Committee to Award Miss Piggy the Oscar.

"Mediocrity abounds in American history. From the day Columbus mistook North America for India—and then got credit for discovering the U.S. even though he only landed in San Salvador—American history has been written with the leaky pen of ineptitude. While our history books have extolled our greatness, it is really in our shortcomings that we find our true story. Names like William G. Miller, Rutherford B. Hayes and, of course, Millard Fillmore are more of what America is really like. We feel it is time to pay homage to the mediocrity in our history—to root for the middledog, as it were. We are a nation of misfits. This tradition needs celebrating.

"Our publication is the only newspaper in America dedicated to mediocrity. Others may achieve the same results, but we're the only ones with this as our purpose. It conveys the news of the organization, including awarding the annual Millard Fillmore Medal of Mediocrity to the most mediocre person in America (1979 recipient, Ed McMahon; 1980, Billy Carter). It features foto-features of Fillmores. So far we've fotofeatured Fillmore, California ("It Never Rains in California, or in Fillmore Either"); Fillmore, Illinois ("Where 62032 is More Than a Zip Code, It's a Way of Life"); and Fillmore, Indiana ("The Town that History Forgot"). The *Bu(n)gle* has also featured an interview with the *Millard T. Fillmore,* a tugboat in Seattle; interviews with Kansas and New Jersey, the most mediocre states; and the ongoing biography series, Profiles in Mediocrity.

"Perhaps our most average glory came when postage rates went up to 13¢. There had been, in 1938, a 13¢ Millard Fillmore postage stamp which, of course, no one ever used. It featured a bust of Fillmore, and was part of the 'Presidential Bust' series. We wrote to the Postmaster General arguing that the taxpayers could save lots of money, and Fillmore could finally get his due, if the 1938 stamp was reissued rather than spending unnecessary money for new commemoratives. Besides, we argued, since Fillmore was by all accounts a presidential 'bust' it would be truth in advertising. The Postmaster replied that there were no plans to reissue the stamp. So we wrote back, asking respectfully if at least they couldn't print Fillmore's face on the back of the new stamps. We never got a reply. Perhaps it got lost in the mail.

"Membership entitles one to the *Bu(n)gle,* a membership card (we use playing cards), and the Millard Carta (the 13-point Plank of Broken Promises) in which we pledge to fight the ept and to rail against American greatness if and when we ever find it. Our readers walk the gamut from lawyers, dentists and dermatologists to yachtsmen, newspaper and media types and missionaries. Their only common denominator is an appreciation for the common. They remember the Edsel, not the *Maine;* shout 'Spiro Who?' instead of '54–40 or fight'; and believe that Bad Taste Is Timeless, that History Repeats Itself, and that Mediocrity in the Pursuit of Greatness is Nothing Unusual.

"Our activities include the annual Mirthday Party for the Old Boy, every January 7 or thereabouts, and the national Bathe For Millard Fillmore Day, every February 23, to celebrate the myth that Fillmore installed the first bathtub in the White House (he didn't, but no one knows who really did).

"We have no president: that's too high. I'm vice president. We never hold elections, because Fillmore was never elected president, and frankly he was lucky to be elected vice president. . . ."

POLITICAL GOSSIP

There are, according to usually reliable sources, over 1,000 newsletters that regularly assess the political climate in the nation's capital. The *Washington Crap Report* is the only one among them published in St. Petersburg, Flordia. This makes it a refreshing antidote to all the hermetically sealed Inside Washington journals.

The *Crap Report* is unabashedly different. It is (it proclaims) "dedicated to exposing the Washington standards of greed, corruption, self-indulgence and the Great American Dream of profit at all cost" and is printed on shocking-pink paper. Three dozen items, few over one paragraph long, are published in each monthly, four-page issue. Many are mini-exposés, based in fact. But the *Report* is not afraid to resort to gossip, either. In the following examples, names are withheld but they're *always* printed in the *Crap Report.*

"It's terrible what some on the Hill are saying about Rep. ———. The rumor types are saying he's a 'Womanizer.' Let's hope the voters back home never hear the rumors."

"Usually reliable sources say Rep. ——— seems to suffer from a bad case of the 'Sniffles.' His friends hope he finds a cure for whatever is causing this problem."

"Just about everyone is whispering about the story of ———, the Jimmy Carter campaign ———, losing $12,000 to actor Walter Matthau in a poker game. ——— says the story is false."

"New Jersey sources say that state's ——— is mighty well 'connected' with some types back home who want to make him governor. From what we hear his backers usually get what they want in New Jersey."

"———, the new junior Senator from ———, is only 38 and a bachelor. After the election he was reported vacationing in the Bahamas with ———, the lovely lobbyist from ———."

The *Report* takes delight in tracking the current doings of those implicated in Watergate: who's buying a restaurant in Washington, who's become counsel to President Reagan, and so forth. The *Crap Report*—appropriately enough—was the only Washington newsletter to report Edmund Muskie, then secretary of state, running into Soviet ambassador Anatoly Dobrynin in a men's room at the United Nations. "They'll have to stop meeting this way," the *Crap Report* commented.

Editor William A. Leavell, a reporter who has covered six national political conventions, says that he selected the name of his newsletter "for its shock value and also because it pretty well tells the truth—we are a 'crap' sheet with the gossip and other stuff you don't find in the straight media. In fact, we have picked up the nickname of *The Crapper* and our people are often known as the 'people from *Crap*.' We don't mind at all.

"While we write about the flock in Washington, that is not our market at all. We scare the devil out of the bureaucratic and elective gang. They do not like anyone or anything that rocks the boat. Our market is the boondocks, the out-back, and the folks who want to know what's 'really' going on in Washington.

"Our sources are mostly young people in or around government who see the picture and don't like it. Many are young reporters who dig up a story and have it redlined by some funky editor. They want to see it in print so they send it to us. We have sources on staff on the Hill and in the White House. I used to be on staff in Washington and have many friends and contacts built up over the years.

"It's a fun thing to do. It will never make a lot of money but it has become an assignment sheet for some editors of major media. We send it to the media free. I realize they're too cheap to subscribe to anything. They read it and select items of interest and assign reporters to follow up with a feature. We just hit the top of the mountains and don't go into details. This broadcasts our mentions to many millions.

"We have a paid subscriber list which grows, thank goodness. We select some shakers and movers and send it to them free. We have a very large free list to the White House and on the Hill. We have become something of a factor in national politics. We can't be of much help to anyone or anything but we have a very strong negative factor. If we get on your case we can do a real dance.

"We are not Demo or GOP," Leavell asserts, "liberal or conservative, and we do not support any cause or party. I think most such types are a little bit crazy. We simply tell our little gossip and let it lay. If it hatches, then well and good. If not, we don't cry. We pass on rumors because in politics a rumor, true or false, is a fact of life. We trot them out to sink or swim. We don't fan them or make them up."

Millard Fillmore

The Thirteenth President of the United States
1850–53

Profiles in Mediocrity

Chapter XIII: "Goodbye, and All That"

Our story thus far: After a lackluster and non-descript Presidency, and having signed his political death warrant with the Compromise of 1850, Fillmore ran as the incumbent for the 1852 Whig Presidential nomination.

For their candidate in 1852, many Whigs wanted not a man who stood in the middle of the political spectrum, but a man who stood nowhere at all. Fillmore met this criterion admirably.

So he announced his candidacy for re-election; or more precisely, for election, since he had never been elected President in the first place. He thought he had a chance, having reversed what would become Teddy Roosevelt's motto in later years; he'd spoken loudly (which satisfied the South) but carried only a little stick (which pleased the North).

It took 53 ballots at that Whig convention in 1852 to nominate a candidate—and it wasn't good ol' Millard Fillmore that they chose. The party which had made a record of nominating old soldiers William Henry Harrison and Zachary Taylor did it again. They named Gen. Winfield "Old Fuss and Feathers" Scott.

Scott did what old soldiers always do—he just faded away. The party went down to defeat to a terribly dismal Democratic ticket headed by Franklin Pierce (who had to wait for his own 49th ballot to get the nod) and VP nominee William R. King (who didn't campaign because he was dying of TB in a Havana sanatorium at the time).

If Fillmore wasn't the Whig nominee, at least he lived long enough to hold the party together—and the nation—as they dragged themselves down to defeat. At the time there was no clear law of succession, and if Fillmore had died as President—with no VP below him—a nation already on the brink of Civil War might have been brought to a standstill. "A kindly Providence once again forgave us our political oversights: nothing happened to Fillmore," writes historian Michael Harwood.

Next: It's the unemployment line for old Millard. . . .

The Fillmore Bu(n)gle

Can you name this internationally known British golfer?

— collected Andrew Lang books.
— visited Pau.
— learned to play golf at Charston and Torquay.
— played at East Croydon.
— was a member of Sunningdale.
— won a tournament at Wentworth with a handicap of 35.
— wrote a book; the dust jacket, which is not consistent with the contents, shows a golf course.

Answer:

Agatha Christie

Golf Collectors' Society Bulletin

Attempted Assassination

There are many parallels between the attempted assassination of Theodore Roosevelt, which took place on October 14, 1912 in Milwaukee, Wisconsin, and the shooting of President Ronald Reagan. Both men survived the assaults; both were wounded in the chest; both showed extraordinary courage. There are, of course, also differences between the two historic incidents. For instance, T.R. was no longer President when he was shot. He was at the time the Progressive (Bull Moose) Party candidate for President against his successor in the White House, Republican William Howard Taft, and Democrat Woodrow Wilson. T.R.'s bullet was never removed. The following account of the Milwaukee shooting was written by Joseph Bucklin Bishop in 1920.

When the campaign was at its height in October its progress was arrested and the whole country was shocked by the attempted assassination of Roosevelt while he was on a speaking tour in the West. As he was leaving his hotel in Milwaukee, on the evening of October 14, a half-crazed fanatic shot him as he stood in an automobile bowing to a cheering crowd. His assailant was only a few feet away when he fired the shot which under ordinary conditions would have been fatal. One of Roosevelt's secretaries, Elbert E. Martin, who had been a football player, immediately sprang upon the assailant and forced him to the ground. The crowd, thoroughly incensed, was crying out, "Lynch him, lynch him," but Roosevelt, who had not been thrown down by the shot, calmed the crowd by saying: "Don't hurt him! Bring him here. I want to look at him." When one of his secretaries suggested that Roosevelt be taken at once to a hospital, he said: "You get me to that speech; it may be the last I shall deliver, but I am going to deliver this one."

He rode at once to the hall where he was to speak, and on arriving there one of his companions exclaimed as soon as they came into a lighted room: "Look, Colonel, there's a hole in your overcoat!" Roosevelt looked down, saw the hole, and putting his hand inside his coat, withdrew it with blood upon it. Not at all dismayed, he said: "It looks as though I had been hit, but I don't think it is anything serious." Three physicians who were found in the audience examined the wound, said the bullet had penetrated his breast, that they could not tell how serious the injury was, but that in their opinion he should be taken at once to a hospital. He refused absolutely to permit this, saying: "I will make this speech, or die; one or the other," and strode to the platform. The great audience, in ignorance of the shooting, broke into prolonged cheering at his appearance, and when quiet was restored the presiding officer said: "I have something to tell you and I hope you will receive the news with calmness. Colonel Roosevelt has been shot. He is wounded." A cry of astonishment and horror ran over the audience and great confusion followed. Roosevelt stepped to the front of the platform and produced instant calm by raising his hand and saying: "I am going to ask you to be very quiet and please to excuse me from making you a very long speech. I'll do the best I can, but you see there is a bullet in my body. But it is nothing. I'm not hurt badly."

He began at once upon his speech. On taking from the breastpocket of his coat the folded manuscript of his speech he saw that it had a bullet hole completely through it, having first passed through a metal spectacle case which was also in his pocket, but this did not check him for a moment, though he said afterwards it did startle him a little. Showing it to the audience, he said: "It takes more than that to kill a Bull Moose!" Several times during his speech he seemed to be growing weak but when persons on the platform rose to help him, he said: "Let me alone. I'm all right." In the course of his speech he said that certain newspaper utterances were to blame for the attempt to assassinate him—that a weak-minded man had been influenced by them. He finished his speech and later in the evening was taken by special train to Chicago, arriving there at half past three the next morning. Looking from the car window and seeing an ambulance standing by the station, he said: "I'll not go to the hospital lying in that thing. I'll walk to it and I'll walk from it to the hospital. I'm no weakling to be crippled by a flesh wound."

On arriving at the hospital a thorough examination of his wound, with X-rays, was made and it was discovered that the bullet had entered his chest at the right of and below the right nipple and was embedded in a rib; it had touched no vital part. One of the examining surgeons said: "Colonel Roosevelt has a phenomenal development of the chest. It is largely due to the fact that he is a physical marvel that he was not dangerously wounded. He is one of the most powerful men I have ever seen laid on an operating table. The bullet lodged in the massive muscles of the chest instead of penetrating the lung."

Mrs. Roosvelt, who was in New York at the time, received news of the shooting while at a theater and, accompanied by her two daughters, went at once to Chicago, where she took personal charge of the patient. Dr. Alexander Lambert, Roosevelt's family physician, also hastened to Chicago and after examining him said: "The folded manuscript and heavy steel spectacle case checked and deflected the bullet so that it passed up at such an angle that it went outside the ribs and in the muscles. If this deflection had not occurred and the bullet gone through the arch of the aorta or auricles of the heart, Colonel Roosevelt would not have lived 60 seconds."

In the official bulletin of October 15, the attending surgeons said: "We find him in a magnificent physical condition, due to his regular physical exercise, his habitual abstinence from tobacco and liquor."

Describing his sensations at the time of the shooting, a few days later, Roosevelt said: "It was nothing, nothing. I felt a little pain, but it was not serious. When I stretched out my arms or reached for my manuscript it made me gasp a bit, but that was all. It was quite amusing when I reached for my manuscript to see that it had a hole in it from the bullet and there was a hole in my spectacle case too."

"Amusing, did you say, Colonel?" someone asked.

"Well, it was quite interesting," he replied. "It was difficult to keep my temper," he added, "when at the close of my speech a half dozen men scrambled upon the platform to shake hands with me. Didn't they know that it is impossible for a man who has just been shot to shake hands with genuine cordiality?"

He remained in the hospital till October 21, when he went to his home in Oyster Bay. The man who shot him was a fanatic, named John Schrank, who was shown by papers found on his person to be of unbalanced mind, and to have been following Roosevelt about the country for some time seeking a favorable opportunity to shoot him. In a sort of diary, among these papers, were entries in which Schrank said McKinley had appeared to him and told him that Roosevelt was his murderer. Another

entry showed that some of the campaign talk against Roosevelt as a candidate for a third term had affected his crazy brain, for it read: "Any man looking for a third term ought to be shot." When he was arraigned in court in Milwaukee, on November 12, 1912, he showed very clearly that this was the case, for when asked how he would plead he replied: "Why, guilty. I did not mean to kill a citizen, Judge; I shot Theodore Roosevelt because he was a menace to the country. He should not have a third term. I did not want him to have one. I shot him as a warning that men must not try to have more than two terms as President." Could there be furnished stronger evidence than this that violent denunciation of public men, in the press and on the stump, incites assassination by inducing persons of unbalanced minds to attempt it in the crazy belief that they are thereby doing a public service? The assassinations of Lincoln, Garfield and McKinley were directly traceable to this source.

The court appointed a commission of five alienists to examine Schrank and report on his mental condition. They reported on November 22 that he was insane and he was committed to an asylum for the insane for an indefinite period.

Theodore Roosevelt Association Journal

Bee Pollen Bars

Just about everyone knows about the love President Ronald Reagan has for jelly beans but did you know he has another favorite between meal snack? Reagan dearly loves BEE POLLEN BARS. He is reported to keep these around and munches on them frequently.

Just in case you've never heard of BEE POLLEN BARS, athletes say they improve their physical performances.

Washington Crap Report

Once when Abe Lincoln was making a speech a drunk called out, "Did I have to pay a dollar to see the ugliest man in the world?" Lincoln said, "Yes, sir, I'm afraid you were charged a dollar for the privilege. But I have it for nothing. Thank you!"

Funny Funny World

Lizzie Borden . . .

. . .took an *ax* (1)
And gave her *mother* (2) *forty* (3) whacks
When she saw what she had done
She gave her father *forty-one* (4)

(1) ax: the murder weapon was never found
but is thought to have been a *hatchet*
(2) mother: the victim was Lizzie's *stepmother*
(3) who was killed with *19* blows
(4) while her father died of *10* blows

But the greatest inaccuracy, of course, is to pin the murders on Lizzie. Details of the crime have been rehashed by scholars and hacks, but one point on which all agree is that Lizbeth A. Borden was found "not guilty" of the murders by a jury of her peers who took only a little over an hour to reach a verdict. Lizzie was born in Fall River, Mass., in 1860; the murders took place there August 4, 1892. Lizzie was brought to trial June 5, 1893, and found not guilty June 20. She died June 1, 1927, at the age of 66, leaving an estate of $1,000,000, including $30,000 to the Animal Rescue League. After the trial she was *not* a recluse but visited, traveled and received friends. She was generous with her wealth in many ways, including providing scholarships to needy students. . . .

—W. T. Rabe
The Woods-Runner

Rod Serling

"There is a sixth dimension beyond that which is known to man. It is a dimension as vast as space, and as timeless as infinity. It is the middle ground between light and shadow—between science and superstition. . . . This is the dimension of imagination. It is an area which we call . . . the Twilight Zone." When the late Rod Serling said this more than twenty years ago, little did he know that his classic show would live long after him. Born on Christmas Day 1924, Rodman Goward Serling was the messiah of television quality. He fought to have everything his way. "Twilight Zone" represented the best half hour one could watch. Writing many of the scripts himself, he also featured writers such as Richard Matheson, Ray Bradbury, George Clayton Johnson, Earl Hamner ("The Waltons"), Reginald Rose

and the late Charles Beaumont. Directors included Don Siegel, Lamont Johnson, Ted Post, Richard Donner and Stuart Rosenberg. Serling died on June 28, 1975 . . . but we can watch him every night at the beginning and end of every episode in the "Twilight Zone."

—Akira Fitton
Psychotronic

The Great Depression of 1929 struck at a critical time for me as I was in transition passing from my teens to my twentieth birthday. Times were hard, banks went broke, people lost their life's savings, their jobs, and almost everybody was declining. Singers and entertainers were no exception to the times because they too declined along with everyone else except for a young singer dying of tuberculosis who got bigger and bigger as times got harder and harder. He seemed to be telling us that everything would again be OK when he sang about trains and better times down the road. Jimmie Rodgers had a message we could identify with because he had been there before us and understood what we felt.

An old timer here in Central Texas told me recently how his family would save eggs to buy the next Jimmie Rodgers record. Not every family could afford each of his records and would alternate the purchase from family to family as they came out, insuring everyone the opportunity to hear him sing. It might be at our house one month, a neighbor's house next month or sometimes down at the drug store where the records were sold. That's about all we had to look forward to except to half-sole the holes in our shoes and cut each other's hair with the old hand clippers.

Looking back it would seem that nature provided him with a quality to fit the times. Because as suddenly as he had arrived at the beginning of that great tragedy, he departed as it began to end. That same quality has propelled his record sales into one decade after another since his departure almost fifty years ago. . . .

Perhaps the most descriptive tribute to Jimmie's musical and lyrical accomplishments is inscribed on a marble statue of "The Singing Brakeman" that stands in close proximity to an old consolidation steam locomotive in a park in his home town of Meridian, Mississippi, which states: "His is the music of America. He sang the songs of the people he loved, of a young nation growing strong. His was an America of glistening rails, thundering boxcars, and rain-swept nights, of lonesome prairies, great mountains and a high blue sky. He sang of the bayous and the cornfields, the wheated plains, of the little towns, the cities, and of the winding rivers of America. We listened, we understood, Jimmie Rodgers—The Singing Brakeman, America's Blue Yodeler—His music will live forever. (Dedicated by his many fans and the Folk Artists of America, May 26, 1953.)"

—Henry Young
Jimmie Rodgers Memorial Association Newsletter

QUESTION: Would you tell us if there was any remorse in Aaron Burr's life after his duel with Alexander Hamilton and how did it affect him?

ANSWER: I think very likely, if Burr had ever had the chance to do the thing over, he would have handled it in some other way, other than by dueling. But, you must remember . . . that dueling was a common thing in that era and when you felt that you had been wronged, if you were a "gentleman" the thing to do was to challenge unless you could get an apology. However, again I remind you—Burr was a stoic and a fatalist. The deed had been done—Hamilton had died. That was it. Why be depressed by it?

Hamilton's first son, Philip Schuyler Hamilton, had been killed in the very same place, Weehawken, by George I. Eaker in a duel with exactly the same pistols, three years previously. But, George Eaker wasn't hounded around and called names and made to feel that he had committed a terrible crime. He continued to conduct his law practice, with no interruption.

Also, please remember that the great duelist in American history is not Aaron Burr! The great duelist in American history is President Andrew Jackson, who fought at least twelve duels and perhaps more. And one of his antagonists was drawn off the field dead before five minutes had passed. But nobody gets up and says that Andy Jackson was a terrible man because he took part in duels but they do it in Burr's case. Burr is called a "terrible man" because he took part in one duel. Well, he really did take part in two. It's said he did take part in a duel with Hamilton's brother-in-law, John Barker Church, a week previous to the one involving Hamilton. That was a duel with pistols, too, and Burr got a bullet through his coat in that particular encounter. Remorse? Well, I don't know. In his old age Aaron said one time when they were talking about some of these events: "My friend Hamilton, whom I shot." And they were friends in many ways, although Hamilton, over and over again, repeatedly, constantly was anti-Burr. But, I don't believe that Aaron sat down and cried about it. As I said before, Aaron was a stoic. . . .

—Samuel Engle Burr, Jr.
Chronicle of the Aaron Burr Association

Written in Blood

To H. L. Mencken, for some years a magazine editor, Thomas Wolfe once submitted a story written on butcher paper that still bore the bloodstains from the meat, according to E. E. Edgar.

When Mencken arrived at his desk, the manuscript, awaiting him, was covered with flies.

"What's this?" he demanded in disgust.

"It's a great new story by Thomas Wolfe," said an associate. "Read it. You'll get something from it."

"And what is that," said Mencken, "typhus?"

The Thomas Wolfe Review

What was Oliver Hardy's Nickname?

"Babe." He was given the name by an Italian barber when he first started in films. In his very early films he is billed as Oliver "Babe" Hardy and sometimes just Babe Hardy.

The Intra-Tent Journal

often that people mistake him for his fictional hero.

"It seems I will never be able to escape from Sherlock Holmes, and I guess it cannot be helped," said Conan Doyle, with a smile.

The Woods-Runner

Wilde About Opera

Asked to buy a subscription to the opera, Oscar Wilde, to whom opera was a bore, refused.

"But your friend bought a subscription," it was pointed out to him, **"and your friend is deaf."**

"If I were deaf, I would buy one, too," said Wilde.

Funny Funny World

A Meeting with Conan Doyle

(Introduction to a collection of Sherlock Holmes stories by noted Russian writer and linguist Kornei Chukovsky, translated by George Gladir.)

I met Conan Doyle in London in 1916. He was a broad-faced, broad-shouldered man, tall in stature with very narrow little eyes and over-hanging seal-like mustache which made him look rather jovial. There was something naive and homely about him.

I started telling him how people in Russia like his Sherlock Holmes. One of the persons present remarked with a reproach: "Sir Arthur has written not only Sherlock Holmes. . . ."

The next day, he kindly came over to pick us up, another Russian writer and myself, in order to show us the places of interest in London.

"Well, what would you like to see, my friends," he asked us when we walked out into the street? "Baker Street for sure," we said unanimously, "the street where Sherlock Holmes lives."

Strolling along with Conan Doyle in London, we could see (ascertain) his colossal popularity. Cab drivers, shoe shiners, reporters, street vendors, newspaper boys, and school boys in every street kept recognizing and greeting him with a friendly nod of their heads. "Hello, Sherlock Holmes," said to him one youngster. Conan Doyle explained that it happens very

"Authors"

On these pages are reproductions of cards from an "Authors" game in the possession of Carl Hartmann. Authors was popular in the 19th century; indeed, Alger himself mentions it. In a letter to George Bacon, dated January 26,

MORAL AND RELIGIOUS.

HORATIO ALGER, JR.

T. S. Arthur.
Henry Ward Beecher,
Edward Everett Hale.

POETS.
—
HENRY W. LONGFELLOW.

James Russell Lowell.
Oliver Wendell Holmes.
John Greenleaf Whittier.

1874, he says, "Your application for a picture and biographical material for use in a 'Game of Authors' has been forwarded to me by my father. It gives me pleasure to comply with your request, . . ." And in a letter to his good friend Irving Blake dated February 2, 1897, he writes, "A new game of Authors will be published in Cincinnati in the fall. I am in it. It will be issued by the U. S. Playing Card Co."

"Mr. Clown"

On May 2nd, 1966, the United States government put its stamp of approval on the world's number one clown when it put "Mr. Clown's" already famous face on a 5¢ stamp. "Mr. Clown" can refer only to the greatest living clown and possibly the most popular clown that ever lived—Lou Jacobs.

Fifty seven years as a clown with Ringling Brothers means that the 78-year-old funny-man has seen more than half of the 109 years of the Greatest Show on Earth.

One wonders how many people forgot their problems for a moment to laugh at the antics of this unforgetable man, in all of those appearances in a show—all of those shows in a year—for all those years. . . .

I talked to Lou on Wednesday, July 30th. It was the day that Frosty Little auditioned three clown college hopefuls at Union Station in Dallas and I sponsored a 19-year-old Richardson, Texas, clown named Poppy Benner, who did a live television interview from the floor of the arena during the afternoon circus performance.

When Dave (Skinhead) Lewis and I introduced Poppy to Lou Jacobs, I thought that she would faint.

Lou said that he had just gotten a phone call last week and he *would* be teaching at the clown college again this fall. "I've been there every years since it started," he said.

Poppy said, "I hope that I make it, and get to go to the college."

"I hope you do, too," Lou said. "I like your face and your costume. They go so well together. You look beautiful. I will be happy to teach you, but most of the young people don't listen too much to us old duffers."

"I will," Poppy promised.

Lou's two dogs, Pee Wee and Buffy, were running around at his feet and one barked occasionally. Lou looked at him sternly, "Be quiet." Then to us, "He's already in trouble—he insisted on dying twice in the last performance."

—Bob Stoddard
Calliope

Charles Darwin was a chronic complainer who was happiest when he had something to gripe about.

One night, he and his wife were guests at a banquet at which everything went wrong. The speeches were dry; the champagne was not; the food was inferior; the service even more so, and worst of all, the naturalist was given a seat in a draft, about which he had a phobia.

Throughout the meal, he grumbled and swore. Later, the sponsor of the affair came over to Mrs. Darwin and said apologetically:

"I do hope your husband will forgive us. We wanted so much for him to have a good time."

"He had a wonderful time," she assured him. "He was able to find fault with everything."

Funny Funny World

Basil Rathbone

Tells how his Sherlock Holmes was born, lived, died, and almost killed him!

A few years before his untimely death in July, 1967, Basil Rathbone—who for much of the world was Sherlock Holmes—attended a Wayne, Nebraska, meeting of the Maiwand Jezails (a scion of the Baker Street Irregulars, an international organization of Sherlock Holmes buffs) which spreads its meetings over several western states. The speech is reproduced here, slightly edited, for the first time.—W. T. Rabe

I am very much privileged to be here, because, after all I think you must recognize, with me, that I am but the shadow of the substance. I thank you from my heart for your generous welcome. I thought it might interest you to know how the pictures in which I played Mr. Holmes came into being in 1939. It did happen in a most extraordinary way. . . .

Marken, Gregory Ratoff and Darryl Zanuck. Now put those three together and try and think what on earth they would be talking about to each other. Dear old Gregory Ratoff, God rest him, is gone . . . with that wonderful Russian accent . . . not a bad director, and a damn good actor. Gene Marken, a very erudite "technical" writer, I call him. And Zanuck, who never went hunting in Africa, they say, because with those tusks he might have got shot.

They were having dinner at Zanuck's home. Why they were meeting had nothing to do with Sherlock Holmes, but somewhat early in the dinner Gene Marken said, for absolutely no reason at all, "Isn't it funny that no one has ever done the Sherlock Holmes stories."

Long pause.

Then Gregory Ratoff said, "And why not?"

Zanuck said, "Well . . . quite an idea; yeah. Any royalties?"

Oh yes, there'd be royalties connected with it, someone answered.

"Bye the bye, that is a hell of an idea, isn't it? But, who . . . who for Holmes?" And Gene Marken said, "Ha! Who else? Basil Rathbone."

And then Zanuck said, "But then, we need Watson," and Gregory Ratoff said, "My friend, Nigel Bruce."

"That sounds like something to go after. Get 'em down here in the morning," Zanuck said.

Nigel Bruce and I were both phoned by our agents to go over to Fox to discuss making "The Hound of the Baskervilles." There was no intention of making anything other than "The Hound." Within 24 hours this series of pictures, which ended up seven years later, was started at 20th Century Fox by these three entirely incongruous people having dinner together. . . .

We went over to Universal in 1942 for 12 more pictures and one of the things about the pictures—and I think we all agree, one has to be completely impersonal about it—they were beautifully made. Photographically, the way they were directed and constructed by the writers. All of this was admirable.

There was a little man called Roy William Neill. He was a comparatively unknown director but he had great devotion to the stories. After the first two, Fox decided not to make any more—I couldn't tell you why—and Universal took it up and little Roy Neill took over the whole thing. He was the producer, the director, and the writer, with a man who helped out in the writing called Millhauser. . . .

We loved Roy Neill. He was mousy, a little guy. A little guy and as sweet as they come. But a damn good disciplinarian. We didn't disobey orders on the set. We were always on time and we always knew our lines. It was thoroughly professional. I am told by the Universal people that the first picture cost $178,000 and the twelfth, $235,000. This is pin money today, compared to almost anything you can do. In fact, it's almost impossible—unless you're doing "David and Lisa,"—to do a picture for $178,000.

They were 14 very special experiences. I treasure the memory of every single one of them. I treasure it now!—at the time it was a different matter. Obviously, you cannot go on continuously playing the same role in pictures and at the same time playing him 38 weeks on radio each year for seven years, so that you are saturated to the extent that you lose your sense of proportion, as well as your sense of pleasure and enjoyment.

Eventually, without realizing it, they came to an end. Universal decided not to make any more pictures and that moment I decided I wasn't going to do any more radio. That drove Jules Stein of M.C.A. into a fit, because he was ready with another seven year radio contract.

I said to myself, "Another seven years and I'll go stark, raving mad."

So I hoiked it off to New York. When I arrived I discovered that I had been so firmly associated with this character that no producer in New York would touch me with a barge pole.

No matter whether it was a play I was suited for or not. In a couple of cases they said, frankly, "Yes, there's no question that the part is right down your street; but you can't walk out on that stage without being Holmes. I don't care whether you have on a toga playing Cassius, or what."

For a year I was very, very disturbed. I thought, "By God, this is the end. There is no more theatre for me." Then, dear Jed Harris—dear, crazy, Jed Harris—gave me "The Heiress."

One night, to the theatre, came dear little Roy Neill in a gray flannel suit and a white carnation. He was going home to Maidenhead-on-the-Thames for the first time in 15 years and was very emotional about this return. He took some keys out of his pocket.

"You see this key?" he said. "That key opens the door to my home in Maidenhead." He had had a housekeeper stay there all that time, waiting for this wonderful moment when, after making substantial monies, he was able to go home and enjoy his life on the River Thames.

He boarded the ship, I learned later, arrived, went to Maidenhead, put the key into the front door lock, turned it, walked into the hall of his home—and dropped dead. . . .

The Woods-Runner

Casey Stengel made his big league debut with the Brooklyn Dodgers late in the season of 1912. Only a few hours before, he had arrived from Alabama, where he had been playing in the Southern Association, reports Joseph Durso in *Whitey and Mickey*, by Whitey Ford, Mickey Mantle and Joseph Durso.

"The first time he came to bat, he hit a single. Then he repeated the trick the second, third and fourth times up. When he stepped up to the plate the fifth time, with four straight hits under his belt, the opposing manager switched to a left-handed pitcher.

"Young Casey countered by turning around at the plate and batting right-handed. This was an act of bravado, as he was not a switch hitter. But the stratagem worked. He had built such a reputation by that time, that the intimidated pitcher walked him."

Funny Funny World

How Shaw and Twain Met

Dear Mr. [Cyril] Clemens,

I met Mark Twain, late in his lifetime, on two occasions. On one of the visits to London made by my biographer Archibald Henderson, I met him at the railway station, and found that Mark had come over in the same boat and was in the same train. There was a hasty introduction amid the scramble for luggage which our queer English way of handling passengers' baggage involves; and after a word or two I tactfully took myself and Henderson off.

Some days later he walked into our flat in Adelphi Terrace. Our parlormaid, though she did not know who he was, was so overcome by his personality that she admitted him unquestioned and unannounced, like the statue of the Commandant.

Whether it was on that occasion or a later one that he lunched with us I cannot remember; but at any rate he did lunch with us, and told us stories of the old Mississippi storekeeper. He presented me with one of his books, and autographed the inside of the cloth case on the ground that when he autographed fly leaves they were torn out and sold.

He had a complete gift of intimacy which enabled us to treat one another instantly as if we had known one another all our lives, as indeed I had known him through his early books, which I read and revelled in before I was twelve years old. As to what impression he made on me all I can say is that he was himself, and exactly what I expected. We got on together perfectly.

Faithfully,
G[eorge]. Bernard Shaw

The Mark Twain Journal

Pinocchio

Pinocchio! The most famous puppet ·of all! Eternally young, this wooden marionette celebrates his 100th birthday this year.

His exciting adventures were penned by Carlo Lorenzini, who adopted the name "Collodi" after his mother's birthplace in Northern Italy. Born November 24, 1826, Lorenzini entered a seminary for the priesthood after completing school, but found he was not really suited for the life, and in 1846 began writing for various local newspapers. He wrote a number of books on a wide variety of subjects—travel, humour, novels. When he was over fifty, he was asked to translate three of Perrault's fairy tales from the French. . . .

In 1881, Collodi decided to try something different and wrote a story about a little wooden puppet named Pinocchio. Hearing that a friend had just been appointed editor of a new children's paper called *Giornale per i Bambini* (The Children's Journal) in Rome, he sent the story along, telling him to do what he liked with "this bit of foolishness." The very first adventure of Pinocchio appeared in the next issue of the paper (July 7, 1881) under the title *Storia di un Burattino* (History of a Puppet) and youthful Italian readers demanded more. Editor Guido Biagi requested more chapters on the adventures of the marionette, which Collodi supplied casually and when the mood struck him.

Young readers, still tender and uninformed, were (and are) enraptured when they see and recognize themselves in a book. They see themselves in a mirror. Pinocchio is not bad; and if it was enough to have good intentions to be perfect, Pinocchio would be a paragon. But he is weak. What he is forbidden to do is always a little more attractive than what he is ordered to do. So it is, after all, a novel with little morals sprinkled throughout in such an attractive way that youngsters are not aware of the lessons the mischievous puppet learns from his adventures.

In 1883 *The Adventures of Pinocchio* appeared in book form and before long a million copies had been sold in Italy alone. The book's original English translation was by M. A. Murray and was published both in Britain and America in 1892. The publisher made a fortune on the story, but Collodi, who never married and never had children of his own, apparently did not realize he had written a classic. He died in 1890 at the age of 63 in Florence, where he lived with his brother.

Pinocchio is probably the best puppet story ever written and probably the best children's book to have come from Italy. His adventures have been translated into more languages than any other book except the Bible. The story of the boy-puppet was even further popularized by the full-length cartoon feature by Walt Disney. Today there are small memorials in Florence and Collodi to honor the memory of the immortal little Pinocchio.

> —Roger Dennis
> *A Propos*
> (Union Internationale de la Marionnette)

Johnny Appleseed

Frontier Hope

"The grandeur, the vastness, the inexhaustability of nature are in man, and the sensitiveness and mystic impenetrability of the soul lies in the bosom of nature."

> —D.T. Suzuki

The eloquence of Suzuki's statement is easily understood as we observe the wonderful cycle of nature. Nowhere is it more breathtaking than in the beauty and fragrance of apple blossoms and the eventual fruition of apple orchards from the Middle Atlantic states to the Midwest. We owe a great debt to the man who left us the legacy of these magnificent orchards which color our landscape providing sustenance for both body and soul—John Chapman, better known as "Johnny Appleseed."

Born in Leominster, Mass., in 1774, his legend continues to live although most people think of him as a folk hero rather than a man of character and purpose who carried seeds and seedlings into the wilderness. For example, Kentuckians still tell tales of Johnny Appleseed giving a bag of seeds and a brightly polished apple to a gangling youngster named Abe Lincoln who was on his way home from borrowing a book from a neighbor. Struggling with stubborn soil and faced with endless lonely lamp-lit hours, the pioneer settlers welcomed this benevolent wanderer who planted not only apple seeds, but also spiritual ones.

Deeply religious, Johnny became interested in the books of 18th-century scientist, inventor, philosopher, and theologian Emanuel Swedenborg. He obtained these books from a Philadelphia importer, Mr. William Schlatter. Johnny acted as a travelling library to the settlers, leaving chapters from Swedenborg's *Heaven and Hell* on one trip and exchanging them for others on his return trip. He called these pages "Good News Fresh from Heaven!"

Johnny never neglected a needy family nor shunned the faithless. He possessed an unusual eloquence and could hold a group spellbound with a discourse on the merits, beauty, importance, and delights of an apple. He used these occasions to speak in parable. It is easy to hear Johnny comparing a tree to love and use: "roots, seeds, branches, leaves, flowers and fruit all work together for the good of the whole—cooperating, creating something proud and strong—a good deed from love and faith."

His profound love of nature won the respect of the Indians, and in the course of this relationship, he frequently acted as an intermediary between them and the settlers. This trusted friendship resulted in his channeling many of the Indian medicinal remedies and herbal knowledge to the early pioneers. It was said that the Indians thought Johnny was touched by the Great Spirit. They invited him to witness their religious ceremonies and he found their convictions and insights in harmony with his own.

By horse, canoe, or on foot, Johnny visited many states, including Pennsylvania, Ohio, Michigan, Indiana, Illinois—and once walked from Iowa to Philadelphia to attend a Swedenborgian church convention. In the process of roaming the wilderness, he became a legend in his own time. In 1817 . . . *Harper's New Monthly* published an illustrated biography entitled "Johnny Appleseed, A National Hero," which brought him national attention. As *Harper's* put it, he was a frontier hero "of endurance that was voluntary, and of action that was creative and not sanguinary."

During the years many honors have been bestowed upon one of the country's true heros. Plays, books, songs and poems have been written about him. Two famous apple species, the "Jonathan" and the "Chapman" were named for him. . . .

Of all the tributes written about him, however, perhaps the most succinct description was by author Ophia D. Smith. "In field and meadow and forest he walked, concerned with the spacious thoughts of God. In his earthly life," she writes, "he was a one-man humane society, a one-man clinic, a one-man missionary band, and a one-man emigrant-aid society. Johnny Appleseed did not need to die to find Heaven, for Heaven was in his heart."

Logos

Henrik Ibsen enjoyed eating out, where he could be stared at by an admiring public.

The playwright never checked his hat in a restaurant. Instead, he would carry it with him to his table. When he took his seat, he would place the hat between his knees, open end up.

One night, a curious waiter came up behind the playwright, looked over his shoulder and saw that the hat contained a mirror.

Funny Funny World

"Can you keep a secret?" Katherine Anne Porter asked Henry Allen of *The Washington Post* during an interview several years ago. She then directed him to hang his coat in the closet—leaning against the wall was her coffin. "I bought it by mail from Arizona for about $150," said Ms. Porter. "I deeply resent this ghastly show and expense. When I die, I have told my executors that I will have a coffin and linen sheet ready for them."

Continental Association of Funeral and Memorial Societies Bulletin

Circus Greats

1. PHILIP ASTLEY, 1742-1814. Father, in England, of the modern circus.
2. JOHN BILL RICKETTS. Brought the circus to the colonies in 1793 and performed for President George Washington.
3. ISAAC A. VAN AMBURGH, 1811-1865. First animal trainer of note.
4. DAN RICE, 1823-1900. Circus manager and America's first clown. Performed for President Abraham Lincoln.
5. GILBERT R. "DOC" SPALDING, 1843-1865. Built a floating palace, a magnificent river showboat.
6. PHINEAS TAYLOR BARNUM, 1810-1891. The greatest showman ever.
7. W. C. COUP, 1836-1895. Forerunner of "The Greatest Show on Earth", famous innovator.
8. JAMES ANTHONY BAILEY, 1847-1906. Helped found R.B. & B.B. [Ringling Brothers, Barnum & Bailey] Circus.
9. JAMES ROBINSON, 1835-1917. Founded acrobatic school.
10. WM. F. "BUFFALO BILL" CODY, 1846-1917. Founded wild-west shows.
11. RINGLING BROTHERS of Baraboo, Wisconsin: Al (1852-1916), Alfred T. (1863-1919), John (1866-1916), Otto (1857-1911), Charles (1864-1926). Became "The Greatest Show on Earth" in 1918.
12. ISRAEL (died in 1973) and IRVIN FELD —Famous circus promoters purchased R.B. & B.B. in 1967.
13. CHARLES PHILIP "CHAPPIE" FOX, born in 1926. Founder of Circus Museum Library at Baraboo, organizer of Milwaukee Schlitz Parade, reactivated 40-horse hitch, circus historian.

The White Tops

Animals & Other Living Things

GRIN AND BEAR IT

Ten years ago Peter Bull, a British actor best known for his role as the Russian ambassador in *Dr. Strangelove,* wrote *The Teddy Bear Book.* Bull, a longtime collector of stuffed bears, recounted the story of Russell McLean, a Lima, Ohio, resident known for donating teddy bears to children in hospitals.

James T. Ownby, a journalist and public relations specialist in Honolulu, Hawaii, read Bull's book and decided to take Russell McLean's message to the world. In 1973 Ownby founded the Good Bears of the World International, an organization in which bear lovers band together to talk about their cuddly animals and donate teddys to needy children. By 1981 more than 9,000 Good Bears were organized in dozens of dens around the world. Ownby makes a yearly pilgrimage to international headquarters in Bern, Switzerland (Bern means "bears," according to Ownby), but the organization is based in Hawaii, where *Bear Tracks,* the quarterly journal, is published.

Ownby feels that teddy bears are an often-overlooked common denominator in the lives of most Americans. He says that six out of every 10 Americans grew up in the presence of a teddy; if you're part of that group, "you're in the 60% bracket," he says. To promote the cause of bears (and donations to hospitals and other institutions) Ownby spends about 45% of his time on the road, talking to the press and presenting bears to leading politicians. He has met several governors; more than a dozen states have held Good Bears days. Ownby is now trying to get Congress to proclaim October 27—Theodore Roosevelt's birthday—national Good Bear Day. A Good Bears of the World Foundation has been formed to handle contributions from members and profits from the sale of an Official Good Bear (a.k.a. "Goodie") by the Ideal Toy Company.

Bear Tracks is a lively, 32-page journal. Like the average teddy it is only eight inches high but filled with good cheer. It contains feature stories (a history of Winnie the Pooh, for example), letters from readers, and "Grrrrr's from Bearo #1" (that's Ownby). We are told that "the wife of British actor James Mason, living in Switzerland, is now a GBW member. She has over 100 bears." Matt Murphy, a banker in Texas, "has counted his collection at over 1300 bears." And, according to *Bear Tracks,* the CBS-TV program *Alice* is planning to present "a skit about us."

Now Ownby is looking to 1985, which he hopes will be named The Year of the Teddy Bear. "Being the founder of an organization of teddy bear people exacts a high and happy price," says Bearo #1. His mission in life is to cause "thousands of people to become more bearminded. . . ." Ownby truly believes "there is room for a teddy bear in the arms of nearly every man, woman and child."

LEAVE IT TO BEAVERS

Hope Sawyer Buyukmihci observes, nourishes, and protects all sorts of animals and birds that wander into the fields near her home in New-field, a small town in south New Jersey. Deer, foxes, muskrats, ducks, snow geese, and dozens of other creatures pass through each year. She calls the 300-acre property—mostly wild woodland and swamp—the Unex-pected Wildlife Refuge. The daughter of a nat-uralist and "bird artist," Edward Saywer, Hope started Unexpected to give her own chil-dren a chance to experience nature first-hand.

During the first years of refuge-watching, Hope put out a newsletter called *Good News from Unexpected.* She wrote a book called *Un-expected Treasure.* "In 1970," she recalls, "I decided to concentrate on beavers, about whom people know so little and who desperately need protection." She wrote another book, called *Hour of the Beaver,* and began publishing a 16-page, illustrated quarterly, *The Beaver De-fenders,* which now goes out to 400 subscribers in the U.S. and Canada. "They are all nature lovers," says Hope, "and especially interested in beavers, of course."

Some of the articles in *TBD* are reprints from other publications with titles like "Bonkers Over Beavers" or "Meet Mr. Beaver: Landscape Modifier." Hope's contributions cover week-to-week happenings at the refuge. She raises sick or orphaned baby beavers (called kits) in her home. The beavers are not relegated to the basement; they have the run of the house. Sometimes when she's not around they drag brooms out of the closet and begin building makeshift dams across doorways. "All during January, February, and March, we had Candy with us," Hope once wrote, "and although never friendly, she was a joy to be with. Beavers smell good, for one thing, and the rhythmic sound of their gnawing is easy on the ears."

Hope kept one beaver, named Chopper, in the house for two years. "He had a furry face full of childish eagerness," she recalls. That's why "it was hard for those who knew Chopper," Hope explains, "to face the fact that beavers just like him could be trapped and killed to make fur coats." In addition to the large numbers of beavers killed every year for their fur, others are destroyed by people whose land has been flooded because a beaver decided to dam up a nearby stream. Chopper was clubbed to death by a fisherman who claimed the beaver had tried to climb into his boat.

Like many "animal protection" publications, *TBD* seeks to dispel what the editor feels are harmful "myths." In the case of beavers, Hope believes, one has to consider their entire contribution. The dams may occasionally be a nuisance but they help conserve water, control soil erosion, and encourage aquatic growth. "Beavers are as much a part of our waterways," Hope contends, "as the water itself."

The new craze for Western wear does not augur well for Hope's furry friends. "They are using beaver fur for the hats," Hope points out, "especially the more expensive ones." She has responded by writing "Away with Traps," which she has labeled The Song of the Beaver Defenders. Members of the group, the song proclaims, would "rather take pictures than wear beaver coats. . . ."

Depend on the rabbit's foot if you will, but remember it didn't work for the rabbit.

Turtle Express

A Brief History of Pigeons

The feral pigeon as we know it today is descended from the wild rock dove. The closely integrated flocks seen in town and city are partly a legacy of the days when lords of the manor kept the pigeon in a semi-domesticated state as a source of winter food. Even in ancient Egypt, pigeons were kept as household birds, and their close association with man goes back even further—with origins in India.

Around the late 18th century, the dovecote pigeon declined in importance as a food source when improvements in agriculture made the production of grain more valuable as a source of bread than of pigeon food and farmers began to frown upon the plundering of their fields by the squire's flocks.

Those wild pigeons which have adapted themselves to co-exist with human civilization—roosting beneath tenement eaves and populating city parks and zoos—are often regarded with a peculiar ambivalence by townspeople. On the one hand, they are fed, by the local tender-hearted citizenry, and on the other, regularly exterminated by officials.

Nonetheless, the many domestic varieties serve very useful and even heroic roles. It was the messenger pigeon who relayed the conquest of Gaul to Rome and brought the first news of Napoleon's defeat at Waterloo to England. Pigeons were put to extensive use in war, serving, for example, the French underground to convey messages back to Britain. And since Neolithic times the fact remains: tender young squab is a great delicacy on the table!

Farmstead

Dateline: Africa

There's trouble in the Sudan. That's the word from Harry Tennison, president of Game Conservation International. The news is distressing because the Sudan is widely viewed as one of the best places in Africa to hunt. "I've heard some very bad news about poaching," Tennison told us. He referred us to Brian Coleman, who led parties into the Sudan earlier this year. "The poaching has simply gotten ridiculous," he told us, "particularly in elephant." Coleman reports seeing bands of 20 or more poachers on horses and camels, armed with automatic weapons. "We found herds of elephants in the bush—sometimes 20 or more—that had been machine-gunned. Right in Juba, at the airport, I saw several tons of ivory ready to be flown out. There were truckloads of it.". . . .

World Wide Hunters

The Great Water Bed Caper

When the Clyde Beatty-Cole Bros. Circus began appearing in shopping centers without sponsors to boost the ticket sales, their press department began looking around for ways to heat up the publicity campaign. If this could be done without buying a lot of media space, so much the better. Photo exhibits and appearances of an "advance" clown were used regularly. Elephant races on the first show day became so regular that Fred Logan & Co.

thought they had qualified for an olympic team.

Then, on their last tent appearance in Louisville, a new idea. The radio newscasters announced that, shortly before the evening performance, a Clyde Beatty-Cole Bros. Circus elephant would test a water bed supplied by . . . . and here the name of the cooperative dealer was enunciated, free publicity for everybody. This demonstration would prove beyond doubt whether one could sleep on the device without fear of it popping a leak and flooding the bedroom. Anyone contemplating new carpets and a water bed at the same time must see this exhibit, which doubtless also marked the entry of the circus into the field of consumer research.

I arrived at the lot and found the dealer's truck parked by the pony ride. He was spreading the rubber mattress on the ground by the curb in front of the ticket wagon, while his wife was passing out literature on the joys of waterbedding to the growing crowd. Evidently the bed frame was not to be used for this particular investigation.

The driver of the water truck had been taking his time filling the mattress and the crowd now filled the front of the midway and the adjacent street. The TV mobile news crew arrived and were escorted to the front, shouldering big video cameras and belts of batteries. The big watch-bed-show was about to begin. Then came Fred Logan around the end of the menagerie top with one of the little punks, no!, with Peter, great big 4 ton PETE. I thought perhaps it had not been such a good idea to get to the front of the crowd after all. We're all gonna get wet. Too late to go to the car for a raincoat. Weighing the merits of getting pictures or staying dry, I decided a little water wouldn't hurt anything and I could brag about it years later. Besides, it might pop on the other side and I could photograph someone else getting wet. Maybe the water bed dealer' or the TV cameramen or Fred Logan. It was worth the chance.

Now the great consumer investigation was announced. The water truck had remained and the TV guys had been spotted where the show name would appear in the newsreels. Logan commanded Pete to go into her act. First she sat on the water bag. It bulged and sloshed but leaked not a drop. Then she reclined on her side and appeared to find it comfortable. The edges of the mattress puffed out around her,

but it remained intact. Finally she did a head-stand on it, getting a round of applause from the crowd. By this time, no one questioned the quality of this water bed. The dealer beamed and his wife handed out more literature.

It was all a great success. Everyone proceeded to the performance dry to the bone. I paused to look again at the water mattress while they were draining the water from it. A few spots of dirt were the only damage. The vinyl toys on the midway should be so tough.

Reflecting later on the water bed demonstration, it was perhaps not as spectacular as it seemed. The mattress was not brim full of water so that, when the elephant's weight was on it, the highest pressure points, bony joints for example, could press the water aside and rest on firm ground. So the water pressure in the bag was not nearly so high as it appeared to be. It was certainly stressed beyond what human weight could accomplish, and proved to be a durable product. If the S.P.C.A. hears of it, Beatty-Cole may soon have to provide a water mattress for each elephant.

—Bill Rhodes
The White Tops

The vast majority of bats are not infected with rabies. Their contribution to our environment, even beyond their important role in controlling insect populations, cannot be estimated. They also continue to be important subjects of basic and medical research which has led to significant technological developments. For almost all persons who work with these creatures for any length of time, bats also become esthetically pleasing. It would be very unfortunate if unreasonable fears of rabies led to policies which resulted in attempts to reduce our bat populations.

NSS Bulletin
(National Speleological Society)

Technological Breakthrough in Preventing Wildlife Deaths by Automobiles

The Austrian Academy of Science has confirmed the highly successful results of an investigation by the Institute of Comparative Behavior on reduction of road accidents involving animals. Animal behavior theory was put into practice by a company that manufactures optical devices. Reflectors were devised for placement 10 or 20 yards apart, giving the appearance of reflected, red eyes glowing in the dark. Thus, animals' natural inborn fear of predators is translated, in behavioral terms, to the fear they need to feel of an oncoming motor vehicle if collisons are to be avoided. Automobiles have been deadly to wildlife because there has been no way to inform animals of the dangerous speed and power of a phenomenon which has had no place in the evolution of any species. The eyes of predators, on the other hand, are instantly recognized as signalling danger. It is a universal language.

Because the car headlights strike a number of the reflectors, many "eyes" flare up instantly, thus producing an "optical fence." The result has been a decrease of 80% of collisions with animals after dark in Austrian roads equipped with these reflectors. . . .

It is noted that thousands of miles of European roads where deer frequently cross have been made safe with these reflectors. In Austria alone, 300,000 reflectors have been installed. Furthermore, unlike fixed fences which interrupt the accustomed paths of wildlife, the optical warning fence is activated only when a vehicle approaches.

Animal Welfare Institute Information Report

Peter Jenkins, chief warden of Kenya's Meru National Park, knows that poaching in his park will be more difficult in the near future. This park's wardens will begin patrolling on the backs of camels. African poachers are now able to hide quickly when a game warden's motor vehicle stirs up dust and comes within hearing distance. The use of camels will change this advantage. Camels are able to travel into the most inaccessible parts of Africa, are able to cover 25 to 40 miles a day, require little upkeep and are quiet.

Mainstream

The Prince Is King

Barba Gemini Prince of Tara Sita has been officially crowned as the American Cat Fanciers Association's "Silver Anniversary Cat of the Year."

This beautiful Orange Eyed White Persian Male was bred by Barbara Thorsen of St. Paul, Minnesota, and owned by Margaret Chunyk of Winnipeg, Manitoba, Canada.

Margaret Chunyk's reaction was that of what might be expected from anyone just told they had Cat of the Year. The initial jubilation then gave way to the feelings of most of the Cat Fanciers, happiness for the cat and its accomplishments, gratitude to the breeder, and a feeling of thankfulness for being so lucky to be owned by such a beautiful cat. . . .

When out of the Show Ring, [B.G.P. of T.S.] then becomes the household pet with full run of his domain. He is a cat of gentle disposition and temperament, but, at the same time, rules the Chunyk home with an "iron paw."

ACFA Bulletin
(American Cat Fanciers)

The Siamese

Though the Siamese cat is extremely intelligent, it does not do to assume that he is always and necessarily better mentally equipped than other cats. In fact, *felis domesticus* is, as a species, very clever, inasmuch as he has exploited man to his own great advantage for countless generations.

In the Stone Age, and probably earlier, the smallest member of *felis catus* found warmth and safety by man's fires, shelter in his caves; he was no doubt tolerated on account of his ability to slay rodents and thus protect man's food supplies, perhaps also for his affectionate ways with man's children. In any case, here he is, firmly established in our homes, benefitted by all our scientific expertise from medical research to refrigeration, thriving on regular meals, sleeping on night-storage heaters, living like a lord without ever working—this is surely clever!! So clever, in fact, that the cat is *ex legis*—no laws can be made for a creature who cannot be arrested!

But it is invidious to compare the mental abilities of the different breeds. Most cat-lovers will protest, if a claim be made on behalf of

one breed, that their own particular variety is unusually intelligent; will, maybe, arise in their wrath to defend the mental powers of the breed they fancy! There are one or two obvious comments that may be made. The long-hair cat, with his weight of coat and his over-typed face, short-nosed and sometimes with overshot lower jaw, is inclined to be more placid, quieter, sleepier than the lively short-hair. Long- or short-haired, individuals vary within a breed: as with other species, there are no two alike, and for us who live with them, there is great charm in noting the differences of behavior, of likes and dislikes, of intelligence, in the cats. . . .

Whether the thought processes of Siamese differ from those of other breeds is a matter for discussion, but not easily resolved! I would say that all cats tend to know their own minds—where they want to go, what they like to eat; that they all tend to possess the determination to achieve their ends; and that they all are skilled in persuading man to provide for them.

These are feline qualities from time immemorial, and they vary in intensity from one individual to another, and so, maybe, from one breed to another. Many comparisons may be made, as between individuals and breeds. Most fanciers have seen a Persian of show quality who knows that it is time for lunch; he is on a heater, or in a patch of sun; his owner is not—as she should be—in the kitchen preparing his meal; he yawns once or twice, rises and stretches in leisurely fashion, moves slowly toward the human who exists to wait on him, tilts back his head with its lambent round eyes, and says very softly, "Mew?"

His Siamese distant relative knows only what the Persian knows—that it is time for luncheon; it is his treatment of the situation that is different. He also wakes, yawns, stretches—but much more briskly; he dashes to the dilatory slave, bashes her leg with his hard head, utters the Siamese roar, maybe leaps to her shoulder, purrs so as to be heard in the next room, firmly asserting his right to immediate attention! His thought processes are the same as those of the Persian, but his actions are much quicker, and his seductive wiles more emphatic. He may or may not be more intelligent, but he will get what he wants sooner.

—Phyllis Lauder
Siamese News Quarterly
(Siamese Cat Society of America, Inc.)

Illegal Polar Bear Hide Trade Supports Cocaine in Alaska

Global trade in polar bear hides is the primary means of financing the use of cocaine in Alaskan coastal villages, according to the U.S. Fish and Wildlife Service's chief law enforcement agent and state drug investigators.

The Marine Mammal Protection Act prohibits the sale of raw polar bear hides to or between non-native Alaskans. But a large polar bear hide measuring 10 feet square can be purchased for about $1,000 in coastal villages and, after being smuggled out of the country, it would sell for more than $10,000 in Japan.

Besides Japan, the other large trade center for Alaskan polar bear hides is the London Fur Exchange, where the hides bring premium prices alongside polar bear hides from Norway, Greenland, Canada and Russia.

Estimates of the kill range from 200 to 400 a year, but the exact figure is unknown. Fish and Wildlife agent Larry Hood says his seven-man force is finding it nearly impossible to

control or keep abreast of the trade. "We're such small timers, we just can't compete," says Hood of the sophisticated hide smuggling and drug selling connection.

"There's absolutely no protection for the polar bear right now," according to Hood.

Animal Welfare Institute Information Report

Otter Espionage?

Remember those news stories a few years back about our Navy's use of porpoises and sea lions as carriers of explosives? Well, you guessed it! Recently declassified materials obtained by the *New York Times* under a Freedom of Information request shows the CIA conducted experiments to determine if river otters could be trained to carry out similar missions.

The otters were part of a larger research program to investigate the feasibility of using animals to carry explosives, listening devices and other items to locations human agents could not reach. Otters were reportedly preferred subjects because they could get around equally well in water and on land, they were extremely intelligent and were very dextrous. The experiments appear to have ended inconclusively but since much of the documents' original text was deleted by CIA censors it is not possible to know for sure if this research is continuing or if it has actually been implemented. . . .

The Brightwater Journal
(River Otter Fellowship)

The Noble Ass

Because of a convulsion in the English language which began back in the Middle Ages, that noble beast, the "ass," our mascot, now finds himself an object of ridicule. His name has become a synonym for the butt end of just about anything at all, and without good reason. We also use "ass" as a derogatory term for people we don't like.

An ass will never drink too much—now how many of us can say the same? But what can an ass do that a horse can't do better? An ass can carry 50% of his weight on his back. A horse can carry only 1/6 of his weight. The ass is more intelligent. He learns quicker and he doesn't forget. An ass will never take you through a gate that is too narrow for the cart that he's pulling. But just try it with a horse. If he can personally make it, the horse doesn't give a darn whether you make it or not.

You ask how the word "ass" came to be misused? Well, I'll tell you anyway. Apparently it began back around 1200 A.D. In those days, "ass" meant the animal and "erse" referred to the human buttocks. Gradually, "erse" became "arse." The theory is that when "arse" crossed the ocean, New Englanders got hold of it and dropped the "R."

Thus, by the 19th century, a proper Bostonian couldn't distinguish his "ass" from his "ahhs." That's why polite society took to calling the ass a "donkey."

Donkey is really an insulting term. It stems from the word "dung" plus the word "key" —meaning hue or color. So "donkey" really means manure-colored.

One of the reasons why the ass has been treated with disdain is that he hates war. Although it is difficult, sometimes impossible, to ride a horse into battle, it was still Don Quixote, on a horse, who charged the windmill. (Alas, no more Don Quixote.) Now Sancho Panza, sitting on his ass, simply stood by and watched. There are many cases in history of people staying out of trouble by just sitting on their asses.

The ass was thus consigned to second class status as a hauler and carrier, a perpetual member of the services of supply. The ass was a peasant's animal, while the dumber horse became the darling of the gentry. The military horse was petted, fondled, and cared for until the day of the big battle; then he was ridden half to death and maybe wound up with an arrow in his—uh, rump.

There have never been any cases of an ass dying from an arrow in the rump, and very few cases of dying from overwork. If his load is too heavy or he begins to tire, he stops to rest.

The horse, on the other hand, will trust to human mercy, and as a result, millions of them have dropped dead while trying to take just one more step for old massa.

Males are called "jacks" and females are "jennies." If you cross a jack with a mare, you get a mule—usually. Incidentally, the father of our country, George Washington, was the first to breed mules in America; he used some asses given to him by the king of Spain. That is not to say that all asses came from Spain.

Turtle Express

The Crafty Crow Is Under Fire

California Takes a Potshot at Crows—Just When People had Learned to Love 'Em

The term "birdbrain" is intended as a slur. And certainly it's a slur on birds. Crowbrain would be something quite different—the crow has a larger brain than most other birds, and he uses it to more effect. That line of crows you've seen perching on a scarecrow proves how easily the crow deciphers an attempt to deceive him. And hunters have learned, to their surprise, that a crow quickly learns to distinguish between a farmer going about his business and a hunter who has a rifle in hand and plans to shoot a crow.

More amazingly, the crow can recognize the hunter who has shot at him even when he turns up, on new occasions, without a gun.

Folklore? No, this seems to be real. In recent years, the crow has turned from a much-maligned bird into one of those creatures of fun and fable that many persons admire. Scarecrow building has become a sport rather than an act of warfare—a new breed of scarecrow sculptors has been found, aware that the crow will hang around anyway, and they build the scarecrows just to put a touch of color in the fields. All's right with the crow, then?

No, in California (which is supposed to be a trend-setting state, remember?) the trend is suddenly running backward. Acting with intemperate speed lest those brainy crows hear about the move and form a committee, the state Game Commission ignored all the recent articles which have suggested that the farmer, too, is discovering that the crow can be more friend than foe. It ignored the spirit of the Migratory Bird Treaty which binds the United States and Canada into the protection of, among others, crows. It ignored those naturalists who have lately pointed out that the crow's diet—about a third of which consists of insects and rodents—can play a key role in keeping farm and ranchland from being overrun by the wrong creatures.

With not a dissenting vote, the Game Commission capitulated to a proposal from "16 sportsmen's organizations and 33 individuals" that crows, on public land, become fair game for the hunter: no limit, a 124-day season starting in early fall.

It had all happened so suddenly that wildlife care groups were caught off guard. Newspapers took it up in a spoofing way. "Eat crow" is a favorite American expression, particularly among politicians, so recipes were dug up to show that you really *can* eat crow and that certain crow recipes supposedly yield a delectable dish. The Animal Protection Institute intruded into the controversy, proposed to try to cut the new crow season off with an injunction, and quickly established that the pesticide division of the fish and game department couldn't even certify that the eating of crow was safe.

Was their flesh carrying a dangerous cargo of insecticide poisons from the bugs they pick off with easy skill? Nobody knew. Nobody had tested. The first to learn might be those who had saved the crow recipes and gone hunting.

API and other opponents of the crow hunt weren't hoping to prove that crow meat can be dangerous for your health, though. They were simply exposing the fact that the Game Commission had acted with precipitous carelessness and in the face of the crow's new and growing reputation as a bird whose habits are helpful even to his former enemy, the farmer.

Besides, there was already latitude in the law to allow farmers to kill crows which depredate crops.

Starting in 1972, it became against the law to own a crow everywhere in the U.S. In the small town of Lyndon, Illinois, they would understand and cheer for that. For in Lyndon, which calls itself "The Crow Capital of the World," there is lasting tribute to a crow named Rocky. The town pet at Lyndon, Rocky was accustomed to riding to school in the morning on the heads of school kids, and he'd be back at recess time to play with them. One day he rode off on the handlebars of a boy who was headed across the bridge. The boy on the bike didn't think about the fact that Lyndon had a law against shooting crows but the law ended at the bridge. Winging for the river, Rocky was brought down by a burst from a gun. "Here Lies Rocky the Crow," says his $300 headstone, "Everybody's Friend." Posthumously, Rocky is more famous than before. Each year he's celebrated in Lyndon's annual event—the Crow Festival.

Mainstream

Profits in Monkey Business

One *Forecaster* source indicates that huge potential profits in raising animals lie ahead . . . not necessarily for those usual barnyard inhabitants. On the contrary, the biggest profits that could be made by specialized animal raising would be to raise a herd of monkeys. Monkeys are badly needed and the 2 countries which shared almost a monopoly in supplying the U.S., India and Bangladesh, have recently cut off shipments completely. Yet, roughly 15,000 monkeys . . . rhesus monkeys to be specific . . . are badly needed for USA medical research and testing alone. It's boiling up into an international controversy. If Bangladesh doesn't relax its ban soon the U.S. may cut off aid. India itself is the largest recipient of World Bank load aid, much of which is forgiven, or never repaid, or repaid in unusual rupees that must by law be spent in India! So the money business in monkey business looks to be profitable if you can figure out how to get the rhesus rascals reproducing.

Monkeys to be exported in Bangladesh recently cost $81.50 wholesale, and could immediately be sold for $185 when landed in the USA. Undoubtedly a quick and sizable profit. Are you Midwestern mink ranchers listening? The monkeys for medical testing are needed a lot more than the mink coats! In fact, the U.S. apparently has a plan for national self-sufficiency in monkeys for the mid-1980s. Private individuals with facilities and experience are encouraged to learn all they can and take a flyer on the rhesus monkey business!

The Forecaster

Sight of Barn Owl Found Deficient at Night

Although the barn owl is known as a skillful predator at night, whose hunting prowess is well suited for the task of feeding its large families of voracious young, its vision is actually so discriminatingly poor in the dark that if a man stays relatively still, wild members of this owl have been known to play on his shoes, perch on his knee, and land on his head without expressing any fear whatsoever!

The Raptor Report

Smokey the Bear

In 1942, there was great concern among forestry officials in Southern California due to the lack of equipment and personnel for forest fire fighting. Because of the war, fewer resources were available to them for this purpose.

State and U.S. forestors appealed for help from the newly organized War Advertising Council, now called the Advertising Council, Inc. This public service agency agreed to sponsor a nationwide forest fire prevention campaign. The Foote, Cone, and Belding advertising agency of Los Angeles contributed its facilities and talents to help conduct the campaign.

Copymen and artists brandished pens and brushes, writing text and designing colorful campaign ads. Several ideas were tried, but in 1945, the advertisers decided that an animal that could be portrayed erect was most promising, as the figure would then be able to use its paws and arms in demonstrating fire prevention activities. A well-known cover artist, Albert Staehle, was commissioned to draw a bear, and the first "Smokey," in dungarees and old-style ranger's hat, and pouring water on a campfire appeared—a natural peacetime symbol which melded the emotional appeal of

an animal with the ruggedness of a firefighter. The caption read, "Smokey Says—Care Will Prevent 9 Out of 10 Forest Fires." This friendly "character" and his slogans slipped into the hearts and homes of millions of Americans; the result—a decrease in forest fires.

Smokey made his public service debut on posters and car cards in 1945. Magazine and newspaper forest fire prevention advertisements soon followed.

In June of 1950, a black bear cub, dazed and badly burned, was rescued in the wake of a forest fire on Capitan Mountain in New Mexico. Nursed back to health by Judy Bell, daughter of New Mexico Game Warden Ray Bell, the cub named Smokey was flown to Washington, D.C., where he found a home in the National Zoo, as the *living* symbol of forest fire prevention.

The original *living* symbol of forest fire prevention died on November 9, 1977, at his retirement home in the National Zoo and his remains were buried at the Smokey Bear Historical State Park in Capitan, New Mexico. Smokey's living symbol continues to greet over 3 million visitors to the National Zoo each year. . . .

Bear Tracks

Biddy Sings: 'I Ain't Got No Body'

Although there are a number of records of chickens flapping wildly round the farmyard for several minutes after being decapitated, there is only one authentic case of a chicken surviving 17 days without its head!

The incredible story started on 12 November 1904 when Mr. Herbert V. Hughes, proprietor of the Belvidere Hotel in Sault Sainte Marie, Michigan, USA, was beheading chickens for the Sunday dinner. Some of them were given to a member of the kitchen staff to pluck and clean. Suddenly the girl let out a high-pitched scream and rushed terror-stricken from the kitchen, and when Mr. Hughes investigated he found a Black Minorca hen . . . headless . . . walking slowly around the room.

The news spread like wildfire and for more than two weeks the Belvidere Hotel was invaded by crowds eager to see the bizarre sight of a living headless hen.

Mr. Hughes fed "Biddy," as she was called, by means of a syringe injected into the raw end of the food pipe and the bird flourished. Sometimes she would stretch up and flap her wings and then attempt to preen her ruffled feathers with her headless neck; other times she made strange croaking noises as if she was trying to sing.

The hen lived until 30 November. She would probably have lived even longer if it hadn't been for the carelessness of an attendant. Each day the end of the neck had been gradually healing up, and by the 17th day the skin had grown so closely over the end of the windpipe that poor Biddy suffocated.

The Woods-Runner

Illustration by Siri Chandler Beckman

Crickets

Carson I. A. Ritchie in his book *Insects, the Creeping Conquerors* gives some fascinating information about crickets in captivity. The ancient Greeks kepts crickets (and other musical insects) in cages made of reeds. In Spain, crickets (and other singing insects) are kept in cages to sing during Mass. Pairs of insects are also hung from the ceiling in homes, in light, two-storied cages. In early American pioneer days, many immigrant German boys kept crickets as pets, a carry over from Germany where most boys had several boxes for keeping insects.

In the Far East, the keeping of singing insects in cages reached the dimensions of a cult or art. In ancient times, there were even cages made to be worn in the sleeve of a garment, so the owner could have constant musical companionship. No home was too poor or to rich

to have some sort of cage for a singing insect.

Cricket cages in the East have varied from crude wood boxes to embossed gourds with elaborately decorated stoppers of jade or tortoise shell, to pieced boxes of wood or ivory in varied shapes, or cages of gold or silver wire or split bamboo, to porcelain cages with openwork sides.

Much simpler cages may be easily devised by contemporaries who wish to keep crickets as pets. "Any well ventilated enclosure with some moist earth will do for a cricket cage," says the Audubon Encyclopedia.

Many naturalists have written of how crickets in the natural state will sometimes fight, often ferociously, over a female. In captivity, the addition of meat to the diet is necessary to keep pet crickets from resorting to cannibalism.

In China, cricket fighting has been a favorite spectator sport, on a par with bull fighting in Spain, sometimes with great sums staked. In ancient days, good fighting crickets were believed by the Chinese to be reincarnations of human heroes, and were called generals or marshals. In tournaments held in the 1920's the victorious cricket had his name inscribed on a gourd-shaped ivory tablet, and when he died was buried in a small silver coffin.

Much serious, scientific study has been devoted to the cricket's "song." Dr. Frank E. Lutz, author of *A Lot of Insects,* says that in its fundamental notes, the chirps of the cricket are in the octave just beyond piano range. Some observers have noted that just as playing a record may start a canary singing, a cricket will also sometimes begin singing in response to man-made music.

More readily observable is the fact that cricket singing is louder, and quicker in tempo, when the weather is warm. The black field cricket is not so attuned to the temperature, however, as his relative, the snowy tree or "thermometer" cricket. (The formula: Count the number of chirps the thermometer cricket makes in 15 seconds, and add 40, for a close approximation of the Fahrenheit temperature.)

There are many kinds of crickets, such as the mole cricket and the cave cricket. But it's the shrill and sweet melodies of the common black field cricket which rise to poignant crescendo in those last days of warm weather in the fields of harvest.

—Georgia Hammack
Farmstead

Thumbs Down . . .

To Dade County, Florida, for legalizing cockfighting. Cockfighting is illegal in all states except Alabama, Arizona, Florida, Hawaii, Kansas, New Mexico and Oklahoma.

Mainstream

Releasing Dolphins

Last year Dexter Cate brought the slaughter of dolphins in Japan to world attention when he freed 300 that were penned up to be killed for pig feed and fertilizer in a small bay off Iki Island. The Iki slaughter is only an example, and a relatively minor one at that, of the inhumanity of some Japanese fishermen toward this intelligent and sensitive creature.

Dolphins are hunted for their meat in 10 locations off the coast of Japan. The meat is the cheapest one can buy in that country, and for good reason. Not only is its taste strong and fishy, but it contains 10 times as much mercury as is allowed in food under Japanese law. With this in mind, Greenpeacers Patrick Wall and Jay McManus set out to provide a test case on the legality of marketing this contaminated meat, with the aim of effectively stopping the killing of dolphins in Japan.

Arriving last November 15, our two-man crew soon established itself in a hotel on the Izu peninsula, 60 miles south of Tokyo, near one of the slaughtering sites. Planning to study the situation to determine the best means of opposing the kill, the two came prepared for anything: Zodiac and motor, a kayak, wetsuits and a good working knowledge of the Japanese language could all be important tools in the upcoming months.

Their first action was a perfectly legal one, one which should have been easy to execute. Using little-publicized Japanese statistics on the mercury content of dolphin meat, the Greenpeacers drew up an advertisement warning of the high concentrations, and tried to place it in a local newspaper. Apparently because of pressure from fishermen, however, the paper refused to run the ad. After repeated attempts to get the information out through traditional means, it became obvious that the two would have to go directly to the hunt to bring the issue to light.

Because of the limited market for dolphin meat, dolphin "roundups" are held only once a week from September to December. The fishermen of the area hunt for dolphins as far as 50 miles out to sea. When they find a pod, they use underwater noisemakers to confuse and disorient the dolphins. The fishermen catch several dolphins and hang them by their tails from the bows of the ships, then beat and stab them until they give distress cries. When the rest of the pod comes to their rescue, the fishermen line up their boats and drive them into the harbor to be slaughtered.

After missing one roundup by just half an hour, Jay did the only thing he could do at the time. Clad in a wetsuit, he entered the water of Kawana harbor to swim among the dolphins as they were dragged to shore to be speared to death; above the water he held a sign that said in Japanese and English, "Don't kill the dolphins." His protest swim was shown on Japanese national television everywhere except on the Izu peninsula. When he went to Tokyo for the next few days, complete strangers pointed at him, calling him *Iruku-san*, "Mr. Dolphin." The slaughters did not occur for the three weeks subsequent to this protest.

There would be only one more roundup this season, and Patrick and Jay realized it would provide their most important opportunity for direct action. In the Futo harbor pen, 650 dolphins struggled, awaiting a slow death that was scheduled for the next morning. At 4:30 a.m. December 23, Patrick launched an eight-foot inflatable boat and rowed to the nets. Carefully untying them (to avoid charges of damaging the nets) he pulled enough of them up into the boat to create a gap through which the dolphins could escape. He tied the boat to a convenient buoy and left it there, himself entering the water in his wetsuit to help the dolphins escape. Swimming back to shore, he made his own escape by walking through the village back to the car waiting at the launch site a mile away.

The next morning the fishermen were surprised to find a bright yellow boat full of net floating in the middle of their dolphin pen, and 150 of their catch, worth $5,000, missing. (Dolphins are very social and do not easily abandon their injured. For this reason many had not taken advantage of the gap in the nets.)

The fishermen informed the police, who were just as surprised when Patrick nonchalantly walked into the police station the next day to claim the Greenpeace boat.

"Sure I let the dolphins go, and now I'd like

my boat back, please," he told the astonished police.

The head of the Futo fishery cooperative was neither nonchalant nor astonished; he was furious. "If you come back here again we will kill you," he said in the presence of police.

After many days of questioning, Patrick Wall was formally arrested and charged with interfering with the lawful business of the Izu fishermen. Patrick didn't mind paying for the dolphins' freedom with his own, recognizing that the publicity the incident would evoke would be extremely beneficial in disseminating the information on mercury content, and consequently, in stopping the slaughter. Given the choice of either pleading guilty and being fined $59, or pleading innocent and standing trial to face a penalty of up to three years in prison, he easily chose the latter.

"I cannot even pretend it was a crime to free the dolphins," he explained.

After 62 days of imprisonment, Patrick went to trial. His defense: that because the amount of mercury in dolphin meat was in excess of Japanese standards, the fishermen's business was not lawful. A Japanese environmental chemist testified that he had conducted many analyses of dolphin meat, and that his findings coincided with Greenpeace's. The prosecutors were reduced to asserting that since the chemist's samples had been provided by Greenpeace, he could not be sure they had come from Izu. Despite the lameness of this accusation, Patrick was convicted. He received a six-month suspended sentence and was deported from Japan.

—John Frizell and Patty Hutchison
The Greenpeace Examiner

The Airedale Terrier

(By F.H.F. Mercer, from *The American Book of Dog*, published 1889.)

An airedale is not a pretty dog—no one can accuse him of being beautiful; but he is a rough-and-ready looking customer, with such a weird head and face, and such human-looking eyes, that one can not help liking him. I have heard people insist that the Airedale had monkey blood, as he looks more like "our ancestor" than a dog, and undoubtedly there is a resemblance.

When my first Airedale arrived by express, the box in which he was delivered, during my absence from home, was carefully deposited in the kennel-yard. On my return, I was met at the door by a friend who "keeps house" with me, and was told excitedly that an "awful-looking brute had come," and that he had left it in the box, being afraid to take it out. I went into the kennel-yard, and there saw this terror-inspiring creature, whom I at once pronounced to be the champion ugly dog of Canada. I let him out, and he was as affectionate a little, or rather big, fellow as you could find anywhere. My friends all ridiculed and laughed at him for the first few weeks, but now their feelings have changed, and I am fairly besieged with applications for "one of those Airedales."

As I am a devoted Spaniel man, I have not yet tested Airedales afield, but I understand that they are most invaluable a dog, all-around. They can "run" a deer, a fox, or a hare; beat for feathered game, and kill a rat, retrieve a duck, and "draw" a 'coon. They are the least quarrelsome of dogs; but when once their wrath is raised, "look out for squalls" — something is going to suffer.

They are much used by poachers in England, being an improvement on the "lurchers" of olden days, and, moreover, less likely to arouse suspicion in the gamekeepers, to whom a lurcher is as a red rag to a bull.

"He's a queer looking 'coon," I overheard a visitor say of an Airedale at a show, "but he looks like a dandy for work"; and I think this breed exemplifies the adage, "Handsom is as handsom does."

They are grand watch-dogs and excellent house-dogs, kind and affectionate with children, and most intelligent. I am afraid, however, that they will never be popular, looks being so much against them. There are but few of them in the country, and very, very few good ones.

Airedale Terrier Club of America Newsletter

By all known laws which can be proved on paper or in the wind tunnel, the bumblebee cannot fly. The size of his wings in relation to his body, according to mathematical and aeronautical science, indicates he can't. It is an impossibility. But, of course, the *bumblebee* doesn't know these rules, so he goes ahead and flies away.

Turtle Express

The Plain Truth

Chicken hawks are still etched in the minds of the American public—despite the fact that no such species of bird has ever existed.

No North American bird of prey, or raptor, feeds entirely or even significantly on chickens and other domestic fowl, as Dr. A. K. Fisher's exhaustive food study and public relations effort proved at the turn of the century.

The popular misconception has its roots in the anti-predator beliefs, and practices, of early American settlers in the South and Midwest, where large *buteo* hawks, characterized by their large wingspread and wide soar, frequented to prey upon wild rabbits and mice.

Farmers and ranchers became accustomed to the hawks perched atop tree snags and fence posts, or lazily soaring in the open fields, and these economy-conscious men began to associate the birds with raids on the backyard chicken coop.

The target birds, usually red-tailed hawks, were wrongly branded as chicken thiefs, even though Dr. Fisher's prey examination for the U.S. Dept. of Agriculture already showed the birds' diet was that of crop- and coop-destructive mammal and rodent pests. Despite such exemplary feeding habits, these birds and their kin were commonly destroyed; in many states their killing was encouraged by government bounties. . . .

Even though official attitudes toward the airborne hunters have since changed and state and federal laws now protect all hawks and owls, most states still allow by permit the shooting or trapping of these birds in times of damage.

Worst of all, the often unreachable rural citizen still clings to the false "chicken hawk" notion, and his and his neighbor's ignorance persists to perpetuate the myth and bring harm to these birds.

—J. Richard Hilton
The Raptor Report

Farewell, Farewell, Rhinoceros

The most immediate threat to rhinoceros survival is the commercial value of their horns. Currently worth more than their weight in gold, rhino horns are the most expensive animal product in the world. Superstitious cultures attribute a variety of curative powers to powdered rhino horn; tribal chieftains carry rhino horn walking sticks as a symbol of prestige, some primitive cultures believe a rhino horn cup will detect poison, rhino by-products are given to alleviate everything from earaches to labor pains.

In North Yemen dagger handles carved from rhino horns are a status symbol. Once available only to the few, Arab oil wealth in recent years has put the $6-12,000 price tag for those jambia within easy reach of more and more Yemeni. Legal exports of rhino horn from East Africa in 1950-71 averaged 4.2 tons annually. In 1976-77, North Yemen imported 7.6 tons per year, a figure which represents the deaths of 4000 rhinos for this market alone.

Even where rhinoceros hunting is illegal, poachers' incentive is great: at today's market value for rhino horn a self-employed farmer can double his annual income by killing a single rhino! There are also professional poachers whose sophisticated techniques enable them to decimate entire populations of rhinos with very little effort. Rhinos are easily approached, and spears and knives have been replaced with automatic weapons and advanced technology. The horns are hacked off, transferred to middlemen and shipped out of the country, probably by aircraft. The value of rhino horn has made poaching increasingly attractive; poachers are willing to take greater risks, and even some underpaid game wardens have been lured into this illegal activity.

Effects of poaching on rhino populations are already apparent: since 1973 the average trophy horn mass has dropped 60 percent, indicating that there are fewer mature animals.

55,000 black rhinoceros were killed in Africa in 10 years—*one every 90 minutes.* At this rate of extermination, the black rhino will be extinct before this century has ended.

Mainstream

Turtle Towing

A new service to our readers . . . . It's auto towing. On mornings when your car won't start, who's to give you a push? We all know about towing costs. NOW IT CAN BE FREE. Thanks to a marvelous invention—The Chojnowski Turtle Whistle perfected while trying to get the bartender's attention.

This long-range two-inch stainless steel whistle was devised to help people stuck in the sand, mud or snow. It has two notes, audible only to turtles. One note signals, "Turtles, come!" The other signals, "Turtles, push!"

One whistle toot brings hundreds of turtles, each exerting one Turtle-Power, to push your car out. A single ad in a local newspaper swamped Chojnowski with orders. Then a serious problem arose.

The turtles often injured their shells when pushing heavy vehicles. Undaunted, Chojnowski devised a harness so the turtles could pull instead of push. The moose-leather harnesses are offered in lots of 200 for $11.95 each, with a free whistle (altered, of course, to instruct the turtles to pull instead of push)

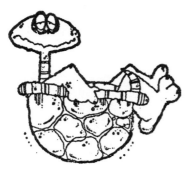

thrown in. Total price, $2,390. Orders poured in so fast that Chojnowski couldn't keep up.

However, it is mighty cold in these parts when most car batteries go dead. To ask the turtles to work on frigid January mornings with no protection would be inhumane. Nothing stops Chojnowski. He has devised a turtle vest of warm fake fur (choice of mink, chinchilla, or tiger). An all-weather set of 200 harnesses and vests is only $4,380.

Turtle Express

Humpback Attacks

On February 4, 1981, two beached humpback whales were discovered on remote islands near the Seymour Canal, 20 miles south of Juneau, Alaska. A large, 45-foot female was found first; later a young male humpback, presumed to be her calf, was discovered on the beach of a nearby island. Biologist Charles Jurasz and veterinarian Cliff Lobaugh performed autopsies which led them to conclude that the mother had probably been killed by shots from a high-powered rifle.

Unfortunately, this is not the first case of whales being shot in southeast Alaska. Earlier this year the owner and the operator of the *Repulse,* a fishing vessel owned by the Ward Cover Packing Company of Ketchikan, Alaska, were fined $15,000 when they were convicted of "heedlessly and senselessly" shooting at a humpback whale. The whale later washed up, dead.

There is a large reward offered under the Marine Mammal Protection Act for information leading to the arrest and conviction of the female humpback's killer.

—Mark Boberick
The Greenpeace Examiner

That's Life

ON FIRE

It began with a title, a wonderful, brilliant title contributed by its founder, the late Joe Hallet: *The Visiting Fireman*. It has since become an (perhaps *the*) annual event for fire buffs, a 400-page journal/directory, with a drawing of what co-publisher Dan Martin calls "the familiar little character wearing his fire helmet and carrying his suitcase" on the cover.

Martin, the 55-year-old photographer who, with a friend, purchased *Visiting Fireman* in 1977, explains: "It has a catchy title that has gained too much recognition among our faithful 'participants' to ever be abandoned now. Unfortunately, that name is not properly descriptive to any who are unfamiliar with what we publish. Newcomers must have it explained to them as follows:

"The Visiting Fireman is the directory of fire buffs and fire buffing. We list all our participants, updating their mailing addresses in this constantly changing world and including their own descriptions of their affections and affiliations. Only the chiefs of two major cities are a bit coy about their positions. Our participants include hundreds of fire department members as well as all of us who are just hobbyists.

"In addition we publish listings of fire-buff clubs, fire history museums, fire radio frequencies, articles on making fire apparatus models, a guide to some restaurants featuring fire station decor, the winners and their scores from the New England Hand Engine Musters, lists of movies that have featured fire fighting actions, book reviews, and many, many photos of fire apparatus, fires, and anything else that would interest the fire buffs. Finally, classified advertising for buffs wanting to increase, dispose of, or exchange their treasures."

These listings, interspersed with action photos and still-lifes of fire vehicles, make up more than half the book; articles make up most of the rest. The 1981 edition had a report on the Hall of Flame Museum in Phoenix, the South Australian Fire Brigade, and Fire Protection in Shizukoa (Japan). There was a long article on "Buffing Overseas" and an ad for a restaurant described as "New York City Firefighters' Favorite Spot."

VF emanates from Martin's basement, in Naperville, Illinois. Dan's wife, Mae, is bookkeeper and major promoter. It goes out to more than 2,400 readers, some as far away as Italy, Australia, and New Zealand. There are two subscribers in Saudi Arabia, one a "chief" at Jubail Industrial City and the other a "fire buff" in Riyadh. In his *VF* blurb, Takeshi Miyawaki of Kyoto, Japan, describes himself as a "paid firefighter, captain" who is interested in "plastics fire car model, badges, helmets. . . ."

Until he bought *VF,* Dan Martin had a lifetime fascination for fire fighting, thousands of photographs of fire equipment, a 24-foot-long 1926 American La France fire engine in his back yard (he used to blow the siren every New Year's Eve), and nowhere to show any of them off. When Dan's wife told him she had heard that someone was looking to sell *VF,* he rushed into the breech. Now he says: "We are just life-long Midwesterners trying to get favorable attention for our annual publication. The *Visiting Fireman* is undeniably a cheap, chintzy operation as publications go. However, it does benefit its participants a lot and us, its publishers, a little."

MAIL ORDER MADNESS

Bob Orben works at his job seven days a week but he rarely has to go to an office. "I try to write 25 jokes every day," he says. "But if I'm hot, I might come up with 50 or 60 jokes."

Sometimes he gets inspired by current events, sometimes by personal experience. A few years ago, when his newsletter, *Orben's Current Comedy,* reached subscribers a week late, imperiling the topicality of some of his gags, "I sat right down," Orben recalls, "and wrote five vitriolic anti–post office jokes and got it out of my system."

Orben has been "a human joke writing machine" (in the words of *The Wall Street Journal*) since his teens. He wrote the first of his 45 joke books, *The Encyclopedia of Patter,* in 1946 when he was 18 years old. In the early 1960s he wrote for the Jack Paar television show in New York and from 1964 to 1970 for Red Skelton in Hollywood. He also provided material to Dick Gregory. His most-publicized period was in the mid-1970s, when he served as a special assistant to President Gerald R. Ford and was director of the White House speechwriting department. (He did not, however, orchestrate any of President Ford's trips, stumbles, or falls.)

Since Ford left office Orben has faded out of the public limelight a bit but his very successful newsletter keeps him busy. It's a four-page weekly made up of about five dozen one- and two-liners that he puts together at his home in Arlington, Virginia. He calls it "a humor service providing topical new laugh material for public speakers, entertainers, emcees, toastmasters and business, political and community leaders"—anyone who needs to spice up a speech or routine with a few fresh barbs.

Orben pokes fun at practically everything and is militantly bipartisan; when the Democrats are in power he chides them, and when the Republicans are in charge they really get it. Some of his jokes end up being used in the media as conventional wisdom. One joke—"If God had really wanted us to have enough oil, He would never have given us the Department of Energy"—was quoted in *The Wall Street Journal, Time* magazine, and a Mobil advertisement.

Does this mean Bob Orben is pro–Oil Company? "As a craftsman," he explains, "my jokes don't *necessarily* reflect my views. . . ."

Pot Power

U.S. customs officials in Florida used to burn confiscated marijuana on unused airport runways. But then people began gathering downwind. So they worked out a deal with the Florida Power and Light Company, which now uses the flammable substance (1.2 million pounds in 1979) to help fuel its oil-fired generators. Complains one customs official, though, "It's unreliable as a fuel. One week you get 30 tons and then you're dry for three weeks."

Executive Fitness Newsletter

Thwarted Ambitions

(Introduction, by Sherwood Anderson)

The small town is rather like a large family. Living in it has great possibilities—for ugliness, for real human loveliness in relationships, and for fun.

Family fun is a kind of special thing.

Many big city dailies have become standardized. All stories are handled in the same way.

In the small town or county paper, on the other hand, there are infinite possibilities. You can write what the farmers and town people who take the paper call "good reading."

There is a chance for the individual who edits the paper to let go, to be serious, honest sometimes—to have fun.

I submit the piece, reproduced here and written by my son Robert Lane Anderson, as a sample of country newspaper—family—fun. It was published as a bit of regular news reporting in our Smyth County (Virginia) News *and our* Marion Democrat *at Marion, Virginia.*

The great steer trial between Mr. Henry Staley and Mr. Roscoe Wilkinson at the court house. Early in the morning a great concourse of steer experts began to assemble in the court room. The cattle men were out in force. When the trial began none of the fair sex was in the court room; all had delicately withdrawn.

Mr. Preston Collins was the attorney for Mr. Staley. Mr. Andy Funk represented Mr. Wilkinson.

"Both men look fit," Clerk Sam Kent said when they entered the arena, each followed by a group of supporters.

Judge Stuart was on the bench. Mr. R. C. Hash, foreman, Mr. W. S. McClellan, Mr. H. C. Farris, Mr. R. L. Copenhaver and Mr. Conley Copenhaver were in the jury box.

Mr. Staley was suing Mr. Wilkinson for $181 rent for the pasturing of nineteen of Mr. Wilkinson's steers in the 190 acre pasture up back of the golf course for six months last summer. Mr. Wilkinson had a counter claim for damages.

It seems that Mr. Wilkinson turned his steers into the pasture in April last year. He testified that Mr. Staley told him that only his and twenty other steers belonging to Mr. Keesling were to go on the pasture during the summer. He claimed it was understood that no heifers were to be pastured in the boundary.

Mr. Staley, on the stand, denied that anything had been said about heifers. "We spoke of cattle," he said.

Well, Mr. Wilkinson's steers were turned in the pasture. They lived along quietly and put on flesh. The pasture was at that time, apparently, a sort of steer heaven. Everything was O.K. with the nineteen steers.

Then, along in July or August, Mr. Doug Keller made a deal with Mr. Staley and put in about two dozen calves for a month. That was all right as Mr. Keesling had never put his steers in and there was enough grass. Mr. Wilkinson didn't complain about that.

The steers, according to testimony of Mr. S. M. Parks, who lives near the pasture, kept to themselves and the calves kept to themselves.

October came. Along about the tenth or twelfth Mr. Wilkinson took Mr. Doug and Mr. Legard Keller up there and sold them the steers for delivery on the 24th, when his rent period ended. Mr. Keller and Mr. Keller looked at the steers. They were a fine, fat bunch that would average about 1050 lbs., they testified at the trial.

So Mr. Wilkinson had sold his steers but they were still in the pasture. But, on the 6th, Mr. Staley had rented the pasture rights to Mr. Bowman Long, of Flatridge, Grayson county, and Mr. Long soon after sent over a bunch of heifers. Then the trouble began with his steers, according to Mr. Wilkinson. Romance entered their lives.

The steers, Mr. Wilkinson claimed, lost all sense of how a respectable, just-ready-for-the-market steer should live and conduct himself. They looked at the heifers, they neglected their eating, they couldn't, in the words of the witnesses, "keep their minds on their business."

They played tag with the lady cows all over the 190 acre lot. Their days and nights were spent in fruitless revels. There was no peace in Mr. Staley's pasture, the serpent had entered in.

On the 24th Mr. Wilkinson and the Kellers came for the steers. They were so bad off, Mr. Legard Keller said, that he had trouble recognizing them as the same bunch he had bought some days before. Gone was the sleek fatness, the contented steerful look. Instead there was a bunch of wild-eyed, worn, ruffled, thinned down, sleepless and disappointed animals. When they were weighed they only averaged around 950 pounds.

This was Mr. Wilkinson's counter claim: Mr.

Staley had allowed heifers to be turned in and his steers had consequently run about an average of 100 pounds each off themselves. The steers had been sold at about ten cents a pound. Not to be selfish, Mr. Wilkinson said through his attorney, he was only claiming a loss of 60 pounds per steer. That made him due, he claimed, about $119 damages from Mr. Staley.

And it was here the drama began. Mr. Funk and Mr. Wilkinson had assembled all the foremost authorities on steer psychology now living in Smyth county. They were massed on the left. One by one they took the stand and told of the secret thoughts of the average steer. . . .

The steer, they agreed, is a sensitive animal. He has an imagination. He is perhaps a neurotic of a sort. When by himself or with other steers he is generally happy and carefree. He eats, drinks, lies in the shade, grows fat and is sold for beef.

It is when heifers come into his life that he changes. A heifer, it was brought out over and over again in most delicate language, has times in her life when she is filled with romantic thoughts. She thinks of a little home and fireside and babies playing around the cottage door. Her heart is full of yearning.

At such times somewhat the same thoughts get into a steer. He too has romantic imaginings, and they are bad for his digestion.

It was quite possible that some such things came into the lives of Mr. Wilkinson's steers and Mr. Long's heifers, the experts agreed. Under such circumstances, it was variously estimated, a steer might lose from 50 to 100 pounds in coquetting with a lush young heifer over a 190 acre lot. It was quite possible, even probable, they agreed.

On the other hand were assembled expert authorities for Mr. Staley.

These gentlemen had a different view of what a steer thinks about. Their steer's lives are not filled with thwarted ambitions. Innocence rules in their flocks, they said.

Afterwards came the closing arguments by the attorneys. Mr. Collins spoke doubtfully of the great loss of weight suffered by Mr. Wilkinson's steers. Mr. Funk began with the history of man. He traced a parallel with the fall of Mr. Wilkinson's steers. "Who can blame a steer," he asked.

Then the jury retired. They stayed out a good long time. Finally they came back with the verdict. Mr. Staley, of course, was awarded his $181 rent. But from it they deducted $25 to pay for damages to Mr. Wilkinson's steers. The verdict put the trial costs on Mr. Wilkinson. He has to pay the fees of the experts. Mr. Funk moved for a new trial but no action was taken on the motion.

The Winesburg Eagle

Back to Meadows

American houses were once surrounded by shaggy lawns instead of the close-cut gardens we're accustomed to today. It may be time to reconsider devoting a portion of our land to the shaggy lawn or meadow. Besides being cheaper to maintain, a meadow is a potential source of new pleasures attractive to wildlife that varies by season, and is geographically distinct. Meadows also save fuel, time, fertilizer, herbicides and water.

American technology and salesmanship changed the look of homegrounds in the late 1860's by providing an inexpensive close-cutting lawn mower. At the same time, a machine aesthetic was introduced into American culture that enabled us to obtain a nationally recognizable lawn idiom: The close-cut garden lawn. . . .

To start, simply let your lawn go. Just be sure to alert your neighbors to your plans. Explain that meadows are the first step towards letting land revert to its natural forest state. While you're not planning a forest in your back yard, you are going to revitalize the land and entice some wildlife to your neighborhood. Assure them you will pay attention to the borders (and be sure you do), so that your meadow doesn't encroach upon their manicured lawns. . . .

The Old-House Journal

At the first meeting of George Bernard Shaw and novelist George Meredith, both of whom had well-deserved reputations as non-stop talkers, mutual friends laid wagers on who would out-gab the other. Meredith got the jump on the playwright and chattered away without giving Shaw an opportunity to interrupt.

Shaw felt humiliated. Two years later, when another meeting was arranged, he was determined to make a better showing. He came on with tongue wagging, and did not stop talking for a moment.

Meredith was silent. It was a sweet revenge for Shaw, but one that was short-lived, for as he was leaving, he learned that since their previous encounter, Meredith had become quite deaf, and probably hadn't heard a word.

Funny Funny World

Origins

Fenton, MI: The town was originally called Dibbleville after Clark Dibble. When he moved away, two prominent citizens, Colonels Fenton and Leroy, played a game of cards, and the winner had the town named after him. The main street was named after the loser, Leroy. The names remain as they were in 1836. Other streets were named after women in the card-playing families.

Cash, TX: was named for the first postmaster, J. A. Money!

Frostproof, FL: This community was originally known as Keystone City. In the winter of 1896-97, though, two severe freezes engulfed the central part of the state and destroyed most of the citrus crop as well as many trees. The five miles square area of Keystone City and its environs escaped. Next spring the residents renamed the town. Later the freeze of December 1962 left the town undamaged again.

Atlantic, IA: When the railroad was located here, a decision was to be made between the names Atlantic and Pacific, since the distance to each was approximately the same. Two pioneer citizens decided to flip a coin, and Atlantic was the winning name. Complications arose, however, when an engineer planning the town decided to call it Avoca. It was at this time that a community leader learned of the change and convinced the railroad that Atlantic should remain the name of the city. It was incorporated in 1870.

Seattle, WA: When Pioneers named their settlement after Sealth, chief of the Suquamish tribe of western Washington, he was very disturbed. A Suquamish superstition said that if anyone mentioned his name after he was dead, his spirit would be troubled. If the superstition is true, Sealth's spirit must be troubled often, as Seattle is a frequently-mentioned city.

Mann's Choice, PA: The name dates from 1890, when a post office was petitioned for by Mr. Job Mann, a congressman. At the time, the town was known as Foot of the Ridge. Mr. Mann went to the P. O. Department and requested a post office. The request was immediately granted, but when asked to furnish a name, Mr. Mann hesitated to suggest one. The clerk merely shrugged and entered Mann's Choice.

Lebec, CA: Named for an unfortunate traveller named Peter Lebec who was killed by a grizzly bear there in 1837. His friends carved "Lebec" into a huge oak tree and it was found in 1889.

Quicksand, KY: Before any bridge was built in this area, a man was returning home on horseback and began to cross the stream at this spot. As he neared the center of the stream his horse began to sink underneath him. Frantically, he cried for help, but before onlookers at the bank could reach him, rider and horse sank from sight. Quicksand stuck as the name of the site of this tragedy.

—Barry Yeomans
PMCC Bulletin (Post Mark Collectors Club)

Tomb It May Concern

It may not work in the rainy Northwest, but any place that has at least four days of sunlight a week works for a new invention—a solar-powered talking tombstone. The owners of U.S. patent No. 4159970 say the cost, including installation, is $10,000 now, but they hope to get the cost down into the $1,000 range someday.

The invention is a spin-off of space age technology. A plexiglass enclosure is placed in a hollowed-out tombstone, which contains a small speaker and a three-inch solar panel. A tape recorded statement can run up to two hours. Only someone with correct keys can activate the recording and listen to the last words, or whatever, of the grave's occupant.

Continental Association of Funeral and Memorial Societies Bulletin

Fowl Play

On Monday, March 16, 1981, Officer Russ "Crusher" Haley, I.D. 3011, was working commercial detail out of Susanville. Officer Haley was assigned complaint detail to conduct an investigation into a dead chicken being thrown out of a car window while on U.S. 395 south of Byer's Pass, Lassen County.

"Crusher" Haley interviewed the complaining party and determined that the complainant had "seen" the male subject, about 40 years old, 20 pounds overweight (complainant has very critical eye), 5′ 8″ to 5′ 11″ in height with normal length brown hair driving a small reddish-brown station wagon with California license (supplied correct license number). Complainant had taken the fowl, a Bantam rooster, dead, as evidence. Complainant did advise "Crusher" Haley that he noted rigor mortis had not set in when he took fowl into possession.

Officer Haley doggedly tracked the suspect down and learned that the suspect had struck the rooster with the right front of the station wagon and the rooster became airborne. The complainant mistakenly thought the chicken was litter, but in reality it was a victim of trying to cross the road for whatever reason.

Evidence was to be buried or held in evidence in deep freeze until Lassen County District Attorney determines if there is sufficient evidence to prosecute for anything.

The California Highway Patrolman

Ford Motor Co., the most vocal of the U.S. automakers in asking government action against Japanese imports, isn't setting a very good example. Ford gave away a variety of trinkets to an international collection of automotive writers who gathered to see FoMoCo's 1981 models in Dearborn recently.

Writers who excelled on a test about auto servicing were awarded watches—made in Japan. And the writer who scored highest on a fuel economy driving competition walked away with the grand prize, a Japanese-made television. The winner, appropriately enough, works for a Japanese car magazine.

The California Highway Patrolman

What Makes an Old House "Significant" and Worth Saving?

- Is it in sound physical shape? In an era of limited resources, we can ill afford to waste sound buildings.
- Is it connected in people's minds with a landscape, streetscape or neighborhood? Would people miss it if it disappeared? That a building is architecturally significant is a point that can be understood by a handful of architectural historians. But the people who live near or pass by a building can tell you if they *like* it. Isn't that enough? These vernacular landmarks give stability and a framework to our daily routine.
- Is it beautiful or visually entertaining? Given the sterility of so much of modern construction, we should cherish beautiful old buildings that bring joy to our lives.

A house or building that fulfills even *one* of these criteria is a structure that should be taken seriously . . . and is worthy of attention from *everyone* who cares about what kind of world we live in.

The Old-House Journal

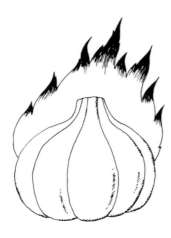

Anti-Garlic Law Lingers

There are many whacky food laws in cities and states across the USA. Many are no doubt left-overs from earlier days. Since garlic was scorned by our Puritanical fore-fathers, it's not surprising that anti-garlic laws would have been passed. In fact, garlic was seen as a punishment in Colonial America. One surviving law is on the books in Gary, Indiana: It is illegal to take a streetcar or go to the theater within four hours of consuming garlic.

Garlic Times

Double Theft Leads to S.F. Lawsuit

In San Francisco an insurance company has filed a $25,414 claim against the City of San Francisco to pay for a luxury car that was stolen twice: once from a dealer and once from a police garage where it was stored for safe-keeping.

"How someone could go in and drive off with a car in the care of the police department—well, it's an embarrassing situation. It shouldn't have happened," said Charles Wiersch, manager of the San Francisco branch of Motors Insurance Company, which filed the claim.

San Francisco police recovered the silver four-door Mercedes six weeks after it was reported stolen from a San Jose dealership.

Inspector Al Weatherman of the police auto-theft detail said the car was taken to the garage at the Hall of Justice.

The car, which was recovered early in the morning, was missing again less than seven hours later. "It's a mystery where it went," Weatherman said. "I guess the city is just going to have to buy a new car."

But the city claims adjuster, Bernard Shew, denied the claim on the grounds that the car was left locked and there was no negligence by the police.

Police Times

U.S. Park Police Claim World's First "Reverse Medevac" Flight

Washington, April 1—World's first recorded "reverse medevac" flight has been made by a Bell 206L of the U.S. Park Police in Washington, D.C. Sources at the department said the flight was made after the driver of an empty dumptruck was blinded by the sun as he rounded a sharp curve, lost control of his vehicle and struck a tree. "I guess the combination of the heavy rainstorm and his being over gross weight with those bricks helped cause the accident," the sources said. Conditions at the time were said to be foul but sunny.

A Park Police helicopter was dispatched to the scene and took the injured driver to the trauma unit at Metropolitan General Hospital. Half an hour later, he was again flown to the accident scene, located on a long flat stretch of road.

"It was a perfectly routine situation," said the Park Police spokesperson, "we got him into the trauma center and before they could even put a bandage on him, the woman from the Admissions Department came in and found that the victim didn't have any sort of hospitalization insurance. She ordered him flown back to the accident scene before anybody laid a hand on him." Contacted for a comment on the unusual procedure, the hospital spokesperson said there was no truth to reports that the Park Police had tried to refuse the return trip and just leave the victim at the hospital. "The person we saw here (she refused to call him a 'patient') did not have any form of coverage to make sure the hospital did not lose money on the case. We are, after all, a public service organization," she snapped, adding that the case was being blown up into an unjustifiable cause celebre even though the truck driver did not object in the slightest to being taken back to the accident scene and left there. "He was, after all, unconscious."

—Self-parody issue,
Helicopter News

A federal district judge has ruled that *El Pueblo,* a Texas monthly newspaper, may print names reportedly taken from a list of 3,000 clients of a local brothel.

Dissolving a state court order blocking publication, the judge agreed with the paper that it was an unconstitutional prior restraint on the press. Defending the bordello's madam's position, lawyers argued that the newspaper had obtained the list "improperly" and had no right to publish it.

Maria Cabral, spokeswoman for the newspaper, said that 45,000 copies of the paper were printed initially, and the newspaper had been deluged with calls from distributors wanting more. Attorneys have advised the newspaper only to print the names of public figures on the list.

Cabral noted that publishing the list would expose a "double system of justice," revealing that some men who make and enforce laws have been violating the laws against prostitution.

Freedom of Information Digest

Watch. *Fake furs.* Down coats took away lots of fake fur business, but with emergence of *hairy* surface fabrics as one of key stories for winter '81-82, fake furs will have their day. And with quilted real furs appearing in fur market, quilted fake furs sure to follow.

The Fashion Newsletter

Count Your Blessings

- A mother is only 19 and has six kids. She gave birth at age 15 to a singleton; at 17 to twins; and at 19 to triplets. She uses over 250 diapers per week for her six children under the age of 3.
- A Texas mother has a 5-year-old; a 4-year-old; a 3-year-old; 2-year-old triplets; and 1-year-old twins.
- A ten-year-old girl gave birth to twins last year in Indiana. An OB/GYN Professor at Indiana University School of Medicine was quoted as saying ten-year-olds have given birth there before; 11-year-old mothers are almost common, but a multiple birth for a mother that young is extremely unusual.
- A 21-year-old Missouri mother recently gave birth to her third set of twins. Her mother had given birth to six sets of twins and bore 24 children altogether. One of the Missouri mother's sisters had borne five sets of twins, while another sister had four sets. Thirteen more of her mother's children had three sets of twins.
- In the 1920's an Indiana woman gave birth to three sets of triplets and two sets of twins in five years, for a total of 13 children.
- In 1961 a Florida mother at the age of 37 gave birth to her seventh set of twins.
- A Sicilian woman bore 11 sets of twins in 11 years.
- An Ohio mother had seven sets of twins, five sets of triplets and three sets of quads for a total of 41 children.
- A Russian peasant in the 1800's fathered 66 children, all multiples. His first wife had quads four times, twins three times and triplets seven times. His second wife bore triplets seven times and twins once.

NOMOTC Notebook
(Mothers of Twins Club)

Jean Saint-Germaine of Canada wants to build a gigantic pyramid-shaped mausoleum that would have crypts for 200,000 caskets and niches for 1,000,000 urns. At 534 feet high, with its base covering 17 acres, it would be larger than Egypt's Great Pyramid, which is 450 feet high and occupies 13 acres.

Beginning prices would be $3,000 for vaults and $250 for niches. There would be a restaurant on the top floor. Mr. Saint-Germaine doesn't have a building permit, yet, and if unable to build it in the Province of Quebec, may move his $600,000,000 project to Ontario.

Continental Association of Funeral and Memorial Societies Bulletin

Fire Sale

Mr. Starnham Silber lost his favorite pipe while hunting in the Fish Switch Mountains near Pal o' Mine, Montana. A Forest Ranger later recovered the cherished briar (which had Silber's name & address on the shank) and delivered it to him in person, along with a bill for the $429,000 worth of timber it burned down.

The Pipe Smoker's Ephemeris

You might say this is one speedster who really paid out a heavy fine. Apparently not too happy about being arrested for speeding, James McBride, a Dover, Del., tombstone maker, paid his $30.50 with a check etched on a 40 pound slab of granite. The court decided to keep it. Not only as a memorial but because the granite is valued at $225.

•

When Detroit policeman Fraser pulled over a 1974 Plymouth, he thought the car looked familiar. No wonder. The auto turned out to be Fraser's own, stolen from his home just one month before. The driver of the car was absolved, but not the man who had sold it to him.

•

A car driven by Jane Spindler and another by Helen Will collided at a Wausau, Wisc., intersection. After police wrapped up their paper work on the minor crash, the two women drove off in different directions. A block away the two collided at another intersection.

•

A Seattle, Wash., jury found Leroy Anthony Pines guilty of taking $800 at gunpoint from a service station attendant. After delivering its verdict, a juror read a letter on behalf of the entire jury panel praising Judge George T. Mattson on his performance at his first Superior Court trial. While this was going on, the defendant escaped.

The California Highway Patrolman

Tell It to the Judge

The following is a sampler of drivers' explanations on accident reports filed this year with the Middlesex County, N.J., Police Department.

- "Coming home, I drove into the wrong house and collided with a tree I don't have."
- "I had been driving my car for 40 years when I fell asleep at the wheel."
- "The other car collided with mine without giving warning of its intentions."
- "I thought my window was down, but I found it was up when I put my hand through it."
- "The guy was all over the road. I had to swerve a number of times before I hit him."

Police Times

They Build Sand Castles in Malls—for Money

It's beach time near our Florida office and summer's approaching rapidly throughout the rest of the country. One new firm . . . of Del Mar, Calif., specializes in building sand castles—what else?—as special promotions.

A sand "Town of Bethlehem" in a center in St. Louis generated more than $120,000 worth of free media exposure last Christmas.

The promo could be tied to local contests, and tie-in opportunities for mall merchants should be obvious. The firm charges $9,000 plus airfare from San Diego for a 60-ton, 12 to 14-foot-high sand castle. The airfare's for the staff of five that would prepare a promo that size: smaller models can also be built.

National Mall Monitor

Crime

Providence, R.I.—Joseph P. Stevens did a double take as he drove to work on Interstate 195 and spotted his car, stolen the day before, going by on the back of a flatbed trailer.

The car was smashed into a hunk of metal six inches high and 18 feet long.

Stevens, 51, of Fall River, Mass., knew the car was his by the insurance company sticker still fastened to the bumper and the rag hanging from the mangled trunk in the same spot he put it before the car was stolen.

He followed the truck until the driver stopped at a diner and then he called police.

The police arrived to find an intact federal sticker with an identification number that proved the 1971 American model car belonged to Stevens.

They impounded the entire shipment of cars, which they said came from a salvage company in Westport, Mass. The truck driver was released pending further investigation.

•

Ann Arbor, Mich.—Police said yesterday a 66-year-old robbery victim was shot in the head and walked around for three days before going to a hospital with a headache.

"The victim claims he didn't hear a bang, didn't see a gun and didn't realize he had been shot," Ann Arbor police Staff Sergeant Harold Tinsey said yesterday.

The man, a Ypsilanti resident whose name was not released, said he thought he had been hit with a chain Friday as he returned to his car in a shopping center parking lot. A mugger escaped with the man's wallet and $23, Tinsey said.

Doctors at University Hospital found the bullet lodged behind the man's left ear on Sunday night after taking an X-ray.

Funny Funny World

News & Notes

According to Phil Kloer, columnist for the Jacksonville, Florida, *Times-Union,* WABC radio in New York once asked its listeners to "send in a postcard with your name written on it." By the time all the cards were in, 50,000 had "Your Name" scrawled on them.

Contest Newsletter

The Arts

THE HORROR!

When Michael Weldon was growing up in Cleveland in the 1950s his grandfather was manager of a movie theater. Mike got to watch four films every weekend. Quite often they were Grade B, C, or D horror or science-fiction flicks. When Weldon grew up (slightly) and moved to New York he pursued his interest by attending triple-features on 42nd Street. In 1980 his private passion went public—with *Psychotronic,* a 10-page, hand-written tabloid billed as "New York's Weekly TV Movie Guide." A few months later the *Village Voice* hailed *Psychotronic* as "literate, well-researched, and always sent on time," and by mid-1981 it was becoming quite hip in certain film and video circles in Manhattan.

For an average issue Weldon reviews approximately 45 offbeat films scheduled to be aired over network and New York-area television channels the following week. *Psychotronic* is must reading for sci-fi and horror film addicts, whose only source of information on these movies, Weldon says, is "the one-line, sarcastic put-down" found in other publications. Weldon has all the dope on the most obscure films, and while his reviews are witty, they always contain accurate plot summaries and fascinating bits of biographical trivia. In reviewing a film released as *Voyage to the Planet of Prehistoric Women* in 1968, for example, Weldom revealed: 1) The film originated as a serious sci-fi film produced by the Leningrad Studio of Popular Science Films in 1962. It featured Soviet cosmonauts and a giant robot exploring Venus. 2) In 1966 Roger Corman and American International Pictures bought the film, added scenes with Basil Rathbone, and released it as *Voyage to the Prehistoric Planet.* 3) Three years later Corman hired (then-unknown) director Peter Bogdanovich to shoot new footage starring Mamie Van Doren as the leader of a tribe of women who wear clamshell bikinis and worship pterodactyls. When the film was re-re-released, according to Weldon, Bogdanovich hid under the pseudonym Derek Thomas.

"An incredible number of low-budget films get made and forgotten each year," Weldon says. "Some are done purely as tax write-offs and go directly to TV. There's also a large number that open on 42nd Street, play three days, and then show up on the home screen. There's no source of information on these movies." Weldon saves the original advertisements for these films and uses them as illustrations in *Psychotronic*. Weldon's small apartment in New York's East Village is decorated with old posters, including one for *Caged Heat*, directed in the early 1970s by Jonathan Demme, who would win several Best Director awards in 1980 for *Melvin and Howard.*

Weldon has struggled to keep *Psychotronic* going on the money he makes as a clerk in a record store. But he doesn't want to go head-to-head with *TV Guide*, just yet. "I just want to make *Psychotronic* support itself," he says.

PICKIN' 'N' GRINNIN'

The license plates on the van that sits outside Hub Nitchie's house in Greensboro, Maryland, read: "BANJO." For Hub Nitchie, it's more than cute self-promotion. Banjos are a way of life and the reason Hub is, he maintains, "the happiest guy in the world."

The former junior high school librarian has been putting out *Banjo Newsletter* for almost a decade. It began "as a hobby" in 1972, Nitchie says, "a frustrated banjo player looking for company." He looked and he found; *BN* now has over 9,000 subscribers, including several in Eastern Europe and one in the Australian Outback who "lives 1,000 miles from the bank," according to Hub.

At bluegrass concerts and folk festivals, Nitchie is approached by strangers who recognize him from a sketch that accompanies the logo on the cover of each *BN*—a bald man with a walrus mustache playing a banjo. "I wouldn't let my hair grow now even if I wanted to," Nitchie says.

The first issue of *BN* contained "a little gossip and a few tips" on how to play the 5-string banjo, according to Hub. Nitchie knew that there was an audience out there—several banjo books by Pete Seeger and Earl Scruggs have sold 400,000 copies or more, he says—and so he quit his library job to take a crack at full-time publishing. "When you own a mail order business," he explains, "you can live where you want to and keep your own hours."

Hub recalls that when he finished his first issue back in November 1973 he turned to his wife, Nancy, and said, "That's it! I'll never get enough material together to fill another one!" But soon he discovered that "on the contrary, the major difficulty in putting *BN* out every month is finding space for all the things I have." *BN* has grown into a 32-page monthly, neatly laid out, magazine-style, and typeset by him on his own machine. Hub also bought a typewriter that creates musical notations—"banjo tabs"—for songs that *BN* readers might want to learn. Nancy handles the subscription department; and the family cat, the Nitchies contend, licks the stamps. The Nitchies live in an enormous Victorian residence and an almost identical house next door serves as their office.

The publication hardly resembles a newsletter anymore but Hub refuses to change its name. "I like to keep it loose and informal," he explains. A typical issue has an interview with a banjo star (Butch Robins, John Hartford, Carl Jackson), a couple of record reviews, shop talk, and a lot of instruction and songs.

What does Hub Nitchie do to relax? Plays the banjo, of course. Some of it is "work"—people send him banjos to "test." Occasionally a bunch of banjo pickers will come around. Hub will pick up one of his many banjos and jam with them. He keeps an upright bass on hand just in case someone else wants to join in.

Piecing It All Together

Quilts are in vogue. More women are quilting now than any time since the Depression and quilts themselves are being recognized as true art forms. . . .

Part of the appeal of quilts, naturally, is the immediate visual effect of the overall coverlet design. Jonathan Holstein and Gail van der Hoof have done much to open the eyes of the public and the art world to the visual attributes of American pieced quilts. In 1971, they organized the first major museum exhibition of quilts selected solely on the basis of design and color. The art world has always needed to see a consistent body of work before it can give its nod of approval and recognition to an artist or group of artists, and so it was with quilts. The bold, easily identifiable Amish quilts, dating back to the 19th century, especially turned the heads and changed the minds of the art world and the viewing public once they were exhibited together as a portfolio. Now only ten years after the 1971 Whitney Museum show, quilts have been recognized for their palette possibilities and, as a whole, are treated as an up-and-coming mode of artistic expression. . . .

The Goodfellow Review of Crafts

Why *Look Homeward Angel* Was Rejected

The late William Sloane "returned many times over the years" [according to John Ciardi in his introduction to Sloane's *The Craft of Writing,* Norton, 1979] to his mistake of having rejected *LHA*. Sloane read about 200,000 words of Wolfe's huge Ms before giving it up. "It was, I suspect, Wolfe's damnable unreadability that finally moved Bill to ship back that crate of manuscript." After the book came out, Sloane read it "and found in it not one word of the 200,000 he had read." Maxwell Perkins read all of it because he had promised Wolfe's agent to do so and quarried the novel from the manuscript's later pages.

The Thomas Wolfe Review

Moby Tick, a play by Emanuel Peluso, is now in print. It is in the format of the TV panel show *To Tell the Truth* and features three men who all say "Call me Ishmael." The real Ishmael never stands up, but Melvillians should have no trouble in identifying him.

Melville Society Extracts

Q: What is the one sentence that Ishmael addresses to Ahab [in Moby-Dick]?

A: "But at every bite, sir, the thin blades grow smaller and smaller!" (from "The Chase—Third Day"). Except for Ishmael, who, as we learn later from the Epilogue, replaced the Parsee as Ahab's bowsman, the crew of Ahab's boat consists of "tiger-yellow barbarians." Their knowledge of English is presumably quite limited. The complaint that the sharks have chewed up the oars, making them almost useless, is not attributed, but since Ishmael is the only member of the crew with a command of English, we can infer that the sentence is his.

Melville Society Extracts

How America Got "Porched"

The idea of verandahs as living spaces was introduced into the U.S. in a roundabout fashion. In England, during the late 18th and early 19th centuries, the "naturalistic" landscape designers developed the idea of harmonizing architecture with the landscape. Men such as Lancelot "Capability" Brown, Humphry Repton and John Loudon stressed that a house and its gardens should be carefully integrated into nature. This was a radical departure from the formalistic landscaping popular up to that time.

Because of the cool English climate, however, these English designers never developed the idea of the porch or verandah as a way to further integrate house into nature.

It remained for an American, Andrew Jackson Downing, to seize upon the verandah as a logical device for transplanting the English concepts of naturalistic landscaping into American building. Downing's background was as a nursery man and landscape designer. But his desire to construct buildings in harmony with the surrounding landscape soon caused him to embrace architecture as part of his total practice.

Porches and verandahs became a central element in Downing's designs. Along with the practical function of keeping the entrance dry, a broad porch was a "necessary and delightful appendage" in a country with hot summers. "Hence a broad shady verandah suggests ideas

of comfort, and is highly expressive of purpose."

Although porches had been used on some houses in the southern U.S. prior to Downing, it was the impact of Downing's published works that caused "verandah mania" to spread across the country in the mid-19th century. Countless old farmhouses were "modernized" with porches or verandahs, plus that other Downing favorite: the bay window. (The bay window permitted a wider perspective on the landscape and thus allowed more room for viewing artfully constructed "prospects.") And no new home, of course, was complete without its porch, verandah or piazza. . . .

The Old-House Journal

Sherlock Holmes Makes a Dodge Commercial

Sherlock Holmes, as never before, continues to make his presence ubiquitous, not only in criminology, science, and letters, but in commerce and mass communications. Books, films, plays, recordings, television drama, ephemera of all kinds enjoy unprecedented success on the strength of the most dubious association with the Holmes name. None of this has been lost in the creative cells of Madison Avenue. . . .

This brings us to a consideration of a recent and perhaps the most pervasive use of Sherlock Holmes in the history of advertising. Holmes's most publicized case is certain to be immortalised by students of the Holmesian canon as "The Case of the Curiously Seductive Diplomat." In structure it resembles the classic detective story, a case including circumstantial evidence from which Holmes deduces the solution to the crime.

The Dodge Division of Chrysler Corporation began an advertising campaign in 1977 intended to introduce the Dodge Diplomat to the mid-price automobile market. According to Dodge marketing officials, the Diplomat was designed to appeal to young, upwardly striving

professional and managerial people who wish to "step-up" from Ford or Chevrolet ownership. . . .

Dodge's four-week media blitz brought the Diplomat message into 90 percent of all U.S. TV households an average of 10 times. This means most Americans probably saw Holmes and Watson selling Diplomats at least once. Even Basil Rathbone never brought Holmes such notoriety.

The television commercials came in 30- and 60-second versions. The basic version featured Holmes, Watson, and Toby the bloodhound lurking about fog-shrouded Baker Street in search of Ford and Chevy owners who have disappeared without a trace. Holmes deduced that they have been car-snapped by the "fiendishly seductive new car by Dodge."

Print advertisements featured scenes from the television spots, or placed Holmes in special situations unrelated to the basic theme. For example, in an ad appearing in several golf publications, Holmes and golf star Tom Watson were shown examining a Diplomat. "Looks like another great drive, Holmes," said the golfer. "Elementary, my dear Watson," replied the detective.

Perhaps this is all good fun. But we might well remember Holmes's admonition that we see but we do not observe. The seduction theme was worked into the copy for all the ads; and in some of the television spots, Holmes succumbed to what he called "an overwhelming desire" to drive the car, despite Watson's protestations. It was not clear whether Watson feared that Holmes would become "car-napped," presumably abandoning his own Ford or Chevrolet, or would be arrested for the theft of the Diplomat, certainly an embarrassing prospect for the world's greatest detective.

This was not the first time Holmes sullied the law while endeavouring to preserve it, nor was it the most serious crime he has committed. But what is unsettling is that Holmes, a strict rationalist, succumbed to a purely emotional appeal, and blatantly invited the observer to do likewise. Here, the emotions play a decided part in the judgement, there is reasoning from insufficient data, the conclusions are unscientific, invalid, implicitly illegal, and immoral. *The detective now becomes a metaphor for the twentieth century.*

There is something disheartening in the use of Holmes in such ways. Perhaps the oblique solicitors know something others do not of the emergent professional and managerial classes that is not pleasant to admit. The Holmes of the Diplomat campaign is a parody of the Holmes who could serve as a rôle model for the intended audience. But perhaps young managers and professionals no longer care for reason, in the way that it was idealised in the Victorian detective.

—Paul G. Ashdown
The Baker Street Journal

Saving the Boater's Terrace

A sunlit moment at the end of a meal on a restaurant terrace in 1881 crystalized the halcyon days of Renoir's youth. It also immortalized the village of Chatou and the restaurant Fournaise. It was there, under the red and white striped awning, Renoir painted his masterpiece "Luncheon of the Boating Party." Today there is a crusade brewing to save the site before it crumbles into the Seine.

The restaurant, a three-story brick mansion, sits on the isle of Chatou, a 20 minute train ride from Paris. In the 1880's it was a magnet for painters, writers and actresses, with their straw hats and parasols and a passion for boating. Renoir painted an idyllic picture of the summers he spent there. "It was one continuous party," he wrote, "I was always hanging around at Fournaise. I found there as many superb young women as I could possibly wish for."

Letter from Paris

James Thurber philosophized: "No man who has wrestled with a self-adjusting card table can ever be quite the same man he once was."

American Humor

Lucky Underwear

As anyone knows, even if their only acting experience has been as a flower in a kindergarten pageant, getting up on stage before an audience can be a thrilling—but frightening —experience. The actor's life is not an easy one.

And so actors are superstitious people and rely not only on their looks and their charm and their talent but also on rabbits' feet and a whole host of superstitions. If charm should fail, maybe charms will work.

Some stage superstitions are purely personal, but others have been picked up from tradition (like the general belief in our society that breaking a mirror or walking under a ladder or having a black cat cross your path is unlucky) and are treasured by those who have no idea how or why the superstitions originated. . . .

For years I wondered what the explanation was behind the tradition that real flowers, though very welcome after a performance, are unlucky for stage decorations; prop flowers are almost always artificial. Of course real flowers would fade during a run and have to be replaced frequently and artificial ones would not, but that did not explain why actors had such an aversion to the real thing. Then I read in Wilfred Granville's *Dictionary of Theatrical Terms:*

"The reason for this is probably that the petals or leaves, falling from a vase, are apt to cause an artiste to slip on the stage as happened to a leading Shakespearean actor when real leaves were strewn about the stage in *As You Like It.*"

I'm certain that most actors who told me how unlucky real flowers can be never heard of that explanation. Still they clung to their belief.

Granville also notes that to fall on the stage augurs a long run and mentions that the Hamilton Deane version of Bram Stoker's *Dracula* saw a player trip over a doorsill and fall heavily onto the stage. "The play ran for two years in London, and had a New York run." Indeed, the count is still "undead" as a theatrical figure. But the tradition goes much farther back than the end of the last century, when Stoker wrote *Dracula*. Maybe it's connected to the tradition that it is bad luck to wish an actor good luck in a new play. (You have to say, of course, "Break a leg.")

When *Macbeth* failed recently in New York, everyone was reminded that it is an "unlucky" play. It's even "unlucky" to quote from it. Many actors never will; they consider it a jinx, like lilies, peacock feathers and yellow in the set. In fact, all quotations from Shakespeare are banned during rehearsals of plays by lesser dramatists; some lines from *Hamlet* are considered damn near fatal to the success of a production. (At least so I have heard, and do—in part—believe.)

Tradition has it . . . that something going wrong in rehearsal means it will be "all right on the [opening] night," and they worry when things are going too well. They firmly believe a bad dress rehearsal heralds a smash opening night and they are sure that a case of nerves before a performance is a good sign. . . .

They dislike seeing friends backstage before a performance almost as much as they like seeing them backstage after one. They do not approve of peeking out at the house before the curtain goes up or appearing out front during the show when they are not on stage. Backstage, especially in dressing rooms, they forbid anyone to whistle. That's as bad as putting shoes on a table or a hat on a bed.

Many have certain articles of clothing or jewelry which they treasure as amulets or talismans and like to wear on stage if they can. Some think it very bad luck to remove a wedding ring, and if they are not supposed to wear a ring in a play will put tape and makeup over it rather than take it off. Old shoes comfort them.

An actor is going to be nervous if some costume designer who doesn't know the traditions (or can see no way around it because the role is, for instance, Robin Hood or Peter Pan) has dictated he must appear in green. The cast won't feel secure until the last bow, when flowers should be handed over the footlights rather than being delivered backstage. Until opening night has safely passed it is thought unlucky to mention the exact number of lines you have in a show or to read congratulatory telegrams or to write on the mirror in your dressing room. After opening night, it is okay to send out your laundry, a superstition that may derive from simple caution. . . .

One former chorus boy who is still around after a long and successful career as a leading man in the movies still likes to wear red socks on all occasions. Several actresses of note (whom it would be ungentlemanly to name) wear their "lucky" underwear, some of which must be pretty tattered after all these years, on important occasions such as opening nights and "command performances" at the White House. Lucky earrings are not uncommon, and some actors have attempted to hand down the mantle of stardom from one generation to another more or less literally: a Shakespearian star might, on his retirement, give a junior colleague of promise the dagger he wore as Richard III or the sword he wore as Hamlet.

Luciano Pavarotti looks for a bent nail on stage before he feels right singing in opera, a branch of theatre that is full of old superstitions and traditions. There is a story—how reliable I do not know—that for a long time it was a tradition in a certain opera for the tenor to turn his back on the audience (in the theatre this is thought to be bad), go to the back of the stage, and only then turn around and step forward to sing his big aria. Eventually, one tenor found out that it was Caruso who seemed to have set this business and he asked the great singer why he did it. Caruso said it was because he liked to spit before singing that aria.

When one considers all the stories of things that went wrong in opera—the swan boat manipulated offstage too soon ("What time does the next swan leave?" was what Leo Slezak asked the stunned audience), the pillars that fell too soon (cutting off Samson's big scene), the fat *diva* who bounced back up over the parapet after supposedly jumping to her death in *Tosca,* and on and on—one can hardly blame opera singers for seeking confidence and protection through good-luck charms and such. They may not be able to wear their battered "lucky" old hat (as John Ford did when directing films) but they can carry "lucky" coins somewhere, even if there are no pockets in tights.

Dancers are equally superstitious. Any chorus girl knows that if you spill powder while you are in the dressing room it is a good idea to do a little dance on it. And anyone who knows ballet will tell you to spit in your shoes before a performance.

For some reason, expectoration is a fairly common element in stage superstition. If you want to encourage an actor, in a play or at an audition, you can spit on either side of him. If anyone sprays you with spittle on stage by accident, don't wipe it off until the curtain falls. If anyone whistles in your dressing room, go outside, turn around three times, and spit before re-entering.

You can't be too careful.

I wonder how many of the old theatrical superstitions, just a few of which I have had space to mention, remain. I wonder how they are being adopted or adapted in the new media such as cinema and television.

Finally, some helpful advice: never play the part of an invalid if you can possibly avoid it. Moliere did in his own play and died, practically on stage!

—Leonard R. N. Ashley
Dramatics' Curtain

When D. W. Griffith was filming *The Birth of a Nation,* he ran out of money moments before he was to shoot the ride of the Klan, the highlight of the picture. He had planned to use scores of horsemen in the scene, but Griffith didn't have enough to pay one of them.

As he pondered his predicament, the director noticed up the road a crowd of cowboy extras, who were working on another picture. He had his cameramen set up his equipment. Then he signaled to an assistant, who began to shout: "Lunch! Come and get it, everybody!"

Whooping it up, the extras galloped their horses at breakneck speed past the camera to the studio commissary. The scene that resulted was acclaimed for its realism and elevated Griffith to the top stratum of Hollywood directors.

Funny Funny World

Ghostly TV Critic

Though Heinz Ehlert died 18 years ago, he is still monitoring his widow Eleonore's TV watching. If he objects to a program, Eleonore reports, the TV set is supernormally turned off. Psychic researcher Hans Bender, who visited Eleonore's home in Solingen, West Germany, to investigate the phenomenon, could not explain it. "It's a strange power that hates popular music," he reported.

Parapsychology Review

More gloomy statistics: It has just been revealed that the United States has only a five year reserve of guest hosts for talk shows.

Orben's Current Comedy

Laurel & Hardy's First Film

Stan Laurel considered "Putting Pants on Philip" (released on Dec. 3, 1927) as their first film as a duo, although it was the 13th film in which both of the boys appeared. But Roach Studios says that the first film in the "Laurel & Hardy Series" was *Should Married Men Go Home,* released in 1928. . . .

The Intra-Tent Journal

Nasty Corner will provide occasional relief from all the praise and celebration in *The Real Art Letter;* however, its vituperations will never be leveled at a struggling artist, no matter how distasteful the work. No, the spleen venting will be directed strictly at those artists who have benefited the most in acclaim and money for the least amount of sensitivity, talent, or hard work. This month's award goes to Jasper Johns, creator of the painting *Three Flags,* which was bought in 1979 by New York's Whitney Museum for $1 million. I believe this is still the highest price paid for a piece of artwork by a living artist.

The painting in question is a three-tiered representation of American flags (the forty-eight star variety, since *Three Flags* was painted in 1958). The op art effect is interesting enough—but $1 million?! Come on. I wouldn't mind so much if the body of Johns' work were noteworthy in its entirety, and they just happened to single out this rather weak piece. Sort of like giving the Oscar to Liz Taylor for *Butterfield 8.* Sadly, my overall impression of Johns' career, based on a retrospective of his I saw at the Pompidou Center in Paris in 1978, is that *Three Flags* may be the high point aesthetically as well as financially.

To give the artist every benefit of the doubt, maybe it was the out-of-the-way exhibit space they gave the Johns show and not the comparison with the permanent exhibit that put his work at such a disadvantage. Whatever it was, the result for me was the repetitive, monotonous exercise viewing this type of "formula art" usually is. Besides flags, Johns' other obsession is with bull's-eyes. It's almost as if he were inviting critics to make a target of him; but few of us are taking him up on it. Mind you, this isn't imagery from one period of his career to be replaced constantly by new visions. Johns has painted virtually the same pictures over and over again for twenty years. Only the most complex compositions of color schemes could still intrigue after this kind of repetition.

It's heartening to see a living artist receive the kind of commendation a $1 million price tag connotes; the disappointment is in the continued glorification of the least challenging, least committed school of art.

The Real Art Letter

Why Christopher Reeve Is a More Satisfying Superman then George Reeves

Remember the Superman comics? Of course that's the real Superman, isn't it? Remember how in the comics Superman was incredibly innocent? Remember the time a bunch of thugs held someone hostage and got Superman to promise he'd give them anything they asked for? And they asked for, in true thug fashion, the biggest hunk of "ice" in the world, and Superman brought them an iceberg? Remember that then they stamped their feet and demanded the biggest "rock" in the world and Supe brought them a boulder? Then they threw tantrums, yelled at our hero, called him stupid and demanded the biggest diamond in the world, and Superman made them a baseball field. That was the true Superman we knew and loved.

How about George Reeves? Wasn't he satisfying? Of course he was. It didn't really matter that his muscles were padding. It didn't really matter that those of old movies and TV shows were in black and white and we were used to red and blue. It didn't really matter that George was fair haired and we knew he should have black hair with one curl down his forehead. He did all the things we wanted him to do. He stood with hands on hips and let bullets bounce off his chest. He bent guns, rifles, and crowbars like rubber. He knocked thugs' heads together with regularity. And he always arrived in the knick of time to save Lois and Jimmy from death's clutches.

So where did George fail as Superman? In the way he played Clark Kent. George's Clark was a competent, superior, almost smart guy type, if you think about it. Remember how Lois always chased Superman and Clark would be standing in the corner leaning nonchalantly against the building, tongue in cheek, lording it over Lois that he beat her to the story? Remember what a superior creature he was when he talked to Lois and Jimmy and how he'd look at us out of the corner of his eye as he feigned a swoon so that we'd know he was putting one over on them. Remember how, even as Superman, he always eluded Lois with a chuckle that never failed to exasperate her? Remember how you knew he liked Lois, but never could be sure if he loved her? George Reeves, you see, was a satisfying Superman, but he failed at portraying Clark Kent! And that's where Christopher Reeve succeeds.

Chris' Clark Kent is pure innocence and incompetence. He is a 25 year old with the puppy love of a 12 year old as far as Lois is concerned. He lets her get the scoops because he loves her blindly. He can't even see where he's going when she is around. He steps in front of cars in traffic (naturally endangering the cars more than himself) and he becomes so lost in his love for her that the world faces total destruction while he satisfies his deepest yearnings to hold Lois in his arms and give up all his powers for her.

Chris Reeve as Clark Kent stumbles and bumbles. He stammers and blushes around Lois. He closes his thumb in an orange juice squeezer and trips over his own feet. He plays Clark so well that his own portrayal traps him when, in the honeymoon cottage, he trips over the bearskin rug landing with his hand in the fire. No amount of explaining will persuade Lois that he isn't Superman.

How does he act when Lois discovers his secret? Is he superior and glib? Does he rise up with a wise answer, as George would have, to put Lois in her place? No, he tears at our hearts by becoming the guilty little boy who's caught in his own lie, speechless with his love for Lois. He shows his anguish, and our hearts skip a beat. He tells Lois, "I've wanted to talk to you about him," meaning Clark, and she says, "But he is you." And he is, you see. Even as Superman he is Clark Kent where Lois is concerned. Chris Reeve captures our hearts and imagination as George never did.

Chris Reeve brings alive our childhood fantasies of Superman in two ways. He looks the way we want Superman to look, with the black curl on his forehead and the deep blue eyes. The new Superman movies are in vivid color so we see him dressed in red and blue the way we want to see Superman, not in the shades of grey we saw George Reeves in. His muscles

are real (didn't it thrill us to hear that he worked out till he dropped from exhaustion to acquire those muscles so he wouldn't have to disappoint Superman fans with padding), and to keep the illusion pure, out of costume with his hair undyed he doesn't look a bit like our hero so he's preserved for us exclusively on the screen. Second, and most important, he doesn't try to be realistic, up-to-date or sophisticated in any way. He remains the comic-strip character, innocent, loving, trusting, and pure. And in so doing he becomes the real Superman to us.

—A. I. Seret
Movie Trends

When Charlotte Henry, the star of Paramount's 1933 *Alice,* died recently, *Time* magazine in its obituary remembered that "she played Alice to Cary Grant's Mock Turtle, Gary Cooper's White Knight and W. C. Fields' Humpty Dumpty." This film remains the best of the *Alice* motion pictures. . . . A new *Alice* produced in Poland and France with mainly French actors arrived a year ago in England, and may have sneaked across the Atlantic. It's an up-to-date version with an Alice "with blonde hair and fishnet tights and stiletto heels who dances on a table among champagne glasses." The *Daily Mail* didn't think much of it. . . .

Knight Letter

A writer at MGM came to executive producer Louis B. Mayer for a raise in pay.

"And why should I give you a raise?" the studio chief wanted to know.

"Because I am underpaid."

"Do you have any idea how many people in this organization are overpaid?" L.B. demanded.

"Quite a lot, I imagine," the other conjectured.

"A helluva lot," Mayer assured him. "And that's why some people like you have to be underpaid," he added, bringing the discussion to an end. "Fair is fair."

Stunned by this logic, the writer retreated, to pursue the matter another day.

Funny Funny World

Tarzan Finds a Son (1939)

In the original print of MGM's fourth Tarzan adventure, Jane died. Before it was released Edgar Rice Burroughs said they had no right to kill off his character. The ending was re-filmed and Maureen O'Sullivan was talked into (paid more) doing two more entries. . . . Screenplay by Cyril Hume *(Forbidden Planet)*. Directed by Richard Thorpe *(Jailhouse Rock)*.

•

BEWARE! The Blob (1972) ("Son of Blob")

This sequel to the popular 1958 movie was recently re-released by some smart ass as "The Movie J.R. Shot!" That's because the world-famous Larry Hagman directed this silly comedy with guest star victims of the red man-eating mass of protoplasm. Godfrey Cambridge is the first to go (he drinks some of it and is consumed from within). Carol Lynley, Shelly Berman, Burgess Meredith and Hagman himself all show up briefly as blob food. Robert Walker Jr. and Gwynee Gilford are the survivors. Producer Jack Harris also presented the original *Blob* with Steve McQueen.

•

The Thing with Two Heads (1972)

The ultimate blaxploitation horror movie, not to be confused with the previous year's all-white *Incredible Two-Headed Transplant* (starring Bruce Dern). Both are from A.I.P. This, believe it or not, features star Ray Milland as a racist brain surgeon with terminal cancer. He arranges to have his head transplanted onto the healthy body of a volunteer convict from Death Row. Milland first creates a two-head gorilla (created by Rick Baker). When he awakens from his operation he finds his head on Rosey Grier's body. You've got to see him (them) running around, riding a motorcycle, yelling at each other and punching each other in the face. . . .

•

Navy vs. the Night Monsters

We've got some *bad* ones this week but this release is the top must-see feature. The casting director deserves an award. Blonde bombshell Mamie Van Doren (real name—Joan Olander) stars with suave Anthony Eisley. Pamela Mason was the 60's TV Dodge Girl. Bill Gray was

Bud on *Father Knows Best*. They're all at the South Pole but it's hot! Acid-bleeding, walking plants are after the cast! The cast is after Mamie! (Mamie now runs an antique shop in California. . . .)

•

The Fakers (1970)

Bikers, neo-Nazis and the Mafia in Las Vegas all come together under the sledgehammer direction of the notorious Al Adamson. It became one of Al's 5 big drive-in releases in '70. Broderick "Highway Patrol" Crawford stars with fellow over-the-hill actors Kenty Taylor, Scott Brady and Adamson regular, John Carradine. Photographed by Laslo Kovacs in Utah. . . .

Psychotronic

No Werewolf Classic

I was watching that masterpiece of French New Wave cinema, *Abbott and Costello Meet Frankenstein,* for maybe the hundredth time the other afternoon (Costello's powerful performance reveals new depths of metaphor with each viewing), and it occurred to me that out of Universal's gallery of those monsters we've all grown up with, the Wolf Man was just about the only one who was created for the films—the others (Dracula, Frankenstein's monster, the

Invisible Man) having crept onto the screen from the pages of classic works of fiction.

The point is that there hasn't been a "classic" werewolf novel that has achieved the stature of *Dracula* in the public's imagination to the extent that Dracula and vampire are virtually synonymous by the time a kid is two years old. Lord knows how many times Dracula has flashed his toothy smile on film, and his innumerable reappearances in novels, short stories and comic books probably hold the all-time record for pastiches. *Dracula* seems inevitably to be the standard of comparison for every vampire novel written since; it's either "a gooseflesh chiller in the tradition of. . ." or else "a terrifying new departure from the tradition of. . ." Pretty impressive when you remember that Bram Stoker's Dracula only appeared in one novel, and that some eighty-five years ago.

It does seem curious that there has not been a werewolf novel that has achieved similar dominance within this particular subgenre—no leader of the pack, if you will. Both the vampire and the werewolf are creatures hallowed by centuries of legend and folk traditions, as opposed to being mere creations of some deadline-haunted novelist's imagination. Both creatures have the potential to inspire sympathy as well as fear, for they are themselves victims of the curse that has robbed them of their humanity and made them objects of dread—children of the night who cannot control their compulsive need to feed upon human flesh and blood. Romantic, mysterious, terrifying—their murderous assaults evoke repressed sexual fantasies, creating the underlying eroticism essential to horror fiction. . . .

—Karl Edward Wagner
Fantasy Newsletter

awareness of temporality engenders the ethical phase (he will not kill himself because of his religious belief), which in turn is abandoned and the religious stage emerges (after fighting on board ship, he returns to Elsinore to avenge his father). After going through these three phases, Hamlet's religious melancholia is resolved when he is capable of accepting his father's ghost as a divine messenger after reading Claudius's treacherous letter which substantiates his discovery at the mouse trap scene. Then the Kierkegaardian existential leap into faith is made and eventually culminates in a providential choice of the "moral" act in a Christian existential tragic sense compounded by Unamuno (awareness of the greatness of man yet "quintessence of dust").

The Shakespeare Newsletter

Hamlet and Christian Existentialism

Shaakeh S. Agajanian of the State University of New York at Plattsburgh writes that the cause of Hamlet's procrastination and irresolution is a complex kind of religious melancholia analyzed by Kierkegaard as Aesthetic Melancholy, Romantic Sadness, and Feelings of Sinfulness. These correspond with three stages in an individual's life: aesthetic, ethical and religious. After the collapse of the hedonistic first stage (Hamlet's love for Ophelia), the

Eight Songs Recorded by Elvis Presley *and* Bob Dylan

1. "Don't Think Twice, It's Alright"
2. "Tomorrow's a Long Time"
3. "That's All Right Mama"
4. "Early Mornin' Rain"
5. "A Fool such as I"
6. "Blue Moon"
7. "Let it Be Me"
8. "Can't Help Falling in Love."

Elvis Now

Film Jargon

Film criticism has relied more and more on French phrases as the quality of movies has decreased. The more the economics of the medium has forced the industry toward the box office hype of gratuitous violence, the more the movie critics rely on arcane philosophic thought based on the French theorists. J. Hoberman, writing about the latest Hollywood masterpiece, *Dressed To Kill* ("Dazzling"), tried to place the movie in the context of film art a la Hilton Kramer. The effect is bathetic, since the subject hardly justifies the effort. Note the casual references to works that anyone who is anyone would recognize—to say nothing of the foreign words. "Mise-en-scene, oeuvre, auteur" all raise the level of discussion above the level of Angie Dickinson's vagina, which is, after all, the central attention of the film:

"There should be no doubt that De Palma is auteur. Consider what he managed to do with the telekinetic claptrap of *The Fury.* Though *Home Movies* doesn't work, its casting and situational cross-references to *Dressed To Kill* make it a weightier film in the context of De Palma's oeuvre." In another part of this Voice essay, Hoberman writes of a certain scene:

"Beginning as a study of the sex life of a museum [sic], it slugs you with the psychopathology of everydaylife, takes on the oneiric hide-and-seek symbolism of Max Klinger's *Story of a Glove,* then reaches an outrageous climax . . . De Palma's mise-en-scene among the works of art is hilariously smutty." Whereas pretentious art criticism is designed to make art inaccessible, mannered film criticism is calculated to give stature to a business. To compensate for the guilt of dealing with pure entertainment, film critics tend to invest *all* films with significance beyond belief. Every Maria Montez-Jon Hall jungle movie is given the full intellectual treatment, as if it were Bergman's *Seventh Seal.* Thus all movies become works of art, and the medium itself becomes a valid object of aesthetic study as opposed to mere sociological analysis.

Robin Wood, writing in Film Comment, analyzes *Once Upon a Honeymoon,* a Ginger Rogers and Cary Grant film.

"The whole passage may be taken as epitomizing the film's characteristic rapid alternation and juxtaposition of the comic and the appalling, its audacious and disconcerting mixing of modes.

Specifically, two conventions are here set against one another. The imminent assassination of Borelski is clearly signposted . . . and its mechanism hinted at, arousing suspense and demonstrating the ruthlessness of the Nazis, ready to sacrifice their own men as means to an end; yet the young Nazi is depicted as both comic and touching, the sort of character who won't come to much harm—certainly won't meet an abrupt, violent and bloody death. His 'Heil Hitler' is funny, pathetic, and horrible all at the same time, the precise point where the two conventions operating coalesce."

Remember, this is a Cary Grant-Ginger Rogers movie! A movie, that, according to Wood, "at its exact midpoint, brings its two popular stars right to the verge of surgical sterilization," whatever that means. . . .

Nothing escapes this type of over-intellectualizing when it comes to movies. I can provide an entire bibliography of scholarly analyses of The Three Stooges, Fay Wray, William Bendix and Laurel and Hardy!. . . .

The Cultural Watchdog

Moby-Dick and Vietnam

Like other great works of literature *Moby-Dick* is a symbolic matrix in which readers of different times discover different meanings. During the late 1960s it was impossible to teach the book in an American college without recognizing analogies between the situation of the *Pequod* and our government's relentless prosecution of the Vietnam War. Both seemed to be animated by a concept of manifest destiny, a fatalistic and potentially self-destructive aggressiveness. Both also embodied the racial bias whereby white Americans used their "brains" to organize non-whites to accomplish their physical ends. Like the American presidents who directed the war, Ahab seemed impervious to criticism, and under the sway of an irrational and irresistible compulsion. But Ahab was endowed with an intellectual and emotional depth of insight our presidents lacked. Nonetheless, they tended to project all evil on to a single Enemy—the hated whale for them being Communism. As for opposition to Ahab's doomed purpose, it was expressed only by Starbuck and Ishmael. (All the others were under the sway of the magnetic doubloon and Ahab's charismatic leadership.) Starbuck's inability to break the law (by using the musket) in order to save the ship's company illustrates "the incompetence of mere unaided virtue." Ishmael's mode is comparable to the opposition of the dropout culture of the sixties and its emphasis on private salvation. In the case of opposition to the war, too, no organized movement aimed at changing the underlying structure of power emerged. Our individualistic responses to power are politically ineffectual, and they tend, as in *Moby-Dick,* to lend credence to an apocalyptic view of the nation's destiny.

—Leo Marx
Melville Society Extracts

Golden Days of Radio

Did it ever occur to anyone if Edgar Bergan ever made a mistake and used Charlie McCarthy's voice when Bergan was supposed to be speaking and vice versa? He had Charlie's lines typed in red and his in black, making it almost impossible for him to forget to change his voice.

•

In 1946, Wally Maher complained that his directors cast him only as an evil character, playing bad guys on the *Suspense* show. In three years, he killed 31 persons, embezzled 5 million dollars, was killed 18 times himself, and served 1000 years in prison. Some record!

•

Personal Quirks: Sammy Kaye hated mustaches and wouldn't permit any member of his swing-and-sway orchestra to grow one.

•

It was estimated that in eleven years Prof. Quiz gave away $200,000. Remember, this was between 1937 and 1948.

•

Cecil B. DeMille had quite a problem in how high to place a microphone head. It came about on the *Lux Theater* production of "Jane Eyre," starring Helen Hayes and Bob Montgomery: Helen Hayes stood 5′ 1″ while Bob stood one foot taller.

Hello Again

Nabokov in Wonderland

Vladimir Nabokov's mature works are rather Carrollian in their word-play, their mirroring, their play with fantasy. It is therefore not surprising that at the start of his career he translated *Alice's Adventures in Wonderland* into Russian. Some of the changes he made while translating simply give *Wonderland* a Russian setting (1000 roubles instead of 100 pounds) or capture the spirit of Carroll's wordplay (instead of literally translating, say, "reeling" and "writhing"). But other changes stray farther from the original and hint at Nabokov's own later style and vision.

In general, while not radically altering *Wonderland,* Nabokov harries the boundaries between the fantastic and the realistic, making the two harder to distinguish and hinting that reality is itself rather fantastic. He allows alliteration, for instance, to extend to repetition of additional sounds within words and to creep out of the verse and dialogue and into the narrative text. He reduces our reliance on Alice's perspective, on the perspective of the representative of the "real" world, so that it is harder to judge the fantasticality of Wonderland. Similarly, he eliminates many of the specifications of Alice's height, which in the original help to orient us to how different Wonderland is from the "real" world. He also disorders numerical sequence and relates otherwise unrelated numbers, as if to suggest that the absolutes of cause and effect, of logical progression, of numerical sequence, are no longer absolute, and reality has become relative. In Nabokov's *Wonderland,* fantasy is kept less firmly in its place as something to be carefully differentiated from and excluded from reality, as something that creatures from reality can assault and then retreat from with impunity. . . .

—Beverly Lyon Clark
The Knight Letter

I'm against video tape recorders. I just don't believe God intended us to watch the Super Bowl and the third game of the World Series on the same day.

Orben's Current Comedy

—Louis Bodnar Jr.
Newsboy
(Horatio Alger Society)

Music

Composer-conducter Gustav Mahler, for ten years the director of the Imperial Opera in Vienna, was an irascible and unpopular eccentric, who ruled with an iron hand. Few dared to criticize him openly, however, because it was recognized that he alone had raised the Imperial Opera to international stature.

Mahler was present at almost every performance. When he wasn't conducting, he would lean over the rail of his box and hiss at those who came in after the curtain had gone up. One night, he was hissing at his loudest when the emperor Franz Josef made his entrance. The appearance of royalty did not silence Mahler.

For some moments, a confrontation seemed inevitable. Then the emperor looked up and recognized the director.

"Oh, it's Mahler," he said, and he waved a hand to his fellow autocrat and proceeded to his seat, without further comment.

•

A young composer brought his latest composition to Igor Stravinsky to seek his opinion.

"This music is beautiful and new," said the Russian-born master, who was not usually generous with his praise.

The other was overjoyed.

"However," added Stravinsky soberly, "the part that is beautiful is not new, and the part that is new is not beautiful."

Funny Funny World

Serious Stuff

I. F. SMITH

A few years ago *The Washington Post* called *Privacy Journal* "the most talked-about Washington newsletter since *I. F. Stone's Weekly*." A few weeks later *The New Yorker* said that *PJ* was "the most interesting publication to come out of the capital since [you guessed it] I. F. Stone's walloping *Weekly*." Apparently I. F. Stone concurred. He visited *PJ* editor Robert Ellis Smith in his office—a room over his garage seven blocks from Capitol Hill—and dubbed him "I. F. Smith."

High praise indeed for the editor of "An Independent Monthly on Privacy in a Computer Age," founded less than 10 years ago. Smith graduated from Harvard in 1962, edited the *Southern Courier* weekly for a while, became a lawyer, and put out a newsletter for the American Civil Liberties Union until it "ran out of money. I decided I could do it better on my own." In 1974 he withdrew $1,000 from his savings account and *Privacy Journal* was born. *PJ* is an eight-page, sparsely illustrated monthly made up of somewhat technical but entirely readable articles on data banks, lie detector tests, state and federal privacy laws, and the possible abuses of cable television. One of *PJ's* regular writers is a Dr. Veggie Legume, "the *nom de plume* of a well-known mole placed in the heart of the federal government."

Smith has spotted the beginnings of consumer rebellion against invasion-by-computer. "It's hard to get people riled up about a trend," he explains. "It's all so gradual. You've got to give up some privacy, after all, to get some benefits. You tell your Social Security number, you tell your age for your driver's license because you don't want to hold up the line arguing. People have a basic inclination to be open. And people don't know what's being done with the information. But people are going to get more aware. They'll begin to shop around for, say, the bank that requires the least information from them for a loan. . . ."

Like I. F. Stone, Smith gathers most of his material from very public sources—from material published by the government and business. Smith attends computer conventions and readers send him tips. He enjoys being self-employed. "Every journalist dreams of putting out his own publication," he says. "The capital required to start or buy a newspaper is impossible, but the capital required for a newsletter is quite modest."

The two thousand subscribers to *PJ,* he says, are about equally divided among business people, lawyers involved in civil liberties and privacy cases, and citizens who've felt "invaded" themselves. Perhaps relatively few Americans have really suffered, so far; but nearly everyone, Smith believes, is a potential victim.

HOME FINISHINGS

"We went to a party in Brooklyn and fell in with brownstones," says Clem Labine. "I thought a stone house was a sensible purchase—sturdy, low maintenance and all that. Restoration is like opening door after door after door. Who knows where it all will lead?" For Clem Labine it led to *The Old-House Journal,* an amiable, extremely attractive, and very successful monthly for those who love (and live in) what he refers to as "antique houses."

This was not exactly what Labine had in mind when he and his wife purchased a row house, built around 1880, near Prospect Park in Brooklyn for $25,000 in 1967. After five years of plastering, patching, stripping, and painting, the Labines had a delightful new/old house and the notion that they knew almost all there was to know about such projects. Labine, who has worked as an engineer, editor, and advertising salesman, quit his job at McGraw-Hill in November 1972 to try to get together *The Old-House Journal.* (Labine is not related to the Brooklyn Dodgers pitcher of the same name. With his dark mustache the baseball pitcher he resembles most is Rollie Fingers.)

"I literally sat down at a drawing board and tried to figure out what an old-house journal looked like," Labine recalls. He found his old mechanical-drawing set in his attic and withdrew nearly all of his $4,000 in savings. When the first issue of *OHJ* came out in October 1973 it had three paid subscribers, according to Labine—his mother and two of her friends. To attract interest he distributed thousands of free copies at flea markets. Eight years later its circulation had climbed to 50,000 and Labine was making a living out of it.

For the first several years *OHJ* was published out of the Labines' basement. Clem did the very adequate typesetting himself on his typewriter. His wife, Claire, an Emmy Award–winning co-writer and co-producer of the television soap opera *Ryan's Hope,* helped in the planning stages and wrote an *OHJ* column for a couple of years. But eventually Labine hired a staff and *OHJ* outgrew the basement; it moved, as you would expect, into a rehabilitated brownstone around the corner. This means, Labine says, "I can still walk to work!" Several employees—editors and circulation people—help him get *OHJ* out each month.

Along with *The Chocolate News, The Old-House Journal* is one of the most attractive "amateur" publications in America. It is printed on cream-colored stock with many line drawings and photographs scattered throughout. Labine describes the contents of *OHJ* this way: "We specialize in how-to information for people who own houses built before 1920. We are devoted to restoration and sensitive rehabilitation, as opposed to remodeling—or as we call it, 're-muddling.' " There are tips on how to repair cracks or where to find Victorian wallpaper to cover them up. Other topics covered recently include Turn-of-the-Century Chintz, Refinishing Floors, Dumbwaiter Design.

Typical subscribers, according to Labine, are young couples "who have just purchased their first old house because they loved its character—but find themselves a bit overwhelmed by the sagging beams and the cracking plaster. They had visions of gracious living in their elegant restored parlor and hadn't really counted on having to cope with antiquated plumbing and a wheezing heating plant. So the job of *OHJ* is to give them lots of practical, helpful information, plus a bit of inspiration, through case histories, to prove that it *can* be done!"

The Tumbleweed (or Russian thistle), probably the most successful and widespread wild plant in the world, is being studied at the University of Arizona, Tucson, Arizona, as the principal ingredient in burnable "tumblelogs" for your fireplace. The project, supported by the U.S. Department of Energy, may result in large commercial plantations of the weed for that purpose. The researchers are also developing harvesting equipment and methods and a mini-processing plant to make the fireplace logs.

Solar Energy Digest

All Points Bulletin

A study of employees who steal from their employers show that they have other habits that investigators can check with employment records. In general they take long lunch breaks, are noted for sloppy work, are known to use drugs or drink on the job, often come late and leave early and use up sick leave even when not ill. These traits should serve as warning to employers that if internal theft begins—they are likely suspects.

Police Times

The road to riches is lined with I.R.S. toll booths.

Orben's Current Comedy

I haven't been feeling well. I think I'm suffering from the 24-hour news.

Orben's Current Comedy

Collector-Investors

Illustrations remain a good investment for beginning collectors . . . at any price level. Some originals bring five and six figures such as Rockwell, Remington and Leyendecker, while works by lesser-known artists range from $2,000-$7,000. One dealer told THE GRAY LETTER a wise $2,000 investment can be expected to double in value in the next few years.

Look for dramatic composition and action . . . in illustrations, as well as attention to detail. Collect specific illustration categories and learn which artists represent them best, such as family, pictorial magazines (The Saturday Evening Post); fashion, cosmetics magazines (Ladies Home Journal); general marine covers; and western covers.

•

Now may be a good time to buy jewelry made in the 1940s and 50s . . . Francois Curiel predicts this area will be hot in 10 years, as collectors interested in Art Nouveau and Art Deco jewelry find less and less in that area available. "Forties and fifties jewelry will be a period in the future, very definitely. It's starting on that road now," says Peter Schaffer, of New York's A La Vieille Russie.

The Gray Letter

What's Mine is *Yours*

Will solar save our nation from being victimized by OMEC? OMEC is a mineral cartel, not yet formed but almost sure to be, which would set the price of imported metals in the same way as OPEC now does with oil.

This Organization of Mineral Exporting Countries would find the United States very vulnerable because we have to import 22 of the 27 metal ores considered vital to our economy from foreign countries, many of which are just waiting to get even with us for actual or fancied wrongs.

So it behooves us to start planning without delay to find substitutes for these metals or to find deposits of them in our own country.

The main problems with the latter approach are that such deposits, if found, are likely to be of low grade, requiring much energy to extract, and be located in areas far removed from conventional power sources.

But sunshine is everywhere and we now have the technology to harness it to provide the power needed for mining and refining these ores.

The Bureau of Mines, Department of the Interior, has information on more than 135,000 U.S. mineral locations—including active and abandoned mines, geothermal wells, smelters, and refineries—which is stored in the Bureau of Mines Mineral Industry Location System (MILS).

For each mineral location, MILS includes its name, map coordinates, mineral commodity, type of operation, and other relevant data. This information is available for a variety of government and private purposes, including mineral exploration. . . .

So, if your editor was 50 years younger, we would be pestering the Bureau of Mines to find out where the metals of our choice were located and what power and other problems would be encountered in mining them. Then we would try to interest investors in forming a company or companies to extract the metals, using the latest solar technology for power if appropriate.

There can be no doubt that a market exists for these metals and at a good price, or that our government would not encourage their mining, so what are you young lads and lassies waiting for? Reach out and open the golden door of opportunity!

Solar Energy Digest

Paint Pointers

Many people ask, "What color should I paint my house?" The following guide should help you find color combinations that are historically appropriate and suitable for your taste.

Pre-1800 houses were painted whatever colors were obtainable. White paint was not available in a pre-mixed form before the 19th century, but white lead was used to make white paint on site from early colonial days. Those people who could not afford or did not have access to white lead used whatever natural pigments they could (when they didn't simply leave their clapboards to weather) such as rust which made "spanish brown" and "indian red."

Between 1800 and 1840, houses were mostly painted in whites and creams with green shutters. The classical revivial styles were most

popular partly because Thomas Jefferson fostered them, thinking them best suited to the democratic ideals of the young American republic. After 1840, Andrew Jackson Downing helped start a fashion for romantic Gothic and Italian style cottages that were better painted in soft stone and field colors than in the more severe colors of the classical revival styles.

The 1860's and 1870's introduced more imposing formal styles like Second Empire, Renaissance Revival and Italianate. These larger houses were suited for their role in the expanding cities in which they were built. They were sometimes painted in pale colors to suggest the formality of stone palaces, but more often they were painted in dark greens and reds suggestive of the masonry and brick buildings they emulated. These darker colors were used by architects such as James Renwick, who designed some of the buildings in one of America's first national museum complexes: The Smithsonian Institution in Washington, D.C.

By the 1800's and 1890's, colors were not only dark but vivid and plentiful. Queen Anne and Stick styles both boasted a wealth of detail and color to heighten the effect of all those balusters, shingles, porches and towers. And these colors became more vivid as the century wore on. Initially they were predominantly painted in earth tones of green and rust, reminiscent of the natural pigments used in the glazes that distinguished Craftsman style Rookwood pottery. Later the hues were increasingly bright and joyously fanciful, similar to the luminous colors used by Tiffany in his art glass.

The turn of the century witnessed a colonial revivial that brought back plain white and creams. The many-colored late Victorian Queen Anne houses were masked in white, as were houses of every other earlier style, whether they were built in a colonial revivial style or not. The movement from pale to dark and back to pale had come full circle.

Choose by Style

When selecting colors, the best place to start is with your house's style. If you choose colors that were initially intended for the style, you will show it in its best light. Even if your house was built years after its style was at its peak, (a Greek Revival built in 1870, for example), you should still paint your house in the colors suitable for that style.

The Old-House Journal

An angry man in Great Falls, Mt., was arrested when he attacked an aide to right-wing-type GOP Rep. Ron Marlenee. The weapon used was a copy of the liberal New Republic.

Washington Crap Report

Two Catholic nuns in Denver, Co., spend their days building pine caskets in an effort to help the poor fight the high cost of dying. They make their coffins at the Denver Catholic Work House, which offers hospitality to the homeless and food to the hungry. They turn out about a dozen coffins a month, and hope to make enough money selling them to help pay the rent. As members of the Sisters of Loretto, they took vows of poverty before joining, and have no plans to expand into the construction business.

Continental Association of Funeral and Memorial Societies Bulletin

---

RCA says it has produced a system that will automatically adjust, by radar, a car's speed to meet traffic conditions. The system has been made to hook up with cruise controls on cars and, when an auto so equipped comes up behind a slower vehicle, it automatically slows down. It is also designed to resume its speed once the slow auto is out of the way.

The California Highway Patrolman

Parker Brothers print about the same amount of play money each year for their Monopoly games as the U.S. government prints for us to use.

Washington Crap Report

Soldiers for Peace is Taylor Morris' idea for easing the escalating arms tensions in the world. The ultimate exercise in networking would be for 100,000 young Russians to exchange places with 100,000 young Americans. Their personal relationships would spread and immediately relax tensions. Morris' proposal strikes at the heart of the world's military problems. Solutions lie in bypassing the governments and allowing people to deal with one another, unencumbered by political baggage. Contact: Taylor Morris, % Soldiers for Peace, 46 Union St., Peterborough, NH 03458, USA.

●

The concept of a volunteer economy that would eliminate the need for work for pay is being explored by Ernest Mann (715 E. 14th St., Minneapolis, Mn. 55404, USA). He believes there are many people ready and willing to operate such an economy but feels lack of communication hampers people from realizing that others are interested.

●

A village designed and planned by the people who will live there is taking shape in Pennsylvania. New Village (New Village Office, 253 South Mt. Vernon Ave., Uniontown, Pa. 15401, USA) will be a community dedicated to economy, environmental soundness, and self-reliance. All 190 dwelling units, and all of the other buildings will be energy efficient. Economic development and business centers will be included in the plans. Housing will mix people of all incomes and services will be provided to keep New Village affordable for everyone. The residents work with the Institute of Man and Science to bridge the gap between the developers of technology and those who must live with the results.

TRANET

We deal with a very strict bank. It's called the First Savings and Lien.

Orben's Current Comedy

Last Public Hanging

Rainey Bethea had drifted to Owensboro, Kentucky, from West Virginia. Little was known about his background, but this did not keep him from finding employment as a chauffeur for a middle-aged lady. This in itself was no mean trick in 1936, since 20 percent of the people were unemployed. Bethea raped, killed and mutilated his employer.

For this, he was tried, found guilty and sentenced to die on the gallows. At that time, Kentucky used electrocution as a means of executing criminals, but hanging was reserved for rapists.

Rainey Bethea was a black man and feelings had run high during the trial. But now that the verdict and sentence had been rendered, people settled back and waited for justice to be served.

In my eight-year-old world, politics did not exist. My hero was Jack Armstrong, the All-American Boy, and the arch-villain of all villains was Robert Ford, whom I had seen waste Jesse James at the old Princess Theater in Calhoun.

I realized vaguely that a man was going to die. But transcending that gruesome thought was the knowledge that I was going to spend the day in Owensboro, some 40 miles away. To a farmboy growing up in the Pond River Bottoms section, Owensboro was a wonderland of candy stores, food shops and bright, flashing lights.

It was still pitch dark when what seemed

like the entire population of the Shutts Community started loading into the back of Grandad's International truck. No extensive efforts had been made to clean the truck and traces of animal waste still clung to the sides of the truck bed, a token of Grandad's many trips to the stockyards.

The sun had yet to make its appearance when we arrived at the execution site. In the gray pre-dawn it was obvious that the crowd was in a festive mood. A local reporter later described it as a "Roman Holiday." The gallows stood stark and bare on a lot now occupied by the Executive Inn. Droplets of resin oozed from the death structure's green, unseasoned pine. Vendors were much in evidence. . . .

By now, the sun had ascended in the east and as execution time drew nearer, the crowd became more subdued. Abruptly, there were shouts of, "Here he comes." "They're bringing him out." It was indeed time. For coming into view, riding pillion behind a policeman on a motorcycle, was the condemned man. Rainey Bethea was experiencing his last moments of life.

It must be said that Bethea met death in a cavalier manner. For a man barely 20 years old, he showed remarkable composure. Halfway up the gallows steps, he asked to be allowed to change his socks. This request was granted. Bethea asked if the trap door would hold if he walked out on it. He was assured that it would. After the traditional last words of solace from a minister, the noose was placed around Bethea's neck and a black hood was draped over his head. The hangman and his assistant quickly moved Bethea out to the center of the gallows floor and the trap was sprung.

Death must have occurred instantaneously. There was not even so much as a twitch from Bethea as his body swung back and fourth in an ever-decreasing arc. Bethea had requested that his body be sent back to his mother in West Virginia for burial. This request was not carried out.

Bethea was buried in potter's field among the indigent, the infamous and the unknown.

Shortly afterwards, Kentucky abolished hanging as a means of executing criminals. The hanging of Rainey Bethea was officially recorded as the last public hanging in the United States.

—Mel Tharp
Joint Endeavor

The Republicans have finally come up with the answer to the question: "What do you give to the person who has everything?" More.

Orben's Current Comedy

Coming California Catastrophe

The United States is unprepared for the catastrophic earthquake that is more than 50% likely to strike California during the next three decades. This was the conclusion of a study conducted by an *ad hoc* committee of the National Security Council, assisted by other federal agencies. The NSC committee, which was organized in response to President Carter's concern about disaster preparedness after viewing the destruction caused by the eruption of Mt. St. Helens, found that current preparedness and response plans are probably adequate for moderate earthquakes, but that a very large one will present the state and nation with damages, casualties, and social and economic impacts unparalleled in magnitude since the Civil War.

In the committee's report, an analysis of the disaster readiness of local governments and state and federal agencies reveals that response to such a great earthquake would be disorganized and largely ineffective. The plans of different governmental units, levels and jurisdictions have not been coordinated. In addition, the possibility of a prediction has not been incorporated into the plans, long-term recovery issues have not been considered, and communication problems would be formidable.

Natural Hazards Observer

The Pentagon reports that in 10 years the Russians will have the capability to wipe out 200 million Americans. That puts them exactly 10 years behind the I.R.S.

Washington Crap Report

Afraid of Computers?

Are we afraid of computers? Well, yes, says a spate of articles and surveys. . . .

John Leo, writing in *Discover* magazine, profiles the "computerphobe." "Deep in his phobic heart, the resistance fighter knows that computers are designed to destroy privacy, eliminate jobs, carry the TV generation even further away from literacy, read little squiggles on cornflakes boxes so the grocer can cheat his customers more easily, and allow World War III to be launched entirely by technical error." Leo quotes the chief psychologist at the Equitable Life Assurance Society as saying, "We've always had a love-hate relationship with machines. . . . We're entering the epoch of technology believing that computers are taking us over, pushing us out, alientating us."

Many companies employ specialists to adjust their workers to new computer applications. If this isn't done, there's ample evidence to show that workers may sabotage systems, feed phony information, or make naive mistakes out of fear. Other corporations find it essential to work out a strategy to orient their customers to computers (called "hand-holding").

We may be on the verge of widespread electronic video and computer units in the home, but computerphobia is a main reason that the electronic revolution hasn't come sooner to the home. A new survey by International Data Corp. in New York City "found that many Americans harbor concern that the latest advances in electronic home products could intrude on their lives." Most respondents in the survey were enthusiastic about interactive systems in their homes to access diverse data bases, but 30 percent were concerned that too much personal information would be recorded about a person in one place.

More than half of those polled in a 1978 survey released last year by the American Council of Life Insurance in Washington, D.C. stated that they would rather deal with a person than with a machine in routine business transactions, even if this raised the cost of the service.

And, 56 percent feared that large numbers of persons will be displaced by automation.

These attitudes are negative despite efforts by manufacturers to make computer hardware "more personal." "Lines are soft. Terminals have rounded edges and have lost their boxy look. Colors range from muted beiges and pastels to vivid blues and oranges. . . . Cluster work areas look like comfortable conference tables," reports *Behavior Today* newsletter in its Oct. 27, 1980 issue. And, of course, the trend in software is English-language programming rather than "computerese." More systems accept handwritten data.

"Human speech as input to computers and computer speech as output to humans —otherwise known as voice processing—will come to the forefront, during the first half of the 1980 decade," according to a market report from Frost & Sullivan Inc. in New York City.

Another trend is the use of desktop computers. . . . One trade magazine calls them "the friendly alternative in the 1980's." This is because they allow for individual use, can do small tasks, and will accept simple languages for input.

The fear of computers is not unrealistic, especially with regard to the displacement of workers. A cogent report from Worldwatch Institute discussed the revolution in microelectronics: "In three decades, a roomful of vacuum tubes, wires, and other components has been reduced to the size of a cornflake." It added, "One thing is clear: microelectronic technology will have a pervasive and long-lasting influence on international trade, patterns of employment, communications, industrial productivity, entertainment, and social relationships."

Privacy Journal

I've always been a firm believer in that old adage: "If you have to ask, you can't afford it." Somehow I never expected it to apply to postage stamps.

Orben's Current Comedy

Chaco Canyon's Ancient Astronomers

Modern scientists are gradually discovering and appreciating the sophisticated knowledge and extraordinary use of astronomy among the ancestors of modern-day American Indian people, and reinterpreting archeological finds accordingly.

One dramatic example of such finds is a construct located on isolated Fajada Butte, at the entrance to Chaco Canyon, New Mexico. Each noon light passes between three rock slabs leaning against a cliff near the top of the butte. Behind the slabs, illuminated by the light, are two spiral petroglyphs carved perhaps a thousand years ago by Anasazi Indian people, whose descendants are today's Pueblo people living along the Rio Grande and its tributaries.

Until recently these petroglyphs, like others on Fajada Butte, were appreciated for their artistic merit alone. Modern scientists now realize, however, that the shape, movement, and timing of the light beams falling on the two spirals vary with the changing altitude of the noonday sun to provide an accurate measurement of solar positions throughout the year and the approach and arrival of solstices and equinoxes. Scientific evidence indicates that the stone slabs once fit together to form one block on the cliff face nearby and that they were probably moved and perhaps shaped to create the sun marker.

Particular marks denote special solar events. The summer solstice is indicated by a dagger-shaped vertical beam bisecting the precise center of the larger nine-ringed spiral; the winter solstice by two beams that frame the larger spiral on its outer edges; the equinoxes by a slender inverted triangle of light passing through the center of the smaller spiral. . . .

Fajada Butte is a natural site for astronomical observation, as it rises 430 feet above the valley floor and has a clear view to distant horizons. The butte is difficult to climb and guarded near the sun marker by rattlesnakes. Yet pottery shards, rock art, and ruins of small buildings discovered on the butte all indicate its active use by the Anasazi.

Indian Affairs

Marrying a Twin
An Interview with Wives of Identical Twins

I've known Jim and Sam since we were in high school. I mixed them up only once—before I started dating Jim. Now I never mix them up because my husband is more serious, quiet and shy. When we got married, Sam was best man.

Many times Jim tells Sam things before he tells me. They still go shopping together. This used to annoy me. I never knew any twins when I was growing up, so I didn't know what to expect. When we were first married, I was really jealous of the time Jim spent with Sam. As a new bride, I felt that I should be the most important person in his life.

I understand much better now. People who are thinking of marrying a twin should know something about twins beforehand because they will have to share their spouse with the twin. Twins need that special contact with each other. When you are married to a twin, you have to understand and accept this bond and learn not to be jealous of their time together.

When I first met Sam I did not know he was a twin. Months later when we began to date, I met Jim. I was shocked! I mixed them up only once and that was right after I met Jim. My husband is more outgoing, outspoken and stylish.

I didn't have much trouble adjusting to being married to a twin because I have twin sisters. The hardest part about being married to a twin, who is close to his co-twin, is the lack of private time. I'd like to be able to entertain our friends without having to always invite Jim and his wife.

Our wedding was unique because not only were the groom and best man identical twins, so were two of the bridesmaids, my younger sisters.

My advice to a person thinking of marrying a twin, is to be sure you know about twins and meet the co-twin, and be sure to talk it over with your fiance.

NOMOTC Notebook
(Mothers of Twins Club)

Super Secret

One of our top-secret weapons laboratory operations is the Sandia Laboratory in Albuquerque, N.M. They have a $100 *million* computer to help them. An investigation by the Energy Department has found some 200 employees have been using that computer to store games, personal letters, jokes and to help a local bookmaking operation. Who's minding the store?

Washington Crap Report

I sure hope this new economic program is right. Sometimes I get the feeling that every time we start seeing the light at the end of the tunnel—the government sends out for more tunnel.

Orben's Current Comedy

Blimps were once commonly used as long-range patrol vessels. Today they may be making a comeback, overseeing the new 200-mile fishing limit for the Coast Guard. And the U.S. Forest Service may use a hybrid version of the helium-filled craft to airlift logs from remote areas. Both possibilities are being federally tested. Meanwhile, European Ferries is reportedly considering airship service between London and Amsterdam.

Leading Edge Bulletin

Computers are getting more like people all the time. They say that they can do everything but think.

Orben's Current Comedy

Reading *Privacy Journal's* Mail

From Cincinnati: "In a publication of the American Entrepreneur Society, there is a report of a department store in California playing high-speed messages over the Muzak that encourage shoplifters to desist. Surely, this could be used more broadly. . . ."

Answer: You are right; this "subliminal communications" technique is being used by retailers, employers and others to modify behavior. The theory behind the technique is that sounds too quiet for the ears to hear or sights too fast for the eyes to see can nonetheless reg-

ister responses in the brain, according to *Technology News of America's* December 1980 issue. Professionals disagree as to the validity of the theory.

A company in Louisiana markets a service that, with the use of a minicomputer, plays programmed messages at a level just below that of the background music in a store or factory sound system. A message in a store may say, "I will not steal," or "I need to buy that"; a message in a workplace may motivate workers to higher productivity. In a dental office, the message in the music may be "This doesn't hurt." In a theatre, subliminal communications may flash an imperceptible caption on the film saying, "Buy more popcorn," or "I am thirsty."

These messages, negative or positive, can be repeated about 3000 times an hour in current systems.

The Federal Communications Commission has said that it would act on complaints of subliminal communications on the regulated airwaves, and the Federal Trade Commission has said that its use on highway billboards may be deceptive and unfair. Use of the technique in places not subject to government regulations is legal. There is no evidence that the technique is used widely—nor that it works.

Privacy Journal

In the 1950s, a TV antenna on your roof was a status symbol. Now all it means is you can't afford cable.

Orben's Current Comedy

Regeneration: The Ultimate in Body Repair

Were you a salamander, you could regenerate a forearm in about 60 to 90 days. Amputation alone would be enough to trigger the process. As Michael Snow, Ph.D., Anatomy Professor at the University of Southern California, puts it, "Salamanders are fully equipped to do a remarkable job."

Were you a frog, with the help of human intervention, you could regenerate an arm in about a year. All you'd need would be a scientist—like Stephen Smith, Ph.D., Professor of Anatomy at the University of Kentucky—to trigger the regeneration by electric current.

As a human being, what are you chances of regenerating a limb? As Dr. Smith notes: "If our experiments go really well this month, it could be next month. If not, maybe ten years." But, he adds optimistically, "Sooner or later, we'll do it." Dr. Smith estimates that it could take a human being about three months to regenerate a limb, much less time than a frog, because the human metabolic rate is much faster.

How is it that salamanders manage to regenerate arms, legs, eye lenses, tails and heart muscle all by themselves? Dr. Snow is studying muscle regeneration and exploring two possibilities. One is that reserve cells in normal tissue—called satellite and pericyte cells—trigger the regeneration. The second is that the cut ends of muscle undergo de-differentiation; cells in the muscle fragments change into primitive, undifferentiated cells.

Solving this puzzle has important implications for overcoming the horrors of degenerative diseases such as muscular dystrophy. As Dr. Snow explains, if we can learn how to stimulate the damaged muscle tissue to repair itself, we can counteract the disease's destruction.

In any case, one important thing researchers have learned from salamanders is why we don't regenerate our lost limbs. Unlike salamanders, we form scar tissue and close up wounds. Salamanders, Dr. Smith explains, "don't have systems that shut off leaks."

> *The Amp*
> (National Amputation Foundation)

Some people want to send a message to Russia via El Salvador. I'm in no hurry. I'm for sending it via the post office.

> *Orben's Current Comedy*

I don't know how many mortgages they're giving out, but they're now calling them Savings and You Should Live So Long Associations.

> *Orben's Current Comedy*

Staff Status

To make it all seem so important, White House staffers play status games. The size of the office, the distance from the Oval Office, dining room privileges, an assigned parking space, etc., are part of the game. The latest status symbol is a model ship in your office. The Navy has a bundle of these and they loan them to the White House staff to "show the flag." The rules are the top staff have the models of the largest ships. Not to worry. It will pass. Boys will be boys, you know.

> *Washington Crap Report*

Teenagers are people who look out the window on a gorgeous spring day and say, "It's just too beautiful to stay inside. Let's go to a movie."

> *Orben's Current Comedy*

A Swedish pathologist, Dr. Sven Olof-Lidholm, has designed a new casket made of wax-impregnated corrugated cardboard. As durable as a pine box, it can be shipped flat to reduce transportation costs.

> *Continental Association of Funeral and Memorial Societies Bulletin*

Metric System Strangely Inhuman

Wearing light cotton on a hot day and putting on a wool sweater when the weather gets cool indicates an understanding of temperature. Similarly, when stepping into a hot bath or taking the first ocean swim in the late spring, we exercise our innate understanding of temperature.

It is this human scale that provides the foundation of our customary Fahrenheit system and accounts for Fahrenheit's unequalled convenience and elegance. Zero-100 is, as Daniel Gabriel Fahrenheit well knew, the temperature range most frequently experienced by human beings. 100 is roughly the hottest day we know, and it is unusual for the thermometer to dip far below zero in winter.

The metric system's temperature scale is not based on human perception, but on the freezing and boiling points of water, a scale which has no relevance to our living conditions. This same unrelatedness between our physical world and the means by which we measure it recurs frequently in the metric system. A gram, for instance, a 28th part of an ounce or the weight of a paper clip, is too small a unit to cook with; a meter (39.37 inches) is too big and clumsy a unit to measure everyday objects with ease.

Fahrenheit has 180 increments between the freezing and boiling points of water—nearly twice as many increments as the centigrade system (now referred to as Celcius in the new SI metric system), thus allowing almost twice the degree of accuracy in measurement. Increasingly, the general public is voicing disapproval of weather broadcasting in metric.

People do not have a clear understanding of the metric temperature scale. Celcius is too impersonal. It establishes body temperature on a scale that causes an unwieldy amount of tempoerature to be expressed in negative terms (minus). . . .

Because the customary system is so much in harmony with every aspect of our dialy experience, it is engrained in our culture and our way of life. It has survived because it is more than a contrivance. We are halfway through the supposed ten-year voluntary conversion period, and fewer and fewer requests for assistance in conversion are appearing. Metrication is not on its way in—it is on its way out.

—Seaver Leslie
Footprint

Shock Rods

If you are running a laboratory rat through a maze to see how long it takes and how many blind alleys it goes into, you can't just put it down at the "Enter Here" sign and say, "Now see how fast you can find the food. Go ahead." Unfortunately it can't understand plain English.

Prof. Lashley, one of the early experimenters, used to whack the rats a hard pop on the tail to make them start. It worked. They went all right. But the exploding industry in the twenties was electricity. Inventing new uses for tamed lightning, like making clocks go without winding, like spinning ammonia to make a box cold without blocks of ice cut the winter before and saved in straw, and like making a street light turn red and then green every 45 seconds—these were the creative ideas that sprang from inventive minds. One invention, the cattle prod, proved useful in steering cows toward the slaughter chutes. It didn't damage the hide. Some unsung inventor made an adaptation of this for use in the psychology lab. Starting rats to run mazes was easily done with a shot of electricity and saved the effort of beating on their tails. The shock rod was born.

Some unhappy children don't—or won't—understand English either. Some are retarded, some are autistic, and those whose parents don't want them are shunted into institutions. How to put them through their paces? Attendants, wearied of beating on their tail places, which often left marks on their hides, welcomed the new and improved cattle prod scaled to human dimensions and renamed the "hand held inductorium." Decorated with a new name, "behavior therapy," it was endowed by its creators with magical powers to "alleviate human suffering," when responsibly practiced. . . .

—Adah Maurer
The Last Resort

The Electronic Cottage

As commuting becomes more expensive and time-consuming, as both parents take on jobs, and as office time is taken up with distractions, an increasing number of employees are working at home. These are not self-employed individuals, but workers who stay in touch with their large bureaucracies through computer networks.

Alvin Toffler predicted in *The Third Wave* a shift of work from both office and factory into the home. Computers and long-range telecommunications make it possible.

Control Data Corp., fourth leading manufacturer of computers in the nation, is experimenting with "an alternative work station program." The company finds that the decreasing cost of communications makes this plan possible. Two years ago Control Data began retraining disabled employees so that they could do computer-based work in their homes. After the success of this experiment, the company launched the present program for a larger number of employees. Computer programming, courseware design and editing and educational consulting lend themselves to homesite work, according to Gail E. Bergsven, vice president for human services. Employees who work at computers in their homes receive tasks with a definite beginning and end and periodically they are summoned to the office for consultation with supervisors and co-workers. "After one year of alternate worksite program, we have found that the productivity of the participating workers has improved," Bergsven told a conference on Communications in the Twenty-First Century, sponsored by Phillip Morris Co. last month. "With little or no time required in going to and from work, employees have more time to spend working [and] because working at or near one's home is desirable to many, their motivation is higher."

Isolated employees in their "electronic cottages" miss the socialization of a joke in the hall or lunch with a co-worker, says Bergsven, and so they have developed an electronic substitute—"an on-going computer-stored series of conversations, jokes, games, non-sequiturs, and running commentary. It can be called up at any time anywhere in the world, and it instantly puts an employee in touch with his or her peers." There have been problems to iron out. Many of the original participants in the experiment have chosen to return to the central office ("out of sight, out of mind" is a real concern of ambitious employees), and many supervisors feel out of touch with their subordinates. . . .

Privacy Journal

Three solar-powered traffic lights have been installed in Tokyo, Japan. Each has a battery which can store energy for up to 200 hours of operation and a built-in microcomputer which regulates turning, parking, and other traffic instructions according to the time of day.

Solar Energy Digest

Michael Ashley of McKinney, Texas, held police at bay with a shotgun for more than five hours. No one was injured and he was charged with aggravated assault. He was acquitted by a jury after psychiatrists testified that it was a combat flashback that caused Ashley, who had been undergoing treatment for this problem, to go temporarily insane on the night of the standoff. It appears that the attack was triggered by the turning on of a barbecue, the gas and fire reminding him of burned flesh. Defense attorneys believe that the successful defense based on the post-traumatic stress disorder is a landmark in Texas law.

Vietnam War Newsletter

Original Researcher of Infamous Jukes Family Indicted Environment, Not Genes

The famous Jukes family, long cited as an example of hereditary factors in crime, pauperism and moral degeneration, apparently got its bad name through journalistic carelessness and subsequent academic distortion.

Elof Carlson of the State University of New York at Stony Brook has discovered that the original 19th-century researcher of the family members attributed their behavior not to genetic weakness but to their circumstances. Ironically, the Jukes family (a pseudonym) was held up as an example of the importance of environmental factors.

For generations, psychology textbooks have cited the example of the Jukeses and the Kallikaks (an equally notorious New Jersey family) as possible evidence of negative familial traits.

Richard Dugdale, a young penal reformer, compiled the case histories of the Jukes family members and published them in a report to the New York State Prison Assn. in 1874. "The correction," he wrote, "is a change of environment."

He recommended public policies for health care, remedial education, penal reform and assistance to the poor as an antidote to the conditions that produced the family. His report was republished several times.

But when Dugdale died in 1883, an obituary in the *New York Times* mistakenly asserted that "every [Jukes family] member was a criminal of greater or less degree." It concluded that

"the whole question of crime and pauperism rests strictly and fundamentally on a physiological basis."

In 1889 David Starr Jordan, then president of Indiana University and a disciple of Francis Galton, the famed British eugenicist, distorted some of Dugdale's findings to support his own view of hereditary degeneration and argue against immigration. (Jordan later became the first president of Stanford University.)

A later writer embellished the Jukes story, attributing a specific weakness to each of the sisters.

Brain/Mind Bulletin

In its great wisdom the U.S. Senate has struck a blow for censorship. That flock added to the Intelligence Authorization Act a provision asking for a legal injunction against a T-Shirt. That's right, a T-Shirt. The T-Shirt is made in Arkansas, sold by ads in magazines, and says "INSTRUCTOR: CAMP PEARY, VA." This doesn't make sense unless you know that Camp Peary is the CIA training center. Of course the rest of the world might know this but Americans are not supposed to know it.

Washington Crap Report

Trust the People

Many of our leaders may go around saying "Trust The People" but most wear bulletproof vests or clothing when they go out among the "People." Former Secretary of State Henry Kissinger has a topcoat and a raincoat that are bulletproof.

Washington Crap Report

Lilly Simulates Natural Opiates

The pharmaceutical search for a synthetic painkiller modeled after the brain's natural opiates (enkephalins) has produced a potential contender—metkephamid, an analog of met-enkephalin, one of the brain's inhibitory neurotransmitters.

The new synthetic peptide, developed by a Lilly Research Laboratories team, has demonstrated greater analgesic effectiveness than morphine in rodents, with fewer negative effects—respiratory depression, tolerance, addictiveness. It is now being tested in human subjects.

Enkephalin-like analgesics tend to degrade rapidly in the presence of the body's enzymes and to be filtered out by the blood-brain barrier. The researchers restructured metenkephalin to make it less degradable and more accessible to the brain.

The most difficult problem presented by synthetic analgesics is their addictive tendency. The synthesis of a non-addictive painkiller could be a biochemical breakthrough of Nobel Prize stature.

Brain/Mind Bulletin

What may be a major breakthrough in collecting and storing solar energy has been developed by a group of researchers at Kyoto University, Japan, according to a recent story in the *Asahi Shimbun,* a leading Japanese daily.

The article says that the substance, not yet named, is a synthetic material composed of norbordiene, methylbase, and cyanobase. Norbordiene is derived from dicyclopentadiene contained in crude oil.

It is reported that, if the substance receives sunlight, it changes in form as it absorbs energy from the sun, but the temperature of the substance remains unchanged.

Asahi reported that the substance stores 92 kilocalories per kilogram, or almost enough to raise the temperature of one kilogram of water from 0 to 100 degrees Celsius.

Asahi also reported that, in order to draw energy from the substance, all that is necessary is to contact it with a very small amount of silver. When the energy stored in the material is released, it returns to its original condition, ready for the next cycle. . . .

Solar Energy Digest

It's Obsolete

It appears that American ingenuity has triumphed once again. *Chemical Business* magazine reports that combinations of cattle hooves, alcohol and fish oils have soothed nearly all regrets over the ban on the use of sperm whale oil ordered in 1972.

When the Marine Mammal Protection Act,

passed that year, made the importation of whale products illegal, most companies that used sperm oil sent their researchers to the drawing boards to find replacements.

And according to National Marine and Fisheries Services special agent Eugene Bennett, the concoctions they came up with were so efficient that most of those businesses now snub the original as obsolete.

In 1976 a dispensation gave sperm oil dealers three years to use up their supplies. Apparently, though, they had so much trouble unloading the stuff that the deadline had to be extended three more years.

Consumption has sunk so low, Bennett said, that it looks like the current stockpile can be eked out another 30 years.

The Greenpeace Examiner

What has been called the world's first sun-powered laser has been developed at NASA's Langley Research Center. Many applications are envisioned, especially in outer space, where a narrow laser beam could be projected from the vicinity of Earth, for example, to power a space station by converting the beam back to conventional power with on-board equipment.

Solar Energy Digest

More Like It

The new great seal of the Interior Department now has the buffalo facing right instead of left as in the past. Some who don't agree with James Watt suggest a new seal showing the buffalo dead, on its back, with rigor mortis setting in, would be much more appropriate.

Washington Crap Report

You Don't Say?

The Office of Personnel Management and the Merit Systems Protection Board recently sent out similar questionnaires to 19,782 high-ranking federal employees asking them how they liked their jobs. These goodies cost $126,729. Guess what they found? Those making the most money liked their jobs the most.

Washington Crap Report

One John, Two John or No John?

It may seem funny to the folks out in boondocks but prestige in Washington comes in strange ways. After the last election, the one that cleaned out some of the mossbacks in the U.S. Senate, the office assignments on the Hill were re-shuffled. Some of the larger Senate offices were split. As a result, some offices wound up with two toilets while others had none.

The latest prestige symbol is to have one of the offices with two toilets. It's a disgrace to have an office with no toilet. To find out where your senators stand in the Washington pecking order, ask if they are a ONE JOHN, TWO JOHN, or a NO JOHN senator.

Washington Crap Report

People in California are so laid back, this is the only state I know where smoke detectors come with snooze alarms.

Orben's Current Comedy

Tidbits from Turtledom

Peru — Scientists have found ancient lost airstrips. They've also found ancient lost luggage.

•

Greenfield, N.J. — A Turtle wrote that he got a new job and he has 500 people under him. We later found out he was cutting grass in a cemetery.

•

South Holland, Ill. — A Turtle reports that the city just bought a new fire truck. At the city council meeting they decided to keep the old fire truck and only use it for false alarms.

Turtle Express

If I understand the gun lobby, we shouldn't ban guns—just have more Vice Presidents.

Orben's Current Comedy

Collecting & Hobbies

PLAYING A ROUND

What do Golf Collectors collect? Mainly old golf programs from major tournaments and old golf clubs—the older, the better, especially if they have wooden, not metal, shafts. Joe Murdoch's obsession is books about golf—he has over 2,500 of them, which must be a world's record. He claims he's read them all. He also publishes, out of his home in Lafayette Hill, Pennsylvania, what he calls "an 18-handicap publication," the *Golf Collectors' Society Bulletin*. "It keeps me out of bars," he explains.

Murdoch has played golf since he was eight years old, half a century ago, but his journal is only a little more than a decade old. The average issue is 16 pages long and is typeset neatly on a typewriter. Articles are about equally divided between straightforward accounts of golf history and the lighthearted antics, on and off the links, of the society's members. Murdoch does not take himself entirely seriously. He calls the *Bulletin* "a rather crazy publication I put out for the (questionable) benefit of nutty golf collectors."

With a fellow "golf nut" named Robert Kuntz, Murdoch launched the society in 1970, and mailed the first *Bulletin* to 63 prospective members. More than 60 *Bulletins* and 800 members from 43 states and 11 countries have fol-

lowed, including a few top pros, such as Ben Crenshaw. Murdoch says that he specified from the start that he would not publish the *Bulletin* on schedule—that is, every other month—and "I make sure," he says, "that I do not. I like to keep them guessing."

And having fun. It seems that every journal for collectors has a large and extremely *serious* buy/trade/sell classified-ad section. But in the middle of one listing in the *Bulletin* was this item: "J.S.F. Murdoch will trade member of Saturday morning foursome: nice enough fellow, handicap 15 but can't play to it. President of medium-sized bakery, former football player, excellent martini drinker, has been looking for a 6-foot rabbit for 15 years. Make offer. . . ."

THE KEYS TO LIFE

Over the years, Don Stewart has collected coins, stamps, subway tokens, railroad memorabilia, and old phonograph records. "When you're a little bit odd and a little bit introverted it all makes sense," Stewart explains. "Collectors are all pack rats. If I see something I want, I'll buy the damn thing and eat beans and bacon for a month." But after years of grubbing around for all sorts of junk and prizes, Stewart settled on an obsession shortly after World War II: henceforth the key to his collecting would be . . . keys.

Stewart stumbled into this hobby, quite literally, while poking around the ruins of buildings he had razed (he was in the construction business at the time). He found a lot of old and interesting-looking door keys. He started hanging on to them. Then he branched out into watch keys and railroad switch keys; in Europe on a vacation he picked up some keys from the Middle Ages. He ended up with so many keys he couldn't count them, but estimated there were well over 2,000 of them. When he looked for research in the library he couldn't find anything, so in 1975 he wrote (and edited, typeset, printed, bounds, and marketed) the 200-page *Standard Guide to Key Collecting, United States, 1850–1975*. And in 1978, out of his home in Phoenix, Arizona, he began publishing a bimonthly newsletter called the *Key Collectors Journal*. Stewart's *Guide* and *Journal* have become the "key" reference books in this field.

Over 300 members of Key Collectors International receive the less-than-professional-looking but extremely informative *Journal*. (Stewart has his own printing shop, which he salvaged from a demolition job in Idaho.) The *Journal* features rough drawings and pictures of dozens of keys (going back to Roman times), the latest auction news, and terrific bits of key history or key trivia: The Invention of Padlocks, Chinese Handcuffs, All About Locksmiths, and so forth. These stories inspire many messages from readers. "The letters I get are virtually impossible to decipher," Stewart says. "They write with crayons, anything . . . I feel right at home amongst them."

A tall, burly man with black hair and a mustache, Don runs a small stamp and coin store in Phoenix but considers himself "retired." He says he's pushing 60. "I've lived in every western state," he explains, "just bumming around. I grew up during the Great Depression and that affected my mind. I grew up as a bum and I can't break the habit." He says he's not into keys for the money; he feels collecting is an "emotional thing." He loves keys because of their "history and beauty." There are lot of keys around because once they've outlived their usefulness, people just "throw 'em away."

But perhaps the biggest kick Don gets out of his hobby and his *Journal* is the fact that the New York Public Library and the Smithsonian Institution sometimes write to *him* when they're looking for information on antique keys. "That boggles the imagination," Don Stewart comments.

An inebriated man stumbling up the stairs of the New York City subway station waved to passers-by by saying, "C'mon down and see what a set of trains this guy has in his basement!"

The Train Collectors Association Quarterly

Mushroomers Beware:

From Eugene, Oregon, comes a note that the Lane County Sheriff issued a warning last fall that mushroom collecting could lead to jail. This is due to the many complaints of local trespassing by collectors. If convicted, the offender could get up to one year in jail and $1,000.00 in fines. . . . A more serious case is that of a member in Illinois. He is charged with the possession, manufacture and intended sale of a substance containing psilocin. This grew out of the culturing of mushrooms at home and displaying these to others, one of whom was a local narcotic agent. Since so many cultures and spawn are now being made available, we advise extreme caution. The culture involved was that of *Psilocybe cubensis*. If you are inclined to take a trip, take the bus!

The Mycophile

How About a "Hangin' in There" Award?

Sitting here sipping on a cold Rolling Rock, I'm tempted to mount a campaign for this durable design as "Can of the Year." Well, not really, but they're the only U.S. brewery I can think of who has not succumbed to the pressures of design or logo changes, specials or commemoratives, different brands and brews, etc. All they make is a good pale brew in their familiar green packages. So this month let me salute, not my favorite brew or brewery, but a truly steady maverick among a field of shaky, label grabbing competition.

The Beer Can

American Flyer Boys Were Right on Track

Strip away college degrees and inheritances, and the prominent differences between American men hinge on whether they grew up American Flyer or Lionel.

From 1906, when Lionel first produced its Standard gauge electric toy trains, until 1966, when the last genuine American Flyer train was sold, the two titans of tinplate lines warred for the loyalties of boyhood. . . .

On one point, all boy trainmen will agree: Lionels and American Flyers served admirably as the preeminent toys for boys of any age.

Evidence of memorable toy train loyalties pop up every year.

Only a few days ago, for example, the Spokane American Flyers Club had a Christmas party. And these trainmen weren't kids.

"You're not really old enough to have a train until you are 30 or 40," Flyer aficianado John Kelley said before his party. Kelley's basement contains maybe the best American Flyer layout in Spokane, at least of post-war trains. Kelley is near retirement age.

About a dozen other old friends of Flyer ate cookies and talked trains in Kelley's knotty pine basement room and they all said the same.

Trains were the toys they remembered most vividly from childhood.

And something else came through about toy trains.

"I bought my kid an American Flyer train when he was two years old," Ernie Horr, publisher of Spokane's little American Flyer 'S' gauge newsletter, said at the party. "I thought he was old enough to enjoy it."

That was the enduring attraction of trains. They were fun for dad.

They clanged and chugged and whistled and offered the right combination of mechanics and entertainment.

More than that, dad looked good when he put up the train.

Only he could haul the boxes out each Christmas and string the track together.

The trestles had to be fixed to each section, the cow-on-the-track and barrel loading accessories had to be wired, and lastly, the cars had to be unwrapped from the newspapers and placed in certain order on the rails. That was all dad's work.

Trains carried on a tradition year to year. Father and son could talk over new accessories and then dad could make sure Christmas day was an instant success when the new electric switches arrived.

Yet the people at the American Flyer Christmas party reflect the deep trouble in trainland.

Only one train buff under 20 was there to watch the old American Flyers.

In the toy stores, it's computerized Space Wars and talking chess boards that fill the shelves.

Business Week magazine, quoting a computer whiz in California, predicts that the talking, bleeping computerized gizmos will become "the railroad trains of the 80's."

And where are the trains?

American Flyer is long gone. New sets disappeared 10 years ago with the bankruptcy of A.C. Gilbert.

Collectors get up to $3,000 for the surviving trains.

Lionel bought the old American Flyer molds but then General Mills, the cereal people, bought Lionel.

Now dad has to be into computers.

Maybe it's up-to-date, but it won't be as much fun. And dad will feel dumb trying to learn computertalk. . . .

Bah, humbug. Save the rec room for trains.

—Chris Peck
The Train Collectors Association Quarterly

Who is the Indian on the Front of the Buffalo Nickel?

He is a composite portrait of three men: a Sioux chief, Iron Tail; a Cheyenne chief named Two Moons; and one employee in a Wild West show named Chief John Big tree. The buffalo on the reverse, Black Diamond, was a resident of the Central Park Zoological Gardens in New York.

The Numismatist

Ronald Reagan (signature)

What's in a Name?

Q. Which has a greater value, autographs which are signed directly on the photograph or ones signed on the back of the photograph?

A: Autographs signed directly on the photograph. It's easier to display and, therefore, more people would want it, hence, a greater value.

Q. Inscribed photographs (to a specific person) or a photograph which only has a signature. Which is worth more?

A: In most cases, especially with living people, a simple signed photograph is worth more. The demand is greater. More people would want a photograph signed "Ronald Reagan" than one signed "To Archibald Fregosi, Best Wishes, Ronald Reagan" unless your name happened to be Archibald Fregosi. If the person the photo is inscribed to is an important person, its value increases (e.g., "To Alexander Haig, Best Wishes, Ronald Reagan"). For persons no longer living, it does not matter that much. In fact, the more a person wrote on the picture, the greater the value in those cases. For example, a photograph signed "Mark Twain" would be worth less than a similiar photograph signed "To John Edward Charles with the kind regards of Mark Twain, Jan. 5, 1899." No one would expect you to have an inscribed photo of Twain with your name on it. Other famous people are so much in demand in signed pictures, an inscription would not matter.

Q. Are envelopes personally hand addressed but not signed by a famous person of any value.

A: Yes. Not as much as the signature, of course, but there is some value.

Q. Is an autograph the same as a person's legal signature?

A: Not necessarily. U.S. Senator Edward M. Kennedy always signs autographs "Ted Kennedy" which is not his legal signature. Similarly, former V.P. Walter F. Mondale signs "Fritz Mondale."

Q: What is the value of just a signature of a notable person on a card or piece of paper?

A. It only proves that the person was able to sign his/her name. It is the least valuable of all forms of autographs (letters, documents, notes, etc., are worth more).

The Pen and Quill

Marbles as Collectibles

Marble play, anthropologists avow, is as old as man. There is something about a ball—any ball—that engages the interest of anyone, plus generating the idea of throwing it, tossing it, bouncing it, rolling it, or else. There are even crystal balls.

Just how many million boys have played marbles in our American past is anybody's guess. But whatever you may guess, multiply it by a modest one hundred to estimate how many marbles were played with. You may be sure, however, that few boys played exclusively with the types and kinds of marbles described here. These are really rich marbles, for example—the sulphides. They are balls of glass ranging from one to two inches in diameter, in which are imbedded clay figures looking like silver in the glass. Dogs, horses, sheep, ducks, chickens, cats, mice, fish are of record, decorating the interior of a play marble.

The marbles of swirled glass filigree were known as Venetian swirls and, someday, as marble collecting takes on the concurrent nomenclature of glass collecting, may be called Lutz type. They are as beautiful as any Lutz glass; as smartly colorful as many paperweights. A mixed group, displayed in a glass fish- or flower-bowl, against the light, offers one practical as well as decorative suggestion for their use. The very same glass balls were, in Europe, sometimes drilled at the point, fitted with an eye, and used as a curtain or bell pull.

Other marbles of note are the cobalt onyx balls, made from the native stone; carnelians, similarly turned from native mineral; genuine jades and jaspers; and the glass and tin glazed stoneware imitations. Proud and opulent indeed was the father who paid two dollars a dozen for genuine carnelian marbles for his son.

Marble Mania

The First Beer Can

With the bottle so well entrenched, neither glass companies nor brewers were anxious to witness the beer can's birth. Glass companies, of course, wanted to protect their market; brewers had millions invested in bottling equipment. To top it off, the beer can was initially far costlier than the bottle.

Fortunately, the can had some pluses, too. It was shorter, smaller, and lighter than the bottle, so it cost much less to ship. But most of all, it could be thrown right into the trash heap when empty (fortunately for can collectors, this wasn't always what happened).

A strong element of consumer psychology was at work, so bottle proponents quickly seized upon all cases of evidence showing that beer cans were of questionable quality or even outright dangerous. Stories circulated about people who had become ill or even died after drinking beer from cans. Bringing science to their aid, bottle companies tried to show can linings were unsafe and would deteriorate with age, that metal poisoning cases were being kept out of newspapers, that all kinds of vermin hid in the opaque cans, and so forth. The anti-can prejudice persisted in spite of one famous incident when a brewmaster scraped the linings from three cans and consumed them with no ill effects.

So, it was with mixed feelings that on January 24, 1935, the American Can Company and Gottfried Krueger Brewing Company of New Jersey marketed the world's first beer can—Krueger Cream Ale. Bearing the "Keg-lined" vinylite trademark, the can was a "flat top" (today's universal shape).

American Can had been dickering with Krueger for a long time about test marketing a can. Kreuger had insisted on a careful study of marketing areas first. It wanted a special type of city: neither too large nor too small, and its sales and distribution patterns had to be such that the newcomer's impact could be clearly measured. Richmond, Virginia, seemed to meet those requirements.

Test results weren't long in coming. Within two months, Krueger Cream Ale had upset the market pattern, capturing a large portion of sales from such national brewing giants as Anheuser-Busch, Pabst, and Schlitz. The can's chances of success looked bright.

Large and small breweries alike watched developments closely, and many of the small ones quickly signed up with American Can. But American, realizing it needed more than small regional breweries to make an impact on the total beer market, was anxious to sign up a national power. This came in July, when Pabst began canning its blue and silver Export label (its leading brand, Blue Ribbon, wasn't canned at first). Continental Can Company captured Schlitz in September, 1935. By the end of the year, 23 brewers had jumped on the canned wagon, and the can versus bottle battle was underway.

The Beer Can

The "Super Shopper"

You must have seen a "Super Shopper" by now. You know the type. While cameras roll, these zealous shoppers charge through store aisles, heaping their carts with products we all dream about. As they approach the checkout we hold our breath, but the "Super Shopper" only smiles confidently. The register rings on endlessly and the total is very impressive . . . one . . . two . . . even three *hundred* dollars! She reaches into her purse (for a checkbook?). No! She pulls out a fistful of coupons and the cash register begins to whir again. Two more yards of tape are spewed out of the machine and reveal a final bill of an incredible 59¢!

Your coupons don't save *you* this much money, so what's happening? Some of the more even-handed "Super Shoppers" admit that such incredible performances are not possible every week. However, most viewers miss this most important point. Instead, they're busy jotting down addresses and subscription rates for the "refund bulletin" that the "Super Shopper" just happens to be selling. Unfortunately, many viewers imagine themselves clipping coupons and repeating the shopping spree they just witnessed . . . forever.

Problem: What is a "Coupon"?

The problem is one of definition. "Coupon" can mean a discount certificate that can be clipped from a newspaper or magazine. They allow you to receive an immediate discount on an item at the time of purchase and have a value from 10¢ to 50¢.

"Coupons" can also entitle a shopper to a free package of a product. These are popularly known as "Free Product Coupons." They are rarely "found" anywhere (in newspapers, etc.). They are usually obtained as the result of "refunding." This leads to the obvious question. . . .

What is "Refunding"?

Recently, we showed viewers a box of Maypo. A yellow banner was displayed across the front of the box announcing "one box free." Details on the package explained that if a customer *bought* two boxes and *sent in* the box tops, a *coupon* for a free box of Maypo would arrive by return mail. This procedure is called "refunding" and it figures heavily into how a "Super Shopping" trip is performed.

The Super Shopper's Secret Revealed

Imagine participating in many such refund offers (hundreds of similar offers are made each year), and imagine collecting a large stack of Free Product Coupons. If you went to your local grocery store and turned in all of your Free Product Coupons at the same time, you would only pay the sales tax on those items. You would have performed your own "Super Shopping" trip! You would have received a large number of items and paid only a few pennies. (See? You, too, can amaze your friends!)

You must remember, however, that the "free" package is obtained only after you have *purchased* something else, and spent some time and postage. There are a few exceptions to this procedure, but they are rare. We like to think of refunds as high value coupons. For example, in the case of the Maypo offer, we were able to get three packages for the cost of two. It represents a discount of 33% on each of three boxes. This is why your suspicions about the "Super Shoppers" not really getting such good deals is correct. They fail to mention all of the products they've had to purchase to make the one "Super" trip possible.

Double Your Pleasure

Sometimes "Super Shoppers" do their demonstrations in areas where "double couponing" is available. At times, stores will go to extensive and expensive lengths to get customers. In some parts of the U.S. competition is so keen that stores offer to double the value of manufacturers' coupons. Put simply, if you bring in a 50¢ coupon, the store will double the face value. You will receive $1.00 instead of 50¢. The additional amount is paid to you by your merchant. Although he is reimbursed by the manufacturer for the face value of the coupon (and, even, given a handling fee), the "double" value comes out of his own pocket.

One thing to keep in mind: if you find a store offering double or even triple coupons . . . beware. Although it may be an excellent opportunity to save be sure to check that the regular prices are not so inflated that your coupon savings are lost.

Shopping News

Value of Autographs

- 1965 Army–Notre Dame football scorecard signed by "Dick Nixon." Pristine condition. $50.
- Autograph signed letter of Charles Manson from prison. $130.
- Signed photograph of the Shah of Iran (posed with the Carters at the White House, 1977), color. $325.
- Pencil autograph signed letter of Jesse James, 3 pages, to Mr. Flood ("What did you mean by telling in Laexington that we stole Dr. Yates horse . . . if you dont go to my mother & explain why you sed what you did we will hold you responsible & you will be brought to grief. . . Do you suppose if we were thieves we would steal a horse from one that has been so kind to mother as Dr. Yates has . . . they are no men in Mo. who score horse thieves more than we do . . . if you value your life you had better retract your Slander. Jesse W. James."). $11,000.

The Pen and Quill

The Code-O-Graph Cipher Disks

The cipher disk is an old and established encryption device. For many, it reached its peak of popularity during the days of radio drama, where a number of shows offered cipher disks as premiums to listeners. Hundreds of thousands of such premiums were issued to listeners of a program titled *Captain Midnight,* which was an adventure serial.

The program, which was highly aviation-oriented, has best been remembered for its cipher disks, known as Code-O-Graphs. In fact, the Code-O-Graphs frequently became plot elements in the show. Also, at the close of two or three programs a week, an announcer would conduct a "signal session," wherein an ecrypted message concerning some element of the following episode would be broadcast.

Interestingly, the code motif of the show even touched the central character. "Captain Midnight" was not the real name of the character; it was a code name conferred upon him as the result of a World War I mission.

The show was highly popular, with adults as well as with children, even to some of the air crews that saw action in World War II, which might account for some stories that Code-O-Graphs were occasionally used by combat forces. However, such stories were never substantiated.

During its Code-O-Graph years, the show was sponsored by Ovaltine, a milk supplement. The cipher disks were obtained by sending in a seal or label from an Ovaltine container; to collectors, Code-O-Graphs today retail from $35.00 to more than $75.00, depending on condition.

The "signal session" messages broadcast to users were very short, almost invariably less than 20 characters long. However, the manuals that accompanied the Code-O-Graphs suggested that the listeners form clubs ("flight wings") to learn more about aviation and to practice sending and deciphering messages. The messages sent to the listeners were, of course, monalphabetic substitutions. The show did, however, seem to show a more extended view of secret messages than the Code-O-Graphs' use would imply. In an early episode (pre Code-O-Graph) a base of the organization that Captain Midnight headed (the Secret Squadron) was raided to obtain its code books. This implied that in addition to the ciphers later used, base-to-base communication was effected in the more secure manner of code manuals.

One interesting bit of cryptanalytical technique was taught to listeners. In one episode, one of the enemy (a beautiful female spy) asked Captain Midnight to send a long message in code. As she explained to her henchman, since she had a copy of the plaintext, she would be able to compare it with the cipher and thus recover the cipher alphabet (though not in those words). Since a brand-new Code-O-Graph had just been issued, Captain Midnight obliged, using the old cipher—not fool he—and in simple substitution. Needless to say, the spy was able to recover the alphabet, for all the good it did her (she was chastized by her superior, who had the captured old Code-O-Graph); but the technique she used was certainly a valid one.

In some of the manuals, there were word games and other instructions on forms of secret communications. There were even special cipher keys for "flight commanders" (a sort of inner circle for listener-members). It is interesting to speculate on how many people got their first exposure to cryptology through Captain Midnight's Code-O-Graphs.

—Stephen A. Kallis, Jr.
Cryptologia

Cannon Fodder

At the University of Washington Stadium, in Seattle, the football season opened with a BANG! Right. *CHAOS* was there, with a crew of four proven cannoneers, and a naval cannon that spoke with equal authority.

The University asked, and got, *CHAOS*. Would we provide a cannon to salute Husky scores at the home games? Answer: "Yes." Thus began a colorful three-year tradition of the Husky Football Cannon. . . .

The *CHAOS*/Husky Cannon signalled the entrance of the band and saluted Old Glory as she reached the peak of her mast. Newspaper stories . . . heaped glory on cannon and crew. It seemed that the cannon had become an inseparable part of Husky football. Well, almost!

Cannoneers, rise in wrath at what follows: At the termination of the season, the athletic directors of the Pac-8 [Pacific Eight Football Conference] met in Seattle to thrash out the many serious problems facing college football. All we can guess is that they had difficulty in solving these problems, thus struck upon *CHAOS* as a solution. Unanimity had been achieved. They agreed to outlaw cannon at all Pac-8 home games!

In fairness to the University, . . . the U of W athletic director indicated that the organization might re-consider the decision at their next meeting. This would eliminate the necessity of implementing one of the two alternatives proposed to the University in the *CHAOS* letters: 1) Shooting the gargoyles off their buildings or 2) manning a cannon barge in the Lake which lies just offshore the Stadium.

Who will win? Who knows? But we do know this: "When Cannon Are Outlawed, Only Outlaws Will Have Cannon."

> *CHAOS*
> (Cannon Hunters Association of Seattle)

Friday Night Date Fever

I don't know how you start. Maybe you don't really start, more like something in your blood that one day you just succumb to. Start slow and say to yourself (usually your best audience) that one case, one doll and a few outfits will satisfy the need. But like any addict you know that that won't satisfy the need, the craving, the desire for more. You've got the fever, the Barbie Fever.

You drag friends, relatives and anybody close who will go with you to garage sales, flea markets and antique shops to look for that familiar form and face among the crock pots, broken toasters and junk. You wait till the shop is empty to meekly ask if they have or hope to have soon, any Barbies. They look at this six-foot-four, thirty-year-old man standing in front of them as if he had just asked if they carry plutonium. You leave empty-handed. Empty-handed and unsatisfied because you need more.

Then you start another route. Ask friends if they know anyone—you again explain you collect Barbies. Again the plutonium look!! A few will take pity on you and dig through attics and basements to satisfy your cravings. But the dolls are worn and the outfits need shoes and hats and you realize you are getting greedy. Did I say I wanted one doll, one case and some clothes? No, I meant one doll, one case and some clothes from each year. (Maybe I can move *my* clothes into my car to make more room for the collection!)

Now you're really hooked. It is the point of no return. Everyone who comes to your house to visit must be shown your prize items. I am truly offended when someone doesn't want to see my ski outfit, with boots, skies and poles. And in my opinion it is un-American not to want to see my #2 wedding gown. (We're still looking for #1.) Company doesn't come around as often now.

Now, I ask strangers on the street, I call all remote leads and I have found Ruth. I call, thank God I live in New York too, to ask questions. Really I call to pick her brain. Part of this fever, like any fever is an insatiable thirst, a thirst for knowledge. I wonder if I paid too much for something or might this be a true find? I never yet had a real find! I'm still a novice in the old collecting game. Sometimes I feel like I've gotten to the party after all the onion dip is gone. . . .

But no matter what, it is all a nice addiction, something all of us have. It is all part of the fever. We all have it. Some have had it for years, I'm just starting and there will be people coming out of their closets after me. Someday, though, I think I'll have all I want. I'll stop collecting and just give everything to my niece. Someday.

> —Leonard Planes
> *The Barbie Gazette*

A solar-powered toy train in an attache case is now available for $4,000. It comes equipped with 14 solar cells and all you have to do to set the train running around a tiny track is to open the case in a sunlit area.

> *Solar Energy Digest*

Letters to the Editor

To be happy one must have a job, a friend and a hobby. Raising and displaying gourds is a good hobby. It would be a better world if everyone would raise at least one gourd to brag about.

•

We love gourds. Do you have a pattern or instructions for making a guitar out of gourds?

•

My wife and I were given a complete tour of Jacob Tyndall's Gourd Fantasyland.

•

Until recently we made gourd pipes from gourds we grew in West Virginia. Now we live in California and raise a better quality of gourds. We sell gourd pipes for $35.00 each. We have sold them to people all over the world.

•

Although gourds are not part of the Thanksgiving feasts they are a part of the fall decoration. There are a few edible gourds. One of the most colorful, the Turk's Turban, can be baked and eaten like a squash. The New Guinea Bean is an edible gourd but the coarse texture makes you feel like you are eating cattle feed.

The Gourd

Directory

A highly arbitrary listing, and brief description, of some of the most interesting or unusual newsletters, journals, and very special interest magazines published in the United States. Except were noted, quoted material, describing the publication, comes directly from the publisher. In some cases the publisher will respond to inquiries by sending one free issue.

ACFA Bulletin, PO Box 203, Point Lookout, MO 65726: 12 pages, published 10 times a year by the American Cat Fanciers Association, for people who raise, breed, and "show" cats.

Advance Notice, Box JH, 256 Washington St., Mount Vernon, NY 10550: A bimonthly newsletter that keeps readers abreast of new federal regulations and changes in existing rules, published by Consumer Union's Regulatory Information Network. It aims to educate consumers on the regulatory process and encourage their participation in it.

Airedale Terrier Club of America Newsletter, % Barbara Strebeigh, Birchrunville, PA 19421: A 42-page bimonthly for 500 dog owners.

American Astronautical Society Newsletter, 6060 Duke St., Alexandria, VA 22304: A 4-page bimonthly from a "scientific and technical society devoted to space activities of the United States." Similar to the British Interplanetary Society.

American Canals, Box 310, Shepherdstown, WV 25443: An 8-page quarterly from the American Canal Society, to encourage the preservation, "interpretation," and use of historic navigational. At one time there were 4200 miles of canals in the U.S., most in the East and Midwest, but with the advent of the railroads, they were pretty well ignored starting around 1860.

American Checker Federation Bulletin, 3475 Belmont Ave., Baton Rouge, LA 70808: The 24-page bimonthly "has the goal of increasing and promoting interest in Checkers in the U.S. and throughout the world." It reports on local tourneys and analyzes matches on a move-by-move basis. The ACF, in conjunction with the English Draughts Association, arranges matches for the World Checker Championship.

American Gold News, Box 457, Ione, CA 95640: A 20-page monthly tabloid whose 3500 readers want to know everything about gold, past and present—mining, coins, companies, etc.

American History Illustrated, Box 1831, Harrisburg, PA 17105: A 52-page magazine published 10 times a year by the National Historical Society.

American Humor, American Studies Program, University of Maryland, College Park, MD 20742: Twice a year, in 40-page issues, it looks at American humor in a serious, "multidisciplinary" (literary, historical, cultural) and "multigeneric" (film, TV, folk humor) way.

American Lock Collectors Association Newsletter, 14010 Cardwell, Livonia, MI 48154: A 6-page bimonthly for 300 collectors of locks, keys, handcuffs, leg irons, and related material.

The AMP, 12-45 150 St., Whitestone, NY 11357: For 35 years, this 16-page monthly has been published by the National Amputation Foundation "for the benefit of amputees, civilians and veterans, all over the world."

Anabiosis, Box U-20, University of Connecticut, Storrs, CT 06268: A 90-page semiannual scholarly publication, circulation 250, put out by the International Association for Near-Death Studies. "Out of the body" experiences sometimes occur when someone *almost* dies—and *Anabiosis* speculates why that is.

Animal Welfare Institute Information Report, PO Box 3650, Washington, DC 20007: A 4-page quarterly made up of fairly brief and occasionally witty news items about the treatment of animals.

The APBA Journal, 5705 Williamsburg Way, Durham, NC 27713: For owners and fans of the popular baseball board game,

APBA. A 16-page monthly that reports on results of tabletop "leagues" and new cards (based on the performance of real major-league players).

APRO Bulletin, 3910 East Kleindale Road, Tucson, AZ 85712: The Aerial Phenomena Research Organization, one of the oldest and most respected "UFO" study groups, investigates flying saucer reports, and the results are released through this 8-page bimonthly. Sometimes the *Bulletin* drifts from hard news to ask questions like: "UFO Contactees — Collaborators or Cosmic Citizens?"

A Propos, Browning Rd., Hyde Park, NY 12538: A 30-page twice-yearly journal from the Union Internationale de la Marionnette—an organization, affiliated with the United Nations, of puppeteers from over 60 countries. Jim Henson (of Muppet fame) is president emeritus.

The Arrow, 135 Edgerton St., Rochester, NY 14607: A quarterly with historical stories and many photographs of the early Pierce-Arrow automobiles.

AVS News, 708 Third Avenue, New York, NY 10017: A 4-page quarterly from the Association for Voluntary Sterilization.

Baker Street Journal, % John Linsenmeyer, 9 Hendrie Ave., Riverside, CT 06878: A 64-page quarterly from the renowned Baker Street Irregulars, a Sherlock Holmes appreciating society, founded in 1934 by Christopher Morley, 2,000 subscribers.

Banjo Newsletter, Box 364, Greensboro, MD 21639: See profile, "Pickin' 'n' Grinnin'."

Barbie Gazette, PO Box 79, Bronx, NY 10464: A 12-page monthly newsletter for collectors of Barbie Dolls (and all the accessories).

Bare in Mind, Box 697, Perris, CA 92370: A monthly from the "Nudist News Service"—everything you want to know about nudist colonies, "naturist" clubs, and "free" beaches. Circulation: 2000.

Baseball Fact Sheet, PO Box 3529, Trenton, NJ 08629: See profile, "Base Paths."

Baseball Historical Review, PO Box 323, Cooperstown, NY 13326: A 180-page annual journal for 1300 members of the Society for American Baseball Research, based in the town where the sport was supposedly born. Articles take a serious look at the most famous and obscure moments in baseball: from "Cy Young's Final Fling" to "Unrecognized No-Hit Umpires."

Bear Tracks, GBW, PO Box 8236, Honolulu, Hawaii 96815: See profile, "Grin and Bear It."

The Beaver Defenders, Unexpected Wildlife Refuge, RD #1, Newfield, NJ 08344: See profile, "Leave It to Beavers."

The Beer Can Collectors of America® News Report, 747 Merus Ct., Fenton, MO 63026: A 28-page bimonthly for over 10,000 members of the club. Profiles brewery owners and looks at the oldest and newest in cans, with pictures.

Big E, % Perry Piper, West Liberty, IL 62475: A slick quarterly for 2000 owners of Edsel automobiles.

Billiards Digest, John Hancock Center, 875 N. Michigan Ave., Chicago, IL 60611: "The first magazine devoted entirely to billiards." Founded in 1978, it's a bimonthly with 6,000 readers. Tips, trick shots, and tournament coverage.

The Binnacle, % Abraham Taubman, 11 College Dr., Jersey City, NJ 07305: A 22-page "Log of the Shipcraft Guild" for "marine artists" and people who build model ships. 225 readers.

Birding, Box 4335, Austin, TX 78765: A bimonthly that helps 3000 members of the American Birding Association find and identify birds. Includes maps.

Blake: An Illustrated Quarterly, Department of English, University of New Mexico, Albuquerque, NM 87131: Reproductions, on high-quality paper, of sketches by Blake, and scholarly articles about him, abound in each 60-page issue.

The Blind Bowler, 150 N. Bellaire Ave., Lousville, KY 40206: A 16-page monthly newsletter for members of the American Blind Bowling Association, founded in 1951.

Boulder, Lake Superior State College, Sault Ste. Marie, MI 49783: See profile, "Citizen Rabe."

Brain/Mind Bulletin, PO Box 42211, Los Angeles, CA 90042: A 4-page newsletter, founded in 1975, comes out every other week and has 10,500 subscribers. Marilyn Ferguson (author of *The Aquarian Conspiracy*) is the editor; Arthur Koestler and several other noted writers are on the editorial advisory board. Explores the "frontiers of research, theory and practice."

The Brightwater Journal, Box 2061, Irwindale, CA 91706: J. Scott Shannon of the River Otter Fellowship believed that "the river otter lacks good public relations and concern for its plight" so in 1980 he started a 6-page newsletter. Otters in the U.S. are in danger, he says, because of "environmental degradation and overexploitation."

The Brown Family, 430 Ivy Avenue, Crete, NE 68333: A six-page quarterly for people named Brown who are interested in tracing their genealogical roots. 300 subscribers. Grew out of editor William Rapp's interest in tracing the Brown side of his family.

CabArt, 320 S. Division #11, Ann Arbor, MI 48104: A periodic literary tabloid, conceived by Ann Arbor Yellow Cab driver/poet Bart Plantenga in 1980. Publishes "works coming out of the cab culture." Gives a whole new meaning to the expression "hack writing."

The California Highway Patrol-man, 2030 V St., Sacramento, CA 95818: A slick, 100-plus page monthly, first published in 1937, for CHIPS and the motoring public—about 16,000 readers in all. It boasts that it is *not* a "law enforcement magazine." Material in each issue includes general-interest profiles, safety tips, and reports on offbeat CHIPS encounters around the state. Sprinkled throughout are photographs of accident scenes, with drivers and passengers strewn across the road, perhaps meant to shock readers into driving safely.

Calliope, PO Box 3906, Baltimore, MD 21222: A 40-page monthly magazine for 10,000 members of the Clowns of America, "The Greatest Club on Earth," open to one and all. Includes profiles — circus and neighborhood clowns alike.

The Carriage Journal, PO Box 3788, Portland, ME 04104: A slick, 54-page quarterly for 2000 members of the Carriage Association of America. Restoration hints, driving tips, and historical data for those who love old buggies and sleighs.

Center for Conflict Resolution Newsletter, 731 State St., Madison WI 53703: A 26-page semiannual that looks at "alternative" ways to settle disputes and reach "consensus" decisions. Sample observation: "There are always at least a dozen criticisms that can be made about *any* statement. . . ."

CHAOS, % Don Clark, 1326 E. Bercot Rd., Freeland, WA 98249: For 1000 members, around the world, of the *Cannon Hunters Association of Seattle.* It's a 56-page journal—half serious, half tongue-in-cheek—published "now and then." Members who recover one or more cannons are "cannonized."

Chicago Playing Card Collectors Bulletin, 1550 W. Pratt Blvd., Chicago, IL 60626: A monthly 8-page newsletter, founded in 1951, for members who collect antique cards.

Chimney Sweep News, 41663 Keel Mountain, Lebanon, or 97355: A 12-page monthly for about 650 people in the chimney-cleaning business, which has been booming ever since Americans started turning to wood stoves and fireplaces for heat in the late 1970s.

Chip Chats, 7424 Miami Ave., Cincinnati, OH 45243: A slick, well-illustrated bimonthly, from the National Wood Carvers Association, with 16,000 amateur and professional woodcarving readers.

Chocolate News, PO Box 1745, FDR Station, New York, NY 10150: See profile, "Cocoa Loco."

Chronicle of The Aaron Burr Association, RD #1, Route 33, Box 429, Hightstown, NJ 08520: Editor Samuel Engle Burr, Jr., believes that his ancestor has gotten a raw deal in the history books. His 8-page quarterly has about 1000 readers.

Church & State, 8120 Fenton St., Silver Spring, MD 20910: A 24-page newsprint magazine, published 11 times a year. According to editor Edd Doeer, who wants "to preserve the great American constitutional principles of separation of church and state," it is "the voice today of Roger Williams, of James Madison, of Thomas Jefferson."

Civil War Round Table Digest, PO Box 7388, Little Rock, AR 72217: A 4-page monthly for 1000 members who strive to preserve famous battlefields from the ravages of commercial development.

Clearwater Navigator, 112 Market St., Poughkeepsie, NY 12601: An 8-page journal that goes out to 4000 friends of folksinger Pete Seeger and the Hudson River 11 times a year. Seeger raised the sail of the 106-foot sloop *Clearwater* in 1969 to arouse public concern about the befouling of the Hudson, and he has sailed up and down the river, singing songs and giving speeches, ever since.

Compassionate Friends Newsletter, PO Box 1347, Oak Brook, IL 60521: A 6-page quarterly from "a self-help organization offering friendship and understanding to bereaved parents . . . to promote and aid parents in the positive resolution of the grief experienced upon the death of their child."

Contest News-Letter, PO Box 1059, Fernandina Beach, FL 32034: A 12-page monthly report on the dozens of sweepstakes and contests open to the public. Editors Roger and Carolyn Tyndall describe prizes offered and entrance rules. It's not uncommon for *CN-L* subscribers to win half (or more) of the grand prizes offered by sponsors.

Continental Association of Funeral and Memorial Societies Bulletin, Suite 1100, 1828 L St., N.W., Washington, DC 20036: A surprisingly "lively" 8-page monthly for the trade. Its idea of a filler—a little poem—"It isn't the cough that carries one off/It's the coffin they carry one off in."

COSMEP Prison Project Newsletter, % *The Greenfield Review,* Greenfield Center, NY 12833: A 28-page semiannual for, about, and by writers in prisons. Inmate authors present their best work and explain how writing workshops help them do it. Sponsored by the Committee of Small Magazine Editors and Publishers.

Counterforce, Box 26804, El Paso, TX 79926: A 40-page monthly for "executives and security directors in business, industry and government concerned about the threat posed by terrorists around the world." Established 1977. Circulation: 2000.

Covered Bridge Topics, 31 Federal St., Beverly, MA 01915: A 16-page quarterly from the National Society for the Preservation of Covered Bridges.

The Cryptogram, 39 Roslyn Ave., Hudson, OH 44236: A 24-page bimonthly, filled with puzzles, ciphers, and "double quagmires," for

1000 members of the American Cryptogram Association, founded in 1932.

Cryptologia, PO Drawer 388, Houghton, MI 49931: A 64-page quarterly for 1000 readers who are into codes, cryptograms, ciphers, and other scrambled messages.

Cultural Watchdog Newsletter, 6 Winslow Rd., White Plains, NY 10606: An 8-page monthly. Editor Louis Ehrenkrantz likes to "review the reviewers" and shoot down "cultural super stars" such as Joan Didion, John Gardner, and Noam Chomsky.

Deltiology, 3709 Gradyville Rd., Newtown Square, PA 19073: For 1600 members of the Deltiologists of America. They collect antique postcards. The first card came out at the 1893 World's Fair in Chicago and the "Golden Age" transpired in the early 1900s.

Dollars & Sense, 38 Union Square, Somerville, MA 02143: A 20-page monthly bulletin that looks at the causes and effects of current economic problems in easy-to-read charts and articles. Circulation: 7000.

Doris Lessing Newsletter, % Paul Schlueter, 314 McCartney St., Easton, PA 18042: A 12-page semiannual. One of the few journals of this type devoted to *living* authors.

Dramatics' Curtain, 3368 Central Parkway, Cincinnati, OH 45225: A bubbly 12-page tabloid "dedicated to Secondary School Theater." Began as a mimeographed house organ of the International Thespian Society in 1971 (an offshoot of their magazine *Dramatics,* hence the name); now has 42,000 readers. Occasionally looks at school censorship issues.

The Drummer, 994 Broadhead Rd. Coraopolis, PA 15108: A 16-page bimonthly newspaper put out by *The Ruffed Grouse Society.* "Dedicated to improving the environment for ruffed grouse, woodcock, and other forest wildlife."

Early American Life, PO Box 1831, Harrisburg, PA 17105: A 94-page bimonthly, published by the Early American Society, to advance the "understanding of American social history and modern interpretations of early arts, crafts, furnishings, and architectures."

EFO Collector, PO Box 1125, Falls Church, VA 22041: An 18-page bimonthly newsletter for stamp enthusiasts who collect the post office's mistakes—stamps that are considered "errors, *f*reaks and oddities."

ELNA Newsletter, PO Box 1129, El Cerrito, CA 94530: A bimonthly, from the Esperanto League for North America, that contains "news of the language problem and Esperanto as a solution." Esperanto was created by Dr. L. L. Zamenhof (1859-1917), a Russian Jew, as an international language to serve as a "second tongue" for all, to improve communication and the prospects of peace. The Universal Esperanto Association now has more than 30,000 members in 91 countries.

Elvis Now, PO Box 6581, San Jose, CA 95150: A 14-page bimonthly newsletter. By the time Elvis Presley died in 1977, editor Sue McCasland had seen him perform more than 100 times, usually from the front row; she has 13 of his scarves. She is president of Elvis's fan club in San Jose, perhaps the most prominent of dozens of chapters around the country.

The Enigma, 4120 Washington St., Niagara Falls, NY 14305: See profile, "Mind Games."

Enjine! Enjine!, PO Box 450, Eastwood Station, Syracuse, NY 13206: An illustrated 24-page quarterly from the Society for the Preservation and Appreciation of Antique Motor Fire Apparatus in America.

The Enthusiast, 3700 W. Juneau, Milwaukee, WI 53208: Published by Harley-Davidson for "motorcycle riders of all ages, educations and professions." A quarterly established in 1916.

Evelyn Waugh Newsletter, English Department, Nassau Community College, Garden City, NY 11530: All about the brash and eccentric author of *The Loved One* and many other books. 8 pages, 3 times a year.

Executive Fitness Newsletter, 33 E. Minor St., Emmaus, Pa 18049: A biweekly from Rodale Press for 55,000 businessmen looking for ways to stay or get healthy.

Exploring the Bible, Box 20331, West Valley City, UT 84120: Judy Pearce uncovers discrepancies or "contradictions" in the Bible. Pearce says she simply wants "to help those people who want to be set free from Bible-produced guilt and being controlled by others."

Facets, 535 N. Dearborn St., Chicago, IL 60610: Its former title said it better: *M.D.'s Wife.* A 32-page quarterly for doctors' spouses.

Fantasy Newsletter, PO Box 170A, Rochester, NY 14601: Originated in 1978 as a mimeographed sheet, it's now a 36-page magazine, with beautifully illustrated covers, but it hasn't dropped the "newsletter" from its title. News and reviews of upcoming science fiction and fantasy books and conventions, and interviews with authors. Also covers "The British Scene" and "The Fan Press."

The Fare Box, PO Box 1204, Boston, MA 02104: Goes out to 750 collectors every month. Editor John Coffee owns 10,000 subway, streetcar, toll road, cable car, and bridge tokens, some worth $1000.

Farmstead Magazine, Box 111, Freedom, ME 04941: A 90-page magazine (on newsprint), published 8 times a year. Tells its 200,000 readers "How to Milk a

Goat," "How to Run a Roadside Stand," and answers the question: "Can the Small Farm Go Organic?"

The Fashion Newsletter, 743 Fifth Ave., New York, NY 10022: Published 10 times a year, this 4-page "international forecast of incoming fashions" claims to be "the only Newsletter on fashion in the world." Has correspondents in France, England, and Italy.

Federation of Homemakers Newsletter, PO Box 5571, Arlington, VA 22205: This 4-page quarterly has been "fighting for wholesome foods since 1959." Particularly concerned about chemically treated food. Pet peeve: excessive caffeine added to soda pop.

Fiddlehead Forum, The New York Botanical Garden, Bronx, NY 10458: An 8-page bimonthly for 1300 members of the American Fern Society, who are "amateurs interested in growing ferns or in studying them in the wild." Includes a "Home Fernishings" column. Fern scholars are known as pteridologists.

The Fillmore Bu(n)gle, PO Box 712, Cascade, CO 80809: See profile, "Milestones with Millard."

Flat Earth News, Box 2533, Lancaster, CA 93534: A 4-page tabloid published periodically by Charles K. Johnson, who writes articles claiming that there is no such thing as gravity and that the Moon and Mars landings were faked. The International Flat Earth Society was founded in 1888 in San Francisco by Alexander Dowie. Johnson has headed it for 10 years. He contends that there are 1500 members, including a few commercial airline pilots. Johnson believes that the Sun and Moon are 3000 miles away and only 32 miles across. The earth, he believes, does not move, whirl, spin, or gyrate.

The Flyfisher, 390 Bella Vista, San Francisco, CA 94127: A lush 48-page quarterly, printed in 4-color on high quality paper, from the Federation of Fly Fishers, which tries to "cultivate and advance the art, science and sport of fly fishing as the most sportsmanlike and enjoyable method of angling."

Folklore Forum, 504 N. Fess St., Bloomington, IN 47401: Founded in 1968 as a mimeographed sheet, now quite professionally produced 3 times a year by the Folklore Institute at the University of Indiana. Includes record, book, and film reviews but is primarily concerned with what it calls regional folklore, folk crafts, applied folklore, proverb studies, ethnic folklore, and so forth.

Footprint, 47 West St., New York, NY 10006: A 16-page semiannual from the Americans for Customary Weight and Measure. They militantly oppose attempts to convert America's traditional use of inches and ounces to the metric system's centimeters and grams.

The Forecaster, 19623 Ventura Blvd., Tarzana, CA 91356: A weekly, published since 1962 by John Kamin, for speculators in rare coins, gold and silver, old cars, and so forth.

Frank Lloyd Wright Newsletter, PO Box 2100, Oak Park, IL 60303: This 20-page quarterly features interviews with former Wright clients and drawings of the homes he built.

Freedom of Information Digest, Box 858, School of Journalism, University of Missouri, Columbia, MO 65205: An 8-page bimonthly from the Freedom of Information Center, "the only major national clearinghouse for material concerning the flow of information." Assists the media whenever they have "information skirmishes" with the government, but also helps the public gain access to "government-compiled information."

The Friends of Wine, 2302 Perkins Place, Silver Spring, Md. 20910: An 84-page bimonthly magazine for members of Les Amis du Vin, "a group of wine lovers devoted to the appreciation of fine wine and the art of leisurely dining."

From Nine to Five, The Dartnell Corp., 4660 Ravenwood Ave., Chicago, IL 60640: A 4-page semimonthly, for secretaries and clerks, filled with "tips and information for success in the office." Circulation: 27,000. Breezy but not condescending, it balances articles on "when to speak out" with "how to dress."

Funny Funny World, 407 Commercial Center St., Beverly Hills, CA 90210: An 8-page biweekly "comprehensive survey of the wit & wisdom & the funny things that are happening around the world." Mostly made up of brief reprints from newspapers, culled by editor Martin A. Ragaway and 40 "correspondents." 2200 readers—from comedians (Bob Hope, Johnny Carson, George Burns) to ministers looking for a witty, true-life story for this Sunday's sermon.

Gamblers Anonymous Bulletin, PO Box 17173, Los Angeles, CA 90017: A 20-page monthly made up mostly of letters from members of G.A., founded in 1957, "a fellowship of men and women who share their experiences . . . with each other so that they may solve their common problem and help others to recover from a gambling problem."

Garlic Times, 526 Santa Barbara Rd., Berkeley, CA 94707: A 12-page journal published a couple of times a year by The Lovers of the Stinking Rose. They believe in garlic "as a way of life." Recipes, herbal uses of garlic, and reports on Garlic Festivals. Letters to editor Lloyd J. Harris are printed in a column called "The Breath of the People."

Genii, PO Box 36068, Los Angeles, CA 90036: A 68-page monthly "International Conjurors' Magazine" for professional and amateur magicians. Published since 1936. Circulation: 8500. Includes instructional tips and reviews of new sleight-of-hand products.

The Goldfish Report, % Bill Parsonson, PO Box 1367, South Gate, CA 90280: A 20-page monthly put out by the Goldfish Society of America. Describes breeds of goldfish and discusses how to protect eggs from snails (and other predators) and keep your aquarium in tip-top shape.

Golf Collectors' Society Bulletin, 638 Wagner Rd., Lafayette Hill, PA 19444: See profile, "Playing a Round."

Golf Journal, Golf House, Far Hills, NJ 07931: The official publication of the U.S. Golf Association. A slick, 30-page magazine, published 8 times a year, that concentrates on history, lore, rules, and "the amateur game."

The Goodfellow Review of Crafts, PO Box 4520, Berkeley, CA 94704: A 24-page bimonthly newspaper, first published as an adjunct to the *Goodfellow Catalog of Wonderful Things,* but now a "freestanding crafts publication." 10,000 subscribers.

The Gourd, PO Box 274D, Mount Gilead, OH 43338: A 16-pager, 3 times a year, for 1500 members of the American Gourd Society. Encourages the "raising and use of gourds for decorative and useful purposes and the promotion of gourds and gourd craft."

Grass Roots Campaigning, PO Box 7281, Little Rock, AR 72217: Tips for the novice political candidate. A 6-page monthly put out by Jerry Russell, a public relations veteran of 200 campaigns, with (he contends) a "70% winning average."

The Gray Letter, PO Drawer 2, Tuscaloosa, AL 35401: A 4-page weekly that covers "developing trends and investment opportunities in the antiques and fine arts market." Started in 1975 by Gray D. Boone, publisher of *Antique Monthly* (same address).

The Greenpeace Examiner, Box 6677, Portland, OR 97228: A 32-page quarterly, on newsprint, from a leading pro-whale/dolphin/seal group. They believe in actively intervening—coming between the harpoon, net, or club and its victim.

Growing Without Schooling, 308 Boylston St., Boston, MA 02116: A bimonthly for 3000 readers interested in teaching their children at home. Includes information on where to order educational materials by mail.

Hall of Famers, 2801 N.E. 50 St., Oklahoma City, OK 73111: A frequently updated description, published by the Amateur Softball Association, of the sport's greatest players of all time. The ASA also publishes *World Softball,* a 4-page quarterly for players in 45 countries, plus the National Softball Media Association *Newsletter.*

Harvard Medical School Health Letter, 79 Garden St., Cambridge, MA 02138: A six-page monthly, meant to dispel "medical myths," and billed as "the only health letter written for the general public by the faculty of a leading medical school."

Haul Down and Ease Off, 634 Wagner Rd., Lafayette Hill, PA 19444: An 8-page bimonthly for the veterans of General Pershing's World War I balloon corps in Europe. (Balloons were used for reconnaissance.) Editor Craig S. Herbert says that "the average age of our members is about 87."

Heartbeat, 7320 Greenville Ave., Dallas, TX 75251: The Official Journal of the Mended Hearts, an organization of 10,000 heart patients. The 18-page quarterly reveals how drinking, sex, exercise, and other activities affect the postoperative patient.

Helicopter News, 1098 National Press Bldg., Washington, D.C. 20045: A 4-page biweekly for the trade that occasionally takes a lighthearted tone. At the bottom

of one News Briefs section was this item: "Environmental Protection Agency has reassured the public that there is no proven cancer hazard from the use of photocopying machines to illegally copy newsletters. EPA has said total impotence and frigidity are the only confirmed medical conditions thus far."

Hello Again, Box C, Orange, CT 06477: "The oldest monthly newsletter dedicated to the traders and collectors of vintage radio programs." Founder Jay Hickerson, 47, a professional pianist, owns tapes of over 6000 programs from the "golden age" of radio.

The Hollywood Scriptletter, 1626 N. Wilcox Ave., Hollywood, CA 90028: For aspiring film/TV/theatre writers. An 8-page monthly with tips from and interviews with pros.

Hot Springs Gazette, Box 40124, Albuquerque, NM 87196: A 40-page digest "published spasmodically" by Eric Irving and The Doodly-Squat Press. In each issue Irving describes dozens of wading pools in the Southwest for people who *like* to be in hot water. Irving says he agrees with Edward Abbey, who once wrote that "every man needs a place where he can go crazy in peace."

Indian Affairs, 432 Park Ave. South, New York, NY 10016: An 8-page quarterly from the Association on American Indian Affairs, a national citizens organization, which "assists Indian and Eskimo communities in their efforts to achieve full economic, social and civil equality."

Inland Seas, 480 Main St., Vermilion, OH 44089: An 84-page quarterly for 3000 members of the Great Lakes Historical Society.

Institute of Noetic Sciences Newsletter, 600 Stockton St., San Francisco, CA 94108: A 16-page quarterly founded by Apollo 14 astronaut Edgar Mitchell. INS "supports research and educational programs to expand humankind's understanding of the nature of consciousness and the mind-body link."

International Bonsai, % William Valavanis, 412 Pinnacle Rd., Rochester, NY 14623: A magazine for 2000 growers/collectors of bonsai trees. Editor Valavanis, 30, has his own bonsai school and is a nationally known expert.

International Jugglers Association Newsletter, PO Box 443, Davidson, NC 28036: A bimonthly publication for professionals and amateurs.

International Twins Association Newsletter, 114 N. Lafayette Drive, Muncie, IN 47303. 4-page monthly. Association founded 1934 "to promote the spiritual, intellectual and social welfare of twins, and multiples throughout the world."

The Intra-Tent Journal, 8761 W. 85 St., 17-105, Justice, IL 60458: A 12-page quarterly for members of the Sons of the Desert—a sort of Laurel & Hardy fan club. Presents articles on the famed comedians and notices of club activities. Founder John McCabe is the leading biographer of the pair.

Japanese Sword Society Newsletter and *Bulletin,* 5907 Deerwood Dr., St. Louis, MO 63123: The *Newsletter* is bimonthly, the 50-page *Bulletin* an annual. For collectors of 300- to 500-year-old swords, many of which were brought home from Japan by U.S. GIs after World War II. Some are works of art, not weapons, and some belonged to samurai.

Jaybee, Box 39, Valley Park, MO. 63088: See profile, "Refund Fun."

Jimmie Rodgers Memorial Association Newsletter, PO Box 1755, Temple, TX 76501: Published periodically for fans of the so-called "father" of country music. Editor Henry Young spearheaded the successful drive to get Jimmie on a U.S. postage stamp, issued in 1978.

Johnsonian Newsletter, 610 Philosophy Hall, Columbia University, New York, NY 10027: A 14-page quarterly with 1100 subscribers around the world (including the University of Peking). All about Samuel Johnson "and his circle." Founded in 1940, it claims to be "the oldest scholarly literary newsletter in the U.S."

Joint Endeavor, PO Box 32, Huntsville, TX 77340: A 32-page monthly, on a number of crimes and prison-related subjects, which purports to be the only inmate-written magazine published behind bars in this country.

Journal of Genealogy, Box 31097, Omaha, NE 68131: 48-page monthly of history and how-to (trace your ancestors).

Joyer Travel Report, Phillips Publishing, 7315 Wisconsin Ave., Bethesda, MD 20014: "The Newsletter That Brings You The Bargains In Travel—in the U.S.A. and Around the World." An 8-page monthly tip sheet.

Juggler's World, PO Box 29, Kenmore, NY 14217: 28 pages, 5 times a year.

Key Collectors International, PO Box 9397, Phoenix, AR 85068: See profile, "Keys to Life."

King's Korner, 45 Curtis Place, Fredonia, NY 14063: A 16-page monthly through which widely-dispersed members of the Postal Chess Club can play chess by mail. It was found in 1957 at a Norfolk, Va., USO post by four chess players when they learned that one of their group was being shipped overseas.

Kiplinger Washington Letter, 1729 H St., N.W., Washington, DC 20006: See profile, "The Newsletter that Helped Start It All."

Kite Lines, 7106 Campfield Rd., Baltimore, MD 21207: A quarterly for 5000 kite builders and flyers. Includes construction tips and reports on festivals and contests.

Knight Letter, 617 Rockford Rd., Silver Spring, MD 20902: A 4-page semiannual from the Lewis Carroll Society of North America, devoted to the creator of *Alice in Wonderland.* His real name was Charles Lutwidge Dodgson.

KOI-USA, 3906 N. Alhambra, San Gabriel, CA 91775: A bimonthly with over 600 readers. Koi are a colorful breed of carp imported from Japan. Raising koi is popular in California. Koi fans spend a lot of time on their backyard ponds and gardens trying to create a "work of art."

Last Month's Newsletter, Broad-Locust Building, Philadelphia, PA 19102: A 4-page newsletter, issued eventually, by the Procrastinators Club of America. Over 3600 members are urged to "pay your dues late and avoid the big 5% penalty." There are stories about the club's upcoming field trip to the 1964 New York World's Fair . . . and other late-breaking news ("the later it is, the better we like it").

The Last Resort, 977 Keeler Ave., Berkeley, CA 94708: A 24-page anti-corporal punishment journal, circulation 1000, from the Committee to End Violence Against the Next Generation. Made up mostly of reprints of newspaper articles on various forms of institutional assault on children.

Leading Edge Bulletin, PO Box 42211, Los Angeles, CA 90042: A triweekly, launched in 1980, with 4500 subscribers, that studies the "frontiers of social transformation . . . innovations and emergent patterns in all aspects of society."

Le Campion Gourmet Club, 1200 Mt. Diablo Blvd., Walnut Creek, CA 94596: Every month members receive recipes for a 7-course gourmet meal, suggestions on which wines to serve with it, shopping lists, background material (e.g., the difference between "northern" and "southern" Italian cooking), and tiny menus for their guests. John Convery, the director, is a tax attorney but has taken food courses at the Cordon Bleu in France, and other cooking schools.

Letter from Paris, 689 Fifth Ave., New York, NY 10022: An 8-page monthly for Americans who love (but are not living in) Paris. Includes news of current events, restaurant reviews, and historical tidbits.

Life Lines, PO Box 696, San Marcos, CA 92069: A quarterly from the Committee for an Extended Lifespan. Articles about aging and attempts to stretch longevity. Circulation: 10,000.

Lightbulb, 121 N. Fir St., Ventura, CA 93001: A bimonthly 48-page illustrated journal from the Inventors Workshop International. It contains profiles of inventors and the latest news on patents, and trademark and copyright laws. The IWI also produces a catalog from which the public can order new products. Buzz Aldrin, an astronaut, is on the advisory board.

Logos, 139 E. 23 St., New York, NY 10010: The 8-page semiannual Swedenborg Foundation newsletter, with a circulation of 30,000. Emanuel Swedenborg (1688-1772) was a Swedish scientist, mystic, and philosopher. The foundation, established in 1850, "is dedicated to maintaining the flow of Swedenborg's works into the mainstream of contemporary thought." His most famous modern disciple: Helen Keller.

London Club Bulletin, PO Box 4527, Topeka, KS 66604: Members—criminologists, detectives, and laymen—try to crack age-old crime cases, and progress is noted in various bulletins and journals periodically published by the club. Current cases being studied include the Lindberg kidnapping, the Jimmy Hoffa disappearance, and the Lincoln assassination.

Lost Treasure, Box 328, Conroe, TX 77301: A 72-page monthly for treasure hunters, prospectors, and collectors looking for lost mines and sunken treasure.

Lute Society of America Newsletter, % Nancy S. Carlin, 1930 Cameron Court, Concord, CA 94518: A 16-page quarterly founded in 1966 to "stimulate interest in lute music on the part of the general public." People who play the lute are called "lutenists."

Mainstream, 5894 S. Land Park Dr., PO Box 22505, Sacramento, CA 95822: A well-illustrated 40-page quarterly magazine put out by the Animal Protection Institute of America. News and features on endangered species, misuses of lab animals, and so forth. API has 70,000 members.

Maledicta, 331 South Greenfield Ave., Waukesha, WI 53186: See profile, "Foul Play."

Marble Mania, PO Box 222, Trumbull, CT 06611: A quarterly for 500 members of the Marble Collectors' Society of America.

Marianne Moore Newsletter, Rosenbach Foundation, 2010 DeLancey Place, Philadelphia, PA 19103: A 24-page semiannual that examines the life of the late poet.

Mark Twain Journal, Kirkwood, MO 63122: A quarterly, published since 1936, all about the life and works of Samuel Clemens. Editor: Cyril Clemens.

Marquee, PO Box 767, San Francisco, CA 94101: A quarterly from the Theater Historical Society of America. Historical stories, rare photographs, and current news on theater openings, closings, and restoration.

Marriage Enrichment, 459 S. Church St., PO Box 10596, Winston-Salem, NC 27108: With his wife, Vera, David Mace founded the Association of Couples for Marriage Enrichment in 1973 and has edited its 6-page bimonthly bulletin ever since. It reports on the group's activities and offers words of wisdom, such as: "Speak sweet words if you expect sweet echoes."

The Medical-Moral Newsletter, Ayd Medical Communications, 6805 York Road, Baltimore, MD 21212: 4 pages, 10 times a year. Looks at medical ethics and how they intersect with sex therapy, euthanasia, genetic experimentation, organ transplants, population control, etc.

Melville Society Extracts, Department of English, University of Southern Mississippi, Hattiesburg, MS 39406: A 16-page quarterly about the author of *Moby-Dick.* Editor Donald Yannella insists that the publication "be informal and chatty—a sort of family medium—and even humorous. We don't want it ever to become yet another heavy scholarly journal."

Military Collectors' News, PO Box 7582, Tulsa, OK 74105: An occasional newsletter of war memorabilia, from badges to bullets, Civil War to Vietnam.

Miniature Gazette, PO Box 2621, Brookhurst Center, Anaheim, CA 92804: A 100-page quarterly from the National Association of Miniature Enthusiasts. The 5000 readers love doll houses.

Mr. Longears, 100 Church St., Amsterdam, NY 12010: A 48-page quarterly with 1500 readers. The official publication of the American Donkey and Mule Society.

Model Rocketeer, 182 Madison Dr., Elizabeth, PA 15037: A 16-page monthly for 2400 members of the National Association of Rocketry. It tells readers how to assemble, and launch, miniature missiles in their backyards. This practice is legal in all 50 states. Some rocketeers put cameras on their projectiles, which snap pictures of the earth from a height of several hundred feet.

Motor Bus Society Bulletin, 4 Tall Trees Rd., New Rochelle, NY

10802: For 2000 members of the Motor Bus Society, founded in 1948. They collect photos, tickets, transfers—even caps worn by bus drivers.

Movie Trends, PO Box 173, Glen Cove, NY 11542: A monthly 8-page journal of middle-brow reviews and essays that tries to be "jargon-free." First issue: 1981.

Mycophile, 4245 Redinger Rd., Portsmouth, OH 45662: A 10-page bimonthly newsletter for mushroom-lovers from the North American Mycological Association.

Nash Times, Route 1, Box 253, Clinton, IA 52732: A bimonthly newsletter for 1400 members of the Nash Car Club. Remember the Nash? An "economy car" way ahead of its time (it died in 1957).

Nathaniel Hawthorne Society Newsletter, Hawthorne-Longfellow Library, Bowdoin College, Brunswick, ME 04011: A 12-page semiannual specializing in notes about the author and bibliographies of criticism of his work. Circulation: 200.

National Association and Center for Outlaw and Lawman History Quarterly, 4125 West Washington Blvd., Hillside, IL 60162: Presents colorful articles with the aim of preserving the history of Wanted Men and marshals in the Old West of 1850-1920.

National Button Society Bulletin, 2733 Juno Place, Akron, OH 44313: A bimonthly with a circulation of 2500.

National Cartoonists Society Newsletter, 5815 E. Joshua Tree Lane, Paradise Valley, AZ 85253: 8-pages, with (what else?) cartoons, for famous (B. Kliban, Dave Berg, Mort Walker) and not-so-famous cartoonists and animators. Current editor: Bil Keane.

National Mall Monitor Weekly, Suite 500, 1321 U.S. 19 S., Clearwater, FL 33516: A 4-page newsletter about shopping centers. Sample headline: "Needed: more fast-food freaks on zoning boards."

National Supermarket Shopper, PO Box 1149, Great Neck, NY 11023: A 52-page monthly magazine, edited by syndicated columnist Martin Sloane, for 30,000 members of the American Coupon Club. Lists refund offers but also explains how to make the most of a garage sale.

Natural Hazards Observer, Campus Box 482, University of Colorado, Boulder, CO 80309: A 16-page newsletter, with many cartoons, published since 1976 by the Natural Hazards Research Information Center, which is funded by several federal agencies (hence the newsletter is "free," courtesy of taxpayers). Its purpose, says editor Sarah Nathe, is to "bring together researchers and practitioners so that real problems of coping with hazards [hurricanes, earthquakes, snowstorms, and so forth] might better be solved."

Newsboy, Horatio Alger Society, % Jack Bales, 1407A Winchester St., Fredericksburg, VA 22401: A 20-page monthly that often contains a short story by Alger, perhaps the most popular author in America in the late-19th century. The society was formed in 1961 "to further the philosophy of Horatio Alger Jr. and to encourage the spirit of Strive & Succeed that for half a century guided Alger's undaunted heroes—lads whose struggles epitomized the Great American Dream and flamed hero ideals in countless millions of young Americans. . . ."

News from the Hall of Fame of the Trotter, Goshen, NY 10924: A 6-page quarterly for harness race fans.

Nineteenth Century, East Washington Square, Philadelphia, PA 19106: A 66-page, 4-color quarterly from The Victorian Society in America. The society has more than 3 dozen chapters around the country.

The 99 News, PO Box 59965, Oklahoma City, OK 73159: A 34-page magazine, published 10 times a year, by the International Women Pilots Association (founded in 1929 by Amelia Earhart). Readers range from airline pilots and astronauts to housewives who fly for fun.

NOMOTC Notebook, 5402 Amberwood Lane, Rockville, MD 20853: A 12-page quarterly, circulation 10,000, from The National Organization of Mothers of Twins Clubs—"Where God Chooses Its Members." Advice for fathers and grandparents, too.

NSS News and *NSS Bulletin,* Cave Avenue, Huntsville, AL 35810: The *News* is a 24-page monthly, the *Bulletin* an 18-page quarterly, both "dedicated to the exploration, study, and conservation of caves," from the National Speleological Society. Speleology means "cave science," but the activity of cave exploring is usually called "caving" or "spelunking." The society has 5000 members but tries to limit membership to those who realize that caving can be dangerous and is not a "thrill-seeking sport."

The Numismatist, 818 N. Cascade, Colorado Springs, CO 80903: A slick, 300-page monthly magazine, "the official publication of the American Numismatic Association," a congressionally chartered group devoted to the collecting of coins, currency, and tokens. Circulation: 37,000.

The Nutshell, PO Box 1005, Welland, Ontario, Canada L3B 5S2: A 20-page quarterly from The Northern Nut Growers Association, formed in 1910 by "enthusiastic amateur and professional horticulturists." It tells its 2500 readers how they can grow walnuts, chestnuts, filberts, pecans, and hickory nuts in their backyards.

Old Bottle, PO Box 243, Bend, OR 97701: A 50-page digest-size monthly for collectors of antique glassware. Includes a section called the "Fruit Jar Newsletter."

The Old-House Journal, 69A Seventh Ave., Brooklyn, NY 11217: See profile, "Home Finishings."

Old Mill News, Box 435, Wiscasset, ME 04578: A well-illustrated 20-page quarterly from The Society for the Preservation of Old Mills. The society not only believes in restoration—it urges "adaptive use of our country's rich inheritance of Old Mills of all types."

Orben's Current Comedy, 1200 N. Nash St., Arlington, VA 22209: See profile, "Mail Order Madness."

The Original Art Report, PO Box 1641, Chicago, IL 60690: A 6-page monthly, "committed to the Preservation, Comprehension and Progress of Artists and Art." Editor Frank Salantrie considers himself "a devil's advocate on the side of artists."

The Owl of Minerva, The Hegel Society of America, Department of Philosophy, Villanova University, Villanova, PA 19085: A 12-page quarterly, all about the famous philosopher.

The Palace Peeper, The Gilbert & Sullivan Society, % Vivan Denison, 137 Riverside Dr., New York, NY 10024: Published 10 times a year. The New York group is one of 27 branches of the society around the world. Members also receive *The Gilbert & Sullivan Journal,* put out by the London branch.

The PanAngler, 180 N. Michigan Ave., Chicago, IL 60601: See profile, "Wetting a Line."

Parapsychology Review, 228 E. 71 St., New York, NY 10021: A 28-page, slick bimonthly from the Parapsychology Foundation, which for three decades has tried "to encourage and support impartial scientific inquiry into the psychical aspects of human behavior."

Passport, 20 N. Wacker, Chicago, IL 60606: A 12-page monthly newsletter that shares "new travel discoveries" with readers—inns, restaurants, and resorts "the guidebooks haven't found yet." Published since 1966.

Pen and Quill, PO Box 467, Rockville Centre, NY 11571: A 32-page bimonthly journal for 1000 members of the Universal Autograph Collectors Club. Results of the latest auctions, reproductions of famous signatures (from Muhammad Ali to Ayatollah Khomeini), and addresses of celebrities who might respond to a written request.

The Pipe Smoker's Ephemeris, 20-37 120 St., College Point, NY 11356: A 40-page journal, published once or twice a year, crammed with serious and humorous information on pipes, tobacco, snuff, cigars, and other smoky subjects. Often has a section devoted to Sherlock Holmes.

Pitch Pipe and *Rechorder* [sic], PO Box 45168, 5334 E. 46 St., Tulsa, OK 74145: *Pitch Pipe* is a 32-page quarterly, *Rechorder* a bimonthly newsletter, both published by Sweet Adelines Inc., "an International Four-Part Harmony Organization for Women." Over 33,000 members love to sing, and read about, barbershop quartets.

PMCC Bulletin, PO Box 205, Dunkirk, MD 20754: A 16-page monthly from the Post Mark Collectors Club. Circulation: 1200. Reports include the incredible lengths some members go to collect the names of towns stamped on envelopes — and how those towns got their names.

Poetry Comics, Box 585, Iowa City, IA 52240: In each 22-page bimonthly issue Dave Morice "cartoonizes" poems by famous and not-so-famous writers. An Emily Dickinson poem, for example, becomes a modern True Romance. *PC* has been praised by Robert Creeley, James Dickey, and others.

Points, 15237 Chanera Ave., Gardena, CA 90249: A 2-page monthly for members of the International Club for Collectors of Hatpins and Hatpin Holders. Editor Lillian Baker owns a hatpin from the tomb of King Tut.

Police Times, 1100 NE 125 St., North Miami, FL 33161: A 16-page monthly tabloid newspaper. Reports on the latest technology and crime statistics—with a lot of humorous real-life incidents interspersed. Published by the American Law Enforcement Offices Association. Circulation: 50,000.

Popular Culture Association Newsletter, % Michael Marsden, Bowling Green State University, Bowling Green, OH 43403: A 42-page collection of conference news, course outlines, and historical/ sociological essays for the teacher (and student) of popular culture.

Popular Rotorcraft Flying, 11852 Western Ave., PO Box 570, Stanton, CA 90680: A 26-page bimonthly, founded in 1962, "to unite all people interested in developing and promoting rotorcraft for personal flying." 1500 readers, including several airline pilots, get tips on how to buy kits and assemble their own gyro-copter.

Postal History USA, 430 Ivy Avenue, Crete, NE 68333: A 14-page bimonthly for 200 buffs.

Preservation News, 1785 Massachusetts Ave., N.W., Washington, DC 20036: A monthly newspaper from The National Trust for Historic Preservation, the only national, private organization chartered by Congress to encourage public participation in site and building preservation. Circulation: 135,000. If you've ever wanted to purchase a historic home this is the place to look: A classified section in the back shows pictures of dozens of properties, some listed in the National Register.

Privacy Journal, PO Box 8844, Washington, DC 20003: See profile, "I. F. Smith."

Prosit, PO Box 463, Kingston, NJ 08528: A 24-page quarterly for 1000 members of Stein Collectors

International. "Stein" comes from the German word for stoneware, *Steinzeug,* from which most steins are made. Without a lid a stein is just a mug. *Prosit* is a toast, in German, "to your health."

Psychotronic, % Michael Weldon, 341 E. 9 St., New York, NY 10003: See profile, "The Horror!"

Punsters Unlimited:, Lake Superior State College, Sault Ste. Marie, MI 49783: See profile, "Citizen Rabe."

Quarterly Review of Doublespeak, National Council of Teachers of English, 1111 Kenyon Rd., Urbana, IL 61801: An 8-page bulletin from the Committee on Public Doublespeak, a group of 36 English teachers, college professors, statisticians, and newspaper reporters. The *QRD*'s definition of doublespeak: "Presenting things as they really are not, or trying to *make* them into that which they are not." Circulation: 800.

Railroad Station Historical Society Bulletin, 430 Ivy Avenue, Crete, NE 68333: A quarterly containing articles about, and photos of, old stations—some restored, others falling apart. "A large number of our 400 members are serious students of railroad or architectural history," says publisher William Rapp.

Raisin d'Etre, Lake Superior State College, Sault Ste. Marie, MI 49783: See profile, "Citizen Rabe."

Raptor Report, PO Box 891, Pacific Palisades, CA 90272: A semiannual for 800 members of the Society for the Preservation of Birds of Prey. Editor J. Richard Hilton says: "We are particularly hostile to the 'sport' or art form of falconry."

The Real Art Letter, PO Box 31508, San Francisco, CA 94131: Editor Sally Harms believes that much of modern art—abstraction, conceptualism, video—has "little to do with real art." Her 16-page monthly looks at new artists "who

combine the technical excellence of traditional fine art with a commitment to social, political change and psychological verity." This means: muralists, cartoonists, illustrators, animators, with "recognizable skill" who use "recognizable imagery."

The Ricardian Register, PO Box 217, Sea Cliff, NY 11579: A 20-page quarterly for 600 members of the Richard III Society, founded in 1924. They believe that King Richard was smeared by Shakespeare and other writers and historians. The Register provides historical rebuttal, and reviews theatrical performances—from Laurence Olivier to Al Pacino.

Robert's Telling Tales, PO Box 2161, Bellingham, WA 98227: A very informal 10-page monthly "reproduced by hand-crank mimeograph press." Editor Robert Ashworth, 26, rewrites current events from what he calls a "cosmic idealist" perspective. When Israeli jets bombed Iraq's nuclear reactor, for example, he wrote a story portraying it as an "anti-nuke" demonstration. Circulation: 130.

Robotics Age, PO Box 801, La Canada, CA 91011: A quarterly for over 9000 readers who want to keep up with the latest in research on the uses and capabilities of robots.

Romantic Times, 163 Joralemon St. #1234, Brooklyn Heights, NY 11201: A monthly newspaper for readers of "romance" novels. Profiles authors, reviews books, and presents advice on how-to-write-your-own.

Scout Memorabilia, 7305 Bounty Drive, Sarasota, FL 33581: "The only historical Scout paper approved by the Boy Scouts of America." A 10-page newsletter published 5 times a year. The 1500 subscribers like to buy, sell, and trade books, badges, uniforms.

Search & Rescue, PO Box 641, Lompoc, CA 93438: A thick quarterly billed as "The Journal of

Emergency Response." Teaches search, survival, and rescue skills "that mean the difference" between life and death.

The Shakespeare Newsletter, University of Miami, Coral Gables, FL 33124: Longtime editor Lou Marder claims that this 4-page monthly "has the world record for one-person publication—31 years, 170 issues." Presents digests of dissertations, news on Shakespeare festivals, and reports on the latest volleys in the great did-Shakespeare-really-write-all-the-plays debate.

Shopping News, PO Box 117-G, Mukwonago, WI 53149: A 12-page newsletter for several hundred grocery shoppers, referred to as "household purchasing agents" by editors Larry and Sue Koralewski. How to find bargains in the newspaper, decipher product codes, and buy in bulk.

Siamese News Quarterly, 2588-C S. Vaughn Way, Aurora, CO 80014: "Official Publication of the Siamese Cat Society in America, Inc." The society had been around 50 years when its 28-page quarterly first came out in 1959. "Obviously," says editor Sam L. Scheer, who is 86 years old and owns over 300 books about cats, "our readers are Siamophiles, those *homo sapiens* who have a rapport with *catus felis Siamensis.*"

Sipapu, Route 1, Box 216, Winters, CA 95694: A 24-page semiannual "for librarians, collectors and others interested in the alternative press." The Pueblo Indians believed "sipapus" were tunnels to the "other world." *Sipapu* tips readers off on the best in new feminist/Third World/peace movement/literary publications—and covers comic books too. Editor Noel Peattie, a librarian at the University of California at Davis, also conducts interviews with leading small press editors.

Skeptical Inquirer, PO Box 29, Kensington Station, Buffalo, NY 14215: A quarterly from the Committee for the Scientific Investigation of Claims of the Paranormal, a group of 43 scientists and journalists, such as Isaac Asimov, B.F. Skinner, and Carl Sagan. Attempts to separate "fact from myth" on such subjects as the Bermuda Triangle, Bigfoot, UFOs, the occult, and so forth.

Solar Energy Digest, PO Box 17776, San Diego, CA 92117: An 8-page monthly that contains about 75 brief news reports covering every aspect, from photo cells to space stations. Editor William Edmondson has been active in solar research and development since 1944.

Sons of Sherman's March to the Sea Bulletin, 1725 Farmer Ave., Tempe, AZ 85281: A 1-page quarterly. Stan Schirmacher's grandfather was in the vanguard of General William Tecumseh Sherman's march through Georgia in 1864—he was a flag bearer and drummer boy. Schirmacher formed this group in 1966 to assist others trying to trace service records of ancestors who served in the Civil War (they don't have to prove a connection to Sherman).

Sotheby's Newsletter, 980 Madison Ave., New York, NY 10021: Published 10 times a year for clients and potential customers of Sotheby Parke Bernet, the famous gallery/auction house. What's soon-to-be-available in the world of pricey jewelry, painting, prints, furniture, books, stamps, coins, and other objects. Plus: pictures and descriptions of incredible houses and estates. When Richard Nixon was trying to sell his New York home it was pictured here over the words: "Presidential Townhouse."

Sparks Journal, PO Box 530, Santa Rosa, CA 95402: A friendly, 40-page tabloid quarterly from the Society of Wireless Pioneers, "Adventure and Experiences of Professional Brass Pounders Around the World." Founder William A. Breniman has said that the objective of the society is "to record the colorful history and memorabilia of the early days of Wireless. To give

credit due the hundreds of brave and dedicated men and women who saved thousands of lives and untold numbers of ships. . . ."

Spotlight, 1385 S. Colorado Blvd. #512, Denver, CO 80222: Even potatoes need p.r. and that's what *Spotlight,* and its sponsor, The Potato Board, are for. They want "to increase the consumption of potatoes and to develop new markets for potato products." An entertaining quarterly that goes out to 17,000 spud growers in the U.S.

The Surf Report, PO Box 1028, Dana Point, CA 92629: A monthly newsletter that presents "a summary and forecast of surf conditions worldwide" for people who like to ride the ocean's waves.

SWL, 16182 Ballad Lane, Huntington Beach, CA 92649: A 52-page digest-size monthly from the American Shortwave Listeners' Club. Occasionally a listener comes across a Voice of America broadcast emanating from a country where no U.S. personnel are supposed to be situated. (Translation: The CIA has landed?) Recently, a correspondent reported hearing "Disco Action Radio" coming from Madagascar. His comment: "Hasn't anybody told them that disco is *dead?*"

Table Tennis Topics, Olympic House, 1750 E. Boulder St., Colorado Springs, CO 80909: A 20-page monthly tabloid from the U.S. Table Tennis Association. Current editor Tim Boggan was a member of the American "ping-pong diplomacy" team that visited China in 1971. Circulation: 6000.

Tax Angles, 901 N. Washington St., Alexandria, VA 22314: An 8-page "monthly letter of tax saving ideas, strategies, techniques," edited by Vernon K. Jacobs. More than 50,000 readers.

The Theatergoer, 21 E. 84 St., New York, NY 10028: A 6-page monthly newsletter for people who want to be "in the know" on all aspects of theater. Includes reviews, inter-

views, and tips on how to save money on tickets.

Theodore Roosevelt Association Journal, Box 720, Oyster Bay, NY 11771: A prestigious 32-page quarterly. Recent contributors have included Barbara Tuchman, Edmund Morris, and David McCullough. Circulation, over 2000.

The Thomas Wolfe Review, Department of English, University of Akron, Akron, OH 44325: A 72-page semiannual all about the author of *Look Homeward, Angel.*

Thoreau Society Bulletin, State University College, Geneseo, NY 14454: An 8-page quarterly read by 1000 members, some of whom make a yearly pilgrimmage to Concord, Mass., near where Thoreau wrote *Walden.*

Tin Type, PO Box 4555, Denver, CO 80204: A 20-page monthly for 900 members of the Tin Container Collectors Assn. They favor tobacco and coffee tins.

The Titanic Commutator, PO Box 53, Indian Orchard, MA 01151: See profile, "Titanic Undertaking."

Tournaments Illuminated. PO Box 743, Milpitas, CA 95035: See profile, "Middle Agers."

Train Collectors Association Quarterly, PO Box 248, Strasburg, PA 17579: An illustrated 40-page magazine for 13,000 members of the association. They love toy, tinplate trains—the classic Lionels, Gilberts, and Americans Flyers of their youth.

Train Sheet, 105 Fairmount Ave., Hackensack, NJ 07601: An 8-page, illustrated quarterly from the Railroadians of America. "For individuals whose avocation is the gathering, preserving, writing and publishing of railroad history."

TRANET, PO Box 567, Rangeley, ME 04970: TRANET stands for Transnational Network for Appropriate/Alternative Technologies.

This newsletter/directory briefly describes, every 3 months, dozens of projects and publications, around the world, concerned with such topics as wind power, holistic health, and experimental communes, and tells readers how to contact them.

Tsunami Newsletter, PO Box 50027, Honolulu, Hawaii 96850: A 32-page publication that goes out 2 or 3 times a year to 700 scientists, engineers, educators, government, and civilian protection agencies around the world. A tsunami (soo-nah-mee) is a very large ocean wave caused by an underwater earthquake or volcanic eruption.

Turkey Call, PO Box 467, Edgefield, SC 29824: A 42-page bimonthly, on slick paper, from The National Wild Turkey Federation. It includes recipes, preservation news, and bulletins: Wild turkeys attack joggers in upstate New York. According to *TC* there were only 25,000 wild turkeys left in the U.S. in 1942, but thanks to conservation efforts there are more than 2 million today.

Turtle Express, PO Box 96, Westchester, IL 60153: See profile, "Not for the Swift."

UFO Newsclipping Service, Route 1, Box 220, Plumerville, AR 72127: A 20-page monthly compilation of newspaper stories, from around the world, reporting flying saucer sightings.

Under the Sign of Pisces, % Richard R. Centing, Ohio State University Libraries, 1858 Neil Avenue Mall, Columbus, OH 43210: A 22-page quarterly, founded in 1970, about "Anais Nin and Her Circle," and called (by *Magazines for Libraries*) "one of the best author newsletters." Certainly it's one of the most attractive. Nin contributed to the newsletter "and helped promote it during her lecture tours of America," according to editor Centing.

Vietnam War Newsletter, PO Box 122, Collinsville, CT 06022: "For Vietnam Veterans and others interested in learning more about America's longest war and its aftermath." A wide-ranging 12-page mimeographed monthly. It reviews books on the political roots of the war and has up-to-date reports on the latest vet demonstration or Agent Orange revelation. It mentions new cookbooks for lovers of Vietnamese cuisine and reports on "current events in Southeast Asia." Editor Tom Hebert says the newsletter "is not pro-war, and it's not anti-war. It is pro-Vietnam Veteran."

Vikingship, Box 301, Chicago, IL 60690: A 10-page quarterly from the Leif Ericson Society for Vikings and their fans. Established 1965. 1200 readers.

Virginia Philatelic Forum, % Ed Rykbos, 5221 Carolanne Dr., Virginia Beach, VA 23462: A bimonthly newsletter affiliated with the American Philatelic Society.

The Visiting Fireman, 1024 Elizabeth St., Naperville, IL. 60540: See profile, "On Fire."

Washington Crap Report, PO Box 10309, St. Petersburg, FL 33733: See profile, "Political Gossip."

The White Tops, PO Box 69, Camp Hill, PA 17011: A slick, 40-page monthly from the Circus Fans Association of America, founded in 1926. Presents historical features and the latest news on shows. Association members make Circus Day a big deal in their communities and help circus stars have a good time when the show's over.

WHOA!, PO Box 555, Reno, NV 89504: The title is an acronym—Wild Horse Organized Assistance. An 8-page quarterly from the Foundation for the Welfare of Wild Free-Roaming Horses and Burros. Founded by the late Velma Johnson, better known as "Wild Horse Annie," who helped inspire the 1971 federal law meant to protect the 63,000 wild horses and burros in the Western U.S.

The Winesburg Eagle, University of Richmond, Richmond, VA 23173: An 8-pager all about Sherwood Anderson, the author of *Winesburg, Ohio* and other books.

The Woods-Runner, Lake Superior State College, Sault Ste. Marie, MI 49783: See profile, "Citizen Rabe."

World Federalist Newsletter, 1011 Arlington Blvd., Arlington, VA 22209: A 6-page quarterly for 6500 members of the World Federalists Association. Noted author/editor Norman Cousins is current president of the WFA. Entertainer Steve Allen is an advisor.

The World of Rodeo & Western Heritage, PO Box 1111, Billings, MT 59103: A 32-page monthly tabloid, about equally divided between college, professional, and regional rodeo, with a little nostalgia on the side.

World Wide Hunters, GPO Box 1742, New York, NY 10116: A 12-page monthly newsletter. Subscribers in 11 countries include nobility, board chairmen, "quite a few guys who are simply passionate about hunting and hang the cost."

World's Fair, PO Box 339, Corte Madera, CA 94925: A 16-page quarterly that takes a social, political, and technological view of past fairs and looks ahead to the fairs of the '80s in Munich, New Orleans, Vancouver, Amsterdam, Plovdiv (Bulgaria) and Tsukuba (Japan).